NO SMOKE WITHOUT FIRE

– A NOVEL –

Other books by Jo-Anne

Yesterday's Shadows
A Walking Shadow
Nets of Gold
Keeping Mum
Taking Stock
The Emperor's Women
Doin' It
The S.O.B.
The Quandary
Romany Legacy
A Grievous Burden

Check out the web page at
www.joannesouthernbooks.com

NO SMOKE WITHOUT FIRE

– A NOVEL –

Jo-Anne Southern

PRIMIX PUBLISHING
THE WRITE CHOICE

Primix Publishing
11620 Wilshire Blvd
Suite 900, West Wilshire Center, Los Angeles, CA, 90025
www.primixpublishing.com
Phone: 1-800-538-5788

Published by Primix Publishing 08/20/2021

ISBN: 978-1-955177-31-3(sc)
ISBN: 978-1-955177-32-0(e)

Library of Congress Control Number: 2021917238

CONTENTS

At last the secret is out,
as it always must come in the end,
The delicious story is ripe to tell
to an intimate friend,
Over the tea cups and in the square
the tongue has its desire,
Still waters run deep, my dear,
there's never smoke without fire.

W.H.Auden

GLOSSARY

These words are commonly used in Lancashire but may be unfamiliar to anyone not born in the British Isles.

butties	sandwiches
chuffed	pleased
chunnering	mumbling or muttering peevishly
clemmed	chilled to the bone
gob	mouth
gobstruck	poleaxed, stunned
gradely	nice, attractive
have a crack	have a chat
heck	hell
kalied	drunk
lobscouse	a stew made of lamb, potatoes and onions
mard	easily hurt, soft
mythering	continual begging or pleading
nappies	diapers
nowt	nothing
owt	anything
slag off	deprecate, criticize
skivvy	servant
whingeing	whining, usually with tears
Would I heck as like	I would never

CHAPTER ONE

1954

The sharp rapping of the door knocker broke into Marian's thoughts and she hurried down the hall.

Pausing on the door step, Rita shook the raindrops off her hair. "Hello, Gran."

"Eeh, lass, come on in and take off your wet coat. You look like you've been swimming."

"I feel like it, too. Any more of this and we'll all develop webbed feet and gills. It's terrible out, and the buses!"

"Aye, I can well imagine, lovey. You come and sit in front of the fire and get warm while I make a cup of tea. You must feel right clemmed."

They went down the short hall to the warm kitchen where Rita took off her shoes and set them to dry on the fender. She ran her fingers through her damp hair, knowing it would dry in a thousand wayward curls.

Relaxing in front of the banked up fire, she watched her Gran bustling around the kitchen. What a love, Rita thought fondly. Marian's fair hair was greying although curly as ever, her pink and white complexion seemed hardly lined unless you looked closely, her eyes were bright blue and she had a merry smile. Not fat, but pleasantly plump, the epitome of a loving granny.

"Did you go out today, Gran?" Rita asked as she watched her gran.

"Aye, this morning, early like, before the rain started." Marian poured the boiling water into the teapot and winced as she set down the kettle.

"Your joints bothering you today?"

"Aye, some. That's how I allus know when it's going to rain. As good as a barometer, my rheumatics are. Harry allus asked me what the day was going to be like, with him working outside all the time."

Rita smiled, remembering her grandfather. Even when very young she observed them, intuitively knowing they treated each other differently than her parents treated each other. Time and again she caught them touching, love taps, when they thought nobody was looking. Rita daydreamed of a marriage like theirs, not an alliance like that of her parents who lived in an uneasy truce most of the time. It was no wonder she was an only child. Gran's words interrupted her musing.

"You hungry tonight, lovey?"

"You must be kidding! With that lovely aroma greeting my nose when you opened the door? I could eat a horse, and don't tell me if that's what you're cooking." Rita laughed. Her Gran was a great cook, plain food but delicious.

"Come and sit at the table and I'll serve up," Marian said pulling out a chair.

"Gran! Steak and onions. Marvellous." She nosed the air, inhaling the delicious aroma rising from the casserole. "If you could bottle that smell, you'd make a fortune" She laughed. "Imagine if you sprayed it at your front door before people came into the house, their mouths would be watering so much they hardly could speak."

Marian laughed. Rita always said the right thing to make a body feel happy. Mind you, she had some peculiar ideas as well, but many of them had merit. Aye, how grand. To spray your house with a delicious smell to make your house welcoming.

"You could have lamb and mint sauce, roast pork, apple pie with cinnamon," Rita expanded on her idea.

"Eeh lass, you do come out with some things," Marian said around a mouthful of food.

"Yes, but it's a good idea. Don't you think?"

"Aye, it is an'all, but won't it be the ones who can't cook for toffee who'd buy it? Imagine smelling steak and onion at the door, then sitting down to jam butties."

They laughed.

"Yes," Rita said, her voice full of scorn, ". . . and it would be my Mam who'd buy it by the cart load. She's got to be the world's worst cook, and I can't imagine why, not with you as a teacher."

Marian chuckled. "Lord love you, child, your mother wasn't one bit interested in cooking. She thought she'd have servants when she wed. To cook a meal was the farthest thing from her mind."

"Yes, and it still is," Rita said, chuckling.

After they washed the supper dishes, they sat drinking tea by the fire and Rita told Gran about her day.

As the mantel clock struck seven, she said: "I've got to be going, Gran. Mam is at the ladies' auxiliary tonight and I've got to fix this mop of mine." She ran her hands through the rioting curls of her now dry hair.

"Will you come for your tea tomorrow, lovey?"

"If I can, Gran, but don't count on it because I might have to work overtime. It's month end, you know." Rita worked as a junior clerk at the gas company offices.

She put on her stiff, almost dried shoes and stood, glancing around the kitchen, her home away from home. Rita always thought of Gran's house as more of a home than her real home.

"Goodnight, Gran, lovely supper." Quickly she hugged Marian and kissed her cheek. "Time to go beard the lion in its den, or is it the dragon in its lair?"

Marian pushed at her. "Get away with you, lovey. Your Mam isn't as bad as all that."

"Maybe not," Rita said, privately thinking her far worse. She never told her Gran everything, not wanting to upset her.

In the late afternoon, Marian dusted the mantelpiece after she banked up the kitchen fire. She glanced around seeing the drifts of ash that lay on everything and tutted. "Darn coal fires might make us warm, but they generate enough ash and cinders to pave a road."

For most of her life, except two weeks in Manchester with her parents, and her later year or so in service, Marian had lived in Trawton, a small mining village. For many years it housed only colliers and mine workers, although now people from Wigan and the suburbs rented the small terraced houses, preferring to commute to the dirty city while they lived in comparatively open countryside. Not a progressive village, it offered little more than accommodation, had no factories, plants or big shops. However, the local mines, already working at capacity, no longer needed men, so now sons of miners were forced to travel farther afield if they wished to become colliers.

She grew up in Trawton where her miner father rented a similar terraced house. The village encompassed her small comfortable world and she was content to stay put; had no hankering to travel, no sense of curiosity about the outside world. Pleased with her lot in life, she didn't own a television and had no intention of getting one. Books and the radio would do her well enough, as she liked to use her imagination.

The small kitchen grew warm, heated by the now blazing fire. Some years back Matthew's men had fixed the doors with weather stripping, and caulked the windows to prevent drafts. Her house felt cosily comfortable against the sodden day.

She smiled as she carefully swept the hearth. Fortunately she could still get coal at a discount through the council. Her husband Harry, dead these past twelve years after working for the council as a road worker, had lost his life in a terrible accident. Not a normal accident, though. The ancient steam roller, badly maintained and parked on a hill, lost its brakes and rolled over him. It almost flattened Harry and his death became the subject of many jokes down at the pub over the years. She heard them laughing and speculating, but droll though it might be if told as a music hall joke, she found no humour in it.

Strange how she could recall the day they came to tell her. She was singing *Maizie Doats* along with the new wireless and vividly remembered earlier talking to Ruth next door about Charlie Chaplin's marriage to Oona O'Neill. It was like it was yesterday. In those days the council officials did not carry life insurance on their employees, the excuse being a small community couldn't warrant the expense. It was only right, Marian thought, that they subsidize her rent and coal for the rest of her life.

She popped into the front room to look out the window. The company room, as she thought of it, she kept starkly clean in case someone dropped in for a visit, so she rarely used it for family living. It feels damp, she thought, I'd better light a fire later to take the edge off the chill. Moving aside the crisply starched net curtains and looking down the road, Marian wondered what time Rita would arrive. The day stayed dark, glowering, with rain steadily falling since noon. That meant the buses would be running late.

She thought her granddaughter Rita, a lovely spirited lass, and loved her as much as Rita loved her. Rita visited her when she could because she did not get on with her mother, and, in fact, disliked her. They often talked about this rift and hashed over the reasons for Rita's dislike. The alienation between mother and daughter never failed to upset Marian, though she could well understand Rita's feelings.

She did not much like Sheila herself, no matter that she was her only daughter. As she matured, Sheila became a nasty person, though where she got it from was a mystery. Once married, she became even more domineering. Predictably, Rita rebelled, much as Sheila had rebelled with Marian. It's true that history repeats itself, she thought as she looked back in her mind's eye to when she and Sheila were set against each other.

As Marian set the table a few minutes later, she thought about the past years when if it had not been for the cheerful support Rita brought into her life, she might have put her head in the gas oven. Life without Harry soon became bleak and lonely. She grimaced now, thinking back to those dark days.

Oh aye, when Sheila heard the news of her father's death she came rushing around to make the funeral arrangements. Yes, she and her brother Roger arrived simultaneously, though once the funeral concluded, they beat a hasty retreat. Marian rarely saw them these days, apart from their duty visit at Christmas.

Rita, a chattering six years old, blissfully unaware of the tragedy, provided a spark of life for Marian and, as years went by, Rita became the only light in her dreary existence. They had wept together, comforted each other, and Rita made Marian's life worth living. However, Marian realized she would never get over Harry's shocking and unexpected death. She would grieve to her dying day that she hadn't even had a last chance to tell him how much she cared for him before he died.

How strange, she thought as the radio played softly, the changes in her life seemed connected with songs that, when heard again, brought back the same emotion as in the old days.

Rita walked home, dreading her mother's reception. These days her Mam was always bad tempered.

"What time do you call this, Lady Jane?" Sheila bellowed as Rita entered the kitchen.

As she took off her coat, she took in at a glance the dirty dishes, the low smouldering fire, noticed the dust and clutter crying out to be cleaned, then looked at her mother. Sheila sat at the kitchen table carefully applying makeup, using Dad's shaving mirror.

"Why?" she asked, looking innocent.

"What do you mean 'why?'" Sheila said, her face displaying distrust. "If I find out you've been dallying with a lad, I'll have your guts for garters, young lady. Where have you been to this time? You knew I was going out."

"Sorry, we worked overtime," Rita said, taking her coat and hanging it on the back door with the others. "Where's Dad?"

"Where do you think he is?" Sheila said, her voice derisive. "At the pub as usual, I suppose. Get your teas ready and look sharp about it."

Annoyed, Rita shook her head. Her mother was unbelievable. "No wonder Dad stays out," she said, deciding for once to have her say. "We don't have much joy in this house, do we? Why don't *you* try cooking a meal for a change? I'm not the cook around here, no matter what you think." Rita slumped into a chair, throwing off the magazines and newspapers. "And it wouldn't hurt you to do some housework occasionally."

Sheila snorted angrily, and stood with hands on hips, her face a mask of annoyance.

"How dare you talk to me like that, you little brat. You didn't learn any manners at school, did you? You don't have a brain in your head, yet you defy me *and* your father, stay out to all hours, you. . .,"

"Please, Mam, don't start, or I'll go out again." Rita picked up yesterday's paper and began to flip through it.

"You're going nowhere," Sheila said through gritted teeth. "You'll stay here and make the tea." Picking up the hair brush, she landed a blow on the side of Rita's head.

"Ouch," Rita roared, putting up her hand to feel if the skin was broken. "What did you do that for? Only people of little intelligence resort to violence. I've told you that before."

"Yes, and only people who are looking for a thick lip talk to their mother in that way." She extended an arm to the fireplace. "I can always get the strap."

"You know, Mam, I pity you," Rita said, her lip curling. "You talk about me being stupid, but you've less between your ears than that pot dog." She gestured to the dusty Staffordshire china spaniel sitting on the mantelpiece. "How my Dad puts up with you, I can't imagine. Lay a finger on me again and I'm going to the police. They have laws against child abuse these days."

"Don't make me laugh," Sheila said with a snort, "Huh! Child abuse? You're coming up to eighteen now and that's not a child."

"Don't touch me again, Mam," Rita said grimly. "I'm warning you for the last time."

Sheila usually resorted to physical violence to make her point and Rita often experienced her foul moods. She recalled younger days when she could hardly move for the bruises under her clothes, days when she saw blood in her urine. She had said nothing to anyone, especially not her Dad. Those were the days when she thought she warranted the punishment, when it had been her own fault for being naughty. Then as she came into her teen years and could reason things out for herself, she read about abusive relationships, discovering it was her mother who needed treatment or counselling. No matter how well she behaved, or however hard she tried, she probably could never please her mother.

Those days of abuse and violence were her secret. She told not a soul - not even the suspicious teacher who once talked to her. Now she understood her mother's predilection, she armed herself against it. It had been many months since Sheila had raised her hand to her, but sometimes keeping her mouth shut was difficult, and this was one of them.

Churlishly displaying disgust, she watched as her mother put the makeup in her bag and checked her reflection in the mirror. She was wearing a tight skirt and an off-the-shoulder peasant blouse with machined embroidery. Rita thought she looked cheap.

"Off to see your fancy man, are you?" she asked, eyes narrowed.

"I beg your pardon?" Sheila said, glaring, her eyebrows in her hairline.

"You've got too much muck on your face to be going to the church," Rita said. She smiled smugly, "I don't think the Reverend goes much for the halfundressed look. I bet you haven't got any underwear on under your blouse, either. Talk about dressing like a tart!"

Livid, Sheila rounded on her. "Now you listen to me, young lady. If you make those remarks again, you'll get the strap and no mistake. You've got a vivid imagination, you have. How dare you think such things about your own mother? I'm going to the Ladies Auxiliary, nothing else."

"I'll come with you, then," Rita said, rising.

"You'll do no such thing," Sheila said, hurriedly shrugging into her coat. "You'll stay here and get the supper ready. Your Dad'll be home soon."

Rita smiled grimly. "What shall I tell him? Shall I tell him where you've gone?" Cheekily she winked.

Sheila paused in her coat buttoning. "You know where I'm going. I told you. You know I go to the meeting once a week, like I've been doing for years." She glared at Rita who could almost see her deciding whether to continue the argument.

Rita wanted to say, 'That's not what Mrs. Pearce says. She says you haven't been to a meeting for ages,' but for some reason she did not.

"Where's your mother?" Arthur Goodwin asked as he came into warm kitchen.

"Ladies Auxiliary, Dad," Rita glanced at him and smiled as she stirred the peas.

When her mother left, she tidied up the kitchen, dusted and built up the fire as the pan of lobscouse simmered. It was the easiest meal she knew how to make.

Arthur plopped into his chair by the now blazing fire and blew out a breath of relief as he took off his boots.

"What a day!" he said as he held out his hands to the flames. "Everything went wrong, two machines down, and four spinners out with the flu."

"Sounds like you need a holiday, Dad," Rita said as she ladled out his supper. "Come on, soups on." She would only have a slice of bread and jam and a cup of tea, having eaten earlier with her grandmother.

Arthur sat at the table. He cut and buttered a thick slice of bread as his lobscouse cooled enough to eat. "You're a good lass, Rita, a good lass. Did you go to your Gran's tonight?" Usually when she didn't eat with him, she'd already eaten at Marian's. Aware of her love for her grandmother, he encouraged it, knowing Sheila didn't show her any affection.

Rita nodded. "Yes, Dad. She's been shut in most of the day by the rain. Her arthritis is bad when it's damp."

"You'd have thought your Mam would go around during the day to see to her," he said. Arthur had never understood how Sheila could treat her mother so callously. "She knows well enough her mother isn't too grand when the weather's like this."

"Yes, she knows all right," Rita said, nodding, "but she never goes around to help." She looked at him from under her brows thinking she would ask again. "Tell me, Dad, what is it with Gran and Mam? Why do they dislike each other so much? They never speak to each other properly, do they? I've always wondered what happened."

Arthur chewed and swallowed a mouthful, giving himself time to think. "Like I've told you before, Rita, I think you should ask your mother."

Rita blew out an aggravated breath. This subject she had broached often in the past with little results. "I *have* asked, often, but she won't say, and I can't ask Gran again in case it upsets her."

Arthur nodded. "Well, it seems to me that it's none of my business or yours. Your Gran and I don't see eye to eye on many things, nevertheless, she's a sensible woman, so if she's at outs with her own daughter, then she has a very good reason for it."

She stared at him blankly. "Hm . . . I still I wish I knew," Rita said, her mind searching for reasons, much as it had done a thousand times before. "I don't ever dare tell *her* I've been over at Gran's. You know I've gone behind her back to see Gran since I was a little girl, Dad, but then I suppose she knows it." She thought back on the mystery that had bothered her all these years.

"One thing puzzles me, though, Dad, when my Granddad died, Mam hardly spoke to Gran, except to tell her about the arrangements, and then she was bossy and abrupt. I was only little, but I can remember her tone of voice and it wasn't nice. She was stroppy with me and I daren't even speak unless spoken she spoke to me."

Arthur rubbed his chin with his handkerchief. "I know about the business at the funeral, lass, but it's not my place to interfere. Well, who knows what goes on in your mother's head?" He continued to eat his supper with relish. Rita had made it and it tasted good. If Sheila had cooked it, it would probably be dried out, burned or too salty as she didn't pay much attention when cooking.

Rita laughed. "Maybe we don't want to open that particular can of worms, Dad, do we?"

"Aye, you're right there, lass," Arthur said, wondering why he stayed with Sheila.

Thinking back, he knew why he stayed right enough, it was because of Rita. He wanted to see her settled with a nice young man, wanted to escort her down the aisle. If he left the house, God only knew what Sheila would do to the young woman. All those years past when the child was thin, white faced with huge eyes full of hurt and sorrow had not escaped his attention. He put the look of her down to Sheila, who could be a cruel bitch when left to her own devices. Yet Rita never complained and, when he mentioned it to Rita, she shyly said she was all right, nothing was wrong. When he broached the subject with Sheila, she always said Rita was going through a phase. No, he would stay and suffer in silence until Rita had found her way in life.

He looked now at his daughter and what he saw made him proud. Rita looked really beautiful sometimes, though always attractive with her abundant reddish-blond hair and blue eyes. She looked like her grandmother, had her drive too and her smart figure - not too thin, with a trim waist and shapely legs. Aye, the lads would soon be chasing her.

Mind you, to make his own life easier he had Molly, warm loving Molly, who catered to his every whim. She owned a cottage some miles outside the village and he spent many happy hours with her. Aye, when Rita was safely married, he would leave Sheila, divorce her, and he and Molly could be wed. Probably until then they would live together. Things had changed a lot since he was a lad. Now 'living over the brush,' as they called it, or common-law, had become almost acceptable.

He heaved a sigh of contentment as he rubbed his full stomach, wondering if his nerves could hold out. Only last week he had almost decided to stay at the cottage and to heck with the world. Still, Rita was almost eighteen now so it was not too long to wait, probably only a year or so, he guessed.

Arthur sincerely hoped Rita would meet a young man at work, someone with prospects.

Sheila laughed merrily as she accepted the second glass of port and lemon from Kevin. Always flush with money, he paid for the most expensive drinks.

Kevin Walton, a retired iron worker, lived only four doors from the Goodwins. He was a good looking man, still had all his hair and his own teeth, tall and straight with a cheeky grin, After meeting by chance one day at Wigan Market, they shared a meal together and discovered a mutual attraction. It was not long before they were meeting regularly in out of the way pubs and cafes. Kevin owned a car, which was a plus in her eyes, since the local men only ran to buying a bicycle, or, at the most, a motor bike.

"You have roses in your cheeks, Sheila, lass," Kevin said as he raised his glass. "To the roses."

She noticed he seemed nervous. "To the roses," Sheila sipped her drink. Port always gave her a warm, comfortable feeling and tonight she didn't care if she did get squiffy because Kevin always remained sober if they drove any distance.

Rita's words earlier had driven a chill into her heart, a chill she must disperse. Anyway, she told herself, who would believe Rita, a mere child? She could make sure the girl kept her mouth shut and felt sure she had covered her tracks in the village because no one had ever seen her with another man near home. Yes, she was sharp. She knew how to play the game and always met her paramours away from the sharp glances of her neighbours.

"Well, have you given it any thought?" Kevin asked, timidly smiling at her.

"Lots and lots," Sheila said, putting her hand on his. "I think about nothing else." She batted her eyelashes and lowered her gaze, thinking it sexy. Kevin thought she had something in her eye and patted his pocket for his handkerchief, wondering if he should offer to remove it.

"And?"

"And what?" Her ludicrously plucked and pencilled eyebrows rose. "I can't leave them, not to come and live four doors away. Surely even *you* can see that."

Kevin blew out a breath through pursed lips. "If you wanted to, you could do it," he argued, "You'd still see your girl, or she could live with us."

Sheila put down her glass and stared at him hard. "No way. I can't do it, Kevin. It's too much to consider, so we'll leave things as they are." Putting her hand over his, she caressed it with her thumb. "We see a lot of each other and nobody knows about us. Let's leave it that way, eh? Anyway, now I sneak into your house through the back, I spend more time with you than I do at home."

He looked suddenly grumpy and she knew things were not going the way he planned. "It's not good enough, Sheila." His voice became a whine that grated on her nerves. "I don't like this hole in the wall business. I want to be up front with it, to walk down the street with you on my arm, to live with you as a partner."

Well, who wouldn't want me? she thought, pleased. A good-looking woman, she had a terrific figure. For months she had promised Kevin she would leave Arthur to live with him, but even though she was a fast and glib talker, Kevin became impatient.

"Please, Kevin," she hissed, noticing people were looking at them, "Don't go on about it. You know I can't. Let's be happy with what we've got right now."

"No," Kevin said in a strong voice. "I'm not happy with it. It's not good enough, and it's been going on too long. I've thought about it a lot, and I've decided if you can't make the move, then we won't see each other again." His eyes narrowed with something akin to distaste

"Kevin! Please don't say that," she pleaded, her voice a hoarse whisper. "What will I do without you?"

"Same as you did before," he said bitterly, "Go without, or find another sucker."

Sheila sipped her port and stared at him stonily.

"You only use me as a convenience," Kevin said, his voice harsh and unforgiving. "I've thought it all out. If it wasn't me screwing you, it'd be some other poor sod. You and your promises . . . and that's another thing, coming to my house in the middle of the day, expecting me to bed you. I'm not a bloody machine, you know, I don't have an 'on and off' switch."

Her face reddened with rage and she spoke through hardly opened lips, trying to keep her voice down. "Well, really! When you're randy, you expect me to come across fast enough, and the same applies, Kevin, to women as well as to men. All I can say is, if you can't get into the mood for me, you're no use any more." She tossed back her drink in one huge swallow. Standing, she picked up her handbag. "Come on! You'd better take me home."

Kevin glared churlishly. "Get home on your own, Sheila. We're finished."

She put her hands on her hips, staring down at him resentfully. "Hey you, how'm I going to get back? They have no buses out here, no trains, and its miles back to Trawton."

He snorted and stared at her with a face like a hanging judge, his expression evident of aversion.

"Serves you right for picking this place," he said, his voice filled with icicles. "It was you who wanted to get as far from Trawton as you could, and this is it. Dump that it is."

The listening regulars bristled. How dare anyone cast aspersions on their local?

Sheila blew out an indignant breath. The man was impossible. What on earth had she ever seen in him?

"Call yourself a gentleman?" she snorted. "How could you do this to me?"

His temper rose. "I could ask the same question," he said. "You're no lady, Sheila, and it takes one to know one. I mean, what gentleman would be consorting with a neighbour's wife? What lady would be committing adultery under her husband's nose?"

Sheila suddenly noticed their voices had risen, how the other patrons listened with interest to their exchange.

"Come on," she hissed, "We're making a spectacle of ourselves. Run me home and we can discuss this on the way."

"Sorry," Kevin said, rising and picking up his glass. "I'm staying here and getting well and truly sloshed. You're welcome to join me get kalied . . . at another table, though. Pay for your own."

Sheila watched him through narrowed eyes as he made his way to the bar.

"A large brandy, please," he said, not looking back.

So the stupid sod was going to get drunk, was he? What *was* she going to do? She glanced around the small snug seeking help, but they were all couples, not a single man among them. Taking in the accusing stares, she glared defiantly and they slid away their eyes.

"D'you want to know what colour my underwear is, too?" she asked, in a contemptuous voice as she stalked out and into the saloon bar. Twenty voices started to babble as she left.

In the crowded bar lounge, she struck up a conversation with a commercial traveller heading for Wigan. After a couple of drinks, he drove her to Trawton, in exchange for her favours in the back seat of his car. They parted on the understanding they would meet the following week at the bus stop.

CHAPTER TWO

Rita sang as she scrubbed the hall floor. "Put another nickel in, in the nickelodeon, all I want is . . .,"

As Marian made an apple pie, she listened and smiled. The lyrics of songs these days, you wouldn't credit it. Still, it was tuneful, lively enough and had been around a couple of years now. Then Rita switched to Mr. Sandman, a jolly song, 'boinging' the fill-in parts.

Rita always helped by doing the heavy housework, especially when the weather turned damp. It was Christmas next week and the children, if you could call them children now, would drop in for dinner on Christmas day. Strictly a duty visit, of course. Again they would delight in nudging each other, pointing out every smut and spot, their faces revealing what they thought of her housekeeping. Well, never let anyone say all she had going for her was good housekeeping.

"Never mind, Gran," Rita said, when she voiced her concern, especially about Roger's wife. "I bet their house is like ours, all ash and soot. My Mam isn't house proud, like you are."

"Oh nay, lass, Roger's Mavis won't have any soot or smuts *She's* got a gas fire. No mucky coal for Madam Azonga. It's what she said last year, anyroad." Her acerbic tone surprised Rita as Gran never usually said anything bad about anyone.

"Well, lah-di-dah! Shows to go how lazy she is, then," Rita said. She laughed. Every day she saw the new gas fires on display in the gas company shop and thought them ridiculous. They looked so artificial with the flames all the same size and the baked clay backing so pale.

She liked to see coals blazing and later glowing redly as they warmed up the room.

Everyone in Trawton heated with coal, as did most in northwest Lancashire. She recalled at school the teacher talking about the new Clean Air Bill Parliament put into effect to cut coal fire emissions. It became absolutely essential because of the dreadful pea-soup fogs the north west experienced when sea fog and cold met the clouds of smoke from a million coal burning chimneys. The effluvium caused an acidic, soot tasting fog that penetrated even the warmest clothing and intensified bronchial diseases among the population. However, the English had burned coal for centuries and Rita couldn't figure out what people would do if they didn't allow them a fire. It did not affect householders right now, only large industrial concerns, although she had read articles praising the new clean fuels as people, on discovering the benefits of electricity and gas, switched to the cleaner fuels without being asked.

On her knees, she scrubbed her way from the front door into the kitchen and stood rubbing the small of her back.

"Whew. Glad that's done. Now, what about the kitchen, Gran?"

She sniffed at the mouth-watering fragrance of mince pies and slow cooking ham, of pastry and icing. Christmas was such a lovely odoriferous time and the house already smelled welcoming. In the corner the radio played a selection of Christmas music and made the evening feel special.

Marian looked up from rolling her puff pastry on the marble board. "I'll do that tomorrow myself, Rita. It only needs mopping and won't take long."

"You sure, Gran?"

"You've done more than enough, lass. The hall will be the death of me and I'm glad of your help. I can't kneel like I used to, not in winter. Aye, time was when it was bare concrete and dead easy with a mop, but cleaning the lino is a different matter altogether."

"No trouble," Rita said as she emptied the bucket into the sink. "You want me to help pick over the currants and sultanas?"

"If you like," Marian said as she popped another dozen mince tarts into the oven. "I'm not making a big pudding or cake this year. Not with your mother saying she's on a diet, and Madam Mavis saying there's too much fatty food. There'll only be you and me to enjoy most of it."

"Good!" Rita said firmly as she washed her hands. She loved Christmas day at her Gran's: the good smells of cooking, the warmth of the house, seeing her few relatives again. Most of all she loved being with her Gran, the only person she loved who loved her back unreservedly. "We'll make right pigs of ourselves, I can tell you. Did you know Madam made Uncle Roger buy her a television?"

"Lord love us. What on earth would they want with one of them gimcrack things? They'll never last, you know, they're only a fad."

Rita laughed. "That's what you said about radio, Gran, remember? Yet all the fetching and carrying of those heavy batteries is long gone. Anyway, they say there's over one and half million television sets in the United States now."

"Good place for them, too. I mean, who wants to sit around staring at a box with a picture the size of a postcard? They'll all go blind and lose their imaginations." She washed her and dried her hands. "No thanks, I like the radio plays and books, then you can put your own faces on people. You won't catch me getting one of them new fangled goggle boxes."

Rita's face fell. Her Dad said the same and she dearly wanted to watch a television. Many people had them now, even here in the village where a television aerial attached to the chimney made you better than your neighbours.

She shook off the blues and grinned. "Well, never mind. I'm looking forward to Christmas dinner here, Gran. It's always delicious and we'll dig in like good'uns, eh?"

"Yes, we will, child," Marian said as she brought the oily brown bags of currants, raisins and dates from the pantry.

For an hour they sat at the table removing the seeds from the fruit, and for that hour they talked: talked about Rita's ambitions, about Marian's past life.

Sheila felt gratified with her new affair. From time to time, when she saw Kevin coming or going from his house, she grimaced and stuck up her nose as if she smelled something bad. She could do much better for herself than him, and hadn't she proven it? George was a real man, he had lead in his pencil, or so he kept saying, and proved it often. In fact, he showed her four times one evening and she could hardly walk the next day.

As for George, he felt fair chuffed he had found a married woman willing to open her legs as often as he asked. Surely she was a nymphomaniac, he told his mates. They were dead jealous, he could tell, and made a few vulgar suggestions about what he could do with her, and he had done it. To his great joy she went along with everything and now, when he and his mates met in the pub to talk, the conversation always came round to his floozie. George got as big a thrill out of the telling as he did of the action.

Rita suspected her mother was seeing another man, but had no proof. This knowledge made her nervous as it went against everything the nuns had taught her at school and church, plus she felt terrible for her father: and too, it drove yet another wedge between her mother and herself.

At every opportunity she silently observed Sheila, saw the plucked and pencilled eyebrows, noted the heavy, gaudy makeup, how she fixed her hair, the shoddy low-cut clothes she bought from the market. Why couldn't her mother be like other mothers? Stay at home, warm, plump, cuddly mothers who baked special treats for you, bought you toys and played games? Mothers who talked to you about your fears and ambitions. Her mother never talked to her, only at her, and then only to give orders. Well, maybe it was all in her imagination since her father never said anything, although she noticed they rarely went out together these days.

Then she found the new underwear concealed in the airing cupboard under a stack of towels. This evening when looking for a clean blouse for work, she spotted something black and lacy sticking out between the linen. At first the discovery stunned her, then she became angry. No woman hid such fancy underwear unless purchased for a nefarious purpose. Well, she isn't going to get way with it, Rita thought, as she viciously hung the bra and panties over the wire under the mantlepiece when her mother went to the co-op.

As she came into the kitchen, Sheila's eyes went straight to the fireplace and she spotted the underwear.

"What on earth," she gasped.

"They don't fit me," Rita said, keeping her face straight. "You bought me the wrong size. You'll have to take them back."

Just then her father arrived home and Rita almost burst out laughing with the joy of the situation.

Arthur, a man who noticed little that didn't directly concern him, sat in his chair and took off his boots. Wriggling his toes to the warmth of the fire, he lay back and shut his eyes.

"What a day," he said as usual.

Sheila, moving like greased lightening, grabbed the underwear before he opened his eyes and glared at Rita. "Keep your mouth shut if you know what's good for you," she hissed.

"What?" Arthur asked, his weary eyes opening. "What's going on now?"

"Nothing, Arthur," Sheila said, "You ready for your tea? You'll have to wait because I only got back from the co-op and I've not started it yet. How come you didn't call in the pub like you usually do?"

He couldn't tell her he'd come straight home because Molly had gone to Chester to visit her mother, so he said the only thing that came to mind.

"We closed off early today, end of a run. Anyroad, I was too beat to go to the pub, beer makes me sleepy."

"Oh yes, I know that well enough," Sheila said, her tone caustic. "Maybe you should start drinking tea instead."

Rita stood to one side watching them. Her mother had gotten away with it again, and she wondered whether to tell her Dad.

Arthur blew out a long breath. "All right, all right, don't start, Sheila.

I've had a hard day and I want some peace and quiet." He winked at Rita who smiled.

"You, Rita, peel the potatoes," Sheila ordered.

Rita slowly unfolded an old newspaper to peel the potatoes onto and got the bag from under the sink. Better she not say anything right now. If God was kind, something else would happen, and maybe her Dad would realize what her mother was doing.

"Don't rush, will you?" Sheila said as she watched.

"No, I won't," Rita said, feeling grouchy. "This is your job, not mine. I've been at work all day and yet you expect me to act as a servant when I get home. What have *you* been doing all day?"

"It's none of your business what I do."

"No, that's right, it isn't, but it *is* mine," Arthur said, turning in his chair to face his wife. "What *do* you do all day that you have to rush to make a meal for me when I come home? Rita's right. You've had all day to peel those spuds, and all day to shop for our meal. What *have* you been doing all day?"

"If you must know I did my volunteer charity work," Sheila said with an air of one insulted at the question.

"Aye, well, charity begins at home, they say," Arthur said, his face a study in scepticism. "In future I expect you to have a meal on the table when I get in and that applies to Rita as well. She works hard *and* gives you all her pay, yet all you do is treat her like a skivvy. The girl's right. Now you listen to me and take notice, Sheila, Rita won't be doing any cooking if she gives you her pay. You'll do the cooking. If she keeps all her money, you can expect her help, but not before."

Arthur knew his wife liked money. He often wondered what she did with the sizeable amount he gave her each week, since the meals were not exactly expensive and nowhere was there any indication of new household items. He knew she bought clothes for herself, though. Oh yes, she liked to dress up, did Sheila, but the stuff she bought was shoddy. It screamed cheap, with its garish colours and flimsy material.

When he asked what she did with the housekeeping money, she told him it cost a lot of money to run the house and to buy food. Like a fool he believed her, mainly because he had not set foot in a grocery shop since he was a lad running errands for his mother. He realized that Sheila would want to keep all Rita's pay and did, so he gave Rita pocket money behind Sheila's back.

Sheila glared at him defiantly, the stupid sod. Why *had* she married him? These days she could not stand him to touch her, and yet she had to put up with it occasionally. She knew why she had married him well enough: he'd had prospects had Arthur, was considered a catch. His nails were always clean and he didn't much smell of sweat Arthur more than lived up to her expectations when they promoted him to a foreman at a young age.

Whatever Arthur else was, he was a good provider and Sheila had a sizable bank account salted away about which he knew nothing. Her nest egg she kept tucked away in a post office savings account because in the future she would need money. Once Rita married, or left home, Sheila intended to go to Manchester, Liverpool, or other city where she could live a proper life - a life filled with gaiety, with spirit and lots of rich men. Every day she worked to this goal, not eating anything to cause her to gain weight, exercising to retain her flexibility. It was an investment in her future that would pay off eventually. George, for one, continually raved about her figure.

The house looked spotless, cleaned from top to bottom, inside and out, ready for the onslaught of relatives. Marian would be mortified if Roger's snooty wife saw as much as a speck of dirt, and as for Sheila, Marian knew she would point out the slightest smudge to everyone, bitch that she was.

They had scrubbed the floors and brushed down the walls to remove any cobwebs or ash. Then it was time to polish the furniture and wash the windows. The last job was cleaning the china cabinet in the parlour, Rita's favourite ritual. Reverently she would remove each treasured item from the cabinet and place it in a towel-lined basket. She would dust and wash each piece before returning it to its appointed place. The glass fronted rosewood china cabinet was the best piece of furniture

Gran owned and held pride of place in the parlour. It had fascinated Rita from her youngest years, particularly the many wonderful things inside. To her young eyes it was a magical treasure trove.

Her grandmother left the cabinet to Marian and it was the only thing of value in the entire family. Her grandmother knew how Marian cherished it and, bless her soul, made special mention of it in her will . . . and weren't the other relatives livid? Imagine leaving such a choice bit of furniture to a young woman who lived in a row house.

As they annually cleaned everything in the cabinet, Rita asked her Gran about a certain piece. This had become a Christmas tradition for them and now as she removed each cherished item, Rita wondered which one she should ask about this year.

As she picked up the soapstone seal, she thought to ask again for its story. It was smooth and heavy and smelled like the sea. Every time in the past when she asked, Gran changed the subject, or said it was such a boring story they would leave it for another day.

She had heard the story about the blue silk and lace garter, the garter her Gran wore on her wedding day that originally belonged to Lady Mary Shelton who wore it on *her* wedding day. Gran had been Lady Mary's maid at the time of Lady Mary's wedding. Her parents sent her to work in service at Southport and she got the position because of her previous work at the Manor. Not that Marian remembered too much about Southport itself as she only ever saw it from inside the house.

Her Gran had been working at Trawton Manor for nearly a year, then the Gerrard family temporarily moved to Scotland and let her go, no longer needing her services. She sought another position in service, went to Southport, but later came back to take up her old position when the family returned.

Rita liked the story. To think her Gran, who was so much a part of the village, had once worked at Trawton Manor house, had seen inside it, had even worked there. Would you credit it? The Manor was the poshest place Rita knew of, not that she had seen much of the world outside Trawton, but she had seen such homes in films and in books.

Gran, as she knew from old snapshots, was lovely when she was Rita's age, and if they were both the same age, they could have been sisters.

Marian often showed Rita the tintype of the wedding party she kept in an old biscuit tin in the sideboard. On the back was the date 1911.

"We were lucky we married early in the year," she said, "because we had a heat wave that year the like I've never seen since. Do you know it was over 100 degrees in London in August? Imagine living in a city in such heat. It was stifling! People died, usually old people, but also small children."

Marian kept photos of other people now long dead in the tin, and it was when looking at the pictures it occurred to Rita that she and her Gran resembled each other, and this made her feel ever closer to her. Her grandfather, Harry Haydon, had been a tall, handsome man back then, his strong jaw and clear blue eyes showing clearly even in the cracked old sepia photo.

This is the ash tray from the Metropolitan Hotel in Liverpool, she thought as she held it. What a tale she heard about that because her grandfather had stolen it on their honeymoon. Gran professed to be upset about it at the time, but relented later when she put it among her souvenirs. Now the ashtray had a special place in the cabinet.

"It amazed, and overawed me all at once." Marian said, recollecting the fine time of their honeymoon. "We ate from gold bordered plates, real gold, mind. They gave us napkins as big as nappies, real linen with embroidery. The wine came in crystal glasses so fine my hand shook to lift mine because I was afraid of dropping it, or spilling anything on the white table cloth. Of course, we were out of our depth, lovey. Such places are not for the likes of us, but it was our honeymoon and I've never forgotten a second of it."

Marian's description of the lavish Metropolitan hotel and the bustling city of Liverpool entranced Rita.

"Liverpool was a great seaport in those days, Rita. Steam ships and sailing ships arrived from all over the world to the docks, fetching goods from China and Japan, Africa and India, America and Canada. Them docks were always full and the city teemed with life. Sometimes on our walks we never heard a word of English spoken as men jabbered in foreign languages and wore peculiar clothes. Aye, the little cafes were fantastic and sold all kinds of strange food."

"Did you try any of it, Gran? What was it like?"

"Oh, some. We ate Chinese and Indian food. All mucked about, and some of it was hot, like hot peppers. Tasty though. We spent a day walking around the city centre taking in the sights and we saw all the great shops, restaurants and theatres. We even went to see a moving picture, the first I ever saw. It hurt my eyes, but it was exciting, all right."

Her face changed and she shook her head sadly. "It's all gone now. The Germans flattened it during the last war, so the Liverpool you've visited is nothing like it was in its heyday. Hundreds of people died in the blitz that raged night after night when them Germans bombed and burned many thousands of houses."

"Is it still as exciting compared with what it was, Gran?"

"No lass, it will never be. They've rebuilt, as you know, and that's what you've seen. Shame the old city is gone and with it many old traditions. One thing I don't much care for is the way they put up substandard housing for them who survived the bombing. Aye, after the war, the council built prefabs, them prefabricated houses, hundreds and maybe thousands of them in all them housing estates."

Rita had seen them and thought them seedy looking as they stood in long rows, run down and neglected. Supposedly temporary housing, many thousands were still occupied stood, cheap and dilapidated: today's slums.

Gran often talked about her two weeks in Liverpool. She recalled the ferry to Wallasey, the miles of golden sands, and their day out picnics on the beach.

Pollution changed had everything, Rita knew. When she was small, Gran and Granddad took her to Wallasey for the day. She recalled her excitement at travelling on the large ferry across the River Mersey, and watching the screaming following seagulls, white and gleaming in the sunshine. Unfortunately, oil had polluted the beach and she ruined her best dress when she sat on a hidden patch. Marian had thought it odd to see few people on the beach when they arrived, and too late they discovered why. It took the shine off Rita's day, knowing that when she arrived home, her mother would punish her.

She sighed as she came back to the present. So many things to ask about, she thought, as she laid each item gently in the basket.

"Well, what's it to be this time?" Marian asked as she gently dried the little figurines and placed them on the table.

"The seal?" Rita asked hopefully.

"Not that old thing." Marian did not look at it.

Rita stared at her. "Why not? You always say that."

"We'll leave it for another day, choose something else."

"But Gran . . .,"

"But Gran, nothing."

"Oh, all right, I think the angel this time," Rita said, as she handed her Gran the small matte china angel with its tiny lace wings. "It's lovely, isn't it?"

"Yes. Very pretty," Marian said as she stood it on the mantel. After tea they would sit by the fire and she would tell the story. This little trinket commemorated her loss of virginity, the reason she acted like a scarlet woman. Now as they ate, her mind sought a story to tell Rita.

1901

"You are so, Marian Steadman." Cissie sounded vindictive and tossed her long plaits angrily.

Fourteen-year-old Marian sighed. While she had taken two walks with Graham Hobbs along Gypsy Woods, he did not interest her. It was spite, she thought, going walking with him, because aware of Cissie's great love for Graham, she delighted in teasing her.

Unfortunately for Marian, Graham began to get ideas so she started making excuses not to be near him, a difficult job since they were both in the church choir. Still, she told herself, once she went to work at the

Manor next week she wouldn't see him at all and Cissie would have a clear field.

The Manor, being a four-mile walk from the village along country lanes, meant she wouldn't be home much once she went into resident service. While she would come home to give her mother her pay each quarter, she had no intentions of making the trip every week on her half day. Her half day, she decided, would be spent going to Wigan to window shop, and visit the market to see everything new and wonderful. How she would get there she didn't know, but surely the other servants must go to Wigan. In her euphoria it did not occur to her their afternoon off was probably on another day.

Sunday morning her mother packed Marian's few belongings into a basket and took her to the Manor. When they arrived, her mother handed her into the care of the housekeeper, Mrs. Wilton.

"Be good, child. Don't do anything to shame us," her Mam said before she left to walk back.

"This is the scullery where you'll be working," Mrs. Wilton said sternly as she pointed to a scruffy, unkempt young woman who stood staring like an idiot. "You are to replace Jean here. She'll show you what needs to be done."

Marian looked around with dismay. She was going to work here? In this dank, dark, windowless space? A single bulb hung from a long wire and its feeble light could hardly penetrate the corners, much inferior to their own oil lamps at home. Still, the manor was the first habitation in the county to install this new lighting and now she wondered why they had bothered.

Along one side of the bare brick wall were sinks, low and shallow. Above were racks for draining the pots and pans, while a pump stood in a corner and a large enamel bucket stood beneath. The flagstone floor was now wet and slippery, and large barrels stood on the opposite side filled with sand and the grit used as a scrubbing compound. Another keg held washing soda.

"Jean," Mrs. Wilton ordered, "take Marian up to the room and show her where to put her things. Bring her back down immediately. Then we'll find a uniform to fit."

"Come on," Jean said, pulling at Marian's arm. "I've got all them lot to get clean before cook starts supper." She gestured to a stack of dirty pots and pans. "Still, you can help me tonight, can't you?" She grinned at the thought.

They climbed a set of steep, bare board stairs, which led to yet another set and then another. Each set got narrower and steeper.

"This is the floor where all the servants sleep, except Mrs. Wilton. She's got a room downstairs off the kitchen," Jean said, gasping because it had been a hard climb. "I'll show you. You and me, we're gonna share." Jean pulled her along a narrow dusty floored passage and into a small room.

The room sat under the eaves and had a high set foot-long narrow window, which apparently only allowed in light as Marian soon discovered it was sealed shut. The ceiling was the underside of the roof, the trusses almost at head height. She saw no light in here, no oil lamp, no electricity.

Two narrow iron cots stood opposite an unpainted pine chest of drawers on which sat a cracked ewer and basin. A wire ran along the inside wall to act as a wardrobe. Jean, she saw, had one faded green dress, a spare uniform of grey and a clean apron.

"Here, you can have the bottom two drawers," Jean said. She sounded magnanimous, being the incumbent. "Come on, we have to hurry. Mrs. Clayton'll be mad as a wet hen if we take too long."

"Who's Mrs. Clayton?" Marian asked.

"The cook, that's who," Jean said, grinning with a mouth full of brownish teeth. "She's got a temper like a fire cracker. You'd better watch your head if she gets mad, 'cos she throws things."

"Oh," Marian said, thinking this was nothing like she'd expected. This bare little bedroom, the dank scullery.

In her naivete, she'd imagined soft furnishings, fine china, deep piled carpets, good meals served by servants and butlers. Her Mam continually talked about how they lived at the manor, told her of the luxury, the splendour. Well, she chided herself, how stupid could she be? How could her mother possibly know how they lived? As for her herself, they took her on as a skivvy, for heaven's sake, and why should she expect anything other than she got? Still, it proved a great disappointment and tears prickled at her eyes.

The girls clattered back down the steep stairs. Mrs. Wilton took Marian to a room near the scullery lined with clothes racks. She handed her a blue dress, the only one close to her size, and too large. Mrs. Wilton bundled two aprons, one of coarse grey material for dirty work, and a grey looking white one for clean work, into her arms. She found her a net mob cap with a tiny frill with instructions to wear it when she worked with food.

"At least your hair is neat and tidy. More than I can say for some." She sniffed as she regarded the plaits. Marian's hair was long; long enough to sit on and she wore it in braids. Now as befitted a working woman, this morning her mother had wound the plaits around her head.

Mrs. Wilton handed her over to Jean who delighted in exhibiting the mound of blackened dirty pots awaiting scouring.

"All these?" Marian's mouth fell open.

"Aaw, this is nowt," Jean said with a great deal of satisfaction. "They only had ten for breakfast today. You wait 'til they have a banquet. They've got hundreds of pots then, and you have to work two days to clean 'um all. Of course," she glanced to make sure they were alone, "Mrs. Clayton goes out of her way to make work. I've seen her pour sauce out of one pan into another lotsa times."

They worked for an hour scouring the huge pots, the small sauce pans, the pie plates and baking tins, the roasting pans, the serving platters. By the time they finished, Marian's hands were a mass of wrinkles, her skin fish-white, chaffed and scraped.

"Come on, its time to start the vegetables," Jean said as she made her way into the kitchen with the clattering iron-wheeled trolley on which rested the clean pots. They donned their net caps.

"About time, too," Mrs. Clayton said as she turned from the stove. Her fat red face glistened with greasy perspiration. "You, Martha, put these in their proper place. Who's this, then?" She inspected Marian with a beady eye.

"Marian Steadman, Mrs. Clayton. You know they're making me up to under housemaid," Jean said, her tone smug.

Mrs. Clayton smiled grimly. "Aye, and they need their heads reading, putting you in charge of the fires! I shudder to think you'll probably burn us all in our beds." She turned her attention to Marian. "Well, young lady, let's hope you've got more in your head than feathers. You can help Maggie."She gestured to a young woman who looked a bit dotty. "with the sprouts, and don't peel them too small. This one here," she pointed at a giggling Jean with the ladle, "can make a ten-pound sack into less than two, what with her peeling and pulling."

Jean laughed loudly, safe now from Mrs. Clayton's wrath.

Marian sat at the table near the young woman Maggie and took a sprout out of the sack. Maggie smiled at her sympathetically. Marian thought Maggie did not appear to have much in the way of brains as she watched her clumsy movements.

"You, Jean, get them carrots scraped," Cook ordered.

Tea time found Marian exhausted. Never had she thought working for a living would be so tiring. Even a pause to wipe one's brow brought a reprimand from Mrs. Clayton, a hard task master who seemingly had eyes in the back of her head. Every time she picked on Marian, Jean smirked and tittered.

The servants ate at a long table at the other end of the kitchen. The household employed two menservants, two grooms and a stable boy, three upstairs maids, two ladies' maids, two valets and a butler. The general housemaid would leave to marry soon - it was her place Jean had inherited.

A long row of bells on curled wires hung from the back wall, labelled for various rooms in the house and outbuildings. Apparently the family did not think servants needed sustenance as the bells constantly rang when they were eating.

The kitchen hierarchy was noticeable, Marian thought, taking it in at a glance. Personal maids wore crisp white aprons over dark blue dresses, and the valets, in their wellfitted dark uniforms with white shirts, looked snooty as they sat near the top of the table. The parlour maids wore cast offs from the personal maids and smart white caps with long frilled ribbons down the back. Housemaids and kitchen workers wore grey aprons and faded cotton dresses with mob caps that covered their entire heads. These were the servants none of the family ever saw.

At Marian's end of the table sat the scullery maid, the kitchen maids and the outside workers, the grooms and stable boy. She thought the stable workers smelled at bit, but it was a good honest smell, the smell of hard work.

The butler, Mr. Hodgson, sat at the table head. A regal looking man who looked down his nose at everyone. Clad in a frock coat, grey striped trousers and white shirt with a black bow tie, he sat in splendour in a large armed chair, surveying them all critically. Only Mrs. Clayton, Mrs. Wilton and Mr. Hodgson spoke during the meal.

She thought the food delicious. Marian's customary fare was of bread and butter, or lard and sugar sandwiches, so she tried everything. As she ate, her eyes consumed the mound of newly baked crusty bread and butter, thin sliced ham and roast beef, mustard pickle and relish, scones, cake and fruit. In the middle sat tea or milk to drink, and jugs of beer for the men.

The meal, and the warmth of the kitchen where a huge roast and chickens were turning on a spit for the family supper, made Marian feel sleepy. She could have put her head down and slept, but when Mrs. Clayton stood, so did everyone else. The upstairs workers left quickly, as did the outside workers.

Mrs. Clayton dished out her orders. "Right, Jean, get them trays washed and polished. You, new girl, you help her. Maggie get out the silverware and make sure it's clean. Martha, you swab the scullery floor and don't forget to put down sand." Mrs. Clayton watched as they scurried to do her bidding and sat with Mr. Hodgson to have another cup of tea, to which, Marian saw, they added whisky from a small bottle.

Within two weeks the job had Marian bored to death. If she kept up with the steady stream of dirty pots, they never rushed her. Mrs. Clayton now smiled in her direction and rarely had nasty things to say. Marian figured Jean must be stupid to think Mrs. Clayton had a temper, as she never raised her voice once, and never threw anything.

These days she saw her roommate only at meal times and upstairs in the dormer. They did not speak at the table and at bedtime both were so tired they rarely spoke more than a few words by the light of a solitary candle. Jean, pleased with her new position, told Marian she once saw Lady Esther in a silk morning gown.

Marian's day started at five-thirty and, when company was at the house, ended at ten at night or later. It was not so much that the work was especially hard. It was the utter boredom of it, the endless pile of dirty pots, the continual vegetable processing. Her hands were red with the lye soap and sand used to scour pots, her fingernails worn to the quick. She knew Jean was right when she said Mrs. Clayton used far more pots and pans than she needed. Well, why not, since she had a skivvy to wash them?

Six months later she felt like she had always been there, never known anything other than work. Mrs. Clayton liked Marian, never yelled at her and always had a cheery word so now when Marian was finished early, she had Mrs. Clayton's permission to walk through the vegetable garden to take some fresh air.

One fine evening she met Master Geoffrey as she walked. Marian, unaware Geoffrey was the son of the house, thought he was a gardener.

"Good evening," she said as she approached. Coatless, he stood admiring the runner beans covered in brilliant red flowers.

"Good evening," he said taking in her shining face and rosy cheeks. "Beautiful."

"Yes," she said, thinking he meant the runner beans. Two cabbage white butterflies were courting, flittering between the blossoms and a bee bumbled from bloom to bloom.

"Yes, beautiful."

Then she saw he was looking right at her and blushed redly, lowering her eyes.

"You must be new here. Who are you? " he asked.

"Marian Steadman."

At first glance she fell in love with him because he was both handsome and well dressed. Then again, the youths with whom she usually came into contact were slovenly and dirty.

"Who are you?" she asked, too naive to know one did not address a stranger so familiarly, as she looked up at him under her brows.

"My name is Geoffrey."

"Hello, Geoff," she said, abbreviating his name as she would with any other boy she met in the village.

"Hello, Marian," he said, smiling down at her.

Very young, about fifteen he thought, as her figure was both juvenile and yet strangely adult. Though petite, her breasts were well developed while her waist was small and this enchanted him. Her colouring was rosy, pink and white, and those big blue eyes contrasting with her strawberry blond hair were bewitching. She seemed like a china doll.

Up to this point in time he'd showed little interest in the opposite sex. At college he had wondered if he were homosexually inclined, but after one disgusting encounter, decided it was not for him. Now the sight of this young woman woke something in him foreign to his being. His heart beat faster at the sight of her and he felt a stirring in his groin. At last, he thought relieved, he was a man with a man's emotions.

Geoffrey, an intelligent young man, knew his education and breeding could well go against him if he wanted to get closer to a village educated girl, so he started to use the local slang, flattening his vowels. She suspected nothing, he could tell, and his heart was glad in his deception.

As he got to know her, he realized she cared nothing for the 'gentry' as she called the family, thinking them lazy and vain. Not that she had ever met any one of them, she confided, working as she did in the dark basement scullery. She had, however, listened with great interest at meal times when Mr. Hodgson and Mrs. Clayton slagged off their master and mistress. Some things she told him made him laugh as he heard how the servants regarded his parents.

For three weeks Geoffrey and Marian met often in the garden and she fell deeply in love with him. Each evening, whenever she could get away, they sat on a rustic bench under a bower of clematis and talked. Each time they met they got to know each other better, each liking what they learned, and each intoxicated the other as they fed off each other's admiration.

Marian waited impatiently for Jean to fall asleep. It did not take long because exhaustion always overtook them after their late meal. Tonight, though, Marian's churning excitement kept her awake. Soon she would meet with Geoffrey, and she would discover what true love meant.

Often she wondered about Geoff. His clothes were of good quality for a gardener, and his speech was sometimes precise. Too, he changed the subject every time she asked him a direct question about his family. While she found this peculiar, his adulation easily diverted her. To think such a handsome youth loved her and vowed his devotion was heady medicine. Her every thought was of him, as was her every dream. His touches thrilled her, and she knew where they were leading. Marian knew the basics of conception as did every country-bred female and now she longed for more than a kiss or a touch.

Tonight she would know him physically, she promised herself. A great fire consumed her, a fire only his touch could quench. Soon it was near midnight and Jean snored softly. Dressing quickly and quietly, she crept to the head of the stairs. Under her arm were her clogs. Barefoot and scared of making the slightest sound, she glided out the door and down the corridor. From where she stood she could hear steady beat of the massive long clock in the hall.

She flitted her silent way through the kitchen and opened the scullery door. Terrified of being caught, her heart beat like a frightened rabbit. Cook had retired for the night and the kitchen was dim since little illumination came from the banked up fire, and only a glimmer from a small oil lamp on the table.

Quickly she passed through the scullery to the larger back door used for the removal of household rubbish. Quietly, she pulled back the bolt, opened the door and drew it to behind her and, moving away from the dustbins and coal house, swiftly ran like a shadow along the paved laundry path to the orchard. Moving became easier now as nobody was around to see or hear, and she hummed as she opened the walled garden gate set into a high brick wall kept closed to keep out animals. The gate squeaked loudly, a long shrieking sound of metal on metal, and she drew in a breath of alarm. Then chuckled at her fears.

Making her way across the silent, moonlit garden, she opened the iron gate on the other side. Leaving this garden, she entered the wild part of the estate. Here in the copses the game keeper reared pheasants and grouse. Deer grazed in the open grassy spaces, and long sheds under the trees housed rabbits, geese, chickens and ducks destined for the table. She scurried through the darkened woods.

A white marble gazebo stood at the top of a rise, in a clearing overlooking a valley and the river. Everyone knew of it as it was clearly visible from the village. Beech woods hid the area from the house. Marian had visited the gazebo often as a child when a gang of them made it a game to visit to picnic on windfall apples the boys stole from the orchard.

A Gerrard of old had built the gazebo folly for his lady love. Round and Ionic, inside were marble benches and a small round table where Marian imagined they enjoyed picnics. Of course, servants would serve those picnics and they would have been of gourmet quality, not of bird and insect spoiled apples. She smiled at the thought.

Marian drew close to the white building. "Geoff?" she called quietly but got no answer. No matter, she could be early as she had no idea what the time was, other than it was well past eleven.

Inside the gazebo, she sat on a bench and stared out over the moonlit valley. Below her she saw two deer grazing, and a rabbit scuttered across the clearing. A fox and her cubs paused to play on the grassy field below. Bats flitted on their silent way, swooping down on flying insects. An owl hooted somewhere in the woods. It was warm, although a slight breeze teased the leaves of a huge old oak nearby. She thought she heard the fox bark.

"Marian," he said quietly, startling her.

"Geoff." She opened her arms and he came to her.

"My dear, dear Marian." As he held her close, his cologne was like all the perfumes of Arabia to her. He smelled so good.

"I think I love you," he murmured into her hair and she felt a surge of joy run through her body.

He loved her! He loved her and she loved him. Had anyone ever been this happy?

"And I love you, Geoff," she said, putting her arms tighter around his waist and breathing in the heady aroma of his cologne.

They sat on the bench and kissed deeply. Although aroused, he was strangely frightened of rushing her. His body ached for her as his mind thought of only one thing, When he kissed her gently, he heard her breath come faster.

Pulling back, he looked down into her lovely face and devoured it with his eyes. Her starry eyes caressed the face she loved and she sighed with happiness. Marian lay back on the bench as Geoffrey moved over her. She felt like ripping off her clothes and giving herself to him. Why was he taking so long to do it? Marian could hear her ragged breath, felt the fire in her loins, the rapid beat of her heart seeming to sound throughout her body.

Losing her virginity was the last thing on Marian's mind. Her mother and the church always taught a girl must hold onto to her virginity at any price because no man wanted used goods. A bride must be virginal and pure. How often they said it, and yet now she did not care. She never before felt such warmth, such longing, such need. Before Geoffrey there had been nothing.

He undid her bodice and touched her breasts and she felt such a thrill. She pushed herself at him and kissed him deeply. Impatient now, he lifted her skirt and caressed her thigh. She opened her legs, glad that she had not worn her underwear and waited for him to take her virginity.

It was wonderful, the feelings ran through her like water over a waterfall, she wanted him and he wanted her. It was building up inside her, what it was, she did not know, but she wanted more of him. Suddenly he pulled out and lay gasping. But why? She ached for more, wanted more and she pulled him lcloser to kiss him again,

Later they wandered back through the woods, hand in hand. From time to time they stopped to kiss.

Geoffrey paused as they neared the far gate of the walled garden.

"Will you be all right?" he asked holding her close.

"I'll be fine, Geoff. I'll creep in like a mouse and nobody will ever know." She kissed his soft lips and felt like she was drowning.

"Take care, Marian. I'll see you tomorrow evening in the garden."

It took a long time for them to say goodnight and Marian wandered back to the scullery door with stars in her eyes and hope in her heart. Surely Geoff would marry her now: he loved her and she loved him. Once a man kissed you, it meant marriage, once a man had known your body, he had promised himself to you. All the girls knew that. Yet where did he come from? She knew he did not come from the village. She watched him move away and into the shadows. Where *did* he live?

For some reason, it proved more difficult to sneak in than sneak out, so it took her almost half an hour to gain the room.

CHAPTER THREE

Before five-thirty, Jean poked at her with a sharp bony finger, rudely rousing her.

"Wake up, slug-a-bed. We've got about five minutes afore Mrs. Wilton checks."

The housekeeper was up and about at five and by five-thirty had checked every room to ensure everyone was about their duties. Mrs. Wilton did, however, because of her privileged and exalted position, take a nap at ten, and a nap after the noon meal in her private room off the kitchen.

"Crumbs," Marian rose hurriedly and got into her clothes. She could still smell Geoff's cologne.

"Here, where did you get scent?" Jean sniffed the air. "It smells like the stuff his lordship wears." Speculatively she stared at Marian. "You carrying on with his lordship?"

"Of course not," Marian said, her cheeks flaming. "The old man? You've got to be joking."

"Aye, and he's got a son an' all." She stared at Marian as if to trying read her thoughts.

Marian roughly dragged the brush through her hair, found it too tangled, and covered it with her mob cap. "Come on then, let's go."

By the time the staff breakfast was served, she had scoured the few remaining pots from the previous evening, scrubbed the kitchen floor, and sluiced and sanded the scullery. Soon lack of sleep began to catch up on her and Marian felt as tired as she had ever been. Wearily she dragged around until even Mrs. Clayton noticed.

"You sickening for some'at?" she asked, nudging Marian as she podded peas for the family luncheon.

"No, Mrs. Clayton," Marian said tonelessly, though she felt like death warmed over.

Edna Clayton stared at her. She had looked peculiar all day, had the girl, smiling a lot and humming and, while Marian's eyes looked bright enough, they had dark shadows under them plus she seemed definitely low on energy. Too bad because they were entertaining forty for luncheon and supper today.

"You, Martha, get them potatoes peeled and be quick about it. You, Maggie, help her," she ordered, meanwhile checking her menus to see what else could be done early.

For the luncheon they were to serve cold shrimp salad, sole with almonds, roast beef and Yorkshire pudding with assorted vegetables, a shape of blancmange with raspberry sauce. For supper: lobster bisque, cod stuffed with shrimp, roast venison, partridge, ham, queen pudding, and strawberries with cream. Between these large meals was afternoon tea for which she needed to make finger sandwiches, bake four cakes, scones, tarts, and savoury pies. For late supper they would serve individual meat tarts and sausage rolls, cheeses and fruit, with only Maggie and Marian to help her unless she could coerce Mr. Hodgson into lending her Jean and one maid.

She wiped the sweat from her brow with her arm as she directed Martha to put more coal on the fire. In the stone floored and marble walled butler's pantry she set the eggs, cream and milk to stay cool. The wine stood waiting decanting to replenish the tantalus, both Hodgson's realm.

So much to do, and so little time. Still, she had managed before, and with less help, and she would manage again.

Marian was definitely drooping by tea time and sat at the table so exhausted she could hardly chew.

Mrs. Clayton watched her closely. Something was wrong with the young woman and she was the best scullery maid she had ever had. God forbid the girl was with child. She glared at the stable boy and the grooms, wondering.

At eight Mrs. Clayton took pity on her. "Get yourself up to bed, Steadman," she said, "We don't want you coming down with something, not with a house full of guests."

Marian smiled her thanks and wearily moved to the back staircase. She desperately wanted to meet with Geoff tonight, but how? The only way to the gardens she knew of was right under Mrs. Clayton's nose and tonight would be a late night for the cook who must be on call until all the guests had retired, in case one should suddenly feel peckish.

"I want to get a breath of air before I go up. I'm sure it would make me feel better," Marian said, opening the back door.

"Aye, make sure it's only a couple of minutes too, or I'll be out after you," Edna said, eyeing her with suspicion.

Marian, suddenly alive again, ran to the vegetable garden and sat on the bench under the clematis. Impatiently she gazed around knowing she could not wait long or Mrs. Clayton would send someone to get her. Anxiously she stood looking around the area.

After fifteen minutes they sent Jean to fetch her.

Hodgson opened the study door. "Your lordship, the guests have begun to arrive," he announced in a flat voice.

Hodgson hated house parties. They caused too much upheaval in his wellordered household. The Manor housed and fed the various cleaners, maids and valets.

These servants treated the visit to another household as did their masters.. For them it became a holiday because they had little to occupy themselves. They flirted with the household staff, even had affairs with them.

Though Hodgson frowned on this, he found it quite impossible to police the entire mansion.

Charles put down his glass and sighed. "Come along, Geoffrey, we must do our duty or your mother will be angry."

At luncheon Geoffrey avoided his mother's eye, although she spent much time staring at him. In the afternoon, attired in frilled organza gowns, the older females sat in the conservatory while the young women, watched by their mothers, vied for Geoffrey's attention.

When they later played whist in the parlour, young Cynthia's dazzling eyes soon entranced Geoffrey. By this time, her obvious attraction for him did not go unseen. The other young women noticed immediately and gave him baleful glances, tactfully keeping their distance. Lady Esther smiled as after tea she and Cynthia's mother closeted themselves in the morning room, presumably discussing an early engagement.

For the formal supper, the ladies wore satin and lace evening gowns. Later Cynthia played the piano in the music room and Geoffrey forgot all about Marian, the servant, who only last night was the love of his life. His eyes and heart were now full of Cynthia's refined beauty recognizing her as well suited to one in his position. He did not walk out that evening, but sat beside Cynthia on the piano stool besottedly turning the music.

At breakfast next day Marian listened to the talk at the top of the table and as the story unfolded her blood ran cold.

"Oh yers. He's head over heels about her," Mrs. Wilton said. "Lady Esther has always wanted him to marry a suitably prominent young lady and Lady Cynthia comes from one of the richest oldest families in Lancashire."

"About time he got engaged too, I should think," Mr. Hodgson remarked. "He's old enough and mature enough to support a wife. Time he put a stop to this chasing around the county with his chums."

"Yes, the young master is a presentable young man," Mrs. Wilton said nodding. "Let's face it, his looks are fine and he's had the best education money can buy. Mind you, he takes after his father in a lot of ways, by all accounts."

"Ah, yes," Hodgson said, nodding sagely, "Sir Charles always did have a keen eye for the ladies, and since he's a fine figure of a man, who can blame him?"

Mrs. Clayton laughed. "Nobody if you ask me, what with that old icicle of a wife. Lady Esther's face would stop clocks, it would."

"We should be glad Master Geoffrey is more like his father," Mrs. Wilton said, "He's kind and thinks nothing of giving a word of praise now and then. Not like his mother, who only finds fault."

Geoffrey? Was Geoff the man she loved? Surely not. Her stomach suddenly cramped. Was her Geoff the young master?

As if he had read her thoughts, Hodgson spoke. "Yes, Master Geoffrey is lucky. Mind you, I had my doubts about him. Time was when I thought he was in the other camp, if you get my drift. He showed no interest in the opposite sex, always bringing home chums to stay, always tramping the woods with them, gathering specimens, or so he said."

"I would never have thought it of him," Mrs. Wilton said, shocked. "I heard his father took him to a bordello for his birthday. That probably put him off."

"Really, Mrs. Wilton, and what do you know of bordellos, pray tell?" Mrs. Clayton asked, her interest piqued.

Mrs. Wilton's face darkened, but she said nothing.

Marian sat stock still, listening to every word. They were talking about her Geoff.

"Blake was set to watch him this week," Hodgson said, gesturing with his head at Blake. "Lady Esther asked us to watch him after she saw him talking in the vegetable garden with one of the female staff."

Mrs. Wilton gasped and quickly looked at each maid. None raised their heads. They knew better.

Marian's heart sank like a stone. Geoff was the son of the house, one day to be Lord Gerrard, and she knew then she had lost her virginity to the wrong man.

Four weeks later she was walking in the garden when Geoffrey stepped out from behind a trellis covered in perennial sweet peas.

"Marian," Geoffrey caught at her arm. "We must talk."

"What about?" She was suddenly livid, anger surging through every vein. "There's nothing you can say that will bring back my virtue. You took advantage of me, you, you," her mind sought a bad word, ". . . you bastard. You ruined me."

Her eyes filled with tears. Marian spent many a sleepless night worrying about whether she might be pregnant. Fortunately she was not, though his words of love and betrayal were harder to erase from her mind.

"Marian, my dear, dear, Marian, please forgive me. I do love you, but we are from different worlds. We have no future."

"You led me on," she said, her eyes flashing fire. "You never said who you were. I thought you were a gardener, and every time I asked you about your home, you changed the subject. You lied to me to get your own way."

After lately thinking about his willing young partner, Geoffrey felt ashamed of himself, which is why he sought her out, to set the story straight.

"Yes, I guess I did," he admitted, "but I didn't mean to harm you. You and I had a wonderful night, a night of love and passion we'll remember for the rest of our lives. I'll never forget you, my dear Marian, my first real love."

Her eyes full of tears, she looked up at him. "Nor I you, Geoff," Then as the immensity of it swept over her, her voice grew hard, "or should I say Master Geoffrey now? Still, I'll recall the night with more shame than love. You've humiliated me."

"Here. Take this to remember our wonderful night." He handed her a small angel statuette. "You'll always be an angel in my memory."

Marian drew back. "Then you should keep it, sir, to remind you of your sins against me. I'm no angel now, am I? Who'll want me now? You've ruined me." Not only was she ruined, she found her mind constantly thinking about sex.

He groaned and she stared at him, feeling a sense of some guilt. But as difficult as this was, he surely had made it plain that she was nothing but a lower class servant. Marian could almost read his mind, and decided she must make him pay for that.

"Please take it, Marian," His voice sounded thick with tears and she glanced up at him. Maybe he did have feelings after all. He tried to find something to say to ease her pain. "Don't leave me like this, with anger for me. I do love you, you know."

"Aye, well," she said, regarding him sceptically as she took the small angel and put it in her pocket. "Goodbye . . . sir." Turning her back on him, she walked back down the path, her mind racing.

Her hand on the figurine, she wondered where to hide it away from Jean's prying eyes.

DECEMBER 1954

Rita sat entranced as her Gran told the story of the angel. It was so romantic, all about how her Granddad and her Gran went to Morecambe and strolled the sands on their first anniversary.

". . . and so your Granddad gave me this little angel because he said I looked like an angel on the day we married."

"Aw, Gran, how lovely." Rita's eyes misted over. Never had there been such a great love as between her grandparents, she thought. Looking at the tiny angel, she suddenly put it to her lips and kissed it.

Marian watched her fondly. Much better she didn't tell the true story.

"Time to put it back and get yourself home now, child. Your mother will be sending out the dogs to find you."

"I wish I lived here with you, Gran," Rita said. Wistfully she looked around the cosy kitchen where the firelight cast its warm glow over everything. She often said this, but knew her mother would never allow her to come here to stay.

What was it between her Mam and her Gran? Maybe one of these days she would simply come out and ask both of them. That is, if they were ever together.

CHAPTER FOUR

1955

Sheila was pregnant. It seemed impossible as she had taken every precaution. For days she moped around. She could not say it was Arthur's child as they had not slept together for over six months. She had no idea of how to go about getting an abortion: didn't even know whom to ask about such a terrible thing.

When Arthur came home early one day and Rita was still at work, she blurted it out.

"I'm pregnant," she said abruptly.

Arthur wheeled around and looked at her. "Oh aye? And what am I supposed to do about it?" His face grew white with anger. "Don't ask me to support some other chap's child."

Sheila weighed him up. Good old Arthur, weak willed and easily led, had suddenly developed a backbone. "How could you say that? It could be yours, you know."

Arthur stood legs apart, arms crossed over his chest. A tall man, slim to the point of thinness with sharply chiselled features, his thick curling hair was one of his best features. The fact she thought she could con him into thinking it was his child was clearly the wrong thing to say by the look he wore.

"Aye, and pigs can fly. I've not put a finger on you for months. Take your bastard and leave this house. I'm having nowt more to do with you."

"Arthur!" She had miscalculated his reaction this time.

Arthur suddenly became staunch in his determination. "You've made a fool of me for the last time, Sheila. I feel ashamed to be married to you, and now you've brought matters to a head. Heck, what a terrible thing to have to tell Rita."

"Don't tell her," she begged, "Please, Arthur."

He steeled his jaw. "You pack a case and get out, and get out now. I'll give you half an hour to move." He stood with hands on hips, his face white and set.

Her gaze flew around the small kitchen. "You don't mean it, Arthur," she said, holding out her hands in supplication.

"I mean it, woman, pack your things and get out now." His hands clenched into fists and she felt a tingle of fear because Arthur suddenly seemed strong.

Rita arrived home half an hour after her mother left.

"Where's Mam?" she asked, puzzled as she took off her coat and hung it on the back of the door. Where was supper, she wondered? Since Dad told her Mam off, at least she usually came home to a meal. The kitchen looked clean and tidy, but cold with no smell of food, nor did she see anything on the stove top.

He sounded bitter. "Gone," he said, "and bloody good riddance too."

"Where's she gone?" Rita asked, puzzled.

"Gone to her fancy man, no doubt," Arthur said. Tension strained his voice. "Sorry lass, but you'll have to do the cooking in future. She won't be coming back."

Something about his white face, blank eyes and set expression stopped her from asking anything further. How had he found out about her Mam's fancy man? Did it mean Dad knew all about Mam's adulterous affairs? A sense of relief washed over her. Now she did not have to tell him anything. Her mind raced frantically, her hands cold and she felt like shivering as she looked into the pantry, wondering what was available.

"Bacon and eggs with bread and butter do you, Dad?"

"Anything, lass, anything that's convenient."

Arthur said little that evening, but his mind was active. Now he was almost free to be with Molly, but where would that leave Rita?

Molly was a good sort who would welcome Rita into her home. Yet would Rita accept Molly?

Rita called in at her Gran's on the way home from work the next evening. All day she inwardly groaned with exasperation as the hours crept by, all because she was dying to tell her Gran what had happened.

"Hello, love," Marian said as she opened the door. "Come in and take off your coat. Tea's brewing. You always did smell a cup of tea from a mile off, didn't you?" she chattered as she bustled into the kitchen. "I baked sour milk scones with raisins."

"She's gone, Gran," Rita said, bursting into tears.

"Aaw now, lass, who's gone?" She pulled Rita into her arms and rocked her soothingly. "There, there, lovey, don't be so upset."

"My Mam, she's gone," Rita sobbed. "She took all her clothes and she's gone."

Marian pushed Rita back so she could look into her woebegone face. "Where did she go? Did she leave you a note?" she asked, wondering what her foolish daughter had done this time.

"No, and my Dad won't say much," Rita sobbed, "only that she's not coming back."

"Well now, maybe it's for the best in a way," she said slowly. Marian didn't want to go into details. She should never slag off the girl's mother, even if she were her own daughter, although agreeing with anything Rita said would be easy. "Come on now, my little sausage, less of the miseries. Surely you and your Dad will manage all right? I mean, what did your mother do that either of you can't?"

Rita smiled through her tears, her Gran understood. She always made everything all right. "That's what my Dad said." Wiping her eyes, she tried to grin. Gran did not sound upset, although Rita knew the villagers would gossip.

Why should she be upset, anyway? It was not as if any love was lost between herself and her mother, any more than between her mother and Gran. It was that she felt so betrayed for some reason, people would point at her as the girl whose mother walked off and left her. Too, maybe it had been her fault.

She drank tea and ate a still warm scone to please her Gran, and while she knew it was good, it tasted like sawdust

"I can't stay long, Gran, I've got to cook Dad's supper and I still have to shop."

Marian took down her purse from the mantle. "Here, take this and buy fish and chips tonight," she said, handing her a tenshilling note. "Your Dad will understand. Or you can both have supper here, fish and chips, of course."

"Thanks, Gran," Rita took the money. "I'll pay you back on pay day." She smiled suddenly. "I'll have all kinds of money," she said gleefully, "now Mam isn't taking my pay off me, and my Dad says he'll give me the housekeeping money. Can you make me a list of what I'll need to buy next week? I'm not good at housekeeping."

"Neither should you be," Marian said firmly, "you're only a young lass yet. Anyroad, I'll help you best I can, and it's time for you to learn. I'll come round to help in the late afternoons before you get home. Cooking for three is better than cooking for one any day. Make sure your Dad won't mind, and get me a key."

From gossip she knew the villagers had twice seen Arthur with another woman; the news had gone its rounds like lightning. Not that she ever blamed him, knowing he received no comfort from Sheila . . . nobody did.

"Thanks, Gran," Rita hugged her grandmother. "My Dad'll be pleased as punch if he thinks you're going to cook. He loves your cooking, and so do I. It's right smashing."

Marian pushed at Rita gently. "Get away with you, lass, it's all blather to get out of doing it yourself. Away home now, and ask your Dad."

Rita felt happier as she walked home. With Gran in the picture they would have good meals and the house would be serene and warm. She felt a pang of guilt, but her mother had never been a loving parent, only a bogeyman who from time to time let up on the punishment.

Sheila rented a room in a boarding house in the lower part of Trawton. Lower because it lay below the hills where the big shots lived, and even lower because it primarily housed a lower class of miner who subsisted from week to week. Long rows of identical dark brick houses lined cobbled streets. No trees, bushes or even a blade of grass found a foothold, other than untamed rye grass and weeds growing on the odd empty lot. It looked depressing and poverty stricken.

The house where she stayed was in the middle of a terrace of colliers' homes, her tiny room, was the small room at the back. She shared the house with the parents, four children, and another lodger, a shift worker coal sorter, who slept in the back of the kitchen.

While she had never been a good housekeeper, the dirty kitchen made her retch and Sheila decided to find better accommodation. Up to now she relied on eating out, usually fish and chips, preferring it to whatever the landlady served up on soiled plates. Unfortunately, though she had been so sure of George, he brushed her off when she gave him the news, which both shocked and disappointed her. Now, sadly disillusioned, she made do on her own as best she could and, to conserve her precious funds, taken this room.

The street lay far enough off the beaten track to plunge her into obscurity and, if she didn't venture into the main shopping district, she could stay hidden. Once she started to show, the tongues would wag unceasingly and the least she could do was protect her reputation by keeping out of sight. Who knew? She might want to go back to the village one day.

"Mrs. Goodwin?" The voice sliced through her thoughts. Mrs. Shillingford, the landlady was all voice and shrill with it.

She went to the top of the stairs and called down. "Yes, Mrs. Shillingford?"

"A man's here to see you. He's in the parlour," Mrs. Shillingford, head back, screeched up the stairs.

Mrs. Shillingford kept the parlour door locked. Sheila had no idea when the family used it as she never saw anyone entering or leaving. Furnished with a threepiece suite of hideous brown with orange splotches, the room felt cold and cheerless. Nevertheless, Mrs.

Shillingford seemed proud of her parlour and opened the door to let Sheila see it, showing off like anything, while making it clear the room was not available to guests.

Sheila heard her walk back into the kitchen and the door slam shut before making her way downstairs.

It could only be Arthur, she reckoned. Nobody else knew her whereabouts and he was the only one to whom she had written. After all, Rita might need her for something. Her heart light with hope, she hurried down the stairs thinking Arthur obviously wanted her back: for what other reason would he have come? Pausing outside the door, she smoothed back her hair, thankful she wore makeup and a clean dress.

She opened the door with a jubilant smile, to see her brother Roger standing in front of the cold fireplace.

"Roger!" she gasped, her hand going to her mouth.

"Yes, Roger," he said, looking grim.

"How did you find me?" Sheila didn't suggest they sit, knowing it might make it look as though she were pleased to see him.

"Arthur told me," he said, his voice flat. He stared at her, his gaze running over her body. "He also said you were carrying another man's child so he told you to leave. Before you ask, I ran into him in Wigan at a soccer match. What on earth has come over you, our Sheila?"

Sheila laughed mirthlessly. "Is this why you came? I might have known it wasn't a matter of concern."

Roger glared at her. His sister had become a stranger to him. She had always done her own thing, ignoring him for the most part, unless it was to tease or torture him.

"He only told me you had left home. When I stopped in to see Mam, she told me you were gone. She said Rita told her." He stared at her stomach pointedly.

Sheila grimaced. "Oh, so we have the fine hand of my Mam here, do we? She's nothing but an interfering old biddy, is Mam. She's got no reason to tell tales about me, not with what she doesn't want you to know. Honestly, her gob's the size of the Mersey Tunnel."

"What does that mean? What doesn't she want me to know?" Roger asked. He scratched his head, puzzled.

Sheila compressed her lips knowing she had said too much. "Never you mind, our Roger. What I know, I know, and wild horses wouldn't drag it out of me. You go back there and tell her to stay out of my life. What I do is none of her business, or yours. Why *did* you come here? What's the real reason?"

Roger looked uncomfortable and turned his trilby round and round in his hands by the brim as if it were a steering wheel.

"Look here, Sheila," he said, moving his gaze to a point over her shoulder. "Mam's obviously worried about you since you left Arthur. She's the one who told me you were alone, and then I got worried about you."

"Oh yeah?" Sheila scoffed, "More like she was worried about Arthur, and since when did you ever think about anyone else but yourself, or that toffee-nosed wife of yours? You bloody well came to gloat, didn't you?"

Roger stared at her. Sheila had always been as stubborn as a mule, and when she made her mind up to something, she always stuck by it, right or wrong. Why on earth was he bothering, he wondered? Still, he had promised his mother he would see what he could do, for the sake of his niece, Rita.

"Well, since you appear to have all your faculties, and are as bitchy and peevish as ever," he said as he turned to leave, "I guess we needn't worry about you."

"Well, thank you very much for your concern, I don't think. There's more behind this visit than you're saying." Sheila spat out the words, knowing from experience Roger ignored most things that didn't affect him. She knew it well enough, so what *had* the old bat said to him?

Roger drew back. If it were not for his mother and his worry about young Rita, he would never have come, but the girl was heartbroken by the gossip. He blew out an aggrieved breath through pursed lips. His sister Sheila had never been an easy person to know and she was definitely prickly now, and obviously beyond listening to reason. His mother's suspicions were unfounded, he decided, as he detected no evidence of a man living with her. Anyway, he had only said he would find Sheila, not that he would investigate her financial condition further. Any more talk would be a waste of time.

"Then, I'll leave. Goodbye, Sheila."

"Goodbye, Roger. Give my best to your wife, what'shername."

"Mavis, as if you didn't know. Of course, of course," Roger said as he opened the door. Sheila, he knew, could not stand Mavis, any more than Mavis liked Sheila.

As he walked down the dreary street followed by screeching, ragged urchins begging for pennies, he thought about his sister.

He and Sheila had shared the same bedroom until she was twelve, and subsequently he slept on the parlour couch until his marriage. When they were small, Sheila, the more aggressive of the two, had grown faster than he, was always the boss. Her side of the bed was sacrosanct and woe betide him if he as much as put a foot into it. Countless times she had belted him, times when their mother had seen the bruises and chastised him for fighting with the boys. She never knew it was her daughter who was dealing out the punishment.

One of Sheila's favourite tricks was to put both her damp hands around his wrist and viciously turn the skin in opposite directions, causing what the school kids called a Chinese burn. Through this and her other cruelties. Roger remained silent or else Sheila would have made his, life more of a misery than it was already. Yes, Sheila was a right bitch and cruel with it.

Good luck to her, then, he thought now. His only thought had been to see if she were living with another man, and whether she needed help. He knew it would not be easy for her, not with no means of support and a baby on the way. Yet she essentially told him to get lost, so he did not offer her money nor offer help. He felt not one pang of guilt about leaving her. Well, it served her right, didn't it? Arthur was such a nice chap and a good provider, and yet she had thrown it all away. It flummoxed him, fair boggled the mind. What on earth possessed her? No wonder young Rita was shocked and upset, what with the gossips having a field day.

Rita felt exceedingly happy without her mother. She found it amazing how the house now seemed filled with laughter and comfort. These days her Dad seemed more relaxed; he laughed more than she had ever known, and they talked for hours. She began to know her father as a man and decided she liked him a lot, a lot more than before he opened his heart. She saw another side to him, realized he was an attractive man when he smiled, liked his looks and looked for his features in her own. Without her mother making his life a misery, he stood taller, talked more confidently.

Gran came around every afternoon and started the supper, which she ate with them. They had never been so well fed and Arthur gained some needed weight.

Arthur, also sublimely happy without Sheila, did not miss her, he told Molly. He spent many evenings at her small cottage and Molly felt delighted Sheila had left, though wise enough never to say it out loud.

They were sitting in her garden watching the doves. "Rita spends a lot of time with her Gran these days, Molly." Arthur took her hand in his and squeezed it. "She seems to have adjusted admirably to life without her mother."

"I hope so, for your sake, Arthur. Teenage girls are strange creatures. She might be covering up when you're around and doesn't like it at all."

"No, Marian would know and she's said nothing. She even agreed Rita is happier."

Each Sunday Arthur and Rita ate at Gran's and, after her Dad went to the pub for a pint, one week Rita asked her Gran to tell her a story about one of the curiosities in the china cabinet.

Marian shook her head. "Now, now that's a Christmas tradition, Rita, we'll not start it now."

"Aaw Gran, why not? Tell me a nice story, one to take my mind off my Mam."

Marian looked at her innocent expression and knew Rita was conning her. On the other hand, Rita needed someone to love her and an outward display of affection could well be in the telling of stories. Maybe she should go along with Rita's ploy.

So every Sunday afternoon she told a story and Rita would choose the object.

This week Rita chose the silk and ivory fan.

"Ah yes, the fan," Marian said as Rita handed it to her, her eyes blurring with memories, hearing the melody of the dance. "This is very special."

1915

One fine Saturday afternoon Marian sat on the river bank, arms around her knees. The warm weather carried a sight breeze, the river bank peaceful under the row of willows. The water flowed past slowly, sparkled with sun spots, chased by dragonflies. A family of ducks paddled around nearby and on the breeze wafted the scent of garden flowers from a farmhouse garden across the river. One would never guess a war was raging in Europe or that German airships had bombed East Anglia. British ships were sunk and many local families mourned the death of a relative. Still, Marian cared nothing for war.

This was a beautiful spot. One she and William often used, a place where they could meet away from prying eyes. She had waited now for over half an hour yet William was nowhere in sight. Marian sighed fitfully, knowing soon she would have to return home to prepare tea as the children would be back from Sunday school. Harry, who was at a darts match at the local pub, would arrive home by five at the latest.

She started to leave when William came running down the lane.

"William, where on earth have you been? I have to leave now," she said, her face stormy with anger. While pleased to see him, she felt annoyed. How *dare* he take her for granted?

Marian did not love William. He was simply a means of proving her power and since Harry cooled sexually, she had gone right off men.

Still, she liked sex, so to drag a man along by the physical hold she had over him was an aphrodisiac.

"My mother was sick and we had to send for the doctor," he said, his tone apologetic.

"Oh my dear, I'm so sorry. I understand now," Marian said, feeling guilty.

"One kiss, please, one kiss before you go," William pleaded and she turned her face to his. She drowned in the bliss of it. William had such delightful lips, lips that warmed her soul.

Every Sunday afternoon when Harry was at the darts match, they met by the river. They first met at a church bazaar where Marian was in charge of a baked goods stall. As their eyes met over the rich fruit cake he proffered for purchase, she blushed at the intensity of his scrutiny.

To William, Marian represented the woman of his dreams; her strawberry blond curls, her blue eyes, her trim shape, she was the person he had dreamed of meeting before he married Bess.

Within two weeks they were meeting and talking and William found a peace with Marian he never knew with his wife. Their friendship remained strictly platonic until the warm June afternoon when Marian succumbed to his blandishments and, after they made love under the willow fronds on the river bank, their relationship changed considerably. They made love while the weather was fine, and every week planned to meet again.

"Where does your wife think you are every Sunday?" Marian asked.

"She thinks I'm out with my mates. She knows I like rambling and it's a good enough reason to be away."

This explanation assuaged Marian's guilty conscience. As for Harry, she was sure he had no idea, had no idea she was not at home making the tea or doing her sewing.

She discovered soon after their honeymoon that Harry had little imagination. Because he was a taciturn man who had no art of conversation, she knew as little about Harry now as she did when she accepted his proposal. Shocked when she discovered him completely illiterate, his refusal to allow her to teach him to read and write added to her disillusionment.

Marian originally met Harry at the May Day celebrations in the village. The Gerrard family granted most of the Manor staff a day off as they left for a holiday at Sir Charles' plantation in Bermuda. May Day fell around that time, and since the winter had been long and hard that year, the warm spring sunshine was a blessing.

Harry Haydon chose her for a dance at the evening celebration and as they hopped around the beaten earth floor of the great barn, she glanced up at him. A nice looking man, his teeth were straight and none were missing. He picked her for two more dances, though he held her firmly and too close for her comfort. Nevertheless, she was flattered to notice his eyes never left her for more than a moment. No matter where she was, she looked at him and saw his gaze following her. At the time she had thought Harry Haydon not a patch on Master Geoffrey, so while she firmly pushed Geoff out of her mind, knowing nobody could ever take his place in her heart.

After bumping into Harry one day when walking home to take her mother her quarterly pay, they started courting.

"Oh," he said in answer to her question, "I work for the council offices. We maintain roads and sewers, hedges and culverts. My job's steady."

She asked him where he lived and discovered he lived with his widowed mother only two streets from her own home. "If you live so close, how come I never saw you at school?" she asked.

"I didn't always live in Trawton. I lived in Wigan when Dad was alive," he explained. "We moved to Trawton after he died and stayed with my Grandma, until she died. Then Mam took over the house."

"Oh, I see," she said, "But how did you get a job with the council? Only local residents get those jobs."

"My uncle is a councillor, or should I say, was. Once he got me in, I stayed in. That's about the size of it." His chin rose, sure of himself. "I work hard and I'm reliable."

So it appeared he had a guaranteed job, especially since they kept him on after his uncle stepped down from the council. Marian knew he liked her, and suddenly he became more of a prospective husband in her eyes, for she did not intend to marry a miner.

They married after the death of his mother, who had not liked Marian. However, soon after Mrs. Haydon's death Harry completely redecorated the house and gave Marian the grand tour. She loved the thought of having her own home and accepted his proposal.

Becoming a stayathome housewife, she found both life and Harry utterly boring and sought excitement with William until September 1915 when Harry arrived home to announce jubilantly that he had signed up and was off to war.

At that moment Marian hated him. What was she going to do? The army did not pay well and she needed money for rent, food and fuel, she argued. Yet it was too late, he had already signed on and soon he was on his way.

Her anger coloured their goodbye. She did not even kiss him as he got on the train in Wigan with the other 'fools' as she called them. Around them women were hugging and crying, mothers were moaning and grasping sons they may never see again, toddlers were crying hysterically. A brass band played "Keep the Home Fires Burning," "Auld Lang Syne," and "It's a Long Way to Tipperary," songs she would always detest. Amid the confusion and noise, Marian stood erect, watching the commotion, staring at Harry with loathing, furious he could leave her. Harry put out his hand as if to shake hers, but thought better of it and got on the train.

Through the four years of his absence, she managed by taking in washing or cleaning other women's homes. She worked in shops and at a farm dairy. A lonely Marian eked out a life for herself, but only just.

While Harry was away he never wrote her a letter of course since he was illiterate. However, other wives who had illiterate husbands received letters someone else penned for them and were proudly flashing them about. Marian got nothing, not even a post card. For all she knew, Harry could have been dead.

Obviously Harry arrived back to less than a hero's welcome. Marian had not even known he was coming. She had amused herself with two or three other chaps in his absence, discovering the joy of sex as entertainment. Not that she was openly promiscuous; she took her pleasure only when assured nobody would know - at least, that's what she thought.

In 1919 they resumed their married life. Harry went back to his job as a road worker as though he had never been away. Things had changed between them though, miraculously for the better, as when he was away Harry learned a few things about pleasing a woman so Marian sometimes enjoyed the physical side of their alliance. She shuddered to think where Harry had gained the knowledge, but decided never to ask.

Within two months she was pregnant with Roger and Harry felt exceedingly proud of himself. Marian, a good mother, enjoyed having a tiny baby so reliant on her, but six months after his birth she fell pregnant again with Sheila.

Two small children and a husband occupied her full time for three years. Then, with the habit of marriage, Harry and Marian did not make love much any more and her eyes again started wandering.

1924

Gordon was the only excitement in her life these days and she lived for Sunday afternoons when the children were at Sunday school for two hours.

It was a glorious summer, warm and sunny for the most part. The crops were splendid, as even the most pessimistic farmer admitted, but now the weather was drawing in and soon it would be uncomfortable to meet on the riverbank. Their old haunt was useful when it was fine, but what they would do when the weather turned bad, she did not know; she anticipated dying of longing throughout the long winter. On the wireless when she heard "Lady be Good" she laughed to think it might be about her, but then she was always good to the man in her life.

"I must go now, Gordon," she said, as she shrugged into her coat. "The children will be back soon. Anyway, the weather's getting too cold to meet here, don't you think? What shall we do then?"

"I've thought a lot about it, but I don't know the answer. I think we'll have to winter over without love, Marian. I know nowhere we can meet without being seen."

Marian shed a few tears and Gordon comforted her. "Don't cry my dear, we'll meet again when the weather is fine and the leaves are on the willows."

"We'll see each other at the town hall ball," she reminded him. "You'll be there, won't you?"

"Wild horses wouldn't keep me away, Marian. I'll be there and my eyes will find you. Smile for me and send me your love."

"Indeed I will, Gordon. Save one dance for me."

"Of course," he said and kissed her softly.

Marian went home hugging her secret, content enough to wait until October when they would meet at the ball held at the Town Hall.

Gordon worked as an office clerk for a small manufacturing concern in Pemberton. Tall and red haired, he was upright and well-dressed. Justifiably proud of his white collar job, he dressed suitably in a three-piece suit with a celluloid collar and tie. This manner of dressing and cleanliness dearly attracted Marian, as did his obvious education.

She often wondered why she was not content with Harry. He was affectionate enough, and had married her despite her background. The shame of her lost virginity troubled her so greatly that she confessed when he proposed, saying someone had raped her. Rape was common enough in the lives of those who worked for nobility and it had not appeared to bother him much. Neither ever mentioned it afterward.

Yes, Harry was a good man and she loved him in a way. Not passionately, not like she loved Gordon, but she *was* in love with Harry. The reason, she was sure, that her lack of passion for him resulted from the fact Harry had reverted to the most unimaginative person. His idea of making love was to come to bed aroused, shove it in and have his way.

To Marian, this signified the end of their marriage. Harry did not love her as she desperately needed man to love her, but simply used her body as a convenience. Yet she knew he stayed faithful to her, did not dally with other women. Trouble was he rarely made love to her, or made ever love the way she liked it. Not like with Geoffrey who had taken his time and roused her to great passion, even as she was a virgin. Nor William who was so very experienced, always making her feel so loved and wanted, adoring her with his body. Too, some others she had used until they bored her. Mind you, she found Gordon a better lover than any of them. He took his time, enjoyed arousing her and she needed the stimulation.

Three weeks later she realized she was pregnant. Whose child? Whose child, Gordon's or Harry's? The thought struck fear into her heart. Well, anyway, what difference did it make?

Harry was over the moon with joy, looking forward to having another child. Cheerfully he spread the news around and the village women congratulated her. Marian was not so sure, thanking God she had not gone with someone with jet black hair. Her own hair was reddish blond so they would not question a redheaded child.

Unfortunately she lost the child in September, although maybe it was for the best. Harry became sorrowful, regarding her with eyes that laid the blame at her feet, and soon they were drifting farther apart.

Almost before she knew it, it was time for the county ball. Thankfully, she rapidly recuperated from her miscarriage and got back her figure, though lost some weight. This solved the problem of what to wear. Her one evening gown, a gown she wore on her honeymoon, one Harry liked, still fit, though more snugly so she had to wear a corset.

When they arrived, gaily chattering people filled the Town Hall and they spent much time greeting friends and acquaintances. On the other side of the ballroom she spotted Gordon smiling in her direction and her heart pounded painfully. She sent her love in her gaze and smiled back as everybody else faded from her sight. How soon would he come to claim a dance?

At first Marian was reluctant to allow anyone to sign her dance card in case Gordon asked for that particular dance. Then, since he made no move to her side of the room, she allowed four gentlemen, and Harry of course, to claim dances.

It was almost the intermission when Gordon and his wife made their way over to the Haydon side of the ballroom. By this time the ballroom felt hot and humid from the gas chandeliers and body heat of hundreds. Martian fanned herself rapidly as they approached, glad to hide her nerves.

"Mr. and Mrs. Gordon McIntosh," Gordon said in introduction as he shook Harry's hand, "My wife Elfreda."

"Mr. and Mrs. Harold Haydon," Harry said, "My wife, Marian."

"Pleased to meet you, ma'am," Gordon said, bowing over Marian's hand, squeezing her silk clad fingers. Her heart leaped and how she could have laughed aloud. They had known each other intimately and yet here they were, strangers.

"Please won't you join us for a cool drink?" Harry said. They sat at the table as he poured the tart lemonade.

Gordon took a sip and put down the glass. "May I claim a dance, Mrs. Haydon?"

"Why, of course, Mr. McIntosh," she said, offering her dance card. Pleased to see he chose a slow waltz, she watched as he wrote his name. Harry looked at her strangely so she tossed her head and smiled brightly at Elfreda. They chatted about gowns and jewels.

After the Macintoshes moved on, Harry took her arm. "Why would you accept a dance with the man? We don't know them - and did you notice the look his wife gave him? The man was very forward."

"So? I can always leave the room when they play the waltz, Harry." Marian was spoiling for argument. "Is that what you want me to do?"

He waved his hand as if to erase his remarks. "Of course not. Don't be accused of bad manners because of my jealousy." He took her hand and kissed it.

Marian smiled up at him. He was a nice person, was Harry. Too bad she didn't love him so much these days.

Each time Gordon danced with his wife, and he danced with her a lot, he gazed across to where Marian sat. His gaze appeared never to leave her when she was in sight and Marian sadly recalled another dance when Harry had done the same. Now not because of the music did Marian's heart beat faster and her pulse race. Gordon was so handsome and yet he was married to Elfreda whose countenance was like a pudding - a suet pudding with raisins, come to think of it.

When the master of ceremonies announced the slow waltz, Marian watched as he excused himself to Elfreda, and made his way over to her. Her stomach contracted with anticipation.

Slowly they revolved around the floor and Marian felt as light as air. He held her tightly and she could feel the warmth of his hands through his white gloves. Gordon was a superlative dancer, she had noticed as much when watching him dancing with his wife, whereas Harry was a plodder with no sense of rhythm. She remarked on this to Gordon who threw back his head and laughed merrily.

"I noticed, Marian, I must admit." He put his head closer to hers and whispered. "Can we say his love making runs along the same lines?"

"Why, Mr. McIntosh!" Marian said behind her fan, her laughing eyes betraying her smile.

"That's a lovely fan," Gordon said, the fan close to his face, "It suits you. I like to see your eyes over the top."

She looked down at the lace edging and smiled. They drew closer to each other and she felt her body infuse with heat as she clung close to him.

"Marian," he said as the music neared the end of the melody and they were on the far side of the ballroom. He stopped moving. "I have something to tell you."

"Yes, Gordon." She waited, waited to hear words of love, her eyes sparkling over the lace of the fan.

He looked at the ceiling. "Dash it all. There's no easy way to say this. They're transferring me to Huddersfield. We'll be leaving within a month."

She felt a sudden jolt in her heart. Surely he was not leaving? Yet he was, he was. Her eyes filled with scalding tears and she held back a sob.

"This is the last time we'll see each other, my love," he murmured as he held her close. "My heart will always be with you."

"Oh my God," she whispered. If only they were alone and could make love one last time. Yet it was never to be and he would never know of the baby she had lost, the baby that could have been his child.

As the music ended, he bowed over her hand and kissed it. "Goodbye, my very dearest one," he said softly, "Goodbye. I'll never forget you."

"Nor I you," she said, her face white and stricken. She watched him turn away to leave and moved to the table on suddenly leaden feet.

"Harry," she said, close to tears, "I don't feel well. Will you take me home?"

As she waited for Harry to fetch her wrap, she looked down at the fan she held, the ivory and cream silk lace fan Harry bought on their honeymoon to match her gown. Now it would remind her of Gordon, of their last dance together, and the last time she saw him. She would also keep the dance card with his name inside.

Marian said nothing on the way home, but Harry thought it was because she was not feeling well. It was four days before she could speak to him, but he did not push her. Women who lost a child had fancies men knew nothing about.

"So your granddad bought me the fan to match my gown. Aye, it was right lovely, that gown, made especially for my honeymoon by a dressmaker. My own grandmother bought the gown for me and when your granddad saw me wearing it for the first time, tears came to his eyes. He said I was beautiful, and I guess I was to him then. He couldn't take his eyes off me that night when I was dancing with other chaps. I kept the dance card from the dance. It's also n the cabinet."

"Oh, Gran," Rita said, her eyes misty as she waved the small fan, "You're beautiful now and I bet when you were young, you were a right bobby dazzler. I think you're wonderful." She fluttered the fan around. "How did you use it, Gran? We don't have fans these days."

Marian showed Rita the way to manipulate the fan, how to flirt over its lacy edge, how to show displeasure. It was a lost art, she said, thinking it too bad this fan brought back sad memories.

"What type of music did you dance to? Was it waltzes and stuff, violins and such?"

"Oh, we had a good orchestra After all, they held it at the town hall. They had about six violins and I know I saw a trumpet and a trombone and drums. Aye, a proper dance band and by, but they could play some good music. One of their best numbers was 'Alexander's Rag Time Band'. We all sang along with it."

"Gosh, and I pictured you doing the minuet," Rita said as she laughed at the expression on Marian's face.

"Enough of that, young lady. I'm not that ancient."

"Sorry, Gran, but I need to know these things. I had no idea your dance music was so modern. They still play those songs on the radio."

"Good music never goes out of style, love, never." She looked at the fan as Rita twirled it. Aye, the waltz they danced to was "After the Ball," and she never forgot how appropriate it seemed later.

"Put it back now, Rita, there's good girl. Time for you to be away home."

Marian watched Rita as she went to the parlour, thinking about the real reason she treasured the fan. Well, she was not doing anyone any harm by saying any different, was she?

CHAPTER FIVE

1955

Sheila moved away from Trawton and went to Wigan. After finding herself a job washing dishes at a café, she managed to survive on her nest egg, her wits and a diet close to starvation. She would have been indignant to know that back in Trawton Arthur had changed a great deal for the better. His nemesis gone, he spent more time with Molly, the main reason for his transformation.

One day Rita arrived home from work to find her Dad and a plump woman sitting by the fire, drinking tea and talking animatedly. The woman smiled at Rita. As she hung up her coat, Rita could not help but stare.

"Hello lass, I'm Molly, come and warm yourself," she said, "I've brewed the tea. Your Dad has told me all about you," she said, her voice so warm and friendly. Rita had to smile.

"Hello, Molly," she said, casting a hard glance at her father. "Strange, but my Dad hasn't said a word about *you*. Are you going to be our housekeeper?"

Arthur laughed. "Aye, Molly will be our housekeeper all right, if it's all right with you, but not a housekeeper like you mean."

He looked at his daughter from under his brows, chuckling nervously, already embarrassed. "No, no, lass, it's well, Molly and I are keeping company. You'll be seeing a lot more of her from now on."

Rita looked from one to the other. "You mean like courting?" she asked puzzled. "Only single people go courting, Dad." Although naive, she realised those who were widowed or divorced walked out with other people to get to know them better. Yet this she had never considered regarding her father. "But . . but you're still married to my Mam."

Arthur nodded. Trust Rita to get to the heart of the matter. "Aye, and that's going to change shortly, Rita. It'll take us a while to get the legal business done, then I'll divorce your mother." Arthur took Molly's hand and squeezed it.

Rita saw the looks they gave each other and felt shocked. In front of her? Her Dad was courting another woman in front of her? Rita, no prude, knew about the ways of the world to some extent, especially since her mother had proved a slut, but a father who flaunted another woman in front of his child must be addled.

Her mother now, well, she was a different matter entirely. Somehow her mother's infidelity, once she found out about it and realized it for what it was, seemed all right. Everyone in the village must have been aware Sheila carried on with other men, although people obviously kept their counsel within Rita's hearing when she was small.

Yet once her mother took off, they talked all right, talked within Rita's hearing, too. Now she dreaded to think what they would say about her Dad after this, about him fetching another woman into the house.

Simultaneously Rita realized she was ingenuous of the ways of the world and sometimes shocked at things she read in magazines and papers, and while she had a normal enough upbringing, she was completely unsophisticated. This naivete made her the butt of many scornful remarks at school. She supposed this was because her mother never talked to her about anything that mattered, and her father never had the time. Her Gran, she supposed, was under the impression her parents had told her about adult life, which made her reluctant to ask Gran because it showed her ignorance. It was a strange way to be when she loved Gran so much, but something stopped her from asking questions of a personal nature. Now she wished she were wiser in the ways of the world, understood why her Dad seemed different, could understand what he saw in this woman.

Rita grew silent. She sat at the table with a face like thunder, rudely staring at them as they chatted. They laughed a lot and were so easy together. How different to when Mam was here, she thought, then Dad and Mam hardly spoke, except to argue.

Molly was a nice person, she could tell and her Dad was so different with Molly, jolly, quick to laugh. So why didn't she like this arrangement? Why did it irritate her? Surely her father was entitled to some happiness?

No, she must try, she thought, standing, saying she was going to see Gran. She thanked Molly for the tea and scones, smiled bleakly at her Dad and left.

"But, why, Gran? Why?" she asked again.

Marian felt flustered and worried that Rita would notice her discomfort. "Lord love you, child, men are men and men have needs. It's time you and I discussed the birds and bees."

Rita pulled a face, embarrassed. Silly old Gran. "Oh Gran, they told us all about it at school."

She didn't tell her the biology teacher touched on the subject using frogs and rabbits as examples so she remained ignorant of the real facts, apart from those she gleaned from other girls at school. She found talking about sex with an adult made her feel squirmy and disconcerted. "It's just that I can't understand why my Dad's going out with a woman when he's still married to my Mam. I can't get my mind around it."

"Do you want your mother to come home? Is that it?" Marian eyed her grandchild, now realizing Rita needed educating in the ways of men. Time someone sat her down, she thought, and told her the plain truth about life. Better she learn it from her grandmother, than on the streets.

"No, no," Rita cried, "I wouldn't want that at all." She shuddered as she hugged herself and rocked in the chair. She dreaded going back to those cold, uncomfortable days.

"Well then, lovey, do you want your Dad to sit by the fire and grow old like me without a female to comfort him and look after him? Men can't cope like women can, and you won't be there forever, you know. One day you'll marry and leave him."

"We could get a housekeeper," Rita said, stone faced, wondering why it was taking so long to shift her mind.

"Aye, that's true enough. I do my best for you, but there's more to life than a cooked meal and a clean shirt." She laughed and pushed at Rita with a loving hand. "Oh, not to you at your age, but you'll understand it one day."

"No, I won't," Rita said, irritated that even her beloved Gran treated her like a baby. "All adults say that! That I'll understand it when I grow up. Oh, Gran, everybody will talk. They saw her going into our house and . . .,"

"Oh, so that's it, is it? Worried about what people might say?" Marian put back her head and laughed merrily. "Well, let me tell you, lovey, there's more going on this street than you'll ever know. You're very young, Rita, very innocent. Don't let it worry you."

Marian wanted to keep her innocent, knowing children grew up far too fast, but maybe telling her certain things might be wise.

"Look Gran," Rita argued, "If Dad is still married to my Mam and she comes home unexpectedly what will happen then?"

Marian shook her head. "Trust me, child, your mother won't be coming back." At least Marian hoped she wouldn't. By, wouldn't that be a right turn up for the books?

"Do you know where she is, Gran, my Mam?" Rita picked at her fingernails, not looking at her grandmother.

"No."

Rita concentrated on her nails. "Is there some way I can find out?"

Marian looked at her sharply, why this sudden interest in the long gone Sheila? "Why do you ask, love?"

It seemed all mixed up in her brain and a terrible worry. "I want to tell her about it, about Dad and that woman, Molly. Someone has to tell her what's happening here."

Marian sighed. What on earth did the child want to find *her*? It wasn't as if she much liked her mother, and since Sheila left she had changed considerably. These days she seemed happier, more contented.

"Look here, Rita, I never thought I had say this, but your mother is a bad person." Rita's head shot up and she gasped. "Now, now, don't look at me like that," Marian said, putting out her hand. "She's my daughter, so I ought to know. Leave her be and don't try to find her. Why on earth would you want to do that, anyway? Telling her won't stop anything and would only make her angry. You've heard what they say about killing the messenger? So heed my warning now. You wouldn't her starting on you, would you?"

Rita thought for a moment. Raising her head, she looked steadily at her grandmother.

"Well, there's something else I have to ask her," she said, her mouth a hard line.

"My word, Miss Stubborn, it must be important if you have to go looking for her, after her leaving *you*. What is it?"

Rita shook her head. She desperately wanted to know why her Gran and her mother had fought, and for some reason it seemed vital that she find out about the rift. Maybe it was something to do with why Gran didn't care her mother had gone, nor did her Dad. Rita thought Dad knew more than he said because he never looked her in the eye when he answered so evasively. Suddenly she felt it crucial to first ask her mother the question, because if it upset it her Mam, it didn't matter as she wouldn't have to see her again, wouldn't feel the length of her tongue. Gran always fobbed her off so it was no use asking her. If she knew from her mother, then perhaps she and Gran could talk about it. Anyway, she loved Gran and would never want to worry her.

Rita sighed now thinking about it and Marian watched her expression, thinking Rita never usually seemed pensive. The girl had, she knew, had often asked her father about the quarrel between her and Sheila and every time he told her he did not know. This was probably the same thing. Arthur said he told her that Sheila had never told him how it started, and it was not for him to start prying between a woman and her mother.

She contemplated her granddaughter, now desultorily flipping through the newspaper. Rita was a deep one, full of thought and complexity. She was also so innocent of so many things that speaking plainly was difficult. Marian found it difficult to see where the child was headed with her problems, most of them of her own making, but this wanting to find her mother?

She shook her head as if to clear it and stood. "I'll make us a nice cup of tea, eh?"

Rita glanced up. "No thanks, Gran. I'm going home. Maybe Molly has gone now and I can talk to Dad about this."

"Now don't start interfering where you shouldn't," Marian said in warning, "Let your father have some happiness for a change."

"All right, Gran, I promise," Rita said, kissing her soft cheek.

Marian smiled as she hugged her. Rita was a good child and if she promised something, she usually stuck to it.

It annoyed Rita to find Molly still sitting by the fire when she arrived. She wondered if she were going to sleep at the house and peevishly eyed her Dad.

He put out a hand. "Sit down, Rita. We're going to have a chat, the three of us. We've been waiting for you." As Rita sat, Arthur glanced at Molly who smiled encouragement. "Well now, you don't seem well pleased with things the way they are, so Molly and me thought we'd clear the air."

Rita plonked herself on a kitchen chair, crossed her arms across her chest and looked at him, her face churlish.

He felt uncomfortable, but continued: "Look, lass, this isn't easy. You know your mother isn't coming back. I've told you before."

She felt cross, thinking here we go again, he's still treating me like a child. "Yes, and you won't tell me where she is, either," she said. "I bet you know where she's living."

"Honestly, Rita, I don't know," Arthur said with a sigh. "She left Trawton some time ago and I've no idea where she went."

"Oh, and did you look for her?" she asked. Molly glanced at her sulky expression and nudged Arthur with her toe.

"I can't say that I did," he admitted. "Do you want her back here? Do you miss her? Is that it?"

Maybe the child loved Sheila, although he knew they'd never seen eye to eye on much, and Rita seemed far happier without the stifling presence of her mother.

She shook her head, shame faced. "No, not really. We're better off without her, aren't we?" she confessed, feeling guilty about voicing it in front of Molly, a stranger. She couldn't look at her. Surely she should only feel love for her mother, and to say her leaving made things better was like a betrayal.

Arthur nodded as he knocked the dottle out of his pipe on the bars of the fire. "Aye, we are and all. Now, if we're happier without her, why are you so set against me walking out with Molly here?"

"I don't know. I honestly don't know," she confessed red faced, and she didn't. Molly seemed a pleasant person and obviously made her father happy, so why did it bother her this way?

Then Molly spoke, her voice warm and soft: "Rita, lass, every girl needs her mother. I understand but from what Arth . . . your father told me, I don't think she was very nice to you. Shall we let things stand for now and see how we go?"

She smiled at Arthur who stared at her as if she were mad. Letting a mere child run their lives, whatever next? his expression said.

Rita looked at Molly's smiling face. Maybe the woman was not so bad after all and maybe she could get Molly to ask her Dad about her Mam and Gran.

"All right," she said, dragging the words out, "But you can't stay here, not while my Dad's married to my mother."

Molly looked amazed that she would say such a thing. "Land's sakes, child, I wouldn't dream of it," Molly said, and then she chuckled. "I have my own house, thank you very much, and I'm comfortable there. No, I meant your father and I would see each other, that's all."

"All right, then," Rita said standing, her mind easier for some reason. "I'll wash the dishes."

"We can do them together," Molly said, joining her at the sink. "Four hands make light work, they say."

As she turned on the tap, she started singing. Rita regarded her with amazement. Her mother never sang. Molly's voice was rich as cream, full of tone that pleased the ear. She began singing the latest pop tune and Rita thought it marvellous because to her Molly was an old lady, and old ladies didn't normally like the new music.

The following Sunday Molly came with them to Gran's for dinner and they enjoyed a pleasant meal.

Marian found Molly warm and caring. She had met her before, of course, at the house when Molly came to supper. Aye, Marian thought, Molly was the type of person she would have liked for a daughter.

If Sheila only had not turned out the way she had, she thought, as she listened to the happy banter. It wasn't her fault, nor Harry's: it was something mentally wrong with Sheila, that's all it *could* be. Her constant belligerence, her habit of throwing things, or using her fists to make a point. No, that was not the way they raised her. Marian never raised her hand to either child, much preferring to use reason instead of force.

Too, last fight they'd had, even Harry left the house when it started. A damned good job too, with what they said - more like screamed and shouted. No, they rarely spoke after that day, which was the outcome Marian preferred.

After the meal Molly and Arthur left to attend a concert in Wigan.

"Have a good time, now," Marian said as she waved them off at the door. "Nice lass, that," she said to Rita who stood by her side, "Nice lass, all round."

Molly wore a smart hat and coat and looked like a real lady. Arthur wore his best suit and, with her arm tucked into his, they matched each other step for step. Already they seemed like a married couple.

Rita nodded, but Marian could see her father's lady friend didn't impress her. Still, it was early days yet and Rita was growing up fast.

"So what's it to be this week? Have you decided?" she asked as they went into the kitchen and sat by the fire. Rita shook her head. Her mind had been on other things this afternoon. Marian decided not to make anything of her silence. "I'll bank up the fire and make the tea while you go and choose."

Rita went into the cold parlour and opened the cabinet door. Touching the various items, she tried to make her choice. Last week had been a wonderful story, but then all Gran's stories were fantastic.

After looking on each shelf, she picked up the bone china cup and saucer, then replaced it. Surely nothing was interesting about drinking tea.

Then she saw it, a small plate with a crude painting of Blackpool Tower. Blackpool Tower excited her and she loved it the day they went to the top on a trip to Blackpool when she was smaller.

"This," she said passing the plate to her Gran. "Tell me about this."

1929

Blackpool Tower. It was glorious, the finest thing Marian had seen in her life, and so high, much higher than she had ever imagined.

Today she had run away from home, literally left Harry while he was at work and brought the children. Of course, the kids thought it was a day out, which it was, but wouldn't it be glorious if they never went back?

"Can we go up the Tower, Mam?" Roger asked pulling at her sleeve. A gangly ten year old, he seemed all scabby knees and jutting elbows. Roger, a real tomboy, was always in trouble one way or another and she loved him dearly.

Marian shivered when she thought about going up the Tower; surely it couldn't be safe? She could see elevator cars rising and falling and people on the observation platform. Inside the lacy ironwork were stairs, terribly long flights of iron stairs. Only an energetic person would climb all those steps, she thought. Yet go up in an elevator, up there practically in the clouds? She felt much too nervous to attempt it, and put them off with a Punch and Judy show on the sands, hoping the kids might lose interest.

It was the very first time Marian had visited Blackpool and they had come on a day's excursion run by the local church. Harry would only find out about it when they got back because she had not even left him a note. While she felt a twinge of guilt at spending her housekeeping money on such foolishness, she felt he owed her that much. What with the constant bickering between them, the way he picked on her every move, his miserable face and monotonous tone of voice as if she were a punishment he had to bear. Yes, a day out, she thought, a day out to blow away the cobwebs and have some fun.

The children hopped around excitedly. Even Sheila grinned happily. The weather was warm and sunny, the bright blue sea topped with white crests while white, grey and young brownish seagulls screamed and wheeled overhead. Everyone she saw wore a smile: she noticed no glum faces here by the sea. Marian already felt better, invigorated in the brisk sea breezes. People had red cheeks, she noticed, and everyone looked healthy.

They strolled along the sands. The tide was out and the children found sea shells and bits of seaweed. Roger, especially thrilled with his finds, put everything in his jacket pockets until they were bulging.

"Come along, children, let's see what the front has to offer," she said after an hour. Her legs and feet ached from walking shoe-less on the soft beach, her knitted stockings were clogged with sand, and her face tingled with a wind burn. Her usually neat hair blew around because her hat kept blowing to one side, so now she carried it.

They sat near the pier where a band happily pumped its way through selections from Gilbert and Sullivan and other light operas. Sheila, a changed child, seemed so full of beans that she even danced a silly dance to "Tiptoe Through the Tulips" and watchers gave her a round of applause. Marian laughed as she curtsied and almost fell.

Later they went onto the front and inspected stalls the offering winkles, cockles, shrimps and mussels. At other stalls, men made Blackpool rock. They stood watching the operators put the red lettering inside the white rock, saw how they rolled and pulled it into lengths. They checked fortune tellers, cafes, restaurants, amusement arcades and places where people could have a photo taken with their head in a cutout of a muscle man, a show girl or a hula dancer. Watching, they saw couples stick their heads through holes cut in two funny cutouts of a gorilla and a fat ballet dancer, another two were a muscle man holding huge barbells and a woman dressed as a queen. Stalls sold souvenirs, cheap jewellery, chinaware, tea towels with Tower imprints, clogs in all colours with shining brass nails, and assorted junk of all kinds. To Marian, it was like wonderland.

It was nearly two o'clock by the time they reached the Tower base and Marian put her head back as far as she could, yet could not see the top. The children were pulling at her and squealing to go inside, but from the steps up to the window, stood a long queue. Impatiently they shuffled along to the ticket kiosk as a loudspeaker played marches that jangled her nerves.

A gentleman started to talk to Marian while they waited. He was a dashing sort in his striped blazer and grey flannel trousers; a cord and a button attached his Panama hat to his lapel.

"What a lovely day," he remarked.

"Yes, it is," she agreed, pleased such an obvious gentleman would speak to her. His voice sounded refined and very pleasant. A memory of Geoffrey flooded her mind and she blushed. The loud music from a speaker over the door thankfully hid their conversation. One should never speak to a stranger, she knew, but what was the harm as she had the children with her?

They spoke of this and that, of the children, from where she hailed, and soon they were inside. As they walked through the zoo and the children gazed in wonder at the various animals, he stayed at her side. The zoo was very malodorous as they didn't seem to clean the cages very often. That made her feel nauseous so she kept her handkerchief to her nose.

"Shall we let the children wander around on their own and maybe take some tea at the tea shop?" he asked. "We can see them if they try to leave as it is close to the exit turnstile."

"What a lovely idea," she said as she took his arm, surprised at herself.

Morris West looked down at her and she smiled up at him. Being a tall man, she felt very petite.

She was lovely, he thought, all pink and white like a china doll. Her figure was absolutely right, not too fat and not too thin, not too chesty or hippy, his ideal woman - married with children. Her children were a hindrance, but he would spend some time with them and perhaps in such a way would get to know her better. Morris knew from experience married women made the best mistresses and were usually willing.

In less than an hour Morris knew a great deal about Marian Haydon, far more than she knew about him. By this time the children were bored with the tatty animals and eager to go to the top of the Tower. This they all did, although Marian stayed well back from the rail as the wind felt a like gale up there in the sky. Frightened of being blown away by the stiff gusts from the sea, she grimly hung onto her skirts, afraid the wind might blow them over her head. The smell of wind borne ozone made her nose run as she held onto her skirts while her hair swirled around her face.

After the excitement of the Tower, they strolled along the sands to a wading pool where Sheila and Roger played with the shrimping nets Morris bought them. Later they made sand castles with buckets and spades he purchased. With the children thus occupied, Morris and Marian sat on rented deck chairs and talked.

A gentleman, Marian decided. Morris's hands were soft and white, and she wondered what they would feel like on her body. Thinking like that made her feel flustered and she stuttered and blushed at remarks he made which were clearly double entendres.

By four o'clock she thought she had known him forever, and it was with great regret she called the children, who by this time were calling him Uncle Morris. Sheila, the mercenary little sod, soon found his money attractive and played up to him, begging for sweets. Morris simply smiled and doled out pennies when she asked.

"Will I see you again, Marian?" Morris asked, his voice earnest as a nearby organ grinder's monkey occupied the excited, squealing children.

"I don't see how," she said, blushing up at him. He made her feel like a young girl and, as his gaze reflected his admiration, she blossomed under his gaze. If she were only free to see him, if she dare see him again, if she could only . . .

"Could you come to Blackpool again soon? We could meet at the Tower," he said, his voice full of longing.

Her romantic expectations and imagination made her long for more of him. Oh, how he tempted her and her body yearned for him, although she knew it was wrong. She was a married woman and, as such, must stay home or return only with her husband. However, it had never stopped her before and she had felt this way many, many times.

She shook her head regretfully. "I'm afraid not, Morris," she said, "We must be leaving soon. Our train leaves in less than an hour."

His voice was earnest as she stared into his face. "Please, Marian, I must see you again. I love you, Marian, I fell in love with you the moment I saw you."

"Oh, Morris," Marian gasped, her expression indicating delight at this pronouncement. "Don't say that, please."

In the background the band played "Making Whoopee," and a part of her mind thought it funny, even as another part rejoiced. A man loved her, a man she hardly knew, a man she had only met recently, but he loved her!

Morris watched her facial expressions as Marian reflected on his flattery. She was thinking about coming back to see him.

Women were Morris's life. He was married, although his wife knew nothing of his other life, his life of debauchery and lust. Raised as a lady, she was afraid of physical contact. Even on their honeymoon she had her own bedroom and her money was the glue that kept them together. Now this unsophisticated young woman was probably hot for it, Morris thought. He could see by the way her breath came faster when he touched her and decided he must try to win her.

Taking her hand, he gripped it tightly. "I love you madly," he said a trifle melodramatically, "Please say we may meet again. I want to hold you in my arms and kiss you passionately."

"Oh, Morris," she said softly. He saw she found it difficult to breathe. "I wish I could. I want to kiss you, too. It is impossible, though, quite impossible."

"Please, my darling, please meet me again," he begged. "Maybe you could come for a week or even a weekend - without the children, of course."

"I can't, Morris, I simply can't." She felt close to tears and her throat closed with tension. How she wanted him, how she needed his admiration and his kisses: how she needed to make love with him. If only they were alone, she thought, instead of standing on the busy promenade as pedestrians pushed past, half-clad children ran around screaming shrilly and the wind played havoc with her hair. If she had only met him when she was alone, if she could only . . . But then her conscience got the better of her. She wondered why she was thinking this way.

"Please, my dearest darling," he pleaded, thinking her nearly persuaded. "Please think of a way. Maybe I could come to Trawton to see you?"

"Oh no!" Marian gasped, thinking it would be awful. Suppose somebody saw them? "I can't meet you there. It would have to be elsewhere."

"Please think of somewhere, my darling. I am dying with love for you." His gaze roved over her chest and she blushed at his words and her thoughts.

"Well, I could probably come next month," she said slowly, reluctantly, her mind racing to find a way to meet him again. He was so exciting, so wonderful and refined and her heart beat faster looking at him. If only she could kiss his lips, those warm looking, well-shaped lips.

"My dearest darling," Morris said as he put an arm around her shoulders.

Sheila ran up followed by Roger. "Mam, Mam, come and see! The Reverend Mather is here with the others and he says we have to go to the train," Roger shouted, grabbing her arm. "Come on, Mam, he's waiting for us."

Marian stood and smiled at Morris as Roger pulled on her arm. "I have to go."

"Yet when will I see you again?"

She decided. "I will come this time next month. I'll go to the Tower tea room and wait for you at noon," she said as Roger dragged her away.

As they sat on the train, the many children chattered among themselves about their exciting day. Marian listened to their happy babble as she thought about Morris.

"Uncle Morris took us up the Tower and we stood right at the rail, didn't we, Sheila?" She heard Roger say proudly. "I could see all the way to our house from up there."

As the children argued about the truth in this statement, the Reverend Mather cleared his throat. "I was not aware you had relations in Blackpool, Mrs. Goodwin."

She blushed beet red. "He's a friend of my husband and we happened to meet by chance." Oh lord, what could she say? Then it occurred to her. "He's not a relative, but children need to have some means of addressing adults."

"Ah yes, indeed," the Reverend said, looking at her speculatively.

Marian reddened, knowing her demeanor was that of a person with something to hide.

When they got home, Harry had already arrived. They found him standing bewildered in the cold kitchen looking at the fire - which, of course, was out - wondering where they were.

"Dad, Dad, we went to Blackpool," Roger shouted excitedly, rushing at him. "Look, we got buckets and spades, and we had ice cream, and we saw the lions and monkeys, and we went to the top of the Tower. I saw an elephant too! We could see our house." Gasping for breath, he began to empty his pockets of his treasures. "I had some shrimps, an' all, and look, Dad, look at what I've got, Dad. Look!"

Harry stared at Marian, his mouth open. What on earth?

"Dad, Dad, look at my bucket and spade." A wind burned, untidy

Sheila pulled at his arm. "Look-it, I got some sea shells and everything." She thrust the small red pail at him.

"Very nice too, lass, very nice, and did you have a good day?" Harry asked Marian who bustled about setting the table for supper before she made the fire. They would have to have a cold meal because Harry expected food on the table almost as soon as he got in the door. Well, I've got the shank end of the pork roast, she thought, and I'll boil some potatoes.

"Not bad, Harry, not too bad at all. I got some fresh air and it made me feel like a new woman." She simply could not look at him. Her face felt flushed although she knew it was probably wind burn. Oh lord, in her mind she had committed adultery and that was almost as bad as the real thing. She had sinned again although she realized the guilty feeling would soon wear off; it always did.

"Hey, Mam, show Dad the picture of Blackpool Tower Uncle Morris gave you," Sheila said grabbing for her mother's purse.

Marian flushed. Darn Sheila. She grabbed her purse and put it on the mantelshelf. "Don't you dare go into my purse," she snapped.

"Uncle Morris?" Harry said, puzzled, looking at her and then at Sheila. "Who is this Uncle Morris? Do I know him?"

"He's a chap who went on the trip with us, from the church, you know. The kids needed a day out, Harry, and I took them. Anything wrong with that?" Marian said defensively.

"Uncle Morris wasn't on the trip with the church, Mam," Sheila said, her voice shrill, "He talked to you when we were queuing up for the Tower. Remember?"

Marian could have clouted Sheila, little big mouth that she was, always tattling on people. On the way home from the station she'd warned both of them to say nothing about Morris, not to mention him. Still, what could you expect from children? They told things as they saw them. Well, she was in right trouble now judging by Harry's expression.

Sod him, she thought maliciously, if he treated me properly, I wouldn't have wanted to look at another man. Turning her face to him, she smirked, a self-satisfied smirk and hoped it got through to him.

Harry looked at her, snorted and sat heavily in his chair. He made no move to light the fire, simply stared into the ashes as if mesmerized.

Stupid bugger, she thought spitefully, as she moved around him to clear the grate of cinders, making no attempt to be careful, letting ashes fly. What an awful ending to a wonderful day.

As she swept the cinders into the dust pan and then into the old bucket for removal to the dustbin, she thought about Morris. His white and soft hands, his pleasant face, his fine clothes. Aye, if Harry Haydon didn't watch himself, she would be off to Blackpool and stay there. Yes, she would.

Harry sat like a statue while she made the fire. When supper was ready, he said not a word but came to the table and ate automatically. She could see his mind trying to work it out; his wife carrying on with a man named Morris and his children already calling him Uncle? Was he wondering how long this been going on? Was he trying to think if anyone named Morris live around here. Had they arranged to meet again? She knew he would not talk in front of the children, but would wait until they had gone to bed. Listen to them, chattering away about this uncle, what he had bought them, where he had taken them and Marian knew her cheeks were still rosy and wind burned.

She was aware she looked beautiful with the colour in her face and she felt smug, that was the word - smug. As they ate, Marian's mind sought an excuse. She thought of and discarded lots of scenarios knowing while Harry was not a genius, he was not stupid.

"So, what's all this Uncle Morris business?" he asked as she came back from tucking the children into bed. "Who is this chap and where does he live?"

"I have no idea." Well, that much was true enough. "He didn't say, and I didn't ask."

"Then how come you spent the day with him if he's a stranger?"

Harry seemed determined not to lose his temper. Both knew that losing his temper never got him anywhere and he could never take back an uttered word, no matter how many apologies.

Marian pushed back her hair. "Look, Harry, we didn't spend all day with him. He was simply a nice man who wanted to give the kids a treat. What could be wrong with that?" She kept her voice calm. No use starting an argument.

His face would have stopped a clock and she knew he was angry. "Nothing, if that's all it was, but why should I believe that?"

She stared at him, unblinking. "Because it's the truth. Have I ever lied to you, Harry?"

He looked at her hard, his expression stony. "Once or twice when it suited you."

She turned away and started cleaning the sink. "I never have," she protested. "How could you say that? Tell me when I lied to you . . . go on, tell me."

Harry put back his shoulders and sat stiffly, not liking the question. "Never you mind, that's for me to know, and you to think about."

She turned away and smiled. So he didn't know when she lied, and yes, she'd lied often. However, Harry was gullible. It had become easier to lie convincingly over the years, so she felt no guilt.

"Where's this picture he gave you?"

Taking down her purse, she took out the small china plate with its crudely coloured hand-drawn depiction of the Tower.

"Here." She thrust it at him. "Let's see if you can find anything to complain about in that. It's a gimcrack thing."

"Might as well toss it away, then." Harry made to throw it on the fire.

"Give it here!" She grabbed it quickly. "It's to remember a lovely day out me and the kids had. If you'd been more understanding lately, I wouldn't have taken them without you. Use your bean and think about me occasionally. All you've done is gripe and complain these past weeks. It's like living with Miss Atwood."

Everybody in Trawton knew of Miss Atwood, once head mistress of the village school and known as a right bitch, always scolding about things the kids did, constantly handing out six of the best with a thick, round ebony ruler. She earned a reputation as a killjoy, a tyrant who never smiled. Harry was like her when he got into one of his moods, and God only knew what set him off sometimes.

"Me? Like Miss Atwood?" Harry said, his mouth agape. "Don't

make me laugh. They knew her as Attila the Hun around these parts, didn't they?"

"Right enough. So you think back to the things you've been on about this last month. There's no living with you, Harry. I can't take much more of it, I can tell you."

She glared at him and, morose, he stared into the embers. He heaved a sigh and said, "Maybe you're right there, Marian, but you have no idea of the problems I've got at work. I don't suppose it's much of an excuse, but it's the truth. I've come close to losing my job and then what would we do? I've got no training for anything else, other than two years with my uncle and that only as a labourer." Harry sighed, a deep gut wrenching sigh.

An hour later Marian sat in tears. Poor Harry, what he had gone through and how he'd tried to protect her from the worry of it all. What had she done? She had spent good money, money they may soon need . . . spent it on a trip to Blackpool where she had dallied with another man.

For a few weeks things were good between them and they drew closer. She never did go to Blackpool again, but set the plate in the china cabinet and looked at it with something akin to longing. It reminded her of that beautiful day, spent with a man who loved her at first sight.

"... .and so your Granddad bought me this to remind us of our lovely day at Blackpool."

"Wow. What a great story, Gran. Seeing the Tower for the first time way back then, and think, those same lions are still there in that smelly zoo." She giggled. "So if you think it smelled bad all those years ago, you'll know how horrible it stinks today. They should bottle the stink and sell it as an anti warfare device. It's better than atom bombs."

Rita ran her finger over the painted surface of the plate. Amateurish, but it meant so much to her Gran. She went to put it back in its place. If she could meet a man as romantic as her Granddad, she would be the luckiest woman in the world.

Marian sat by the fire and closed her eyes. Now his face did not come to mind, no trace of him remained in her memory, not a trace of the face that had haunted her dreams all those years ago. Whenever things would get her down, she used to think about the handsome man who had fallen so much in love with her at first glance, idly wondering whether he also thought about her.

CHAPTER SIX

1956

Rita and her father lived in an uneasy truce. They spoke to each other civilly, but the warm loving relationship which developed between them when they were first alone, had vanished. His imminent marriage to Molly bothered Rita. She knew it shouldn't, but it did.

Even as she realized her Dad could not stay tied to her, a child, Rita was young and selfish enough to want him all to herself. She knew one day she would marry, and then what would happen to him? Yet then again, she reasoned, she and her new husband could have him live with them, so things need not change that much.

Now she surreptitiously watched him as he read the newspaper. What went on in his head? Did he think she could accept Molly as her mother? Molly was nice, although Rita felt strange about thinking her Dad slept with her, and if they married that would happen. Men were strange creatures, she decided, Gran was right.

"Men have needs, Rita, love." Gran told her last week.

"Don't women have needs too?" she asked with some embarrassment.

"'Course they do, but different from men. You'll find out when you grow up that men aren't sane when they're deprived of physical release. We women can take it or leave it, but men are so frantic to get it they use prostitutes for satisfaction. You don't want your Dad going with one of them lot now, do you?"

Rita thought about it for a second. "Well, isn't Molly as bad as a prostitute?"

Marian was shocked. "Rita! I don't know where you get these ideas. I shouldn't be having this conversation with you, a mere child, but I guess you're old enough to learn something of the ways of the world. You don't have your Mam now, not that she'd talk to you like this. Oh no, not our Sheila, she'd much prefer you to learn a load of rubbish on the streets. Anyroad, where was I?"

"About Molly not being a prostitute. Still, Gran, she sleeps with my Dad, I know she does. How can she be different?"

"Rita, lovey, your father loves Molly. His feelings for her, and her for him make it a different proposition. They're getting married and no prostitute ever marries. If she does, the husband knows all about it and isn't much of a man. Anyway, Molly is a nice woman, and she's right for your father, and you know it. This is a lot of old codswallop, young lady, and I'll thank you to tell me why you're fishing. Sex is something you'll learn about when you're older, though you told me you learned a lot at school when I offered to tell you. Meanwhile, you listen to your elders who know all about such things."

"I suppose. But . . .,"

Marian sighed. The child was making trouble where none existed. "You're making things difficult for your father, Rita. He might be catering to you right now, but don't get the impression that'll go on too much longer. You know he's sued your mother for a divorce?" Rita's head jerked up and she paid full attention. "Well, mark my words, as soon as, and if not before that day, he'll be living with Molly, who he's going to marry whether or not it pleases you."

Rita sat sulking. She did not want Molly in their house and how awful to think about them sharing the same bed. The fact her Dad acted so happy and jolly when Molly was around made her resentful. Why couldn't he be nice and jolly without the woman?

The problem was getting the better of her and she spent some minutes pondering how she could make herself accept the relationship. If she were grown up, she would know how to handle it, and no matter what her Gran said, it was not right, not right at all. Yet she was nearly twenty and why couldn't she accept things the way they were? She felt lacking in intelligence.

"Gran?"

"Yes, lovey?"

"May I ask you something?"

"Go right ahead, I'm all ears," Marian put down the duster and gave her grandchild her undivided attention.

"It's about my Mam."

"What about her?"

"Why didn't you and she ever speak to each other? Properly I mean, talking like we do, not giving orders. I can't remember you talking to each other in all my life. She hated you, you know, she often told me that. So what happened to make her that way?"

Marian pursed her lips. "That's nothing to do with you, child. Don't ask me any questions on that score and I won't tell you any lies."

"I want to know," Rita said, her face stubborn and Marian knew she would worry the subject to death unless she stopped her.

"Well, Missy, you can want all you like, but I'll not talk about it, ever. Now, change the subject or go home."

Rita glared at her Gran. Inside she was dying of curiosity, so she saw nothing for it but to find her mother and ask her.

She stopped with one arm in her coat and looked at Marian.

"Where's my Mam? I'm going to ask her since you won't tell me."

"Oh, so that's what this is all about, eh?" Marian felt annoyed. "Nosy little thing, aren't you? Take no for an answer for once. I already told you nobody knows where your mother went."

"Yes, they do!" Rita snapped. Why did everyone treat her like a child who had no knowledge of the world? Then her face lit up with a triumphant smile. "They *have* to know where she is if Dad is asking her for a divorce."

Marian shook her head. The girl was far from stupid. "Well then, there's your answer. Ask your father."

Rita already had, but he wouldn't tell her. Now each day she watched the mail for surely he would be getting legal letters. Yes, that's the way she would get the address.

Marian walked to the door with Rita, worried she was going to start making trouble between Molly and Arthur.

"You know, Rita, this curiosity of yours is going to get you into trouble one of these days," she said as she opened the door. "They do say curiosity killed the cat."

Rita grinned cheekily. "But I'm not a cat."

"No, you'll get hurt worse than one caught in a mangle, though, if you keep this up, young lady."

"Oh, do leave off, Gran," she said, waving her hand airily. "Nothing will happen if I talk to her. I mean, she's my *mother.*"

"I'm afraid it will, lovey, it will indeed. She can poison your mind, turn you against me and your Dad." She stopped as she saw Rita's expression. "Oh well, never mind. Anyway, as I said, I know nowt of her whereabouts."

"Are you sure?"

"Are you calling me a liar, child?" Marian's face showed her shock.

Rita gasped. "Oh no, Gran. I'm sorry."

Marian almost lost her temper. "So you should be, so you should be. You go home now. I've no more patience left. Come back when you've come to your senses and not before. You'd do well to forget your mother. Better you spend some time doing some bottoming on that house of yours. I can't do it all, you know."

Rita walked home slowly and the hundred yards from her Gran's to her own house seemed like miles. How could she have upset Gran that way? Surely she becoming a real bossy britches, maybe taking after her mother. Rita recognized her grandmother as wise, she knew so much and here she was, making facetious remarks and accusing her of lying.

As she made the tea and set the stew Gran had made this morning on to heat, she thought about things. If she wanted to find out about the big secret, she would have to do things differently. She would find her mother, she *must* find her. However, nobody must know, not her Dad and not her Gran, because it upset them to talk about it. The secret must be something terrible. Rita's imagination ran riot as she visualized all kinds of improbable events.

As the tea brewed, she stepped into the front room and looked around critically. Gran was right, the place was dusty and uncared for, primarily because they rarely used the front room these days. The sofa felt damp, the crocheted antimacassars looked decidedly grimy, and she couldn't recall the last time she had lighted a fire. The aspidistra in the front window appeared decidedly sick so she went to get it some water.

Yes, her Gran knew all right. The house had become run down and looked shabby. While her mother had not been half the housekeeper Gran was, at least she looked after the entire house, not just the kitchen like Rita did. Now it was Molly who now washed the sheets and linens, a job Rita hated.

While she should forget her mother and concentrate on making her Dad's life easier, she knew she would not rest until she had found her mother and asked the question.

It took her until Sunday to apologize to Marian, who forgave her.

"How about this, Gran?" Rita asked on the following Sunday as she handed Marian the small frame with a preserved butterfly.

"Ah yes, the butterfly. That's some story," Marian said as she stroked the ebony case.

The iridescent blue, green and yellow tropical butterfly had started life in the Brazilian jungle.

1931

The market was packed with shoppers, all seeking bargains. Marian knew the best time for bargains was at day's end when the tired vendors wanted to pack up and go home. Stalls teemed with shoppers as barkers called their wares, men sold helium filled balloons, others had feathery birds on sticks that twittered when you whirled them in circles around your head. French onion vendors walked around festooned with their wares, berets atop gallic mustachioed faces.

As she poked through produce on the market stall, she heard a voice behind her. "Mrs. Haydon?"

She spun around to find Mrs. Netherton, the new Vicar's wife, wearing a large smile on her fat face. Like a lunatic Cheshire cat, Marian thought maliciously.

"Mrs. Netherton. How nice to see you," she said, not meaning a word, knowing the woman wanted something. The Vicar's wife never made small talk or smiled so widely unless it accompanied a request in one form or another.

"You too, Mrs. Haydon." With a wry smile she reached out and adjusted Marian's white collar. "I wonder if I may ask a favour?"

"If I can help, I will be glad to," Marian said, hoping she wanted something simple and not time consuming. What did she mean by touching her like that? It was not as though they were even friendly. She glanced at her freshly laundered shawl collar, wondering what had needed adjusting.

"As you know, we are holding the bazaar next week and we need another person for the jumble stall," Mrs. Netherton never spoke, she gushed. "One of our ladies is near her time and I'm afraid labour might soon start. In view of that, I'm going to reorganize the work schedule. Could we impose on you for two hours Saturday afternoon?"

Marian smiled. Whew, not bad at all, only two hours on one day. She'd gotten off lightly.

"I think so, Mrs. Netherton," she said, feeling relieved. "Let me get back to you after I check with my husband."

People pushed past, unheeding. Someone trod on her foot and she winced with pain. "I'm sure Mr. Haydon won't mind because it's in such a worthy cause," Mrs. Netherton said, her tone changing to one of enthusiasm. "The church needs a new roof, even *he* knows that. We must all pitch in and work hard to raise the funds."

Sure, Marian thought, we'll all work and you'll be overlooking and doing nothing other than ordering people around, like every other Vicar's wife, except more pushy.

The fateful Saturday found her standing behind the jumble stall from two to four. Now messy, it looked like a pile of rubbish by the time she reached the hall. People had tossed and turned the various offerings every which way and she found it hard to make it look attractive. As she sorted things out in a lull attempting to restore order, a man picked up a frame containing a colourful butterfly.

"Well, I say," a cultured voice exclaimed. "This is too much. This is mine. Excuse me, madam, but who donated this item?"

"I'm sorry, but I have no idea." She looked up at the man and with a heart stopping thump realized it was Geoff, the man who took her virtue all those years ago, except now he was Lord Gerrard.

She stood with a hand at her throat, speechless for once.

Looking up from the frame, he glanced at the woman behind the stall thinking she looked vaguely familiar; but then most of the village people looked familiar to him as most worked at or around the Manor.

"Did you hear me?" he asked, his voice brusque. "From where did this item come? Did my mother, Lady Esther, donate it?"

She shook her head and shrugged simultaneously, mute, incapable of making a sound.

"This is my personal property and I have no intention of buying it, especially since I never gave it in the first place," he said, putting it in his pocket.

Her voice came back. "Geoff?" she squeaked.

Of course it was he, she knew, but this was the only attempt she could make at speech, so shocked was she to see him.

He looked at her closely. "Marian?"

She nodded.

His face lit up and he looked handsome as he smiled. The memory of their lovely time in the gazebo flooded back and she smiled back, patting at her hair.

"My goodness," he said, "You have changed considerably."

"Well, so have you. It's been a long time."

He was Sir Geoffrey now. His father had died two years earlier and an aura of power seemed to hang around him. Yet what did that mean between them? To her he was plain Geoff and would always be plain Geoff. Who would have thought they would have come face to face again?

Her gaze wandered over him, past the good tailoring and the custom made riding boots, to the man himself. Geoffrey seemed broader and his handsome, now ruddy, face had filled out, his frame was well padded by good food and good living. In fact, he looked decidedly stocky, unlike his youthful slimness. His hair looked still as thick but shorter. She noticed how his ears stuck out, but, all in all, he was a fine figure of a man. She blushed at her thoughts.

"I see you're married," he said, looking at her ring. "I trust things are well with you."

"Very well," she kept her voice low so the other customers could not hear. In the crowded noisy hall, they were alone. "I still have the little angel you gave me, and I still think about you, Geoff." Right on cue, the strains of "Memories" floated from the PA speakers.

He smiled at her words as he rocked on his heels, his glance eyes raking her still trim shape. She could see his admiration and blushed, knowing her eyes were shining and her cheeks rosy.

Marian knew he had married Cynthia Armstrong, now the Lady of the Manor. Age and sickness kept old Lady Esther confined to her bed these days. Everyone in the village knew he was not particularly happy with his lot in life because Cynthia had become a barracuda. Her twittering and sniping annoyed the staff, and probably him. Still, even if he had made a big mistake in marrying Cynthia, what did it matter when he had his choice of all the available village women, or others farther afield?

"Do you work?" he asked, keeping his voice low.

She stared at him steadily. "No. I have no need."

He glanced around, keeping his voice low and leaning over the stall. "I wondered if you would like to work at the manor. Not an outside job or in the kitchen, but on the family floors as an upstairs maid."

"I don't know," was all she could say. Her heart beat fast, the blood constricted her throat.

Suddenly he took her work-worn hand and bowed over it. Marian, her gaze flashing around, noticed people openly staring, but Geoff didn't care and why should he? He was Lord of the Manor. For her part, Marian felt flattered when he stood paying her such attention and had paid her a compliment. Imagine, a Lord bowing over her hand! Let them look, she thought, putting up her chin and glancing around triumphantly, her cheeks flaming.

"Could I let you know, Geoff?"

"No, it's not possible. I must know now," he said, looking at her so forcefully her heart skipped a beat. He still loved her, she knew it and the knowledge flooded her body. Right then, she thought she still loved him.

"All right, I'll take the job," she said, reluctantly taking back her hand.

"Be at the Manor at eight on Monday morning," he said, his florid face smiling. Too much port or whisky, too much high living, she thought.

Job? No job existed: she knew it and he knew it. It was a subterfuge to get her within arms' reach. Geoff wanted to make love with her again, that was what this was all about, and she wanted him, Lord or no Lord, because he was still her first real love.

When His lordship came to her attention, Mrs. Netherton bustled over importantly. Nobility overawed village people, but she, in her exalted position as Vicar's wife, was well accustomed to dealing with the upper classes.

"Good afternoon, Lord Gerrard," she said far too loudly, offering her gloved hand as a familiar.

Geoffrey, too well bred to ignore the gesture, held it for a second but did not shake it, or bow over it. Marian saw him wondering who the woman could be, saw the sudden look of recognition as it dawned on him this was the Vicar's overbearing wife.

"I do hope you'll find something of interest, sir." She gestured expansively as if she'd done everything herself. "This is our most interesting stall. One never knows what treasures one might discover here."

"Yes," he said, winking over her wagging bonnet at Marian, who blushed and lowered her eyes.

"Can we find anything to interest you, Lord Gerrard?" Mrs. Netherton said, poking among the clutter of objects and glaring at Marian as if it were her fault everything was not neater.

Geoffrey assumed a haughty, regal stance, hands clasped behind his back. "I do not think so, Madam." He looked disdainful. "I have found what I want. Thank you." Turning, he strolled away among the stalls.

Mrs. Netherton glared at Marian. "What did his Lordship buy?" she asked. "His purchase should considerably increase the receipts."

Marian felt a great deal of satisfaction as she said, "Nothing, in fact, he took back something belonging to him someone donated in error. A butterfly in a frame. It was his, he told me, and what could I say?"

Mrs. Netherton bridled, her mouth a thin line of displeasure. "Lady Cynthia donated the item. She handed it to me herself. Why, she told me his Lordship has hundreds of them mounted on the wall in his study. He surely would not miss one."

"It was obviously not hers to give," Marian broke in, suddenly defensive of Geoff. "So he took it back. Go and ask him to return it, if it's that important." To hell with Mrs. Bloody Netherton. She had found Geoff again and nothing else mattered. Not now he still loved her.

"Marian!" Harry said again more loudly. "What's the matter with you, woman? You're wool gathering all the time."

"Sorry," she said, looking up from her darning. Since she arrived home from the church bazaar, she mulled over a million ways of telling him she would be going out to work. Harry prided himself in that he could support his wife and family, so it wasn't going to be easy, but would be even harder if she didn't pay attention.

"I asked you three times where my shirt studs were," he said testily. "I can't find them."

"I'll get them," she said, putting down the darning egg and moving to the fireplace. "I put them safe on the mantlepiece in this vase since you can't keep track of them."

She handed him the studs and he put the back one into his collar.

"I might be late tonight," he said, grunting as he fastened the front stud. "It's the lodge election and they've nominated me for treasurer."

She smiled. Harry loved his lodge, and every year ran for something, though he never won.

"Good luck. Maybe tonight is the night."

Let's hope he wins, she thought, it will make it easier to give him the news.

Harry put on his jacket and checked his reflection in the mirror over the sink, patted his pockets to make sure he had everything before he went to get his overcoat, and turned to face her.

"By the way, Mrs. Higgins says Lord Gerrard offered you a job at the manor."

She gasped. Nosy old trout, Ethel Higgins, big ears, too. Well, it was out now, she realized with dismay, and she might as well make the best of it.

"Yes, he did, but he didn't tell *her*. She's got ears like a rabbit, that one."

"So? Are you going?"

"I thought I might," she said not looking at him. "It all depends on you."

"You might as well take it," he said, surprising her so much her head shot up. "We could use the money, and it's not as if you chased after the job. It's a royal command, you might say. You take it, Marian."

She stared at him. What was this? Him allowing her to go out to work? Surely his job was safe now?

"Are you thinking of retiring?" she asked, her tone gentle in case things were worse.

He shook his head. "No, and they aren't thinking of sacking me either, so put the thought right out of your head. You go out to work, lass. It'll give you an interest in life. You've been stuck in this house for years, and the kids are in school all day. Let's face it, Marian, there's not much to keep you amused here, so you might as well make yourself useful."

Marian gaped at him. Wonders would never cease. She soon could see Geoff every day and her heart raced as she thought about the fake job. Soon she would be near him, her first love. What Harry said was true because she hardly talked to a soul during the day other than shop keepers and Ruth next door, because the children were at school. The children would miss her when they got home, but then again both usually played on the street with their pals until supper time. They could always go to a neighbour if the weather was bad.

On the Monday morning she set off to the Manor at seven-thirty not knowing what to expect, or even if Geoff had told them to expect her. Going round to the servant's entrance, wiser now in her maturity, she knocked.

Blake answered the door and looked at her, a stranger.

"We don't want none," he said, and made to shut the door.

"One moment, please," she said, leaning on the door frame, "His Lordship asked me to report for work this morning."

"Oh well, then you'd better come in and speak to Mrs. Malone," he said, standing aside. His gaze took in her every aspect and his vulgar stare embarrassed Marian. Obviously he did not recognize her.

"Mrs. Malone?" she asked.

"Aye, the housekeeper. She does all the hiring and firing."

"What happened to Mrs. Wilton who was here the last time I worked for the manor?" she asked.

"Dead this two years," he said with a snort, as if she should have known. "Wait here while I fetch Mrs. Malone."

Mrs. Malone arrived with her nose in the air and a snobby attitude as befitted the housekeeper of such a fine establishment. She acted even more condescendingly than Lady Esther, Marian thought, stifling a snigger.

"What is the name?" she asked, looking down her nose.

"Marian Haydon."

"His Lordship said nothing about anyone called Haydon. Are you related to Marian Steadman?"

She smiled, showing her good teeth, one up on Mrs. Malone who wore a top denture and had rotten teeth below. "That's my maiden name," she said, smiling, realizing Geoff could not know her married name.

"Hm," Mrs. Malone said, her nose inching higher. "I suppose he knows what he's doing. I only hope Lady Cynthia will accept his selection. Well, we'll soon find out."

Marian accompanied her to the uniform room where Mrs. Malone handed her a blue cotton dress and a frilled white apron and cap. She was to be a day parlour maid and would work from eight to four. Much to her amazement she had every weekend off, because a live-in maid would then cover her position. It was easy work, in fact, it was hardly work at all. Above stairs, the sumptuous surroundings fascinated her. Eeh, to think people lived like this and what had she got? A small terraced house with two up and two down. She gawped at the splendour.

A marble paved corridor with a Wilton runner down the centre led to the front hall, its echoing marble floored space used as ballroom for big events. Family crests blazed from each section of oak panelling. War banners of ancestors waved from rafters and a huge fireplace, large enough to hold a tea party in, held a blazing log fire though it was warm outside. The massive square oak staircase, covered with fine Persian carpet with twinkling brass carpet rods, split into two sections at the first floor.

Mrs. Malone showed her into the second floor parlour where she would work, and her dazzled gaze took it all in at a glance. The plush carpets, the heavy brocade draperies, shining furniture, gilt mirrors, heavy oil paintings, the huge floral arrangements standing on tables in fine crystal and silver vases. It fair took her breath away. This luxury was what she had been expecting to see when she first went into service.

She grinned. Aye, she had landed on her feet here all right. Talk about money for old rope. Her job, Mrs. Malone said, was to dust and polish, to serve tea or snacks, and fetch anything requested. More importantly, she must hover silently and invisibly when the family were present in case they required her services.

At the rear of the parlour was a small closet-like room holding a single upright chair and a cupboard where cleaning materials were kept. It also had a bell to summon her. She was to sit here, Mrs. Malone told her, if the family came into the parlour, unless specifically requested to wait nearby.

For two days she waited alone. Nobody entered the parlour, other than Mrs. Malone, so she spent her time dusting and polishing already shiny surfaces. She glanced at the leather bound books and poked into cupboards and drawers. They had so many possessions, so many items at whose use she could only guess.

Dinner at noon and tea at eleven and three, she took in the kitchen at the communal kitchen table where the other servants eyed her and nudged each other. They did not speak to her, but then they still did not allow servants to talk at meals. She noticed things had not changed much in the kitchen with Mr. Hodgson still in residence.

Gaunt and frail now, his voice like a creaking gate, it was almost as though he were shrinking inside his suit, Marian thought. His frock coat looked decidedly greenish and from his table top position he eyed the staff with his customary malice. Why he was still working at his age was a mystery. Marian knew he had been at the Manor since he was a boy of fourteen so was practically built in with the bricks.

Mrs. Clayton was either dead or retired and the new cook, a thin woman with a mouth like a steel trap, had suspicious eyes and a waspish way of talking. She kept her hair covered with a thick black hair net that came down over her forehead where a thick knot made a dent in her flesh. This headgear made her look idiotic and Marian figured her for a murderous boss. Whoever heard of a thin cook?

On the third day of her duty, the door opened and Lady Cynthia entered with another lady. Dressed to the nines, both wore large feathered hats and fur stoles.

Marian stopped polishing and stood to one side, gaze cast down meekly, exactly as Mrs. Wilton had instructed all those years ago.

"Ah, you must be Haycock," Lady Cynthia said, looking Marian up and down through a lorgnette. "My housekeeper tells me my husband hired you."

Marian raised her head. Subservience was not her strong point and why should she stand here while they stared at her? She looked right at the pair of them, her nose rising a fraction.

The other woman sat on the couch and scrutinized her rudely, eyebrows raised. Lady Cynthia appeared blatant in her dislike. Marian blushed under her scrutiny.

"As I was saying, what do you think, Gladys?" Lady Cynthia asked her friend as she turned away. "Has he lost his mind or what?"

Both laughed and Marian flushed hotly. What did they mean? Were they referring to her and Geoff or somebody else? She decided they were simply continuing a conversation.

"Fetch us tea and be quick about it," Lady Cynthia ordered and Marian left hurriedly to go to the kitchen.

Cynthia and Gladys watched her leave. When she gently shut the door, Cynthia said, "Honestly, Gladys, he is the limit. This one is as plain as a pikestaff. What is the matter with the man's eyes?"

"Oh tosh, she's decent enough," Gladys said, "You should see some of my staff." She laughed. "At least this one's clean and tidy, not like the last one he brought home. Confidentially, I think her bovine with those big blue eyes and pink and white complexion, although I must say she does seem willing enough."

"Willing?" Cynthia screeched with equine laughter. "Oh my dear, that's the reason he hires them, because they are *willing!* I have had such a procession through this house, my dear. Mind you, he soon tires of them."

"The man is completely mad. I mean, who could match your beauty, my dear friend," Gladys said loyally, although personally she thought Cynthia looked like a horse and often sounded like one.

Cynthia smiled, pleased at the compliment. "My husband Geoffrey has peculiar tastes. Who would have thought he would turn out like this, a lecher like his father? Still, the acorn does not fall far from the tree, as they say, and his mother has told me such tales about Sir Charles. At least Geoffrey plays at home and not away. I suppose I should be glad."

Gladys deftly changed the subject, knowing Cynthia disliked her mother-in-law. "How is Lady Esther?"

"Confined to bed these days. On her last legs, I hope."

"Is she still difficult to live with?"

"Much worse, my dear, now she is bedridden," she was saying as Marian came back with the tea tray. She set it on the table and, retiring to her closet, sat on the hard chair.

After they drank their tea and departed, Marian went back into the parlour and sat with a plop on the couch. What a shrew, she thought, she's almost as bad as Lady Esther. Poor Geoff, married to such a woman. Then her nose detected the perfume they wore and she smiled.

Later when she took the tea things back to the kitchen, she caught a glimpse of Geoff climbing the stairs on the other side and her heart started to palpitate. Soon, she told herself, soon . . .

Sheila was not pleased at being left to play on the street every afternoon, though if it had been her own idea she would have been over the moon. Roger could have cared less as it gave him more time to get into mischief.

"I don't want you to go to work, Mam," Sheila shouted, pummelling Marian with her fists. For eleven she was tall, almost as tall as her mother, and a bully.

"Don't be silly, Sheila. Stop that." Marian pushed her aside and went to get her knitting.

"Aye, stop it, child," Harry said. Sheila had done nothing but whine since she heard her mother would be at work when she got home.

Lots of the women on the street now worked because things were bad economically and the mines were on short weeks. Thank God, Marian often thought, Harry's still with the council, who, while they don't pay well, at least pay regularly.

"I need to get into the house to get my doll and stuff," Sheila whimpered, unwilling to drop the subject.

Marian spoke quietly. Calm reasoning might help, although she doubted it. "Then take your doll to Mrs. Spencer's and leave it there, Sheila. Then you can get it when you want it. Anyone would think I was deserting you, not going to work, and it's only an hour before I get home after you get here."

Sheila's eyes flashed, she resented not getting her own way. "I don't *like* you working. My Mam shouldn't work, my Mam should be here in case I fall down and hurt myself. Who's going to make me milk and jam butties?"

Marian looked at her sharply. Sheila got worse instead of better. "Stop your whingeing, child. Life isn't over because I'm working. You'll soon get used to it."

"I won't! I won't! I won't!" Sheila screamed throwing herself on the floor and kicking her clogs against the flagstones.

As Marian put down her knitting before standing, Harry looked at her.

"Leave her be," he said. "She's nowt but a spoiled brat, and you've made her that way 'cos I certainly didn't."

As Sheila lay screaming on the floor, Roger watched with great interest. Hysteria had been his sister's favourite method of getting her own way since she was a baby, and it usually worked with his Mam. Sheila was turning blue now, another of her ploys. He watched fascinated as she held her breath and kept her mouth open in a silent scream as her arms and legs flailed. Roger wanted to laugh, but dared not or she wouldn't half pummel him when they were alone upstairs. Sheila, a cruel girl, would make him pay. She would tease cats and kittens until she crazed them and he once saw her break the legs on a duckling and laugh. Aye, his sister was a right devil.

The adults watched her, aware it was all an act

"Sheila! Stop it at once and get up off the floor," Marian shouted, losing her temper. "I don't know . . . you're nowt but a play actor, child, a play actor. Anyroad, your performance is wearing thin. We've seen it too often. Stop it at once."

Sheila, furious her mother had not picked her up and promised she would get her wish, had no intentions of quitting until her mother said she would stay home. She lay on the cold floor and grizzled until she could feel the cold striking up through her pinafore. After a while, and because everyone ignored her, she reluctantly pushed herself up onto her knees, her eyes narrowed with petulance. They would pay for this . . . they would . . .she'd show them.

Roger sat at the table ostensibly doing his homework, but watched her. Sheila's peripheral vision was good and she could see him out of the corner of her eye. When she saw his smirk, she drew in a deep breath of annoyance. Blast him, smirking with superiority. Like a whirlwind she stood and throwing herself at him, punched him in the ear with a fist of iron.

"Ouch!" Roger roared and burst into tears. His ear rang and started to pulse painfully. "Oooow, that hurt."

Harry stood and took off his belt, knowing his daughter would have to learn the hard way. She was too fond of lashing out at anyone who didn't stand up to her. One day she kicked him so hard in the shin with her iron shod clog, she drew blood and he thought his leg broken. Enough was enough.

Grabbing her arm, he pulled her into the scullery. "Right, my girl, I'll not have you dishing out punches while I sit and watch. This has gone on long enough. You need more discipline. You've got a lot to learn and I'm going to teach you a few things."

Sheila struggled to get out of his grasp, but he was too strong for her.

"Don't you do it, Dad. Don't you dare. Mam! Mam! Stop him, Mam!" She started to scream with terror.

Harry raised the belt, holding it by the buckle, and let her have it against the back of her legs over her dress. She was like an eel, constantly squirming so he could not get a clear aim. All the while she screamed like a banshee, making it sound as if he were killing her, and yet he did not hit her hard.

"Harry!" Marian said, frightened at his expression, pulled at his arm. "You can't beat the girl. Stop it at once."

He shrugged her off. "Get out of here, Marian. I've had enough of this girl's disobedience, insolence and defiance. She's nowt but a hellcat. Someone has to chastise her and you won't do it. As I said, enough is enough. This one would try the patience of a saint." As he said this he lashed out at Sheila and the belt came down with more force, although he had not meant it to happen.

"Harry, Harry, please don't do it, stop it now," Marian cried, her face awash with tears.

Sheila screamed louder and louder until the sound reverberated through the small flagstoned space and made their blood run cold.

Roger stood in the doorway smiling. Sheila was getting it now and he wondered whether she would like the bruises and pain. He chuckled to himself behind the cover of his book, she was a right screamer, was Sheila. She practised at it too. He'd heard her once out in the woods and you would have thought someone was murdering her.

Marian pulled and tugged at Harry who had become so enraged he didn't know what he was doing. Eventually she got the belt out of his hand and pushed him away as Sheila lay on the stone floor, sobbing hysterically.

When the front door slammed, Marian knew Harry had gone to the pub or the lodge. Roger stood in the doorway still smiling. By, but it had been a grand sight, he thought.

"Come on, Sheila, get up off the floor and get yourself warm by the fire," Marian said, making no move to help her daughter. In her heart she knew, in a way, Harry was right. Oh, not by lashing out with his belt; she didn't hold with that, but Sheila was becoming too difficult to handle. As an adult if she wanted to have any control over the girl, she must never show the guilt she felt because Sheila pounced on any weakness of character like a hen on a bug.

She turned on the radio and the strains of the music from "City Lights" calmed her. Charlie Chaplin, an Englishman, currently reigned in Hollywood, the world's most famous man. Whenever one of his movies came to Wigan, she and Ruth made a special trip to see a matinee. It was the only form of entertainment available to them at their age, apart from the wireless.

"Come on, you're all right now. Nothing is broken. Here, wipe your face." She pushed the towel from the back of the door into Sheila's hands and stood watching as she rubbed it around her face. Her voice was firm when she said, "Right, get into the kitchen. Time to do your homework."

Marian steeled herself not to show any leniency. While Harry was wrong to strap Sheila, maybe she would learn something from the cruel lesson. She never learned the easy way, and would never learn if her parents sent mixed messages. They had often caned Sheila at school, though Marian only recently learned about this from Roger who liked tattle tale-ing.

Sheila sniffed her way to the table and sat on the chair. "My legs hurt," she said, "Maybe I should go to the doctor."

"Nay, I don't think it's as bad as that, child, and they'll hurt a lot more if you start your carry on again," Marian said as she picked up her knitting. She noticed her hands still shook from the stress of the last few minutes. "Your Dad isn't a cruel man, Sheila, but you have to learn. Surely you understand other people have feelings. You can catch more flies with syrup than you can with vinegar."

Sheila turned to face her mother, her bottom lip stuck out churlishly. "What does that mean?"

Marian looked at her. By the heck, she even wanted people to do her thinking for her. "You're a big girl now, Sheila, work it out for yourself."

"I know what it means," Roger said, his face shining.

Marian looked at him and shook her head. "I know you do, lad, but let your sister figure it out for herself."

Roger sat and crossed his arms. He watched Sheila as she silently repeated the words, her lips moving. She was stupid, was Sheila. That's why she always lashed out in anger at her own shortcomings.. The other girls in her form were clever in comparison and she always came bottom of the class.

Sheila muttered the words, unable to understand their meaning. "What do flies have to do with anything?" she snippily asked Roger who simply smiled and turned the pages in his school book. "Come on, you said you knew. You tell me *now*." She kicked him under the table with the toe of her clog.

"Ouch!" He rubbed at his shin. "Mam said you were to work it out for yourself. Didn't you, Mam?"

"Yes, I did, and I meant it," Marian said, keeping her voice calm, wanting this upset ended. "Put on your thinking cap and sort it for yourself. You know, Sheila, you come home every term with bad report cards, and heaven knows why since you've got enough natural cunning to charm the birds from the trees. You should buck up your ideas and try to learn."

Sheila sat back and rolled her eyes to heaven, piqued and resentful, listening to her mother's platitudes with an expression akin to loathing.

"This is another example of how you don't even *try* to learn." Marian continued, "You can't go through life expecting people to work things out for you."

Marian's voice kept her voice low and patient. No need to lose her temper, though she felt angry. Angry with Harry, angry with herself for she blamed her own failure as a mother for Harry's outburst, doubly angry with Sheila who was brainless and stubborn.

Sheila stared sullenly at the geography book. Then taking out an exercise book, she wrote down the saying. Marian hid a smile, knowing that tomorrow she would get the teacher to tell her its meaning. Sheila glanced at Roger who was drawing a map. Her eyes narrowed and he saw her looking at him speculatively. He shook his head. She glanced at her mother who watched her questioningly, then applied herself to her text book.

Later after they washed and put on their pyjamas in front of the fire, Marian kissed them both.

"So did you work it out yet?" she asked her daughter.

"Of course I did," Sheila said as she ran to the stairs and dashed up them before she asked her to explain.

Roger chuckled. "She doesn't know it, Mam, does she?"

"No, lad, I don't think she does. She would have wanted to show off if she had," she said, fondly ruffling his hair. "Mind you don't tell her, either."

Harry arrived home as Roger was putting his school books in his satchel.

"Still up, lad?" he asked looking around, his mood better for a couple of pints. "Where's her royal majesty?"

Roger sniggered. "Licking her wounds, Dad, licking her wounds. By, but she got it, didn't she?" Roger's face expressed his pleasure.

Harry pulled his son against his knee, an arm around his thin shoulders. "Listen, Roger, I did wrong, but she made me lose my temper. You must never, ever raise your arm in anger against anyone, especially a woman or child. I'm right ashamed of myself."

Roger grinned. "Aaw, Dad, it was right smashing. It paid her back for hitting me, an'all." Gingerly, he rubbed at his ear. Red and swollen, it still felt tender.

Harry sighed. What *had* he done? "It was not smashing, son. It was wrong. Your mother was right. I shouldn't have done it, but I did, and now I can't take it back." He looked at Marian who smiled warmly and he knew she had forgiven him. "Maybe Sheila will think twice before she hits you again. By, I bet those other girls in her class must move out of her reach really quickly."

"Yes, Dad, and you know what?" Roger said, eager to tell them all about his sister. Things they would never know unless he told them.

"Roger, time for bed," his mother said in a tone of voice that brooked no argument.

"Aaw, Mam, I only wanted to tell . . .,"

"Don't be a tattletale, son. Off to bed now."

Roger went slowly up to bed, hoping Sheila was asleep, but she sat at the top of the stairs having listened to everything they had said.

Marian did not see Geoff, as she still thought of him, for more than two weeks. Then at the staff dining table, she heard Mr. Hodgson talk about the trip His Lordship had taken to the family sugar plantation in Bermuda.

Each day she had arrived at work full of excitement, thinking maybe today she would see him, maybe today he would kiss her. Now she felt the exhilaration abate. His being abroad changed everything and she had no idea when she would see him. Obviously he was in no hurry to see *her*.

When he arrived home three weeks later, his appearance suddenly energized the entire house. Maids scurried around, the cook began orchestrating large suppers for the guests Geoff brought with him, Mr. Hodgson stuck his nose into every room checking on every little thing, Lady Cynthia even ordered people around. Was Geoff such a hard master? she wondered. Why all the sudden activity? Surely Lady Cynthia would have been the one to have the fuss made. She was *always* home.

Geoffrey and his business associates filled the house with loud voices, bursts of laughter and sometimes song. They rode in the mornings and supped at noon, and hunted every afternoon on either horse or foot. They wined and dined each evening.

Chattering ladies in gorgeous gowns filled the rooms and even downstairs they could hear music from the string quartet hired to play in the large entrance hall. The hurrying footsteps of many servants going about their business was the order of the day. All the servants scurried, Marian included.

Now every afternoon as she walked down the long driveway on her way home, she looked for him, and every afternoon was disappointed.

At Lady Cynthia's invitation, several local ladies joined the party and kept Marian busy in the parlour, fetching and carrying. Lady Cynthia rudely stared at her each time as she issued an order and often talked about her as if Marian were invisible. Marian suffered this indignity because she felt it was worth it, knowing what she knew.

Soon she would be with *him,* soon they would be alone together and soon her dreams would come true. The fact he was married to Lady Cynthia made no difference to Marian who considered Lady Cynthia as cold as ice. None of the staff liked the mistress, and obviously neither did Geoff.

She felt jealous of the beautiful gowns and the jewellery worn by the ladies, envied them their life of ease. Yet, the way they treated her did not bother her since she considered herself better looking without all the artifice and paint. The way they talked, so rude, so vulgar. That was why Geoff liked her, she was sure, she did not use words as daggers, nor paint her face. Hugging her secret, she performed her duties with a small smile of inner satisfaction.

Each evening she arrived home frazzled and out of sorts, and each evening Sheila would go into her spoiled brat act, until Marian was at her wit's end in case Harry took it into his head to beat her again. The lesson of honey and vinegar had some effect, though, (the teacher explained it to Sheila), and now she would be cloyingly sweet and completely phoney in her demands. Harry, gullible as ever, thought she had learned her lesson. Soon, though, he discovered once she managed to get her way, she reverted to her usual nasty self.

Now he would glare at her when she started her sugarcoated requests. Eventually she stopped bothering with sweet tempered requests and Marian waited for Harry to lose his temper again.

"I *have* to have one," she said, stamping her foot. "I have to have it, Mam. I'll be the only one in my class without one."

Marian paused in her beating of the batter pudding. "Don't give me that, Sheila, there's a few girls I know who don't have one. Their parents can't afford it, and neither can we. Stop your whingeing."

Sheila glared at her mother. She moved toward her Dad and, standing with her hand on the back of his chair, put her cheek next to his.

Marian smiled. Sheila was so transparent.

"Daddy?" she said in a small voice, a nice voice, a wheedling voice.

"What is it, Sheila? I'm trying to read here," Harry said shaking out his paper. He knew all Sheila's wiles and voice wouldn't get her anywhere with him, not anymore.

"Daddy? Daddy?"

"What is it, Sheila?" He lowered the paper and stared at her unsympathetically.

"I have to have a bike, Dad, I *have* to. Mam says we don't have enough money and I know she must have because she's working now, and anyway Roger has one."

"Aye, Roger does. Roger's a good lad and knows how to treat people," Harry said raising his paper.

"But Daddy, D-a-a-a-d!" She knocked the paper down, tearing it and Harry glared at her.

"Once more, young lady," he warned, "And you watch out." His hand went to his belt.

"But Daddy . . .,"

"But Daddy nothing! It's only Daddy when you're on the want, isn't it? The rest of the time it's just plain Dad. You're as transparent as that window, child. Your mother's right, we can't afford it so you're not having a bike. Do something to earn it and maybe I'll think about it. Our Roger earned his with his paper round and his good report cards. Think on, lass."

He rustled his paper angrily. Sullenly she sat at the table and picked up her math book.

"Roger, what's this?" she asked him pushing at his arm and making him smudge his essay.

"Do be careful, our Sheil, I lose marks for blots, you know. What's what?"

"This here," she pointed to an example of long division. "How do you do that?"

He grinned. "The same way you always have. Leave me alone. I have to get this finished."

She pushed the book away grumpily. "Dad, can you help me with this?"

"Could be, what is it?"

Harry, careful with the children, had eventually learned to read to keep his job. It took Marian two years to teach him after the children were in bed. Now he could read a newspaper, although he still did not understand many words, he would never let his children see his ignorance.

"Here, this is it." Sheila roughly thrust the book at her father and pointed at the sum with her nail-bitten finger.

They might have written it in Swahili. Figures meant nothing to Harry and apart from one to ten, any combination made almost no sense to him.

Marian, who had put the pudding in the oven, chipped in. "Leave your father alone, Sheila. He's had a hard day. What is it you want? Show me."

Harry looked at her with gratitude. She would never let the children know about his lack of schooling.

"You can do this," Marian said, looking at the problem. "You've been doing long division since you were seven. Don't try your games with me, madam, you're after having someone else do your work for you."

Sheila grabbed back the book. The look she gave Marian would have removed paint.

"Do the sum and show me the results," Marian said. The child was as full of tricks as a monkey. "And don't you go asking Roger, either," she warned.

The next day Marian walked to work with a spring in her step. Today *had* to be the day she saw him, it had to be.

Spring now and mild, a warming sun shone brightly over newly greened fields. Lambs gambolled in grassy meadows watched over by ewes, sky larks sang high in the blue, and butterflies sought out the dog daisies and blue bells. Along the manor driveway rhododendrons were coming into bloom; pinks, reds and yellows sparkled against dark glossy leaves. Green lawns were ablaze with crocuses and daffodils, and a gardener pruned the bush roses. Yes, she could feel it in her heart. Today was the day.

As it was a fine, windless day, Lady Cynthia and her friends were breakfasting on the awning shaded terrace at ten-thirty and Mrs. Malone sent Marian to help the house maid prepare the table. The men servants set up a long table, now covered with a fine damask cloth. Marian put out the silver cutlery and set crested china plates at each place.

Mr. Hodgson stood watching every move. He did little actual work these days, but simply supervised. Holding onto his control as long as possible, he still held the wine cellar keys and was the only person to decant and serve. On his key chain he also carried the key to the liquor cupboard and woe betide even his Lordship (who also had a key), if he deigned to pour himself a drink. His Lordship, and everyone else, must tug the bell pull and wait for him to serve them. In his old age he had become a martinet, ruling staff and family like a tyrant.

A gardener arrived with fresh floral arrangements that he set at the top, middle and end of the table. The cook and her helper brought out the chafing dishes and placed them on a side table. Perfume wafted to Marian's nose as the ladies arrived, dressed in the latest morning gowns of chiffon and silk, and she breathed in the scent of wealth.

"Haydon, you will help attend table," Mr. Hodgson said quietly as she made to leave. Marian obediently stood to one side, hands folded in front of her at her waist.

Throughout the long leisurely meal, Lady Cynthia, Marian noticed, chattered throughout and ate little. In fact, none of the ladies ate much and most plates were left half full. What a waste of good food, Marian thought, then realized the cook would not waste the leftovers but resurrect them as a staff meal.

Back from their ride, the men clattered through the house. They had eaten a substantial breakfast earlier, though now they would take another meal.

"The dining table is set, My Lord," Hodgson said, gesturing to the open French window.

"Never mind about that, Hodgson, we're going to join the ladies, aren't we, chaps? Much more entertaining. We'll eat out here, so get us some chairs and clean plates, there's a good fellow," Geoffrey said, beaming at the ladies.

Blake and a manservant brought out chairs and soon a jolly and noisy party was taking place. Marian, delegated to collecting dirty plates and handing out clean, bringing tea and coffee to the table, and taking back empty platters to the kitchen, was never still. Continually she glanced at Geoff.

She liked what she saw. His business and holiday in the tropics agreed with him. Tanned and fit looking, his teeth were white against sunburned features and she felt her heart give a great thump as their gaze met. His gaze roved her body and, when he winked, she thought she would die of happiness. She could hardly walk because her legs were trembling. Why did he have to be so handsome, why did she still feel like this about him? While no longer a teenager, she suddenly felt like one.

Marian was in her forty-fifth year. Not an old woman by any means, but old enough to know better. What *was* she doing? she asked herself every night before she fell asleep. What was she doing to her marriage, her children, her pride?

Geoffrey watched Marian as she bustled back and forth. A nice looking woman, almost beautiful in her maturity, she retained the bright blue eyes and curly hair of her youth, although surely experienced sexually. Virgins no longer interested him. They were far too much trouble.

Cynthia surreptitiously watched her husband, watched how his gaze followed the servant, the parlour maid, and could not resist saying something.

"Are you sorting out your evening appointments, Geoffrey?" Her shrill voice cut through the table conversation.

He looked at his wife, saying nothing, but raising an eyebrow. Cynthia, as everyone was well aware, had a large mouth and often used it to her husband's mortification.

"I notice the new woman interests you." She raised her voice a fraction, making sure everyone heard, and table talk sputtered to a close. "Exactly what are your plans for her?" Smiling widely, she glanced around her now silent table and lowered her voice as if imparting a secret. "It is one of my husband's little peccadillos, the hiring of my servants." She turned her gaze back on Geoffrey and then back to the company.

"Shall we be seeing her for long, Geoffrey?" She winked as she addressed her remarks to her lady friends, "Or should I ask Mrs. Malone to hire someone who has some actual work experience?"

Geoffrey, his face like thunder, pushed back his chair, stood and left the table. As Cynthia laughed her horsey laugh, the other women giggled because one always agreed with the lady of the house, even when she made a public fool of her husband. The men, uneasy now, started making muttering noises about changing for the afternoon. One by one the men left and Marian kept busy by clearing the table.

"See how stupid she is?" Cynthia asked her friends, "She doesn't even know I was talking about her. The woman is a complete moron."

Marian kept her head down and carried on with her work. What a horrible person Lady Cynthia was, talking to her husband like that. That woman she talked about, which one of the ladies was it?

The penetrating caught her attention. "You, Hayman, Hayseed, or whatever your name is, are you always so stupid?" Marian glanced up to see Lady Cynthia pointing in her direction with her lorgnette.

"Yes, madam. No, madam," she stammered.

"Are you deaf?"

"No, madam."

"We were talking about *you*, you stupid woman. My husband has a thing for servants, you know, which was the reason he brought you into my house." Cynthia glanced at Gladys who sat her side. "You were right about her being bovine, Gladys, she's about as animated as a cow." She brought up her lorgnette and stared at Marian. "I often wonder what Geoffrey sees in them."

Marian blushing furiously, glanced at Mr. Hodgson who gestured to the french window with his head, meaning he dismissed her. His eyes looked hard as flints.

They had been talking about her. How mortifying. Her mind went back over what she had heard. Geoff obviously was a philanderer and brought women here for his own purposes. He was not in love with her at all. Her face burned with shame as tears rolled down her cheeks.

Anger rose in her and she dashed the tears from her eyes. Well, she was not going to stay here another second. As she strode along the hall, she glanced into the empty study. Sticking her head around the door and seeing the hundreds of small frames covering the walls, she grabbed a colourful framed butterfly and put it in her pocket. They must be worth something if he had taken one back.

Rotten sod, rotten bugger, rotten bastard! She cursed her own stupidity. Dense she was, gullible, ridiculous . . and she thought Sheila stupid! Well, it went to show where Sheila's stupidity came from, and it was not from Harry.

Marian left the house and never looked back. When she got home, she put the butterfly in the cabinet as a reminder of her recklessness and naivete.

"That's how we came by this," Marian said as she rubbed her thumb over the glass. "Your Granddad was smart to find it in that jumble sale, wasn't he? I never even noticed it."

"It's so beautiful," Rita said wistfully, "I wish I could have seen it alive. It's as big as a sparrow, but with wings twice as wide."

"Aye, it's lovely all right. From South America, Brazil, they say."

"You're so lucky, Gran. You've got all these lovely memories. I hope I'm as lucky as you were in your marriage. Granddad was a lovely man, wasn't he?"

"Yes, lass, he was a grand man."

Aye, Harry had been a grand man, all right. He had been until she found about his lady friend, but who was she to talk? She had been no angel.

Still, it wouldn't do to disillusion her granddaughter.

CHAPTER SEVEN

Rita searched the bureau and the sideboard drawer, both places where important papers were kept. At the back of the sideboard drawer she found a letter from the lawyer filled with the legal pomposity she had expected. However, it did give her mother's address: 27 Oldham Road, Pemberton. She stuffed it back, not worrying whether her Dad knew she had seen it. Tomorrow evening, she would go to see her mother.

All day long, as she entered figures in her ledger, she thought about the evening. What would her mother say when she turned up unexpectedly? They had never been exactly close. Still, Rita thought it important to discover why her Mam had left, and why she and her Gran were at the outs.

Why this niggled at her she did not know, but every time she asked Gran, Gran refused to talk about it. She then asked her Dad, who would not, or could not, say. No, her mother knew the answer and Rita saw no reason now for her not to tell her the truth of it. The mystery of it niggled at her like an itch that must be scratched.

She paused in her work and thought about last Sunday when Gran told her the story of the statue of Our Lady of Fatima. Gran was not a Catholic and the presence of this small statuette puzzled Rita.

"That belonged to your mother, not me, Rita," she said, "I don't know why I kept it."

"It's a Catholic statue, isn't it? We have none like this at our church, no statues at all, come to think about it."

"Well, this was something and nothing. She had a pal who was a

Catholic, and your mother was a teenager at the time, so I suppose the ceremonies and pageantry attracted her." She chuckled. "Mind you, she knew two or three lads who belonged to the church who she'd got her eye on, and Catholic lads never took out non-Catholics, like it was a sin or something."

It sounded most peculiar to Rita. School, nuns or parents had not taught about Catholic sins, real or imagined. "Yet why would she want to change to a Catholic?"

"Beats me, love, but she enjoyed anything that annoyed me and her Dad. Anyroad, she started taking lessons from the priest. She'd come home with her Catechism and chanted it for hours, determined to learn it as quickly as she could."

"What's that? Catechism, I mean?"

"I think it's the rules and regulations for being a Catholic. I didn't listen to it, but she did it because it got on our nerves."

"Why didn't she keep it up, then? Didn't they accept her?"

"Oh yes, she managed to learn the stuff and they baptized her all right, though her religious antics lasted only a month or two." Marian paused and glanced at Rita "She was too lazy to get up Sunday mornings to go to church." Marian laughed at the thought. "She used to tell me to wake her, then give me heck when I tried to shake her out of bed."

"Am I a Catholic, too? I mean, if she were one, does it make me one?" Rita asked.

The Goodwin family was not religious, although when she was small they had gone to Christmas carol services, and, like the rest of the street, Easter Sunday service to show off their new clothes.

"No, love, you are not, and neither is she."

Still, that was another bit of a mystery about her mother. Strange, she never saw her as a person, only as a cruel mother.

Today by four o'clock, try as she may, she could not concentrate on her work. *Should* she go? Would her mother even see her? What if she were living with a man? No, she decided, she would go, she *had* to see her.

27 Oldham Road was a long terrace of illmaintained houses, home to cotton mill workers. Ragged kids played shrilly on the street and

mothers sat watching on wooden kitchen chairs at their doors as they chatted with neighbours. Most were doing hand work, darning, sewing or knitting. She walked past an old lady who sat snoozing in the late sunshine, lips flapping because she had no teeth.

Since the houses were identical to those of Trawton Village and most Lancashire industrial towns, at a glance she knew they had two rooms up and two down. Not much room for a house full of kids though she saw many children playing outside on the cobblestones. It was a poor area, practically slummy.

As she reached number 27, she looked it over, noticing it seemed no better and no worse than the rest. Peeling and crackled paint covered a front door that opened directly onto the street and someone had stuffed a broken window pane with an old rag. All of that Rita could lay at the landlord's feet for nobody she knew owned such a run-down terraced house.

As she knocked at the door, a group of scuffling children stood staring at her curiously. A stranger was something that made their day brighter, gave them something to discuss. They giggled and jiggled each other, eyes wide.

Then a woman opened the door. In her arms she held a toddler, her dirty pinny suddenly pushed aside as a snotty-nosed four-year-old peeped out.

"I'm looking for Mrs. Sheila Goodwin," Rita said.

"Oh her," The woman said sniffing and wiping her nose on the back of her hand. "Upstairs back." She gestured with her head to the stairs rising behind her.

Rita entered and the children scattered; nothing more to see. The hall smelled of old grease, bad food and cat urine, forcing her to breathe through her mouth. The splintered stairs were bare of carpet or lino and her footsteps sounded loud. As she started up the stairs, the woman stood at the bottom, looking at her though the smoke from the cigarette dangling from her lip. The young boy crawled up the stairs on his knees at her heels.

Rita knocked on the closed warped door. How could her mother live here? she wondered. It was cold and dirty, and the neighbourhood slovenly. She shivered.

Sheila woke as the sound of Rita's knock broke through her dream.

"Just a minute, just a minute," she said, pushing herself off the cot. She could no longer work as her bulk was too unwieldy.

Opening the door to see Rita, her astonishment was evident.

"What the hell?" she said, her hand at her mouth. "What are you doing here? How did you find me?"

As she turned away, Rita saw her mother's shape. Her mother was expecting a baby? How could her father have done it? How could he have let her leave in this condition? Now he was planning to marry Molly. He didn't care about her mother. Feelings and thoughts reeled around her mind and she felt suddenly nauseated.

"Mam," she said eyes wide with horror, stunned at the sight.

"Oh, what do you want, Rita?" Sheila asked wearily, turning away and moving to the wobbly chair under the window. She glanced down at her attire. An old dress, ragged beneath the arms, an ancient cardigan, her old slippers with the trodden down heels. What a way to greet a guest, how embarrassing to found looking so unkempt, unwashed. She sighed and lifted her head as Rita moved closer.

Rita looked over her shoulder and closed the door because the boy was sitting on the top step of the stairs listening. She was sure his ear would be against the door when it shut.

"Mam, what are you doing here, living like this?" she asked, shocked. The poverty of the place, the smell and the dirt made her stomach roil. Her mother's room, small and cramped, held a messy single bed, a chest of drawers, a small table and a wooden chair. Its tiny fireplace held a smoldering slack fire.

"I much prefer it to what I had," Sheila said sullenly.

"Are you expecting a baby?" Rita asked although it was obvious even to her.

"No, I've got a soccer ball in my pinny pocket. What do you think?" Sheila snapped as she sniffed and rubbed her nose with her fingers.

"Mam," she gestured to her mother's stomach, "Is it going to be my brother or sister?" She did not know how to ask if it were her father's child.

Sheila nodded. "Any child I would have is related to you. I'm your mother, Rita."

Rita's face grew miserable. "That's not what I meant."

Sheila barked a laugh, knowing exactly what Rita meant. "You mean is this your father's child?" Rita nodded. Sheila's face closed up and her tone was acid. "No, I'm glad to say, it isn't."

Rita felt a pang of horror. "Whose is it then?"

"Nobody you know." She pushed at her ratty matted hair, ashamed of how she looked. "You came here to give me the third degree, did you? Did *he* send you?"

"No. I wanted to see you. I'm sorry I came now." She looked at the grungy room and its rickety furniture.

"Serves you right. You were always a nosy little sod." Sheila lit a cigarette and blew out a cloud of blue smoke.

No. This woman was not her mother. She was a stranger, a stranger bearing another man's child. Rita gazed at her, disgust churning her stomach. Sheila's hair looked filthy with grease and dust, and her ragged clothes were stained. When she lived at home, her mother always wore flashy things, things full of colour and style, was always well turned out, had always set her hair in the latest styles.

Rita put back her shoulders. Come what may, she thought, I am going to ask, that's the whole reason for this visit. Above all, I have to know what's gone wrong in the family.

"Before I go, I want to know something. It's important you tell me."

"What is it?" Sheila regarded her with suspicion.

"I want to know why you and my Gran never speak to each other. What did you argue about?"

"That's none of your business," Sheila said, suddenly standing and opening the door, gesturing her out. The child crawled to the top of the stairs.

"I *have* to know, Mam, I *have* to. Please?"

"That's something between your grandmother and myself. It doesn't concern you and will *never* concern you. Ask her if you want. She won't tell you, either."

Rita felt exasperated. She had come all this way for nothing, had found her mother pregnant with another man's child, still refusing to answer her question.

"No, she won't," she said now, "and neither will my Dad, but I want to know. I need_to know."

Sheila's face became grim. "You need to know nothing, my girl. Leave here now and don't come back. You hear me? Don't ever come back to this house because I'll leave tomorrow. Your dad got his papers, I presume, and I suppose he'll be marrying again. You go back there and look after him and his new wife." She pushed the door to close it, pushing Rita with her other hand. "Go on, get out of it."

"Please, Mam," Rita said putting out her hand. Tears streamed down her face. How could she walk away and leave her mother in this horrible place? What decent person would like to see their mother reduced to such penury?

"Go on, leave now," Sheila said, her voice harsh and unfeeling. "Forget about me, I'm not worth it . . . not worth a second of worry. Go on, I tell you."

She looked at Rita as if she were vermin, someone she didn't like and Rita felt part of her heart die. Her own mother, turning her away, pushing her aside. How could she? How could she go home to tell her father about this situation? Heaving a sigh of utter distress, she turned to the stairs.

The boy scurried down as Rita came onto the landing. She turned back, looked her mother in the eye, desperately wanting to ask again, wanting to make things right between them, but Sheila shut the door in her face.

Hot tears pooled in her eyes. What a waste of time. Why had she bothered? She felt as upset as she had ever been, her mother living here, in this run down house and pregnant with another man's child. Was the pregnancy the reason her mother left home, or had happened after she left? Rita couldn't ask her Dad, but she would ask her Gran.

All the way home, Rita worried at the problem. Not only had her mother not answered her question, but now she had other worries. She didn't love her mother, yet thoroughly abhorred seeing the conditions in which she lived. Because it weighed so heavily on her, she found she couldn't mention it to her Dad, hadn't the words to tell him without breaking down.

Arthur wondered why Rita was quiet that evening and put it down to women's business. Yet for days Rita moped around the house, hardly speaking and Arthur began to wonder if she were coming down with something.

"Are you feeling all right, lass?" he asked, his face worried.

Rita nodded, her expression sullen. "Oh, I'm all right, Dad."

"Well, you don't look all right and you don't sound all right. All that sobbing and sighing. Why don't you go round to see your Gran? She'll snap you out of it, whatever it is," Arthur dreaded Rita asking him anything personal, like women's troubles.

"I don't feel like it, Dad," she said sighing again. Every few minutes she sighed heavily, as though she couldn't get enough air in her lungs. Something was troubling her, Arthur knew. Could it be the wedding or Molly? Maybe she felt threatened by Molly.

Molly had come over twice this month to cook their supper and she was a grand cook. Even Rita ate more than usual, and that was saying something.

"Is it about Molly?" he asked now, "You can tell me, you know. It'll be between the two of us."

She gave a half smile. "No Dad, Molly's all right. She makes a good roly-poly pudding."

Arthur laughed. "So that makes her all right with you, does it?"

She grinned. "I suppose so. I won't have to call her Mam, will I?"

So that was it, Arthur thought, grinning. "Of course not, Rita. You can call her Molly. You talk it over with her, lass, she's easy to get along with. No, you won't have to call her Mam, she's not your mother. She'll never be your mother, only my wife."

It would ease her mind, he thought, knowing once she got comfortable with Molly she'd be closer to her than she'd ever been to Sheila.

"Oh, that's all right then," Rita said, making an effort to sound cheerful. Her Dad looked so worried that now that she could never tell him the real problem.

Arthur smiled back and lit his pipe. His daughter was a lovely child, nothing much seemed to bother her, although his upcoming marriage seemed to cause her a great deal of concern. Still, if it were only about how she would address Molly, he had nothing much to worry about. He would, however, talk over his concerns with Marian who would surely get to the bottom of things.

Marian was baking when he called in later that evening. Another fruit cake layer, part of their wedding cake.

"Oh, you've come to have a taste test before I ice it, I suppose?" she asked, glad to see him.

"I wouldn't mind, Marian," he said, as he licked batter off his finger."Can I lick the bowl?"

"Get away with you, you silly ha'porth." She laughed. "I'm going to save it for myself, maybe leave some for Rita."

"That's going to be a beautiful cake, rich and full of fruit," Arthur said, smacking his lips. Marian was a fantastic cook, and her cakes were marvellous creations. The wedding cake was her wedding present to them.

"I've come to ask you to talk to Rita. She's got something bothering her," he said, deciding to come right out with it. Marian liked plain talk, no hedging.

Marian nodded. "Aye. I know and I think it's about what happened between me and Sheila. I've told her repeatedly that I'll not tell her. She did say once she was going to ask her Mam, but I reckon if she ever saw her, she would say nowt. I know you wouldn't say owt, seeing as you don't know much."

Arthur nodded as he sat by the fire and poked it to make a blaze. "Not me, I swore on the Bible, didn't I, and as you say, I don't know the entire truth of it. All I know was you'd been fighting about something and you both said words that changed your relationship."

Marian nodded. Arthur, not a nosy person, had stayed out of their quarrel completely. "We both swore an oath. Well, if the child is on that tack again, I'll sort her out. You leave her to me, Arthur. I'll talk to her when she gets home tomorrow. I'll wait until she gets home, so you stay at the pub for an hour after work."

"Thanks, Marian. You take it easy, now. You're getting a bit long in the tooth for all this dashing and around and worry."

"Now, now, less of the old, young man," Marian said although she could not help but chuckle. "It's being busy that keeps me going. Don't you stop me dashing around. It's a long time to lie in a coffin, so they say."

"True enough. Let me know how it goes with the lass. I'm treading on eggs at home right now."

"Leave it with me, Arthur, she's good girl."

Arthur smiled, relieved Marian was willing to help. "Aye, she is. Thanks for the cuppa. See you tomorrow night if you're still at the house."

Rita arrived back in Trawton early Wednesday as it was half day closing. This meant most of the shops were shut, and that, in turn, made the buses less crowded. The other days she to queue for the bus, then stand most of the hour journey.

"Hello, Gran," she said as she took off her mac. "You're late away today."

The kitchen smelled of cooking, something savoury and tasty, and her mouth watered. The fire blazed nicely. Gran liked to bake pies in the fireplace oven instead of the gas stove, convinced it made the pastry flakier.

"Is that the time?" Marian said, looking at the clock as if unaware of the time. "My word, I'll be late for my own funeral if I keep on this way, Rita. Well, I was late getting here and I was late getting up this morning, so I expect I'll be late for bed tonight as well. Come on, I've put the kettle on and we'll have a cuppa and a natter."

Rita chatted normally, but Marian saw something bothered her, like Arthur said.

"What is it, Rita? I know some'at is up. What is it?"

"Nothing," Rita said, her face sulky.

"I don't believe that, any more than you do. You tell me what's going on and I'll help you with it."

"Well . . .,"

Marian waited. Rita would get to it in her own time. Prompting would not help.

"Well . . . well . . .," Rita couldn't say it and burst into tears.

"Now, now, lass, surely it can't be that bad. Come on, spit it out." Marian cuddled her and kissed her hair. "Come on, you can tell me. I don't like to see you upset like this, love."

Rita dried her eyes on the tea towel, blew her nose on Gran's handkerchief and took a mouthful of tea before she could speak.

"It's about her. My Mam," she said and started to sob, how terrible she felt saying it aloud.

Marian rose, took the pie out of the oven and placed it on the stove top to cool. This action gave Rita time to sort out her words.

"Yes?" she said as she sat again.

"She's, she's, she's having a baby, Gran," Rita hiccuped. "It's going to be my relative, she says. Is it. . . is it my Dad's baby? She said it wasn't and you know what that means."

Marian, shocked Rita had discovered her mother's infidelity, tried to conceal it. "I can't say that I know that for sure, Rita," she said slowly trying to find the words, "I do know your Dad, though, and if it was his baby she'd still be at home. I hate to say this, lass, but I think your mother was playing away. She told you the truth there."

Rita nodded miserably, still hiccuping sobs. "Yes. I think I always knew, Gran. I never told anybody, not even my Dad. She was buying fancy underwear and I know she was seeing a man because she said she was going to the ladies' auxiliary every week, but she wasn't, no, she wasn't. I know because one of the women asked me why she never went any more."

Marian shook her head sadly. Trust Sheila to be playing around right on her own doorstep, fouling her own nest. She must have had a chap with a car because nobody ever saw them that she knew of, and in Trawton everyone knew everybody else's business. Still, Marian knew the village regarded Sheila as a tart because of her makeup and her manner of dressing. She once or twice flaunted her affairs in front of them and the villagers regarded her as a loose woman. Yet the poor child, what a shame to have to face this knowledge about her mother.

"Now, now, don't take on, Rita, love. It's not worth it. Only you and I know, and I'll tell your Dad, though I suspect he already knows."

Rita blew her nose and took a sip of tea. She felt better telling her Gran about her troubles.

"It's awful though, Gran, isn't it? She's a disgrace to us, and think what'll happen if anyone around here finds out. It was bad enough when she left, what with people prying and nosing about why she had gone. It was like they thought Dad had done her in or something. At least I didn't know why she'd gone then, so I didn't tell any lies. Now I'll have to lie. I can't tell the truth, can I?"

"Yes, you can . . . if you want to," Marian said, her lips compressing at the thought. She knew lying about family troubles never helped, and the truth usually discovered in the end. "Say it the way it is, if that's what you want. I certainly will, if anyone asks, and she's my daughter. Think how I feel."

Rita gasped and looked at her grandmother. "Oh Gran, how despicable I am." She put her hand on Marian's, patting it. "Talking about her like that and thinking only of how it affects me. Poor Gran, you must feel terrible."

Marian smiled. "Come on now, lass. I stopped feeling anything about my Sheila many years ago."

Rita thought about it for a second. How could you ever forget a child, not feel for the child? But hadn't her own mother done just that to her? "Don't you think about her at all now?"

"Rarely, Rita, love. She destroyed my love for her years ago."

"Why? What did she do?" Rita felt her heart leap with hope, maybe Gran would tell her everything, about the fight and the reason for their animosity.

"Nothing I can tell you, love," Marian said rising and picking up her coat. "Nothing of any interest, other than to me and your mother."

Rita blew out an annoyed breath. Gran had refused to tell her yet again.

Marian paused and looked around. "I've cooked the pie and it'll be warm for a long time yet. I've mashed the potatoes. They only need the low gas kept on under the steamer to keep them warm. Don't forget to top up the steamer. All you have to do is make some gravy and dish up."

"Please, Gran, please don't leave yet," Rita saw her chance to ask slipping away. "Stay and have supper with us again. I want to ask you something."

"Go on, then, but I can't stay tonight. Hurry up. I've got a friend coming for tea."

"What did you and my Mam fight about back then?" she asked and Marian immediately started shaking her head. Rita groaned. "Why won't you tell me? I know all about her now. You can tell me everything."

Marian's face looked grim as she tucked in her scarf. "I've told you everything you'll ever need to know. Leave it be, Rita. I won't tell you, and she won't tell you, and your Dad won't tell you. It matters to nobody but me and your mother, as I said. Keep your nose out of other people's business, lass," she said brusquely as she went to the door. "Watch the supper now," she warned and left.

Rita sat at the table picking at a loose tablecloth thread thinking she was never going to find out. Still, what did it matter anyway? Deeply she sighed, pushing her hair off her forehead. When was she going to give up on it? Never, she decided, she had to know and it wasn't a matter of being nosy, either. Obviously it was going to take a long time before they thought her adult enough to understand.

"Hello, lass," Arthur said as he came in a few minutes later. "What've you been up to today?"

"You been at the pub?" she asked seeing his grin.

"Yes. Something wrong with that?"

She shrugged and grinned. "Nothing, Dad. Supper's almost ready. Gran made it, but I'm making the gravy. Meat and potato pie and sprouts with mashed, it is."

The next evening she went over to Gran's because Molly was making supper at the house. Let her Dad have a private meal with his Molly for once she decided. Anyway, she didn't like sitting with them because their cow eyes and touching made her feel uncomfortable.

Marian sat knitting a fairisle cardigan, which made talk difficult since she had to count stitches and change wools. Companionably they sat by the fire and exchanged odd comments. The kitchen felt warm and Rita noticed Gran had finished the clippy rug and it now sat on the hearth, its colour bright and strong.

"Nice," she said, pointing with her toe.

"Aye, lot of good fabric in that one," Marian said and started counting stitches. "Brew up, lass, I'm parched."

Later as they sat sipping tea, she spoke. "Gran, I'm sorry about wittering on like that last night." After thinking about it all day, she came to realize blatant asking wasn't going to solve the mystery. She would get the information in a different way. How, she didn't know, but she would come up with something. "I won't ask you about it again. I'm sorry."

Marian smiled, she could never be mad at Rita for long. "It's all right, love, don't let it fash you. Least said, soonest forgotten."

Rita sighed happily and rested her head on the spindle-backed settee. Gran was always so understanding, even with something as bad as this, she could forgive. Look at all the heartbreak she had caused, how in her stupidity she'd made her Gran remember bad things. It stood to reason if her mother had done something to cause the rift, it must be something terrible. If it were not, somebody would have told her about it years ago. She had once asked Ruth Beavis who also said she knew nothing. Oh, what could it be?

How she wished she were grown up and less confused. At least adult enough to understand the feelings that bothered her, to understand why people did what they did. Her Dad said it was part of growing up, but she already felt grown up and looked it. Still, she supposed any parent always treated their offspring as a child.

That night she slept better than she had in a long time. What did it matter about her mother's fight with Gran? It didn't affect her own life one little bit and it was making her Gran angry, her constant wheedling about it. No, better forget it completely: better stop being so damned nosy.

Sheila's labour began during the night and she struggled to the hospital alone. She lodged now with a miner and his wife, but unfortunately the man was on the night shift and his wife, a hysterical type, did little other than utter little squeals of panic as she stood around dithering. Walking all that way was difficult for Sheila, but a patrolling police officer helped her. At three the following afternoon she gave birth to a son.

Poor little thing, she thought, gazing at him as he lay on her stomach. Poor little soul, born without a father. His father is long gone, sod him, he ran like a rabbit when I told him I was pregnant.

"What's the little love's name?" the nurse asked.

Up to then she had not bothered to think, hoping beyond hope the child would be born dead. She sighed and looked up at the nurse, better to say something. Sheila, never very maternal, regarded the new baby as a millstone.

"We decided to name him Reginald. Reg when he's older and Reggie while he's little."

As she lay on the ward listening to the happy chatter of the other new mothers, she began to worry. Once she paid this month's rent, she would be penniless. Her nest egg had not lasted long. Who would have known the cost of living would have risen so quickly? Now she had another mouth to feed, a completely dependent baby to consider.

Well, she told herself, she must get her strength back quickly, must find herself a job. Even as she sat in bed, she flexed her muscles, did sit ups. When she went home, she exercised even more and, through constant exercise, within the month almost regained her figure. Those years of diet and exercise had paid off, she thought as she eyed her reflection in the door of the bakery. Already she was fit, although work seemed hard to find.

Over Sunday tea at Marian's they talked about the approaching wedding, at which Rita would be the bridesmaid. Not that it was going to be what Rita thought of as a real wedding because it would be a civil ceremony at the Town Hall in Wigan.

Her earlier dread about her father walking down the aisle with a white clad Molly in a misty veil evaporated and she felt much better. Now people who knew them would not point fingers and talk about sheep dressed as lamb when looking at her father's new wife. To Rita, Molly was an old lady who shouldn't wear a wedding dress, anyway she had been married before. Rita had no idea from where she got her ideas, only knew what she thought correct from books she read, although Trawton's library was hardly progressive, many of its volumes being Victorian or older.

Much to Rita's relief, Molly's wedding outfit was a pale blue wool suit with a fancy hat. Over tea she described in it detail to Gran who oohed and aahed. Rita could hardly wait to wear the new frock her Gran bought her at the market. It was of pink seersucker with a circular skirt and Gran bought her a crinoline to wear under it so it stood out nicely. She felt like a princess when she tried them on, admiring herself in the wardrobe mirror. Her first grown up dress. Not a bad shape, she thought, as she revolved, a neat waist, a perky bust line. Well, even if she wasn't twenty-one, she looked adult at long last.

Now she and Molly were on better terms, she liked her very much. They talked about her Dad and she realized Molly loved him, and as for her Dad, he was jolly when around Molly. Rita liked him then, liked the way he laughed easily, the way Molly and he said silly things to each other. Yes, her Dad could do worse, and Gran was right, he did need a wife.

"We'll move to my cottage, of course," Molly said, "after the honeymoon, and once we get things sorted out at Arthur's."

Rita heard the words. They hit her like a hammer, the bottom dropped out of her stomach and she felt sick. Move from Trawton?

Leave the house she where she had been born, leave her friends, leave the familiar surroundings, leave her Gran? A cold shiver ran down her spine.

"No!" she said, standing and glaring at them. "I'm not moving. You can't make me. I'll stay here."

Arthur's face became grave. He had not expected any argument in that quarter.

He spoke quickly. "Look Rita, lass, Molly owns a lovely cottage. You'll love it. Wait until you see it. It has a garden and an orchard and it's near a large wood."

"I don't care. I shan't go." Her face clammed up and she stared at her Gran, waiting for her to say something. Gran always sided with her, but Marian said nothing.

Molly touched her hand gently. "Look now, Rita, why don't you come with your Dad and see the place? You'll have your own room overlooking the lily pond and the dovecote. Aye, I've got some lovely fantail birds. I have a red setter and a snobby cat who runs him ragged. There's . . .,"

"I don't care what you have," Rita said, her tone sulky, a whine, "I'll live here. This is my house and I'll not leave it. You can't make me." She glared at them with open hostility.

Molly made to put out her hand but Arthur put out his hand and took hers. "Leave it, Molly. Rita and I will have a talk this week." His look told her to drop the subject. Rita thought he probably figured if she thought about it, and then saw the cottage, she would change her mind. "We'll come for our tea Wednesday evening as arranged. How's that?"

However, the tea party lost its sparkle with Rita sullen and uncommunicative.

When her Dad and Molly left, she and her Gran cleared the table and washed the dishes. They chatted as if nothing had happened and Marian wondered what Rita was thinking. She could understand why Rita didn't want to move, knowing she felt pushed aside by Molly in her father's affections. At last she seemed to have accepted the relationship, and appeared excited about the town wedding and the wedding breakfast at a posh restaurant.

"You make the tea, Gran, and I'll choose something," Rita said as she hung the tea towel on the mantel wire to dry.

Well, Marian decided, I must find a way of putting a moral into whatever trinket Rita brings back.

Rita opened the cabinet door, knelt and looked on each shelf. So many things, so much she wanted to know. The egg cups. There they were, two china egg cups in the shape of hens. One was white and one was brown, and both had cheeky smiling faces, their wings outspread with little dents for the salt. Well made and well painted, turning one over she saw the hallmark, 'Royal Doulton.'

"Here we go, Gran, the egg cups," Rita said as she placed one in her Gran's hand. She sat and looked at the other she still held.

"Good choice, Rita, good choice, because these tell an interesting tale."

1918

Marian raced down the hill, her legs almost going out from under her: aware if she didn't get home before dark the neighbours would suspect she had been up to something.

This Friday afternoon, as usual, she'd spent the afternoon with Jimmy. Jimmy, a farm worker, was one of the few young men remaining in the area. His perforated ear drum and an old farm injury kept him out of the forces. Jimmy limped badly, but she could accept that as it did not affect his love making one bit. He was well built from all the physical activity his job brought with it, tall and broad, his muscles rippled beneath his shirt, which was what first attracted her to him.

They had been meeting now for two months now, two months of passion, she thought, her cheeks warm with the thought. Two months of happiness in her drab life. Presently she worked at the farm dairy while Harry was away fighting the war in the catering corps - not that she knew what Harry was doing. She could not picture him fighting.

Then after reading the newspaper reports of the war, she sometimes pictured him stabbing the enemy with his bayonet, or lurking in muddy trenches. Catering was to do with food, she knew that, but Harry, useless in the kitchen, could hardly boil water, so maybe he peeled potatoes or washed dishes.

Maybe, she often thought, he won't come back. She wouldn't want him back anyway if he got injured. That would involve too much more work from her and nothing from him.

As far as I'm concerned he shouldn't have gone off and left me this way. Selfish sod, he is, over there in France or wherever and I'm stuck here bored to tears. Serves him right that I'm having an affair with Jimmy. I don't love Jimmy, but he makes me feel desirable and wanted.

Friday was her day off, and every Friday Jimmy finished his chores quickly so they could meet in the woods. Deep in a glade stood a woodsman's hut that he had fixed up with blankets and cushions. On the small fire, which he always lit to dispel the damp, they would make tea in a billy can and drink from enamelled mugs. They enjoyed lovely afternoons.

It was a time when they forgot the war, when she forgot she was married, when talk of death and destruction was the farthest thing from their minds. The war was a constant topic of conversation everywhere these days, eagerly read about in newspapers and seen on movie screens, although it did not seem real to those who lived in such a small self-sustaining village. While imported goods were scarce, they could always manage.

Now it would be another week before she would see him again. When they occasionally met in the farm yard, one never acknowledged the other. She was kidding herself, though, because everybody knew what they were doing. Nevertheless, each week she would tell herself it had to stop. Obviously she could see no future in it, and a whole lot of unhappiness if it ever became public knowledge, yet when they were together the physical attraction she experienced transcended all her doubts.

Marian was right to be worried because the farming fraternity was a close-knit community, living in each other's pockets, gossiping about everything. It was far worse at Hillside Farm for gossip than it was in the close streets of Trawton and each time the lovers passed each other in the yard someone saw and sniggered. Whom did they think they were fooling?

"She'll get hers, will Marian Haydon," they said, "Lying with another man while her husband is away fighting for king and country." The women chattered and prattled at meal times, talking about what they had seen, or what they had imagined. The men also talked as they worked, most of them jealous of Jimmy because Marian was a trim lass, with a fresh face and jolly with it, not like their miserable wives who thought nothing of nagging from dawn to dusk.

"You two've been going at it now for how long?" Archie asked Jimmy, who often bragged about his conquest. They were cleaning out the stables and moving in bales of fresh hay.

"Almost three months now."

"She's a comely lass, she is an'all. I wouldn't mind having a crack at her when you've finished." Archie rested on his rake and imagined lying with her, his lips almost smacking over his toothless mouth.

"So why don't you ask her?" Jimmy said, being a man who would share his last mouthful. "She's willing enough and I've got no claim on her, you know. She's already wed."

Archie laughed. "Aye, I know." He nudged Jimmy and winked. "It's only that I wouldn't want you to have to go wi'out, lad."

Jimmy lifted a fork loaded with dirty wet hay and tossed it into the cart. "Nah, it's all right, Archie. You ask her. I've had enough of it sometimes. It's like I *have* to do it now."

Archie chortled as he pushed a pile of hay nearer the cart. "Aye, like marriage, that is. You know what they say, the bull doesn't only service one cow. He's got his choice of an entire herd any time he likes."

Jimmy nodded, heaved a bale of fresh hay into a manger and started breaking it down. "True enough, Arch, true enough. Maybe I'll look further afield."

Because of this conversation Jimmy decided to break off the relationship. It was not going to be easy, he knew, and decided to give her something to make the blow lighter. In his room were two egg cups that had belonged to his mother and he would give them to Marian to soften the blow. His Mam treasured the stupid things as the lady she was maid to in Pemberton gave them to her as a wedding present. He had no use for them. Dust catchers, they were. Might as well give them to Marian.

"Ooh, they're lovely, just lovely, Jimmy," Marian exclaimed as she examined them. "Did you buy them?" If he had, he must have spent his savings, she thought. They were china and hand painted, so fine and delicate, yet strong as iron.

"Nah, I've had 'um for years. Mi Mam had 'um when she was wed."

"Oh, then I can't take them," she said quickly, offering them back. "They should go to your wife when you marry."

"I shall'na wed for many years yet. I don't like what's on offer right now. You take 'um, I *want* you to have them."

"Thank you." She couldn't get over the gift. They were the prettiest things she had ever seen, and to think he wanted to give them to her. He must love her very much. She carefully placed them on the blanket and threw herself at him. Her arms tightened around his body and she squeezed. "I do thank you, Jimmy. It's the best present I've ever had."

"Aye, well," he said, uncomfortable about what he was about to say. Anyway, right now with his face over her shoulder, he didn't have to look her in the eye. "We can't go on meeting like this, Marian, lass," he said as he kissed her neck. "We've been talked about and you know what gossips they are around here. Anyroad, the war is over and your husband will soon be back. We can't keep it up then."

"Oh, Jimmy," Marian said, pushing him away. She had read the war was finished, but never equated it with Harry's return.

Harry Haydon, drat his hide. In all this time she hadn't had as much as had a postcard from him. Others in the same Lancashire regiment sent letters to their wives and mothers and it was from these women she heard where the regiment was fighting. That hurt, for surely he could have had one of his mates write a letter for him. The man was selfish, plain and simple selfish. It did not occur to her Harry was too proud to ask someone to write his letter, was ashamed of being illiterate.

"What shall I do without our lovely afternoons?" she said through a sudden blurring of tears.

"Now, now," Jimmy felt uncomfortable. He didn't know what to do with a crying female. "Your husband will be back. That's what you'll do. Anyhow, if you're looking for a spot of the other, my mate Archie said he wouldn't mind meeting you here once a week."

Marian gasped. What was he suggesting?

He grinned, pleased to have good news for her. "Aye, all the farm hands would kill to lie with you for an hour, tha knows. They've been right jealous of me." He put back his shoulders, under the impression he had paid her a compliment.

Marian struggled to her feet. "You've been talking about our meetings with your mates?" she shouted. "What do you think I am? I'm not a loose woman you can hand around. Oh, how could you even suggest such a thing?" The thought horrified her.

"Come on, lass, it's common knowledge you're married, tha knows, and common talk you bed here with me once a week. Don't start playing the injured virgin now. It won't wash."

"Jimmy Cartwright, you are the most obnoxious person I've ever known. How dare you pass me around to your mates! To horrible Archie, him with no teeth that slavers all the time. How dare you talk about me as if I were a whore! How dare you, you bastard!"

She made her way to the door, kicking the blankets away from her feet. "I'll not be back at the farm again. I couldn't show my face there now so you'd better tell them. I'll never come near this place, either. You're a rotten bastard, Jimmy, a right blackguard! I'll never forgive you, never."

As she ran through the wood and along the path through the fields, she kept her hands in her pockets, cradling the egg cups, one in each hand. At least she had something of value out of the relationship, but oh how it hurt. How it hurt they thought of her as a whore, that they were all talking about her all this time.

God! Her blood ran cold at the thought the gossip might have reached the village. When Harry got home, they would delight in letting him know his wife was a loose woman.

For days she sulked, for days she never left the house, ashamed to show her face. Then she had to go out for groceries and that was the day Harry arrived home.

"How lovely they are, and were you happy in Manchester, Gran? It's such a big city and so different from Trawton."

"Well, at first I was like you. I didn't want to go, but there you are, my Dad got this chance at a good job and had to take it. Aye, leaving my friends was hard. At first, I thought my Mam and Dad were rotten, taking me away from everything I loved. It was a selfish way to be, wasn't it? My Dad needed that job and my Mam was chuffed to bits with the chance of moving away from this place, and there was me with a face as long as a wet Wakes Week. Eeh, I must have been a rotten kid. Why my Dad bought me them egg cups, I don't know, but the first pay he got he took me to the finest shop in the city and I got to choose whatever I wanted. I chose them."

Rita looked at the egg cups knowing Gran was trying to make a point. Was *she* now walking around with a face like a wet Wakes Week? Her Dad needed this marriage, he deserved some comfort with a lovely person like Molly.

"Did you like it there in Manchester?" she asked quietly.

She lied. "It was wonderful, Rita. In a big city there's so much to see and do and I soon found new friends. Children should obey their parents, adults always know best, you know. They would never bring any harm to a youngster of theirs, but you know that."

She stared at her Gran, a smile lurking around the corners of her mouth. "I think you're trying to tell me to go with Dad to Molly's cottage. Aren't you?"

Marian laughed, had she been that transparent? "I expect so. I was telling about them," she nodded at the egg cups Rita held. "It's simply a coincidence the story was about me having to move away."

She crossed her fingers in her pinny pocket. Surely God would forgive her for lying again.

"Oh, yes?" Rita said doubtfully. She thought Marian had always lived in Trawton and had invented this story.

"You chose the cups, not me. I can't help it the way things turn out, can I?"

"No, but . . .,"

"No more 'buts.' You put them back and get ready to be off home. Your Dad'll get worried if you're late."

"Oh Gran, it's only a few steps. Anyway, I'd better give the love birds a chance to have a cuddle. You know, Gran, I must admit it makes me feel funny inside when I see my Dad kissing her."

"Serves you right, child," Marian said laughing and pushing at her. "You shouldn't be looking. Would you want me watching you kiss your boy friend?"

"Aaw, Gran, I don't have a boy friend," Rita said, blushing.

"No, maybe not today, but soon you'll have roses in your cheeks and a twinkle in your eye, and I'll know you've met Prince Charming."

Rita chuckled. "Now, Gran, I've not found any frogs to kiss, not on this street." From time to time she'd gone out with a few of the village boys, but she found them all uninteresting. Those fellows she met while at work seemed too urbane to suit her rural outlook and she rarely dated them. They had aspirations, lofty ambitions and she felt inferior when they talked.

"Well, it could be you'll find one on the bus to work one day. You never know."

When Rita left, Marian thought about her story tonight. What a load of old cobblers. Honestly, who do I think I'm kidding? Still and all, if it solves the rift between the lass and her father, all well and good.

Wouldn't it surprise her to know the truth about the egg cups, the butterfly, and the fan? Aye, I was a gay girl in my day and yet I can look back on those terrible days with a touch of pride because I was attractive and loved. How many in Trawton can say the same?

The wedding was over in five minutes and now they stood in a dusty, cluttered office while a man muttered a few words, witnessed the paper they had signed.

What a swiz, Rita thought, feeling cheated. She had not expected flowers or an organ playing, but the depressing office and the crumpled, gaunt whiskered man was a major disappointment.

Her Dad and Molly looked happy, their faces beaming. Gran kissed them both, gave them good wishes for happiness and threw rice at them on the steps. Rita hung back, ill at ease with her father now. Molly hugged her and kissed her hair, but Rita drew back from her, uncomfortable again. Oh, why couldn't she be happy for them?

Much to her surprise, she found Molly's cottage cozy. Situated on a country lane and built of rosy stone, it had a lovely room that would be hers, a room with a French window so she could step directly into the garden. About ten feet away from the window was the lily pond and to one side stood a rustic dovecote where ten white birds cooed and purled. They were so calming, their sound restful.

Well within reach were the woods - beech woods with deep dells between the trees. In spring the woods were hazy with bluebells, Molly told her, and a cuckoo returned each year, announcing his arrival in early April. The local lads played wild games in the woods, swinging from ropes strung from tall branches.

It was the first time Rita had been in a house with no upstairs and she thought it strange yet very snug: strange not to go up to bed, though. Molly's large warm kitchen had an Aga stove and a larder as big as their scullery back home. A long living room with many windows held plushy overstuffed chairs and a couch, and an upright piano at the end opposite the fireplace. Molly had carpets in every room except in the kitchen where the floor shone with red tiles.

No wonder Dad wanted to move here, she thought, looking around in wonder on the day they went for their tea. She had never seen anything as lovely as Wisteria Cottage, which resembled an illustration in a magazine. The wisteria grew over the outside walls at the front and she imagined it looked a picture when in bloom. The surrounding garden was large and well tended. Molly loved the garden and it showed.

Aye, living in this cottage would be grand, she thought, but what about Gran? What would Gran do on her own? Who would she have now to see to the heavy cleaning when the weather was damp? Who would fetch in the coal for the fire?

For days she thought about it and eventually went to Gran's to talk it out.

"Gran, I can't leave you all alone," she said, tears threatening. They talked for nearly an hour. Nevertheless, Marian told her she must go with her father.

"Look, Rita, when you marry, and you *will* marry one of these days, you'll live with your husband and maybe you both will live somewhere else. You can't worry about me, lass. Life is for the young. I've had a good life and now I'm content. Don't worry about the heavy work. My neighbour Ruth is good to me, you know, and she'll help me with the big stuff. You go and live with your Dad, lass. He'll be very upset if you don't."

"Oh, come on, Gran," Rita cried acrimoniously. "He's all wrapped up in Molly. By the way, she said I could call her Molly," she added, thinking calling an elder by their Christian name made her seem more adult.

Marian tutted. "Now, lass, he may be wrapped up in her right at this minute, but that'll change with time. He's right anxious to wed her, but you know he loves you more and always has your welfare at heart. He loves you, in a different way, of course, but he loves you very much, Rita. He worries about you a lot."

"He needn't bother," Rita said, her tone sullen. "He's getting a new wife and a new life. You should see the cottage, Gran. It's in its own grounds. Molly must have a lot of money."

Marian looked at her steadily. "I doubt that, lovey. She told me she inherited the cottage from her parents, but her husband left not a penny. In fact, she had to work to pay off his debts and he left many, from what I hear."

Rita perked up. Some gossip. "How come he owed so much money?"

"He was a gambling man, they say. She's still paying out."

"Oh," Rita hadn't realized Molly's economic condition was on a par with their own.

"Still, she's got to be better off, Gran, she's got a cow for milk, ducks and hens for eggs, and the garden supplies vegetables. The orchard has apple and pear trees, gooseberry and red currants. Yes, Molly is rich in many ways."

Gran shook her head. "There's rich, and then there's rich. It all depends what you want from life, love."

"I want to come here and live with you."

Marian shook her head. "I can't let you do that, love. You must ask your Dad. Anyroad, you're taking it on yourself, aren't you?" She made her face stern. "How do you know I want you living here?"

"Oh, Gran." Her face fell. Rita had not even considered what her grandmother wanted. She was thinking about herself as usual. "Well, will you have me, Gran, please?" She crossed her fingers under the table. Please God, she prayed, please make her say yes.

Marian shook her head sadly. She didn't smile. "I don't know whether I do or don't, lass. I haven't even given it a thought."

She had, though, for hours she had agonized over it and could think of nothing better than having Rita living with her. However, Rita's place was with her father, so it didn't matter what she wanted. "You ask your Dad and Molly what they think, then come and tell me."

Rita sulked over the answer. She so much wanted to stay with her Gran, wanted to be near her old home. Was Gran pushing her aside like her Dad was doing now he had Molly? Did Gran think of her still as a child? In the past few years they had become more than grandmother and granddaughter: they became real friends.

All the familiar things at home were picked over, some kept to take to the cottage, a lot discarded or given away. Obviously, her Dad wanted to start fresh. When she arrived home each day, she glared with dismay at the packed boxes in the kitchen. She didn't speak to her father who sat reading the evening paper. She sat at the table, chin on hands, gazing moodily into space.

Arthur down put his paper and stood. "Wool gathering again,

Rita? It looks like my little girl has a boy friend." Arthur laughed and put his arm around her.

"Oh Dad, I do not!" she said, pulling back, pushing him away. She saw the hurt on his face and smiled. Served him right, after all he was pushing her away for Molly. He wanted a nice cottage and a garden, that's what it was. Molly was a bonus to him, someone to cook and clean. Rita felt proud of herself for figuring out the reason.

The still naive Rita, knowing little of the ways of the world, considered her father her own property, as was her Gran. She was not adult enough to reason things out when it came down to personal relationships. Marian recognized this, so did Arthur and both talked to her about the new living arrangements. Nevertheless, Rita wanted it all her own way. She didn't want her mother back, but neither did she want Molly.

Rita accepted things had changed in her life. Until her father told her he planned to hand the house where she had always lived back to the landlord. That was a shocker and hurt. Still, if she could move in with her Gran then everything would be all right. Gran would surely never refuse if Dad said she could stay. She begged and pleaded, but Gran again told her to ask her father so she knew what the answer would be without asking. The one she loved most did not want her, her father loved another woman, and Molly was practically a stranger. She felt so abandoned. What she should do, she knew, was get to know Molly better, treat her like one of the family. Yet she couldn't, not yet.

The restaurant where they held the wedding reception seemed posh with its white table cloths and snooty waiters. To Rita's delight, a string quartet whittled away on a low stage in the corner surrounded by potted plants.

She tried to be a perfect lady all day, did not speak out of turn, nor sulk or pout. Everyone admired her dress and she felt special in their eyes. As the party grew merrier, she spoke.

"Dad? Can I live with my Gran?" she asked in a pause as a waiter removed dirty plates.

"Rita," Marian said, her tone stern. "This is neither the time nor the place for that."

Her face fell and she looked sullen. "Well, I want to stay with you, Gran."

Molly looked at Arthur's daughter. She had thought winning Rita over would be easy and had catered to her, made her special things she liked to eat, brought her little gifts. Now she looked at her stepdaughter, felt her anguish.

"A teenager is always a problem." She had told Arthur only last week. "Remember what you were like when you were her age?"

Arthur sighed. "It doesn't matter, Molly," he said then, "Stop humouring her. She'll play you like a fish for everything she can get. Children are like that."

"Oh, Arthur, don't be so unfeeling." Molly shook her head and slapped his wrist lightly. "The girl is getting a new woman in her life, one who's replacing her mother in your affections. That no affection existed between you and her mother means nothing to Rita. I understand how she feels. She thinks you don't love her anymore."

I have tried, Molly thought, tried so hard to get close to Rita but nothing has worked. She sighed sadly. Maybe it's as well she left the past behind her, and changing the mood back to liveliness, said, "I think we should have a toast while we have this lovely wine."

She raised her glass. They all followed suit. "To Rita whose birthday is next week," Molly said smiling, "Happy early birthday, Rita."

"Happy Birthday, Rita," they chorused as the birthday girl hung her head embarrassed. Nobody had ever drunk a toast to her before and she sipped her watered wine, blushing furiously.

By the time they left the restaurant her mood was sunnier. They would go to Trawton where her Dad and Molly would spend the week finally deciding what to else to give away. Rita planned to spend the week's evenings talking her Dad into letting her stay with Gran.

CHAPTER EIGHT

1932

"You horrible old cow. You stay away from my husband. What he sees in you, I don't know. You're a slag, a whore, and a trollop," Marian screamed angrily as the recipient of her invective, Agnes Reilly, stood cackling.

Twelve-year-old Sheila peered around the edge of the door, wondering what was causing the commotion, and saw Agnes Reilly. Agnes, known as a sloppy woman who always wore a dirty apron, kept her hair netted in pin curls and iron curlers.

Agnes, angry, tossed her head and yelled. "Yeah, sure, and you're a fine one to talk, Marian Haydon. We all know about you and your fancy men. No wonder poor Harry wants someone else."

Marian raised the broom threateningly. "Get away from here, woman, get back to that hovel of yours. Keep your scabs and fleas away from me."

Agnes Reilly searched her mind for an answer. "I'll have you know my howse is clean, cleaner than yourn."

Marian lowered her voice as she saw a neighbour step onto her front step. The women on the street had ears like bats and flew to their steps when they heard raised voices.

"Aye, you might say so," Marian said, her voice low and menacing, "but the occupants here are a sight cleaner. Who would look at you without shuddering with revulsion, or tossing a bucket of water?"

Agnes, however, did not lower her voice and Sheila heard every word. “You bastard bitch you! You’re like your mother afore you, all mouth and nasty with it. You’re the sort who eats nails for breakfast. Bloody hard faced bitch.” She shook her fist. “Aye, if I told Harry about your past affairs, he’d soon pack up and leave you, you two faced cow.”

Marian roughly brushed the broom at Agnes’s feet, making her jump back.

“You can’t sweep this away, you know, Marian Haydon,” Agnes shouted. “I’ll see the better of you yet. You think you’re too bloody good for the street since you took up with his Lordship. Flying your kite too high this time, ain’t you?” Agnes sniggered at the look on Marian’s face. “Oh aye, I know all about that. My sister works in the kitchen at the manor, you know, and they all know about you up there. Lady Cynthia told Mrs. Malone you were nothing but a whore, and if you hadn’t walked out she’d have thrown you out, arse over tip.”

Marian gasped. That was over a year ago. Why was it coming to light today? Nobody said a word when she told them Lady Cynthia wanted someone to live in, so she had quit. Harry had not remarked on it either. Had they all been talking about her behind her back? They must have. They must all know of her shame, of her lusting after Lord Gerrard. Naturally, she knew they had talked about her before and managed to put it behind her.

Marian often wondered what was wrong with her. Everybody else seemed content with their husband, but she always looked for someone else: not that she would ever have left Harry. In her book that was not done, and the children were a consideration, but why was she always casting her eye around? What was it in her makeup that made her this way? Why couldn’t she be normal and cleave to her own man instead of making eyes at others?

All she knew was that she was forever seeking something. Whether it was love or lust, she did not know. It was as though a need possessed her, a need no other woman seemed to have, yet she could live without sex, and that being so, it was not for the act itself she wanted other men. While sex was enjoyable with the right man, it must be, she supposed, the very need of the man that governed her feelings. The way they looked at her with anguished wanting, the way their gaze devoured her. She loved the reflection of herself she saw in their gaze, felt like a queen, powerful and in charge. Harry had not made her feel that way since they were courting.

In another age they would have called her a courtesan, she mused, the men would have sought her out and she would have cultivated a salon. Nowadays they would call her a whore. Yet even as the years passed, she never stopped eyeing the men. She needed admiration, guilty at deceiving Harry, she did not consider herself promiscuous.

In 1940 she started meeting Howard Halliwell and their affair continued for a few months. Howard, an ex-Brit now a Canadian, was a merchant seaman who worked out of Halifax, Nova Scotia. His usual circuit was Liverpool, Dublin and New York, from there up to Halifax, Nova Scotia then back to Liverpool. He and Marian met at a village dance when he was visiting his brother who lived in Trawton.

Of course it was a long distance affair as she never knew when Howard would turn up in Trawton, although that made it more exciting. His being well known locally made their rendezvous difficult and she often sneaked him in through her back door where they could be together for a couple of hours.

She recalled once meeting him in Wigan. Both spotted a Trawton lady doing her shopping, immediately separated and walked in opposite directions. Eventually these odd meetings became too stressful so they broke off the relationship. Because they did not have any transportation, it became impossible for them to meet elsewhere as the buses were always full of local gossips.

As a goodbye gift Howard gave her a soap stone carving of a seal. This gesture touched Marian and they parted the best of friends. He still came to visit his brother and her heart would still jolt at the sight of him. The song "I'll Never Smile Again," brought tears to her eyes as it had been playing when they said goodbye.

Aye, Agnes Reilly had spit it right out today. Bragging she had slept with Harry, as if I cared about that. Oh, I would care what people thought of me, that I couldn't hold a husband, but I could care less if Harry slept with the entire street because we have little between us these days, apart from mutual companionship.

Agnes spat at Marian's feet as she turned to walk away, the ultimate insult. She muttered angrily as she quickly marched toward the pub.

Sheila stood behind the door watching her mother who started to sweep the pavement. "Who were you talking to?" she asked slyly as she opened the door fully.

"How long have you been there, bugg-a-lugs?" Marian asked, suppressing the urge to belt Sheila.

"Long enough, Mam, long enough," Sheila said. She grinned maliciously.

Marian cleared the last brush full of grit and litter from the house front and went indoors, Sheila dogging her footsteps.

Sheila was trying to think of what she would like. Time to use her new ammunition.

"Mam?"

"What is it, Sheila?"

"Can I have sixpence?" Sheila smirked and twiddled with her hair.

Marian thought the girl was up to something. "No. I don't have sixpence to give you."

"You'd have had lots of money if you'd stayed working at the manor, though, wouldn't you?" she said in a singsong voice.

Marian turned off the tap and turned to look at her daughter. God forbid Sheila heard the slanging match. Her life wouldn't be worth living.

"What has that got to do with anything right now? I don't have sixpence. Ask your Dad when he gets home, and what do you want it for, anyway?

Sheila squinted her eyes slyly. "I want an ice cream from the Woolsack."

Marian put the kettle over the fire. "Forget it, Sheila. Go and pick up the clothes you tossed all over the floor in your bedroom and sort them out ready for washing."

"I'm not your servant, you know." Sheila tossed her head, Marian caught the gesture as she turned. "You want them, you go get them."

Marian landed a sharp blow with her palm across the back of Sheila's head. It didn't hurt, but Marian could tell it shocked her since Marian had never raised a hand to her.

"Don't you talk to me like that, my girl. Do as you're told. Move it. Now!" Marian's insides churned with apprehension and her heart raced. Sheila had heard, that much was obvious, so if Marian as much as gave her an inch she would be sorry.

"Ow! That hurt." Sheila rubbed the back of her head, then fisted her eyes. "I'll do what I want, and picking up stuff isn't it."

"While you live in this house you'll abide by my rules," Marian said grimly, "Get upstairs and do as I tell you."

Sheila stood defiant and stone faced. "Do it yourself. You can't tell me what to do, not with what I know about you, Mam." Marian gasped. "I heard that woman call you a whore, saying you were up at the manor chasing after his Lordship."

Marian's heart thumped painfully and seemed to stop for a second. Sheila *had* listened. Marian kept her voice steady. "You didn't hear right. That's not it at all. We were talking about somebody you don't know." What could she say . . . what could she say?

Why am I defending myself with the child? It's none of her business and if, God forbid, I'm ever the subject of common gossip it would get back to Harry, and probably has done already.

Sheila stood straddling the hearth rug, hands on her hips. "Oh yes? Who were the other men, then? She said you were a trollop. Imagine that, my own Mam, a trollop! What's a trollop? Bet it isn't anything good."

Grim faced, Marian spoke with lips compressed, eyes narrowed. "Leave off now, Sheila, I'm warning you. I'll wash your mouth out with soap if you keep on about a load of old rubbish."

"You can try it, Mam, but it won't wash it out of my memory, will it?" Sheila said, her tone saccharine sweet as she grimaced in her nasty little smirk.

Marian had to win this argument or Sheila would think she could get the better of her. "Go upstairs I tell you, and pick up those things, and do it now before I wallop you with this." She raised the broom and shook it in Sheila's face.

Sheila danced back, putting the table between them. "Yeah, yeah, yeah. Bugger off, Mam. I won't do it. I won't ever do anything for you again. My own mother called a whore, and she can still look me in the eye! I bet my Dad'll be ever so pleased to hear about this, I don't think."

Sheila went out, slamming the front door so loudly it rattled the dishes on the Welsh dresser shelves.

Marian flopped onto a chair and put her head on her arms, face down on the table. She spoke aloud, "What am I going to do? Harry will probably throw me out if he hears it from Sheila. She has a degree in exaggeration, that child. Oh, God help me." Tears came to her eyes. All her chickens were coming home to roost; she had caused the ruin of her life through her own stupidity.

She vigorously scrubbed the kitchen floor. Work always did help her think.

If Harry was carrying on with Agnes, and she had no reason to doubt it for he had not laid a finger on her for at least a year, then he was also at fault. Still, in the last twelve months she had made no move toward him, either. So, in fact, she reasoned, it was all her own fault; she had driven him away by ignoring his needs. Poor Harry, he asked for so little, a clean house, a warm bed, good children and he had always been there when she needed him.

She sat back on her heels. Yes, they would discuss this and when she got the sins off her chest, they could surely get back to normal. Catholics had it made, she thought then. Each week they went to confession and started off with a clean slate. Maybe that was why they were so steady and pleasant: they were the recipients of free psychiatric help.

Harry seemed quiet that evening and read his paper from cover to cover. Marian sat darning, sitting opposite him in her small arm chair. She kept clearing her throat, wondering if Sheila had said anything to him as he was coming up the street.

She put down the sock. "Harry?"

"Yes?"

"I think we need to talk about a few things."

He put down his paper and gave her his full attention. Now she didn't know where to look, so she bustled around making a pot of tea.

"Aye, go on," he said, lighting his pipe.

"It's about Agnes Reilly," she said, glancing at him. His face reddened, which surprised her, and he looked around the room, seemingly unable to look her in the eye.

"What about her?" His voice seemed gruff, strangled.

"It's about you and her. Is it serious?"

She saw the anger rise in him. "God damn it, woman, a man has needs and you aren't forthcoming lately, are you?" Still, his gaze roamed the room, then he looked at the ceiling. He seemed embarrassed, she saw, but not as embarrassed as she would be once she started to tell him of her own sins.

His next words surprised her. "Anyway, it only happened the once when I'd had a few beers. It won't happen again."

"Oh," Her heart leaped in her breast. So it was only the once and that slag made it sound as if it were a continuing affair.

"I'm sorry, Marian," he said quietly, "I shouldn't have, but I did, and now you know."

The look on his face made her want to take him in her arms. "Oh Harry, it's all right. It's only that she's such a low person. It was her who told me, bold as brass she was, too."

Harry nodded. "She is an'all, she is. I must have been nuts, Marian. She's been after me every time I go down to the pub. She sits in her usual spot by the door and collars me as I go inside. That's why I stopped going there. I only go to the lodge now."

"I see," Marian said. She did too, but it hadn't helped when he confessed so easily. Her own confession needed dragging out of her in a screaming row, or at least raised voices. Right now she felt incapable of bluntly saying the words that would bring their marriage to ruin.

"Can you ever forgive me?" he asked, looking like lad, all trembling mouth and misty eyes.

She moved to his side and put a hand on his shoulder. Now *she* couldn't look at *him*. "Of course I can, Harry. I don't think badly of you, only of myself for not paying you more attention. Yet you haven't made a move toward me for so long so it got harder and harder for me to move to you."

He looked up at her. "Do you know why?"

"No."

"It was because of his fancy Lordship up there." He gestured with his head to the fireplace - the manor lay in that direction. "The place was rife with talk about you and him when you were working at the Manor. Then you came home and said you quit."

She sighed with relief and moved around to face him. "Oh Harry. Nothing happened between me and him. You must know that." That much was true, but given the chance, she'd have thrown herself on her back as soon as look at him.

"Nothing at all?"

"Of course not, you big daft lummox. I was working. Lord Gerrard was in Bermuda, then when Lady Cynthia asked if I'd live in and tend to her wants twenty-four hours a day I couldn't do it. You know that . . . I told you."

"Aye, but other people told me her Ladyship sacked you for making eyes at her husband. Anyroad, he was the one who talked to you at the church bazaar and asked you to go up there. I recall them saying he kissed your hand."

Marian grimaced. "Oh Harry, he's a lord, and that's how lords act." She looked aghast now. "That's what people were saying about me? Oh my God, how can I show my face outside the door again?" Putting her head in her hands, she sobbed.

Harry had given her an opening and yet she couldn't tell him of her affairs. She wasn't crying over Lord Gerrard, no, she was crying for the others she had committed adultery with, with the shame of it and the fact she couldn't tell Harry, even now.

Harry stood, arms hanging at his side, reluctant to make the first move. "Now lass. I'm sorry, I'm sorry about the Reilly woman and I'm sorry you're so upset." He gave a deep sigh and opened his arms. "Come here and give us a cuddle."

Marian threw herself into his arms. Harry was such a good man, a reliable man. Here she was a sinner, a woman with a soul as black as pitch and yet he was comforting *her* and apologizing. Now she could never tell him about the others.

That Saturday they went to Southport together, leaving Sheila at home and Roger away with the boy scouts. It was a lovely day and Harry bought her a crystal vase, then bought her one red rose. What a lucky woman she felt then. Harry still loved her and she was fond of him. Aye, she could have done a lot worse.

Sheila tried to convert to Catholicism. In some ways the stern priest made up for the leniency she experienced at home these days, and she liked it because her antics had riled her mother. They hardly spoke, and if they did, it was only when her Mam gave her an order. She would do nothing for her mother, nothing, not knowing what she knew. Strangely enough, her Mam and Dad were the best of friends these days and she thought Mam must have told Dad about Agnes Reilly and the row, because of her Dad's response when she raised the subject.

She waited until her mother was out before she mentioned it. "Dad, you know what happened?"

He did not look up from his paper. "No, what happened?"

"Well, I bet you'd never guess what Mrs. Reilly said."

His head shot up then. "Look Sheila, I have no interest in gossip and Agnes Reilly is a big mouthed liar."

"Dad, you know what she said?"

"Stop it right now, girl, I'll hear no more. Don't mention that woman's name in this house again."

"But, Dad . . .,"

"But Dad nothing. Shut up and leave it alone. I want to hear no more of your vivid imagination and that's what most of your yatter turns out to be. Leave it. Find yourself something to do. Them dishes need washing for a start."

She stared at him, stupid old man. Then it occurred to her that her mother must have confessed. Oh well, nothing more was going to come of the knowledge and that's when she allowed the Catholic church to convert her.

The lessons and Catechism were difficult and, as Sheila's attention span was all of two minutes, she didn't know how she managed to learn a thing. Then it shocked her to hear a good Catholic attended church every Sunday, not only at Easter. It was all right for those born Catholic, but she wanted to be able to choose when she attended Mass, not have to attend under the penalty of committing a sin. After two weeks of getting up early Sunday, she simply stopped bothering. Anyway, who wanted to walk to the church in the pouring rain?

At her private baptism, the priest gave her a small plaster statue of Our Lady of Fatima and this she placed on the mantlepiece, making the sign of the cross every time she passed in front of it or looked at the mantel. She quickly discovered this drove her mother crazy, so then started genuflecting each time she walked past the fireplace.

Marian sighed testily. "I do wish you'd stop it." Knowing Sheila had finally committed herself to something, she couldn't take the statuette away from her. While she and Harry were agnostic, or at best Church of England, she saw nothing wrong with the girl having her own beliefs, but did she have to flaunt them at every opportunity?

"There's a place for that rubbish," she said after Sheila again genuflected. "The fireplace isn't an altar. Go to church. That's where the malarkey belongs."

Sheila spun around on her heel and glared at her mother. "You're jealous, aren't you? God will take me into heaven and *you* are going to fry in hell." She grinned evilly. "I'll laugh when they bury you, Mam, knowing you'll burn in hell for all eternity. Only good Catholics get into heaven."

This damnation did not impress Marian. "Huh! Then you've condemned more than three quarters of the human race. Who'd want to go to a heaven that only had Catholics? It will be boring, all the hymn singing and incense," Marian said sharply, refusing to allow Sheila to draw her into an argument.

Sheila reached up, took down the little figure and kissed it. "Little you understand, Mam. They have got angels and harps and everything."

"You'd better do more research on the subject, Sheila," Marian said quietly. Sheila displayed her stupidity far too often. Imagine believing such rubbish.

Sheila seemed complacent. "I don't need to do research, Mam. I know what Father Wilson told me and what the Book says. If I can get you and Dad to join the church, then I'll get special prayer from him and be assured of my place by the side of Jesus and Our Lady."

Marian snorted. "Aye, and that's another thing. You can take your 'lady' and put her in the front room. I'm not having all your curtsying and crossing yourself every time you come into the house. Go on, get it out of here."

Sheila stood her ground and didn't move. Stone faced, Marian snatched the statue from her hands, went into the front room and put it on top of the china cabinet without saying a word, then firmly shut the parlour door. That was the last time Our Lady of Fatima ruled the kitchen.

It was also the end of religion for Sheila. Now she had no reason to bring out her faith, unless it was to flaunt the Commandments in front of her rotten old Mam.

1956

Rita heard the story about the crystal bud vase, delighted her granddad had been such a good, loving man.

Marian smiled at her granddaughter. The story was about the only true one she had related. Oh, not about his carrying on with another woman, of course. Better to keep his memory spotless with Rita. No, she had told her about their day out at Southport, saying it was their anniversary.

"You've had such a wonderful life, Gran," Rita said, hugging her.

"Aye, I have an'all," Marian thought back, tears threatening. She recalled some horrible times of course, the two wars, the depression, the Spanish Flu epidemic, but overall, it hadn't been bad.

"Tell me again about when you worked at the Manor, and about when you worked for the lady in Manchester."

"Enough stories for one day, love. You'd better be heading home. It's a fair way to go and it's already getting dark."

She had never worked in Manchester. It had been a white lie one she must try to remember because it would never do to contradict herself. Her Dad had worked there for six months, her mother had gone with him, but she had stayed at the manor.

Despite her begging, Arthur adamantly refused to let Rita live with her grandmother. These days she lived at the cottage and Marian came to visit them there.

"Can I come live with you, Gran?"

"Why on earth would you want to do that? The cottage is a grand house altogether," Marian said, looking around her cramped kitchen. Why would Rita want to live here in this poky house with its coal fire and cramped conditions, when she could live in plush comfort. The reasoning was beyond her and this request for more stories was one of Rita's ploys. She wanted it to get dark so Marian would not let her walk all the way home.

"Come on, Lady Jane, get your coat. I'll give you some biscuits to eat on the way. If you run, you'll can catch the next bus to end of Cuckoo Lane."

Rita left in a hurry, annoyed she hadn't waited longer to ask for the story. One of these days she would make it last long enough to stay over and then she'd never go back.

As she walked along Cuckoo Lane from the bus stop, she thought about her new home. Oh, Molly was nice, and Rita liked her. Her Dad was happy now they had moved from the village, and even worked in the garden every evening after supper.

Weren't they lucky to live on Cuckoo Lane at Wisteria Cottage? The name sounded grand said aloud and she had written it repeatedly on her few books. So why *did* she want to go back to Trawton? She didn't know, other than she wanted to be with her Gran. Even to her youthful and inexperienced eyes, Gran had begun to look frail. She had lost weight, her skin seemed translucent and Rita felt afraid she might die with nobody to see to her.

Every weekend she helped her Dad with the garden, Rita doing the weeding as she didn't know much about growing things. They would talk as they worked and repeatedly she asked to move to her Gran's, but he would not countenance it, would change the subject.

Did he love her so much he couldn't bear to let her out of his sight? Surely that could not be the reason, not now he had the loving Molly at his side. They had bought a television with a large screen and Rita sometimes enjoyed watching it, although her Dad selected the programs.

When she arrived home, they were playing cards. Molly left her cards to put on the kettle for cocoa.

"Here, Rita. you play my hand while I get the drinks," she said, smiling at her stepdaughter thinking Rita beautiful now she had lost her puppy fat. Her cheeks, rosy from her walk, seemed more pronounced. Molly mentioned to Arthur that Rita looked like a model. Her eyes were large with thick dark eyelashes, while her hair, more red than blond, framed her face with curls. She was a right bobby dazzler, as her father often said.

Rita played the hand and won as Molly came back with the tray of cocoa and freshly baked fairy cakes.

"Here we are then. Come on, let's sit in front of the fire."

Molly put the tray on the coffee table and poured milky cocoa into the blue and white mugs from the big white pitcher.

It's cosy here, all right, Rita thought, but I need to be with Gran.

"How was your afternoon?" Molly asked Rita.

"It was lovely," she said smiling. "We had roast pork today and home made apple sauce." She turned to face her father. "You know, I'm worried about Gran, Dad. She's lost weight and she's very frail. I worry she'll be ill and there will be nobody there to see to her. Are you sure I can't go to live with her, Dad? Please?"

Arthur sighed and looked at Molly. Marian was his mother-in-law and while she was a nice person, was not his blood relation.

"Has she seen a doctor?" he asked stonily.

Rita shook her head. Marian would not even consider seeing the doctor. "No, she refuses to go. Says it's only old age and she's fine," Rita rubbed at the lines on her forehead. "Still, you know how bad her arthritis is, Dad, and autumn is drawing on. She'll be bad then."

Molly cleared her throat. She knew better than to interfere, but then the girl had a point.

"Maybe Marian could come to stay with us over the winter," she said. Well, it was a suggestion, one she knew Arthur would not sanction, but it made Rita's idea sound better. Rita caught onto what she was up to and winked.

"Oh yes, Dad!"

"No way, Molly." Arthur looked shocked. "We can't have her here. What would she do all day and where would she sleep?"

"She would sleep on her own bed and we could fit it in here easily. We now have the television and it would make company for her." She glanced around the long living room. "Rita would be happy and we would all know Marian was all right. We could all keep an eye on her."

"She isn't coming here," he said firmly. "This isn't a rest home for retired widows. The woman is not close to me, other than being my mother-in-law, though she is Rita's grandmother, right enough." He looked at Rita who hadn't said a word, already aware she had won with Molly's help.

He sighed deeply. "Well, I suppose you'd better go and stay with her if she'll have you, Rita, but you have to come back home in spring."

"Thanks, Dad," Rita said kissing him and giving him a hug.

She hugged Molly also. "Thanks Molly. I owe you one."

That night she slept like a log. Soon she would go back to Trawton and her Gran.

CHAPTER NINE

Marian felt decidedly unwell. During the night she woke with a terrible thirst and got out of bed to go for a glass of water. As she moved to the hall, her head felt like a sponge and things sounded far away.

"Gran? Are you all right?" Rita asked as she came onto the landing as a faltering Marian reached the top step and grabbed at the bannister.

"Of course, Rita. I wanted a glass of water." Her voice sounded weak.

"You know I told you to call me if you needed anything. You can't go wandering around the house in the dark, Gran, you could hurt yourself. Come on, I'll tuck you up in bed."

"Flipping heck," Marian said and chuckled, "You'd think I was a four-year-old. Leave me be, lass. Get back to bed yourself. You've got work tomorrow."

"After I fetch your water, Gran. Go back to bed now."

Next morning Marian heard Rita getting up, go downstairs and start clattering around in the kitchen. She made to rise. Time for her to make breakfast, a good breakfast meant a good day. Dizzy, she sank back on her pillow as her head felt most peculiar, light and giddy.

Rita brought her a cup of tea and gasped at her colour. "You're as white as a sheet, Gran. I'm sending for the doctor."

She went outside and stopped a school boy, giving him a shilling and asking him to drop off the note at the Doctor's surgery.

"Bed rest that what's he said, Gran, and the medicine," Rita announced when the doctor left in the afternoon. "You've got the flu. A bad case of it, too."

"I know what I've got, missy," Marian snapped. "Don't talk to me like that. I'm your grandmother, not your baby."

"Sounds like you're feeling better already," Rita giggled. "You rest a while and I'll fetch you some soup."

Marian struggled to sit upright. "Now you listen to me. I'll have some buttered toast and tea. Toast with lemon marmalade. None of your soup, thank you. Out of a tin, it'll be . . . and why are you not at work?"

Rita looked at her fondly. "Oh Gran, why'd you think? I'm staying home to look after you because I can't trust you to stay in bed."

Marian could not help but smile. "True enough, Rita, but I'll be up tomorrow, I can promise you. There's nowt wrong with me hard work won't cure."

Rita shook her head. "Uh-uh! Not according to the doctor. You've got to stay in bed, take your medicine and eat light nutritious meals."

"Oh, and you're going to make sure that happens, are you, madam?"

"Yes, I am," Rita said firmly, though she grinned. She was a case, was her Gran.

"We'll see, miss bossy boots, we'll see," Marian smiled and closed her eyes. She liked a fuss being made of her, although she would never admit it. Thank God Arthur had allowed Rita to come and live with her. How she would have managed through a sickness, she did not know.

Each afternoon Rita allowed her grandmother downstairs to sit by the fire wrapped in a quilt. They talked about everything under the sun, but Marian would not talk about the items in the cabinet. "Sundays only," she said.

During these talks Rita learned a great deal about life, home economics, marriage and child rearing. Marian was a good teacher.

One morning when Marian was still partially bedridden, Rita paused on the doorstep to lock the door before she went to the shops.

"Rita?" A familiar voice said from behind her.

She whipped around and came face to face with her mother.

"Mam!" she gasped.

"Where's your Dad?" Sheila asked, obviously irritated, "Our house has somebody else living in it."

Rita kept her face expressionless, determined not to show her fear. She was petrified to think she might demand to come into the house. "Dad's at work, I expect," she said. "We don't live at twenty-six any more. After Dad married, we went to live in his wife's house."

Sheila's heart sank. So he *had* married. What was she going to do now? She had not a penny and the authorities who claimed her an unfit mother, had taken her infant child into custody. Alone and penniless, she had counted on assistance from Arthur, knowing at heart he was a good man and wouldn't see her starve.

"Well, 'bye," Rita said and moved away.

"Wait up a minute, Rita." Sheila caught at her arm. "You can't leave me here."

"What do you want? Where's your baby?" She shook off her mother's hand.

"Never mind the baby. What about me? I've not got enough money to get out of this place. I had to walk the last seven miles and now . . .," she grabbed at Rita again, ". . . . you've got to help me. You're my daughter." She again laid a hand on Rita's sleeve.

Rita stared at her, flicked her eyes from head to toe. Sheila looked decidedly seedy with her creased and dirty clothing, her shoes practically falling apart. She realized her mother looked like derelict, a tramp. What could have happened to bring her to this? Where was the man whose child she had carried and where was the child, her half-brother or half-sister?

"Where's the baby, Mam?" she repeated, shaking off her mother's hand.

"It was born dead," Sheila said, unwilling to admit her desertion of him. It was only while she went to look for a job, for heaven's sake, and the bloody nosy landlady had gone into her room and found him lying on the floor where he had fallen. Thinking she would only be away for a short time, she had left him tucked up on the bed with cushions round him.

She had told them, the stuffed shirts who had taken him, about her landlady, an ogre, who demanded too much money to mind him. What else was she supposed to do when trying to find money to support him properly? she asked them. Who would hire her if she turned up with a babe in arms? They had not listened and didn't care how much she wanted him back. Now he was lost to her until she could prove without a doubt she could support him in a decent home, and the way things were going, she saw little hope of that. She quickly became used to being on her own again and glad he was someone else's responsibility.

"I'm sorry to hear that," Rita said sadly, thinking she'd had a brother and he was dead. "What happened to you to get you into this state?" she asked, curious.

Sheila shivered and looked around. "Look, Rita, can we get off the street? It's parky and people are staring."

"Oh, all right," she said not very graciously, "We'll go in the parlour and close the door. Gran is sick and in bed, and if she thinks someone's in the house she'll be down like a shot. Keep your voice down."

They went into the parlour and Rita shut the door quietly. Not quietly enough, though, for a querulous voice came from upstairs.

"Rita? It that you, Rita? What did you buy?"

Rita pushed her mother onto the couch. "You stay here. I'll have to go up and see to her." She hurried upstairs.

"What did you buy?" Marian asked as Rita came into the bedroom. She had little to occupy her mind other than meals these days.

"I didn't go yet, Gran," Rita confessed. She couldn't tell her Gran about her mother otherwise there'd be ructions. "I forgot my change purse."

Marian chuckled. "Talk about feather headed! *You* forget your purse? You've been cloud gathering. So what's his name?"

Rita laughed. Better treat it as something ordinary. She had to get back to her Mam and get her out of the house. "Never you mind, nosy."

After chatting about nothing for a couple of minutes and seeing her Gran settled, Rita dashed downstairs to the parlour. This time she was careful to make no sound as she closed the door.

"Come on now, Mam," she said almost in a whisper. "What's this all about? Don't raise your voice. She's already suspicious because I came back."

"Look, Rita. The problem is I've got no money, I've lost my lodgings and have nowhere to turn. I can't get a job looking like this, and if I don't get a job, I can't support myself."

Rita stared at her mother. She had a nerve. "What did you expect my Dad to do about it? You're nothing to do with him now. You're divorced."

"I know, Rita." Sheila kept her voice low, was close to tears. She had not expected to have to explain her sorry circumstances to her daughter. "Tell me where your Dad is. I'll go talk to him."

"He's at work as usual. Talk to him there. I won't tell you where he lives." She indicated her mother's old and soiled clothing. "Molly wouldn't like you turning up on her doorstep looking like that."

Sheila looked at her skirt, now stained and holed and a terrible mess. She knew how she looked and counted on her appearance to soften Arthur's heart. "I don't have money for the bus fare, Rita. I haven't a single penny to my name. Lend me something to get to his works." She put out her hand, begging.

Begging from me, her daughter, Rita thought, shivering. How low Mam had sunk, and how low she would go to get some cash. She dug in her purse, realizing it was the only way to get her mother out of the house. Already Sheila's voice was beginning to rise.

"Here." She shoved all her loose change at her. "It's all I've got. Come on, you'll have to leave now."

Sheila pulled herself off the couch. It had been a long time since she sat in such comfort. "Can't I stay here for a couple of days?" She looked up at the ceiling. "*She* won't know. She's upstairs in bed. I could sleep on this." She patted the sofa.

"No," Rita said, she never had any real love for her mother, had even less now. I might have treated a destitute stranger better, she thought. "Come on, you'll have to leave."

Rita cracked the door open and listened. Silence. "Come on out," she hissed.

They went into the hall and Rita was opening the front door when she heard a roar.

"What's all this? Who's that woman?"

They turned to see Marian standing at the top of the stairs in her nightdress.

"My God, it's Sheila! What's she doing in my house?" Marian asked, horror in her eyes and a steely clench to her jaw. "What are you doing here, Sheila?" she gasped, "and why do you look like a tramp?"

Sheila shrank back against the wall. She'd been going to beg her mother for help, but knowing the state she looked was worse than she had thought, found it too demeaning to ask the old lady for help.

"Well?" Marian roared. Rita had never heard her Gran speak so loudly. As she moved toward the stair, Marian put up a hand to stop her.

"We had an agreement, Sheila," Marian said, "that you would never darken my doorstep again unless invited, and yet here you are in my house. What are you doing here and why?"

"Hello, Mam," Sheila said, her face creasing in a smile, showing a gap to one side where a drunk had knocked out a tooth. She harbored a tiny hope her mother would let her stay if she knew the circumstances.

The smile did not sway Marian. "We had an agreement, Sheila, and nothing warrants this intrusion . . . nothing. I will ask you again. What are you doing here?"

Tears sprang to her eyes. "Oh Mam, I've got no money and nowhere to live. Please let me stay."

Marian laughed roughly without humour. "That's a joke! What happened to this fancy man of yours? Well, you can't stay here, and I blame you for coercing Rita into letting you in my house. It can't have been her fault. Why have you come back?"

"I came back to see Arthur, but he's moved."

"Arthur?" Marian said forcefully, "He doesn't want to see you, I can assure you. You'd better be on your way and don't come back. You're not welcome anywhere in Trawton."

"Come on, Gran, get back in bed or you'll be sick again," Rita said, starting up the stairs, but again Marian raised a hand and stayed her. Rita stood part way up, looking up at her Gran, then down at her mother.

"No, I don't suppose I am welcome," Sheila said with a show of her old spirit. "Yet you're welcomed, aren't you, old lady? Though you're the worst tramp I've ever known. They all think butter wouldn't melt in your mouth, and to think they call me all those names. If only they knew about you, eh? I can tell them, you know. We made that agreement long ago."

Marian narrowed her eyes. "Aye, it was, but don't forget I can have you arrested. I might have to go to jail, but they would hang you."

Rita gaped from one to the other. What *were* they talking about?

Sheila made a sound that sounded like swearing as she opened the door. She turned to glare up the stairs. "Go to hell, you old miserable bitch. God will make you pay for this. You'll not rest easy from now on, not after turning me away from your door."

"Get out! Get out!" Marian screamed and clutched at her chest. Rita ran up the stairs to her side.

Sheila laughed. "I hope you've had a heart attack, you old harpy. I hope you live for months in your muck with no . . .,"

"Shut up, Mam!" Rita rushed down the stairs, pushed her mother out the door, then fled to her Gran's side. By this time Marian had slid down onto the stairs, gasping for breath.

"You'll be all right now, Gran," Rita crooned as she held her against her body. "It's because you got out of bed too soon. I'm sorry about my Mam, but she was stranded and I had to give her some money."

Marian croaked, but couldn't make a word, then she passed out and knew no more.

"She has lobar pneumonia, and a few other problems." The doctor said to Arthur and Rita. "I'm moving her to hospital for observation."

Marian became upset when the ambulance arrived. People never came out of hospitals, she said. They were her greatest fear, so much so she had given birth to both children at home. Rita knew about her dread after the day they talked about Harry and the hospital. While he was having his appendix removed, Gran felt convinced he would never come home.

Rita thought back to when she had told her the story. Marian laughed about it then. "I'd even been to the co-op funeral director, you know. Picked out a nice coffin and put in an order for lilies. Well, when he came back from the operation and they me he was coming home, I felt mortified. The man at the co-op was nice though, told me that he wouldn't charge me for all his trouble. Still and all, you won't catch me going near any hospital. Not after what I've seen on this street."

Rita tried to reassure her. "That's silly, Gran. A lot of people go into the hospital for operations and to have babies. It's better in a hospital where they get the best care and have all the equipment."

"Promise me this, Rita love, don't ever let them take me into the hospital. I'll never come out of it, I know I won't."

"Oh, Gran, you are talking nonsense." Rita had said those years ago and yet here waited thc ambulance to take Gran away. How terrified she must feel.

Marian lay on the stretcher. "Rita," she said clearly as they placed her in the ambulance. "If you say I have to go, well I suppose I must, but I want you to stay here to look after the house. You know everything here."

Rita climbed inside and took her Gran's thin, cold hand. She could feel every bone. "Oh Gran, don't be so morbid. I'll be here when you come home and you *will* come home. It's marvellous what modern medicine can do. You concentrate on getting well. I'm coming with you now and I'll stay with you until you fall asleep."

Rita made her way home from the cottage hospital with many questions racing around her mind. An agreement between her mother and her Gran? All about her Gran being a tramp. That was bad, wasn't it? Was this incident what caused the big breakup? If only her Gran would tell her the story. What was that about her Gran going to jail and her mother being hanged?

It was an upsetting week. She clattered around the empty house, trying to keep it tidy. She had little else to do and managed to clean the place from top to bottom as well as she was able. Each evening she went to see Gran and told her of her day.

After six days they sent Gran home to recuperate. Marian would have to take it easy now, the doctors said, no heavy work, no excitement, no long walks, although she could do most things within moderation. They gave Rita a diet chart on fat free and calorie reduced foods. She knew Gran would hate it.

CHAPTER TEN

With the money Rita gave her, Sheila made her way to Pemberton Mills. Arthur still worked as foreman and that was a blessing for surely he must be well paid after all these years. They had extended the mill, she saw, and two new buildings of raw red brick sat to the rear close to the river.

It was a grey day, the sky glowering and dull, and she pulled her thin coat closer around her to keep out the sharp wind. As she walked down the long gravelled road to the mill buildings, the clouds opened and a cold rain quickly soaked her to the skin. Soon her shoes squelched with every step and she felt frozen. A brisk wind blew the rain into her face and by the time she arrived at the gate house, she resembled a drowned rat.

Arthur came to the gate when she told the guard she was Arthur's wife and her message was urgent. Arthur rushed over thinking it was Molly, his mind racing over what could possibly be the trouble.

"Sheila!" he felt both annoyed and shocked. He looked at her with distaste. What a sight she looked. He turned to leave.

"Arthur. You have to help me," Grabbing his sleeve, she pulled him back. "Please listen. Don't leave."

Grim faced, Arthur moved away from the gate house, towing Sheila with him. "What do you want, Sheila? I don't need this, you know. You shouldn't have come here. You're no longer my wife, and don't you ever say you are."

It had stopped pouring and now was drizzling. In the distance thunder rolled and the pewter sky flashed with lighting.

She looked at him, gauging his mood. In the past she could always fool Arthur. If he felt magnanimous, he would give her something to tide her over.

"I know, but would you have come down if you'd known it was me?" Even as she asked bitterly she thought Arthur looked good. He had put on weight and it suited him.

"No, and you knew that well enough. What do you want?" He looked her up and down, his disgust evident.

"Arthur, I'm destitute." She tried to keep her voice even but it quavered. "I need some money to help me get back on my feet. Please," she begged.

Arthur crossed his arms over his chest and glared at her, saw the rat tail wet hair, the missing tooth, the lines on her face and the ragged clothes. "Why should I give you money? What did you ever do for me and your daughter? I think you've got a nerve, Sheila, a bloody great nerve, but then you always did have guts, didn't you?"

It wasn't working but she had to make him see her desperation. "Please, Arthur?" She dropped to her knees, ignoring the puddles, and grabbed at his leg.

"Get off me, woman," Arthur shouted angrily. The gatehouse guard watched this display with great interest and stood to get a better view.

Sheila started to wail. "Please don't do this, Arthur. Please, please, you've got to help me." When this did not seem to move him, she started with threats. "I'll come back every day until you do," she said, her voice cold and hard. "I'll stay right here, I will. Anyroad, I've got no money to go anywhere. What will people think if I start begging outside your work place?"

Giving her a look of loathing, he peeled her hands off his pants and made to move away. Still on her knees, her hands extended in supplication, she raised her voice. Arthur saw the watching gate guard, his eyes already out on stalks, prick up his ears.

"I'll tell them I'm your ex-wife if you won't help," Maybe threats would help.

"God damn it, Sheila, get up off your knees. All right, how much do you want? This is all I need. My ragged ex-wife begging outside and my workers talking about me and sniggering."

"Can you let me have a hundred pounds?"

Arthur laughed mirthlessly. "Why not ask for a thousand? Go on. You'd have as much luck. I don't have a hundred. I don't even have fifty. I had a wedding to pay for recently, or have you forgotten that? I can let you have twenty and that's it."

"Not much, is it?" Her lip curled with derision. "Still, if it's all you can let me have, all right. If I need more, I know where to come, don't I? I'll pay you back, you know."

"Sure you will," Arthur said sceptically as he took out his wallet. The money he had with him he had saved for Molly's birthday present. Arthur thought she would surely understand when he told her what had happened; which was more than Sheila would if the shoe was on the other foot.

Rita continued to worry about her Gran and stayed close since the ruckus with her Mam and Gran's return home from the hospital. She knew the doctor would call in on his way back from his rounds and anxiously she scanned the street from the bedroom window. The street was empty apart from three little kids playing boats with sticks in the rain-filled gutter. The rain slick cobbles gleamed like wet coal and everything looked bleak. Even a woman walking with her filled shopping bag wore black, the only colour from her head scarf of bright red and blue.

"What are you doing?" her Gran asked suddenly. Rita had thought her asleep.

"Just looking, Gran."

"*She's* not back, is she?"

Rita turned to face her and smiled. "No, Gran, she's not back. She never did come back and it's been over a week now, so I don't think we'll see her again."

Marian nodded. "I pray not. She's evil, is Sheila."

Rita wondered why her Gran had said that. Evil? Well, she had slept with another man and had a child by him, she had left her husband. Or had her Dad thrown her out? She didn't blame him for that, but why evil? It was a strong word to describe anyone, particularly one's own child.

"Evil, Gran? What do you mean?"

"That's for me to know and you to worry about." Her speech sounded blurry, Rita thought. "Never mind what I said. I'm glad to see the back of her." She closed her eyes and turned to the wall, obviously unwilling to say more.

Dr. Ross arrived shortly after.

"She's had a slight stroke," he said as they talked in the kitchen away from Marian's earshot. "She's weak on her left side and it has affected her speech. She was out of bed, you say?"

"Yes, doctor," Rita said, "but only downstairs, then she got giddy so I put her back into bed."

He nodded. "Make sure she stays in bed for at least another couple of weeks. I'll call in on my way back to the surgery every other day. Now, don't you worry about her, young lady, she's as strong as a horse and comes from a strong family. All of them lived to a ripe old age, you know. Make sure she stays in bed, and give her the medicine. She's not completely over the pneumonia yet, but once it's cleared up, she'll soon get back her faculties. She's a fighter."

"Yes, she is," Rita smiled and, taking the new prescription from him, let him out.

Marian lay in bed for two weeks. Once or twice she wanted to get up, but became disoriented when she tried to stand. It seemed like staying in bed had atrophied her muscles, she said. Now each day she would stand at the side of her bed until the trembling in her legs stopped, and only then would she let Rita help her downstairs.

"Why am I so weak?" she kept asking.

Rita made excuses. She didn't want to tell her Gran about the stroke, thinking it would set her back.

Molly, not working right now, came around daily and helped Rita with the chores. Gran liked Molly. Molly was funny in her own way and made her laugh and it was because of Molly that Marian started to feel better. Rita felt so concerned for her Gran that she would not let her do anything and fussed around until Marian could have yelled she was not a baby but a grown woman. Still, the girl thought she was helping, although it took Molly to put a stop to her constant mollycoddling.

Although Marian lay in bed late each morning, she soon recovered enough to go about her normal business and Rita went back to work.

One day Marian made a pot pie for supper and began crimping the pastry when a knock at the door startled her. Wiping her hands on her apron, she went down the hall.

"Hello, Mam," Sheila said, "Feeling better?"

Marian made to shut the door in her face, but Sheila was too fast and got half her body inside the hall. She pushed open the door as Marian backed away.

"Not very nice, is it? Shutting me out," Sheila said. She sniffed as she moved toward the kitchen. "At least you could offer me a cup of tea. I've come from Wigan to see you."

"Well, you've seen me now, so you can leave," Marian said, her hands clenched into fists.

"Mam, Mam." Sheila laughed as though she had told a joke. "Come on, put on the kettle." She threw her handbag and hat onto the table.

"Oh all right, I'll do it myself," she said impatiently, "Hm, pot pie, eh? There's enough there for four. You expecting company?"

Marian glared, but said nothing. If only Molly were here, but unfortunately Molly had come over early today to take her to the shops.

Sheila glanced at the clock on the mantle. "Soon be time for tea, won't it? Our Rita still stopping here?"

Marian said nothing. Please God, make her go away, please send her off. She was praying so hard she almost said the prayer aloud.

"You're not very chatty today, are you? You feeling all right, Mam?" Sheila poured the boiling water in the tea pot and set it on the trivet. "You want me to put the pie in the oven? We won't want to eat it raw, will we?"

Marian found her voice. "There's no *we* here, Sheila. You pick up your coat and bag and leave this house. I don't want you here and I'll not have you here."

She glared at her daughter, saw the cheap flashy clothes, the permed hair and lavish makeup. Sheila was back to her old tricks, it seemed.

Sheila laughed and clapped her hands. "My, my, you are full of spunk today. That's not very nice, you know. I *am* your daughter and out of the kindness of my heart I came to see how you were."

"Bullshit!" Marian roared, surprised she used a swear word. "You never had a spot of kindness in that swinging brick you call a heart. You've spread animosity and heart ache in your every action."

Sheila's face grew feral. "Now you listen to me, Mother dear." She moved around the table, close to Marian. Putting her hands on Marian's shoulders and narrowing her eyes, she looked straight into her face. Marian shrank back. Sheila was bigger than she and looked threatening. Her gorge rose, and she felt smothered by the stink of cheap scent. "I'm going to stay here with you, Mam. I've got myself a job in Wigan and I can travel back and forth with Rita. I can't live in town any longer. I want to come back to Trawton, and my home is gone, so this will do."

"Over my dead body," Marian said, feeling weak and shaky. No way could she allow Sheila to come back here to live. It was beyond countenancing.

"I *am* coming back and I've got my case in the back yard. You didn't know that, did you? Busy chopping meat and vegetables, you were, when I peeked through the window for a second. So you see, I'm here, and here I will stay."

Stunned, Marian watched as she fetched in a large ugly suitcase and plopped it in front of the fire. It felt like she was frozen, she thought, her limbs would not move.

"You can't stay here. We have no room," she said, her voice weak.

Sheila snorted. "Don't talk daft, Mam. We had four of us living here before and we can surely house three. I'll share with Rita. Don't you worry none. We'll manage very well."

Marian sat heavily, her legs suddenly unable to support her. This was terrible. Rita would be angry. What could she do? She stared as Sheila sat drinking tea, content and unworried. How could she get her out of the house? Her mind searched for the words to make her see they did not want her, but her mind wouldn't seem to function.

"You've got to leave now," Marian said, pointing to the door.

"Leave off, Mam. I'm staying and you can't do a thing about it. Not unless you want me shooting off my mouth."

Marian's hand went to her mouth. "We had an agreement," she said, the blood running cold in her veins. "You can't go back on it. You signed a paper and swore an oath."

"So I did, and so what? I can always find the document and burn it. Then where will you be?"

Marian gasped, realizing Sheila was back for more than a place to sleep. She had come to find the agreement to destroy it.

Her mind raced to find an answer. "You'll not find it in this house. I put it in a safety deposit box at the bank where only I can get at it. I always knew you'd come after it one day, Sheila. You're nowt but a criminal and a slag."

Sheila's face broke into a grin. "Ha..ha..ha! Oh, Mam, you are funny, you know? A regular comedian, you are." Her tone changed to sarcasm. "You talk as though I did it all. You're a right one to take that attitude, when you're as guilty as sin yourself."

She's right, Marian thought glumly, I did a terrible thing, now it's come back to haunt me. What is Rita going to say when she sees her mother sitting here? What were the villagers going to say when they saw the adulteress back among them? What was Arthur going to say? Oh God, what had she done to deserve this?

Rita gasped with shock when she came into the kitchen to discover her mother putting a bowl of peas on the table as Gran stood by the sink, silent and grim faced.

"What the hell are you doing here, Mam?" she yelled. Tossing her coat and bag onto the floor, she stood with her hands on her hips. "Get out of here, and now." She pulled at her mother's arm.

"Now, now, Rita. Let's not fly off the handle," Sheila said, with a smug little smile, shaking herself loose. "Not a very nice welcome, I must say. Oh well, come and sit down. You timed it perfectly." She turned to Marian who was washing some small things at the sink. "Come on, Mam, do sit down."

Rita stood with her mouth open, speechless. What was this? Why had Gran not tossed her out?

"Gran?" she said questioningly.

Marian did not turn. "Your mother is staying here for a while. She'll share with you. She's working in Wigan." Her voice was flat, expressionless.

Rita's face turned white with anger. "What the bloody hell is going on here?" she yelled. "What have you done to her?" Rushing to the sink, she put her arms around Marian, protecting her. "You're a demon, Mam. You can't stay here. I don't want you and she doesn't want you, no matter what you've made her say. She's sick and fragile and your being here isn't going to help her get better. She's under doctor's orders and mustn't have any excitement or stress."

She cuddled her Gran who was now shorter than she, rocking her as she would a toddler. "It's all right, Gran. I'll fetch my Dad and he'll get her out."

Sheila paused with a forkful of food to her mouth, completely unconcerned. "Arthur? Don't make me laugh, Rita. He's about as much use as a one legged arse kicker. Come and get your tea. This pie is tasty. You were always a good cook, Mam."

Rita and Marian stood at the sink. Rita didn't know what to do and looked down at her Gran who clung to her with tear-stained cheeks. Her face seemed absolutely bloodless and her eyes looked strained.

"Come on, Gran, I'll get you to bed. You're whacked out."

They shuffled to the foot of the stairs, watched by Sheila who did not pause in her meal. "She needs to get out more, get some colour in them cheeks. She's too lazy by half," she said around a mouthful.

"Shut up, you heartless bitch," Rita said loudly. "Come on now, Gran."

Sheila shrugged and took another spoonful of potatoes. Her mother looked poorly, but she'd had the flu, and what could you expect at her age anyway?

"What is she doing here, Gran, and why couldn't you get her to leave?" Rita asked when they reached the bedroom.

"Don't ask, lass, don't ask." She found it an effort to talk, Rita noticed. "Let her be, though. She'll soon get fed up with this place. We'll ignore her."

Rita got Gran to bed and tucked her in.

"Well, *I* won't," Rita said, brooking no argument. "She'll hear from me when I go back down. I'm not sleeping with her in the bed. What a bloody nerve she's got, what a bloody nerve." Gran was already asleep.

Sheila sat eating jam and bread when she got back to the kitchen.

"No pudding?" Sheila asked through a mouthful. "How come? Mam always made pudding when I lived at home." Rita watched her chewing her food, thinking her callous and ungrateful.

"We watch our diet and don't eat sweets much. For your information, Gran's had the flu, then pneumonia *and* a stroke and has to take it easy. You've got to leave. You're upsetting her too much. The doctor will tell you."

"Come off it, Rita, she looks fine. This is an excuse. A way of making me feel sorry for her. She didn't say anything about it and I know she's had the flu, so don't try it on."

"Mam! You've got to leave. Don't you understand? She's sick and your being here isn't helping. She doesn't know about the stroke, I decided not to tell her so as not to upset her. Go on, go, get out and don't come back."

"No way! This is my home as much as yours, more when you think about it. I was born in this dump and here I'm staying." Sheila lit a cigarette and blew a cloud of smoke at Rita.

Rita flapped her hands and pulled a face. "God, what a terrible habit. You're not smoking in here, Mam. It makes the place stink."

"Now you listen to me, Rita Goodwin. I'm still your mother and you're not yet big enough to talk to me like that. In fact, you'll never be old enough. I'll do what I want, when I want, and if I hear any complaints from you, you'll feel the back of my hand."

"Oh yes?" Rita said scathingly. "Still lashing out, are you? I told you a long time ago it goes to show how few brains you possess. You haven't learned much for an old lady, have you?"

Sheila got to her feet and rummaged in her large handbag. "Right," she said flourishing an old wooden hair brush. "We'll see who's in charge around here, won't we?" She landed a blow across Rita's head.

Rita grappled with her, trying to take the weapon away. "Stop this, Mam. She's going to hear us."

As Sheila lost her grip on the brush and broke away, she picked up the poker, raising it threateningly.

"Stop it, stop it, stop it," Rita sobbed. Tossing the hairbrush onto the table, she grabbed her coat off the floor and ran to fetch her father.

"So you've got to come and throw her out, Dad," Rita gasped after she wiped her eyes. She tried to catch her breath, after running from the bus stop she was still breathing hard. "She's going to make Gran sicker. I can't understand why Gran said she could stay."

Molly sat with Rita while Arthur got his coat.

"You stay here until I get back," he said. "I don't want you seeing or hearing what I've got to say."

Rita nodded. If it wasn't for her Gran she would never go back there while her Mam was in residence. Molly cuddled her and kissed her forehead.

"There, there, Rita. It'll be all right now. Your Dad will fix it. Come on, you can help me bake a cake while we wait for him. What kind shall we make?"

Rita smiled, grateful Molly understood how she felt. Yes, wouldn't it have been much nicer if her Dad had married Molly and Molly was her real mother?

Arthur waited at the bus stop wondering what he could say or do to remove Sheila. He had to, though, he knew.

"Well, well, as I live and breathe," Sheila said as she opened the front door. "Here he is. Master of the bleeding universe."

Arthur pushed past her and into the kitchen. She was making herself at home all right, he thought, seeing makeup and hair curlers scattered over the table. Not that she had moved the tea things, simply pushed them to one side. She appeared as lazy as ever, still sloppy and sluttish. Seeing her brought back years of acrimony.

"So what do you want?" she asked, "Hurry up, I'm going out."

"Oh yes, you're going out all right, and you're not coming back, either. While you're here, I want the money I lent you."

"The money? My word, you're such a Good Samaritan, aren't you, Arthur?" Her lip curled as she spat at him. "I spent the money getting myself some decent clothes so I could get a job. Second hand ones, though."

Arthur stood motionless, his mind sorting out a solution to the problem. "Apparently you now have a job from what Rita said and I expect you'll be getting paid so you can afford to let me have it back."

Sheila tossed her head, her lips compressed into a thin line. "Is this why you came over here? To get back your bloody money? There's nothing very Christian about you, Arthur, is there?"

Arthur decided arguing was pointless. He had to get Sheila out of the house and quickly."Look, Sheila, I came here to tell you to leave. You can't stop here, not with your mother as sick as she is."

Her face showed her disbelief. "Oh yeah? What a load of old codswallop that is, she looked perfectly all right to me. You and that kid of mine have cooked this up between you. I know there's no love lost between us three. However, she *is* my mother and this *is* my home, and here I'm staying."

"Your mother doesn't want you here, I know without even asking her," Arthur said, his exasperation evident, knowing once Sheila decided on something, nothing would move her. "How you got in, I can't imagine, but then you were always a sneaky sod."

"My Mam let me in." Sheila smiled triumphantly. "Did she say she wanted me to leave? No! Did she say anything at all? No! That child of mine of mine is nothing but a liar."

Arthur looked around the kitchen. "Speaking of children, where's the new baby? I suppose we have to be glad you didn't show up with it under your arm. Where is it?"

"Safe from you and this family, that's where," Sheila said, moving to sit placidly in the chair by the fire where she put her feet up on the fender. "Do leave off, Arthur, you're such a weak Willy, all talk and little else."

Arthur's intuition told him she was lying. "So they took it off you, did they? Or did you sell it?"

She stared at him contemptuously. "Well, Arthur, that is really beneath answering."

Arthur realized he would have to throw her out, she was not going to make it easy by leaving of her own accord. He looked around. "Right, where are your things? Upstairs? Let's get cracking. I want you out of here and now." Arthur moved to the stairs. "Keep your voice down," he said as she drew breath to shout at him. "She's upset enough without hearing a slanging match."

"You leave my things alone, Arthur Goodwin," Sheila yelled. "This isn't your house and you can't tell me what to do. I'm not married to you any more."

Arthur was grim. "Thank God! Yes, I can tell you what to do. I know what you're like, Sheila, from experience and I can't allow you to take over this place."

"Arthur Goodwin, you move one hair pin and you'll pay for it," she threatened, heading toward him.

As he started up the stairs, she pulled at his overcoat and dragged him back.

"You stay out of this, Arthur," she hissed. "I can cause you a lot of trouble and you know it."

Arthur, mad as hell, pushed her into the kitchen where she fell against the table with a great clatter of crockery. "Listen to me, you rotten slut, you *will* leave and you'll leave tonight. There's no home for you in Trawton, not after what you've done. Rita is sick with the thought of it and I'm angry that you tried it on with your mother. She's a breath away from a heart attack."

Sheila stood upright and wiped jam from her arm on the tablecloth. "Oh yes, back to that, are we? Change the bloody record, Arthur, the old woman is about as delicate as a Sherman tank. She'll outlive the pair of us."

Arthur stood, hands clenched into fists. He didn't want to manhandle her, but if he had to, he would. "Get out, Sheila, get out now, or I won't be responsible for my actions."

"Ooh, pwease save me from the big stwong man," she said laughing in his face. "You're bloody pathetic, you know, Arthur? You've got about as much backbone as that doily." She gestured to the doily on the chair back.

Furious, he grabbed her by the arm and roughly pushed her along the hall. She punched out at him with her free arm and her feet, but rage made him strong and he managed to shove her out the door.

"Stay out, you hard faced bitch," he said as he slammed the door in her face and pushed in the bolt.

"Hey! What about my things?" she shouted through the letter box, banging with her fists and kicking at the door.

"Stay there. I'll get them," he shouted.

After he locked the back door, he tossed her makeup, curlers and hair brush into her handbag, then went upstairs to get the rest.

"Is that you, Arthur?" Marian's voice tremulously asked as he went into the back bedroom.

"Aye, it's me, Marian," he called. "She's out and we won't let her back in again. I'll see to that."

Marian smiled drowsily. Arthur was a good chap.

He came into her bedroom with Sheila's case into which he had tossed everything he thought belonged to her. Some things might belong to Rita although he doubted it. His Rita would not wear garish colours and cheap fabrics.

"Cover up well now, Marian, this lot is going out the fast way." Laughing now, he pulled up the window and tossed everything out with a grunt. "Here's your stuff, you stupid bitch," he shouted, "Now get lost," He watched as she scrabbled for her hat and coat.

"You'll pay for this, Arthur Goodwin," she yelled up at him, her face a mask of hate. "You wait and see, you'll pay for this."

Childishly he stuck out his tongue and pulled down the window.

He dusted off his hands and grinned. "Well, that's a grand night's work, I must say. She looked like she'd swallowed a mouthful of wasps out there trying to gather her stuff together. I expect I've given the street some'at to talk about now. Do you want a cup of tea to celebrate, Marian? I could use one myself."

"Go on then, lad. Let's have a drink. Put a spot of whisky in it as well," Marian said, pulling herself up against the bed head. The short nap had restored her and seeing Sheila's things go sailing out was as good as a tonic.

He brought up the tray with tea and biscuits and they sat sipping companionably.

"Why did you let her in, in the first place?" he asked.

Marian swallowed her tea and looked at her saviour. "I didn't, Arthur. She pushed through the door. I tried to stop her when I saw who it was, but then I was so shocked to see her that I couldn't move. Then when she was in, I couldn't get her out. She'd put her case in the back yard earlier, peeped in through the window, and I didn't see that, either. I feel such a fool, Arthur. She put it over on me, right enough."

Arthur thought about it for a moment. "So why didn't you send her packing when she said she was planning to stay? Rita told me that when she said she was staying, you agreed."

"Aye I did, lad. There's bad blood between us, but you know that. Well, she's holding something over my head I should've cleared up a long time ago. Rita knows there's some'at, as do you. You've looked at me strangely at times, Arthur, I know, and you had to swear anything we let slip would go no farther."

Arthur thought it puzzling. Often he wondered what happened to cause the rift and was as curious as Rita. Now he said: "How bad can it be you let her strong arm you into letting her take over your house?"

"Arthur, I can't tell you. Suffice it to say she's got me where she wants me, she always has since she was a teenager, nineteen years old, and maybe well before that. While her Dad was alive, she kept her mouth shut, but after he died she let me have it, all right. When you went off to war, she made my life a misery. Anyroad, we signed a pact, me and her, to protect ourselves from each other. Now she says she's going to find my copy and burn it, like she's already destroyed hers. That's why she wanted to stay here, so she could look everywhere and get herself off the hook."

Arthur stared at Marian. What could it be and how bad was it? What on earth could have started the feud?

"Can you tell me about it, Marian?" he asked, putting his hand on hers.

She shook her head. "I wish I could, Arthur, I wish I could." Marian sighed a quivery sigh. "It lies heavy on my heart, but I daren't breathe a word right now or break the vow I made. I'll carry it to my grave, I think."

He gathered the tea things and put them on the tray. "Well, I'd better see if she's still hanging around and then I'll be away. Rita will be back when she's able. Don't you worry none, Marian. I'll ask the copper to keep watch. I'll tell him somebody tried to break into the house."

"Please don't do that, Arthur," Marian said, with alarm. "They'll start asking questions. Everyone on the street will already know she's been here, and seen you toss her out and her stuff as well. She sure made enough noise."

He scratched his head. "Aye, that's right. I can bet she's down at the pub right now giving them all the gory details," he said bitterly. "Why can't she go away and stay away?"

"Right enough. Here, what happened to that child of hers?" Arthur looked at her with astonishment. How did Marian know about it? He had told no one but Molly.

Marian grinned as she saw his mind ticking over. "It's all right, Arthur, Rita told me ages ago she'd seen her in Wigan, and she was pregnant. Don't forget now you hinted at it yourself back then and I'd already put two and two together. Anyroad, I didn't want to ask Sheila in case she fetched it along tomorrow."

"Rita knew? Our Rita?" Arthur looked shocked. Putting the tray onto the chest of drawers, he stood looking at her, eyes blank and unseeing. Rita had said not a word. How it must have hurt her to find her mother looking like that, and what *had* she thought of him?

Marian saw his expression and knew what he was thinking. "It's all right, lad. Rita is still a child in many ways, but she's got a good head on her shoulders. She was right put out at first, especially since her mother told her to go away and not come back. What a thing to happen, eh? Her own mother turning her away. Like me with Sheila tonight, except Sheila is as hard faced a bitch as they come. She was living in some fleapit on a back street, so Rita told me when she said she'd been to see her. I think that bothered her more than owt else."

"It would an'all, it would," Arthur said, pulling at his lower lip. So young Rita hadn't mentioned it to him or Molly: she had carried the weight of around on her young shoulders. Suddenly he felt a surge of love for his daughter. Whether she was protecting herself, him or her mother didn't matter, she had shouldered it alone.

He picked up the tray. "Right, I'd better go and check the street and then get off home. I'll check and then come back, and if she's not around, I'll leave by the back gate. I'll make sure to lock up 'cos she's a sneaky one, that."

"That she is an' all. Thank you, Arthur, thank you very much," Marian said with a great deal of feeling.

"Think nothing of it, Marian, call me whenever you need me."

Arthur checked the street carefully, walked to one end and then the other. Nobody was around other than clog-shod miners clattering home from their shift. Going back into the house to tell her it was all clear, he left by the back door.

Rita was home within the hour and dashed upstairs to see her Gran.

"It's only me, Gran. I'm home," she yelled gaily as she ran up the stairs.

Marian smiled joyfully then composed her face as Rita burst into the room.

"Good grief, I thought it was a herd of stampeding wild elephants. What a terrible racket! You must have woken half the street, Rita, never mind the neighbours. What a commotion." Her actions belied her words as she held out her arms. Rita sat on the bed and hugged her close.

"She's gone. Hip hip hooray!" Rita said, throwing her arm in the air in a victory salute.

"Aye, she's gone, but it doesn't mean she won't be back, love," Marian said quietly.

"We'll make sure she isn't, Gran. You won't open the door unless you look out the window first. Right? She won't be able to crash in then."

"Right enough, I expect it was my own fault and I'm sorry you had to go through it."

Rita tucked her in and plumped her pillows. "Cocoa and then sleep, Gran," she said firmly.

The next day Rita looked up and down the street before she left for work.

"Nobody in sight, Gran," she called up the stairs. "I'm off to work now and don't you open the door for anyone . . . and I do mean anyone. You never know what tricks she'll get up to next. When Molly comes, she'll shout through the letter box."

Her mother didn't come back and Rita felt pleased her Dad had seen her off, although she realized it must have been difficult for him since he was married to her for so long. He didn't seem upset, though, when she saw him on his return to Wisteria cottage.

Gran settled down enough that by midweek she felt much better. The doctor, pleased with her progress, remarked to Rita how quickly her speech had recovered. The stroke had not gone deep, he told her.

"She'll see the rest of us out, Rita, you mark my words." She laughed, him a doctor an' all, although she knew it was simply a stale joke and one often said around the village about the oldsters.

Sunday after tea Rita went to the parlour and opened the cabinet. What would it be? With all the upset and Gran's precarious health, she didn't want to choose anything that might cause her any distress.

The dance card? No, that was from the time of the fan. The cup and saucer? That too might be a lost love. The valentine card? Definitely not. The pair of tiny china figurines? What could they denote? Yes, she would choose them.

"Well, and what is it to be this week?" Marian asked as she poured the tea.

"These, Gran," Rita said setting the tiny figures on the table.

Marian looked at them for a long moment, wondering what story she could tell. The sight of them upset her but she quickly camouflaged it. "Ah yes. Harlequin and Columbine. Great lovers, they were."

Rita settled down. She loved romantic stories and her Gran told them well.

1938

Marian was over fifty when she met him, the proverbial tall, dark, handsome man of her dreams.

Matthew Harding was a great success. Through hard work and gumption, he owned two factories and many properties; the manor house where they lived being part of his assets. She met him when he did a tour of the streets he had recently bought - thirtyfour terraced houses, all in need of repair.

While on his first inspection visit, he came into number twenty-two. The minute their gaze met, she knew she would see him again. It felt like a bolt of lighting passed between them.

By this time her hair showed some grey, but she still possessed a trim figure, her eyes were bright and her legs were good. He held her hand for one second too long and squeezed it warmly. Marian smiled up at him, an invitation in her look. Well, she told herself, because I have a few grey hairs, doesn't mean I'm dead.

Her husband Harry, though, had not aged well. He had too quickly degenerated into an old man who relished sitting idle, listening to the radio, or reading his paper night after night. Harry no longer went to the lodge, as after falling out with a member, he let his membership lapse. When she asked him, he complained beer upset his stomach. Marian missed her quiet evenings alone because now he managed to be constantly underfoot, not seeming to sense she would prefer the odd evening to herself.

Matthew winked at her with a roguish eye as he followed his agent through to the front room. He inspected the ill fitting window frame, that allowed in the rain, saw where the plaster was falling off in chunks.

"I'll come back to check on the workmen's progress, Mrs. Haydon," he said, smiling down at her and shaking her hand, again holding it too long. The agent openly stared at them, knowing something was afoot. Marian cacked her nose at him. Sod the man. It's none of his business, anyway.

All day long she saw Matthew's face in her memory. He was handsome, so handsome and tall with it too, so she needed to tip her head way back. He was not a young man, oh no, he must be at least her own age by his grey hair and wrinkles.

Well, wasn't it strange how love came at funny times? She didn't doubt what she felt was love, the same love she had felt for Morris, for Gordon, for Geoff. The shame of it all was that she loved them and yet never knew them. No, she'd stuck it out with dull old Harry all these years.

She was singing, "I've got my love to keep me warm," when Harry arrived home.

He glanced at her as he took off his boots. "Oh aye? Somebody's happy today. What happened? Win the football pools, did we?"

She felt flustered but managed to say, "No, sorry, Harry, no such luck. Yet it was a good day because the new landlord was around with his agent, and they're going to fix the house. All the damp in the parlour, *and* the roof, *and* the back wall. We might even get a new front door, from what I heard him say."

Harry gaped at her. "My word, he's a new broom, all right. About time we got somebody in to see to this lot. A couple more years and it would have fallen down around our ears. It's only being in a terrace that keeps half these houses standing."

That was true enough because the old landlord never did any

maintenance. The row houses were jerry-built to start with and over the years they deteriorated into little more than hovels. Roofs at the end of the rows leaked badly and damp rotted every window because none were fitted properly at installation. Nor were the houses painted after the first coat nearly a hundred years earlier unless the tenants did it themselves. Subsidence from the old mines below caused the street drainage to sink and shatter so it was useless in wet weather.

They knew, of course, families who accepted this dilapidation as the normal state of affairs and yet others who worked diligently to prevent their homes from collapsing. Harry always refused to work on the house. He paid rent, he said, why should he improve the landlord's property when the man could tell them to leave any time? If they did do the place up, the landlord could put them out and get another tenant who would pay more.

Marian stopped trying to change his ideas on the state of the house years ago as their house was no worse, and maybe better, than the others. Once the state of the front door had upset her so much that she scraped and painted the door and front window frame herself. That was years ago. She had not bothered doing anything since as Harry told her off for wasting his hard earned money.

"Aye, about time we got some'at for our money. We've paid for this house ten times over since we've been here, and, let's face it, the previous tenants did the same," he said, lighting his pipe. Picking up his paper, he disappeared behind its screen.

Marian did not care what he thought and did not try to argue about it as she usually would. If he read his paper, it left her free to think about Matthew Harding.

Wasn't it strange she felt like a young woman because a man winked at her and held her hand one second too long? Still, he had done it twice. His gaze held all kinds of secrets, so much so she was keenly aware of her own sexuality in his glance. Her, an old lady, well, she sometimes felt like an old lady - until Matthew looked at her like that. Now she felt light as a feather, as giddy as a teenager.

It was nearly a month before she saw him again. He was walking down the street with his agent as she was returning home from the shops.

He tipped his hat to her as she neared. "Mrs. Haydon," he said, smiling. The sun peeped out from behind a cloud and it was as though a spotlight held him. His teeth looked so even and white and his cheeks were pink from outdoor walking. Handsome, he was, and she felt an intense physical attraction for him. Her breath caught in her throat and she blushed furiously. Me, blushing? Who would have thought I still could?

"Mr. Harding." She almost curtsied. Stupid idiot, she thought, stop this. You're making a right fool of yourself.

He removed his hat as he spoke to her. "Have the men seen to your house yet?"

"No, not yet. Would you like a cup of tea?"

The agent glared at her. She hadn't looked at him once. Obviously she did not include him in the invitation.

"That would be most welcome, Mrs. Haydon," Matthew turned to the man. "Reg, I'll see you at the end house in half an hour."

Marian opened the door and stood aside to let him enter.

"After you, please," he said, the prefect gentleman.

"Well, I thought . . . after all, it's your house. You own it." She laughed up at him and went down the hall to the kitchen.

Why did she feel so silly and juvenile? Why did her heart beat so fast? Why did she feel hot and bothered? Why did she feel like throwing herself into his arms? All the time she was hoping she had left things tidy, not wanting him to think her a sloppy housekeeper.

Before she took off her coat, she put on the kettle. "Sit down, Mr. Harding, make yourself at home."

"Well, it is my house, so *you* make yourself at home." He laughed as he removed his overcoat, tossed it on the settee and sat comfortably at the table. At least she had put on a new tablecloth this morning and it was spotless.

Marian made the tea and took down her best china cups, thinking he looked too high class for mugs.

"Can I have a mug instead, please?" he asked when she set the cups on the table. "Those are too fragile and my finger won't fit through the hole in the handle."

That made her laugh and she got down the everyday mugs. "Too bad. You're a country lad like the rest and to think I thought you were a toff," she joked, already at ease with him.

He laughed. "Not me, lass. I was born not two miles from here. My Dad was a miner and my Ma a mill worker. Anyway, a mug is the best way to drink a good cuppa char and I bet you make one of the best, Marian."

Her heart contracted: he knew her name.

"I asked someone your name," he said as if reading her thoughts. "I like you, Marian, you're my kind of lady."

She felt flattered, but then her head told her he was married. "What about your wife? Is she aware of your eye for the ladies?" Her voice came out shaky and she felt embarrassed to have spoken so bluntly.

He snorted. "My wife? You've got to be joking. I doubt if she's aware I'm on the same planet these days. She simply expects the money to turn up in her bank account and hardly speaks to me."

It sounded like the usual lament of a married man, Marian thought, a man who had grown apart from his wife, like she had grown apart from Harry. Somehow, though, it didn't make her think any less of him.

"Tell me, did you marry money, or make it for yourself?" she asked sharply. It was rude, she knew it, but she wanted to know more about what made him tick. Matthew didn't seem to mind her straight questioning.

"Oh, I made a tidy pile when I went into machinery manufacturing, then I met a man who owned a factory manufacturing car parts." He leaned back in the chair balancing it on two legs.

If that were Harry, she thought, I'd push him back and tell him not to do it, that he'd break the chair.

"It was through him that I met my wife. She's beautiful in a hardasnails way, and I was flattered she even spoke to me, a young chap with hardly any brass. Yet it didn't take long after wedding her to discover she had no heart. She likes money and all that it fetches." He smiled grimly. "She's decorative, but that's all she is."

"Do you have children?"

"No, thank God." He chuckled. "Estelle could never give birth, it might mess her hair. The conception alone wouldn't suit her. 'Too messy,' she'd say . . . and does, I might add."

"Oh, you," Marian said, laughing as she poured tea into the earthenware mugs.

Reg knocked on the door an hour and a half later and they were still talking. Marian went through the rest of the afternoon in a daze. She had fallen in love with him: she loved Matthew Harding.

For two weeks he stayed away, for two weeks she was crazy for him as he occupied her every thought. She became so preoccupied that Harry wondered what troubled her, and she noticed him looking at her when he thought she wasn't watching.

Marian felt sick with love. She dreamed about Matthew almost every night, about making love with him, about his lips kissing her entire body. What a silly old fool she felt. At her age she should know better. At her age she should not be thinking about sex, about kissing, she should be doing old lady things, knitting maybe or making jam.

The day he knocked on the door she was putting on her coat to go shopping. At least this time she looked half decent because she had been dressing up in case he stopped to visit. Today she wore her best dress, the one with the lace collar and cuffs. Of fine navy blue wool, it suited her fair complexion and blue eyes.

"Mr. Harding, sir. Please come in," she said, her voice joyous. Then she saw the agent behind him.

"All right, Reg," he said, brushing the man off. "I'll meet you at number sixteen in half an hour."

"Yes, sir," Reg said glowering at Marian. He knew what was going on all right. His expression said ii all.

They went into the kitchen where she put the kettle on to boil.

"Tea time?" He looked at his wrist watch. "I can't stay long, Marian. Don't call me Mr. Harding, please. We agreed you'd call me Matthew."

"I'd like to call you something else," she said flirting with him under her brows. Look at me, she thought, asinine old fool that I am, flirting with my eyelashes like a film star in one of those silly romances.

He moved around the table and took her into his arms.

"I've wanted to do this since I first met you. Marian? Look at me."

She put up her face and he kissed her. He kissed her like nobody had ever kissed her in her entire life. Her bones turned to jelly and she gasped for breath.

"Oh, Matthew," she breathed. "I think I love you."

His voice was warm, as he said, "I *know* I love you, Marian. I know it as surely as I know my own name."

They stood wrapped up in each other. Marian did not want to let go of him for a second and he held her close. She fit so comfortably into his embrace it was like she belonged there.

"Oh Matthew, what are we going to do?" she asked. It was suddenly too much. How could she fall in love at her age? What about Harry? What about Matthew's wife, Estelle? Surely what she felt was infatuation, a physical longing. It surely could not be an emotional ache but it was, it was, and she knew it.

"We'll find a way, my dear, we'll find a way." He kissed her again and they stood, arms around each other until someone hammered on the door.

"Damn and blast the man," Anger blazed in his tone. "I said I would meet him." He strode down the hall and opened the door. "What is it this time?" he barked.

She heard Reg saying: "You've been gone nearly an hour, Mr. Harding, sir. I thought maybe you'd gone back to the office."

An hour? They had been together an hour? Marian glanced at the clock. It had seemed like five minutes.

Matthew was alone when he came the next day. Marian again wore a good frock, one she had not worn for years. Her lovesickness had caused her to lose about ten pounds. It wasn't the latest style, but the shade of blue exactly matched her eyes. Last night she washed her hair and now it tumbled over her head in springy curls. Earlier she spent five minutes applying a discreet makeup. With a touch of mascara and lipstick she looked good, she thought, admiring herself. Oh, she knew she looked nice, and dimpled now under his appraisal.

What *am* I doing? I'm acting like a teenager and it never ceases to amaze me. The feelings I have inside are like when I met Geoff though I was only a teenager. Surely as we age, we become blasé about people, become cynical? Yet here I am as excited as I have ever been. Matthew Harding loves me and I love him.

To hide her feelings in front of Harry and Sheila was difficult. Sheila possessed such a nose for things. It was her innate inquisitiveness that did it, always prying, always alert to any change in atmosphere. Marian realized Sheila had noticed the difference in her when one evening she asked, "What's got into *you*, then?"

Marian looked at her, wondering what she had done differently. "What do you mean?" she asked, looking puzzled.

"I mean all this singing and smiling. You won the pools?"

Marian knew then she must make more effort because Sheila commenced staring at her as if trying to read her mind. Thank heavens the girl finally had a job, she thought, one that kept her out till six each evening.

Sheila served behind the counter at a wallpaper shop, the only type of work for which she was fit. Marian spent two weeks writing out a chart showing the number of rolls down one side and the prices across the top so Sheila could look up how much an order totalled. As Sheila's knowledge of mathematics was rudimentary, she'd lost two previous shop jobs for charging too much, not enough, or giving the wrong change.

Alone now, Sheila and Harry out at work, Marian gaily sang as she tidied the kitchen. Maybe today *he* would come. The nervous anticipation made her heart sing, and it seemed like she kept her ears continually pricked. At one point she turned off the radio in case she heard his footsteps, but then the house seemed too quiet. She turned it on again, low.

When he did knock on the front door, she nearly had a heart attack. That surely must be Matthew, though it could be the workmen coming to fix the front window. She scurried along the hall, her pulse racing.

"Good morning, Mrs. Haydon," he said as a woman passed them.

"Good morning, Mr. Harding," she said, standing aside to let him enter.

As she shut the door and they stood in the hall, he turned to her and pulled her into his arms. She drowned in his kiss.

"Oh Matthew, what are we going to do?" she gasped.

"Marian, I love you more than anything on this earth and I'd move heaven and hell to be with you. I need you, Marian, I need you so much."

Marian pulled him to the foot of the stairs and took him to the bedroom.

"I think you and I were made for each other," he said as he raised himself on an elbow the better to look into her face.

"Yes, I think we were." Marian pulled him down again and they did not talk.

As their relationship deepened, they spent time talking about their difficult situation. Marian was all for leaving Harry and moving in with Matthew. Her, a Godfearing Christian, who castigated anyone else for living over the brush, now talked about it as though it were nothing. These days it wasn't, but it certainly was to her generation.

Matthew, she thought, sounded more sensible, making it seem as if his only thought was of Marian's reputation. She was blithely unaware that, after much thought, Matthew realized he would never be happy living in sin. He told her he had to consider his wife Estelle, a vindictive person, who could make things difficult. Also, he had his businesses to think about, his factories to consider. The trouble was, and he did not tell Marian this, everything was in both their names. That had been part of their marriage agreement, so Estelle held him in the palm of her hand and could break him.

For three months he came around to Marian's as his men worked on each house. The street's residents considered him a wonderful man and Mr. Harding became the topic of many conversations: how much detail he went into, how he insisted everything be done perfectly.

"Oh aye," they said, "the new landlord is a grand man."

He did not always enter the house through the front door - he knew how to get down the back ginnel right enough. Marian usually worked facing the kitchen window, watching for him. While she waited, she would hold conversations with him in her mind. Her mental image of herself showed a witty, delightful woman and she sometimes laughed aloud at her own brilliance. She knew, though, when they were face to face all her erudition left her mind. Then all she could see was Matthew, and all she could think about was making love.

The emotions he aroused in her astonished and confused: tenderness, passion, peace, joy, merriment and plain old-fashioned lust. Life held new meaning and she saw things in a warm glow, brushed off petty annoyances as if they were nothing, spent her days smiling.

They were making love one afternoon when Sheila arrived home unexpectedly. The shop manager had sent her home because she had complained of feeling sick.

"What the hell is going on here?" she yelled. It was the first moment they heard anything because they were so wrapped up in each other.

Sheila stood inside the bedroom door, her face a mask of disbelief. Her mother in bed with another man? She had seen enough to know her mother was loving it.

"Who is this man?" she shouted, pulling at the eiderdown. "What is he doing in my Dad's bed?"

Matthew grabbed at the eiderdown to cover himself, not knowing what to do. Marian wondered how he could get to his clothes and saw his brow become damp with perspiration. She felt sure his mind searched to find a way out of the dilemma. Her own heart beat frantically as she almost panicked.

"Sheila, get out of right now," she said. Angry words would not help, nor would shouting, so she kept her voice flat and quiet.

Sheila slammed out, angrily crashing shut the bedroom door and thumped downstairs: even her footsteps sounded angry. Struck dumb, they looked at each other as they heard her ranting and raving in the kitchen where she started slamming around pots and pans, poking at the fire.

"What are we going to do?" Matthew asked, his face white and shocked.

Marian felt like her life was finished. Her daughter had caught her in bed with a man. They were both stark naked so no one could mistake what was happening and she couldn't say he was raping her. She couldn't deny her sin.

"Come on, get dressed. I've got to talk to her," she said getting out of the bed and picking up her underwear.

Matthew dressed quickly, throwing on his clothes carelessly. All she wanted to do right then was get him out of the house. Oh lord, what had they done to her marriage? Surely she had ruined her relationship with her daughter and Sheila would probably tell Harry. It did not bear thinking about. Fortunately Matthew was unaware of Sheila's vindictive nature.

"So that's your daughter," he said, breaking the stunned silence. "She must look like her father, there's nothing of you about her," he added as he buttoned his shirt with shaking hands, trying to defuse the situation.

"There's nothing of him in her, either, that I can see," Marian said as she ran a brush through her tousled hair, "If I hadn't had her at home, I would think I got the wrong baby. My son Roger is the spitting image of his dad."

They kissed softly and she put her head against his chest. "Please don't worry, Matthew. I'll sort it out," she said with more confidence than she felt.

He left quietly by the front door, unwilling to face Sheila again. Marian went into the kitchen where Sheila sat in the chair by the fire, her face like thunder, beating her hands in a tattoo on the wooden arms.

"How long has this been going on?" Sheila shouted as she shot to her feet. "Tell me, do you charge for your favours, or is this one of your regular lovers?"

"No need to be nasty, Sheila," Marian said evenly as she put on the kettle. Better to keep one's temper and talk it out.

"My word, we are being adult about this, aren't we? How do you think I feel?" Sheila's voice sounded harsh with anger, with betrayal, with some emotion Marian didn't recognize as being in her daughter. "I come home and find my mother in bed with a strange man and you were loving it. You're nothing but a trollop, just like that Agnes woman said."

Marian stared at Sheila, at the hatred on her face. What could she say in her own defence? She began to fuss with the table cloth, unable to look at her daughter, needing to do something with her hands.

Then came the sound of running feet and people shouting.

"What on earth?" Sheila said, as ever snoopy, quickly went out to the front room window. "Looks like somebody got hurt," she said as she came back. "A workman, I expect." She scrutinized her mother.

Marian stayed by the sink, feeling witless and at a loss for words. While she could see no excuse for what she had done, she didn't think it necessary to apologize for anything, but she must say something. She couldn't stand here like a lump of wood and let Sheila whittle away with her tongue. What could she say in her own defence, what defence was there for committing adultery?

"Somebody got hurt," Sheila said again as she sat in the wooden arm chair and glared. "Right, let's have it. Who is he and how long has this been going on?" Her face was closed and malicious.

Marian gestured with both hands, as if tossing something to the wind. "What's that to you, Sheila? The only thing that matters is that you saw me with him." She raised her chin, thinking telling the truth was better. "If you must know, that man is the love of my life, the man I want to live with, a man maybe to marry, spend the rest of my days with. He's the only man I've ever loved."

Sheila raised her eyebrows. "Oh? Is that a fact? So you don't count them other chaps?"

Her heart skipped a beat. "What other chaps? I never knew anyone else." Marian flushed hotly, her world shattered by the words. How could Sheila know about anyone other than Matthew?

Sheila barked a short laugh. "Less of your lies, Mam. I know all about you, you've got ants in your pants, you have. You can't wait to get your knickers off. I know you like the fellows, all right, and so does half the village."

"What?" Marian gasped. She had been so careful with her every affair. How could anyone possibly know? Obviously she hadn't been as clever as she thought.

"Oh yes, I remember Morris," Sheila started to add them on her fingers, "The chap you took up with in Blackpool. I might have been a kid, Mam, but I knew what was going on. Then you had his lordship, didn't you? Agnes Reilly knew all about him, didn't she? My word, you were a busy little bee. In fact the entire street knew about you and his lordship. Them servants get around and they talk, you know. Then a chap who moved away, I never did get his name." Her voice was scornful now and her face evil. "You used to screw him down by the river. Oh yes, I heard all about it from another woman whose mother often talked about you. You were the village Jezebel according to her, and to think I used to defend you. Then I know about Jimmy who worked at Hillside Farm. You and he used to go at it in a hut in the woods. Sounds like most of the chaps who worked up at Hillside would have . . .,"

Marian stood transfixed, dumbfounded but she to say something. "Now wait a minute here, don't I get to say anything? That's a load of old rubbish. I never . . .,"

"You never what? Never met a man you didn't want to screw? You're nothing but a cat in heat, and to think you're my mother!" Sheila spat in the fire to end her tirade.

Marian said nothing more. What could she say? What words would change the charged atmosphere? She had no excuse for what she had done. None that made any sense. She stood gazing at the fire as if to find an answer in the flames. Sheila would myther the subject to death and Marian only hoped she ran out of steam so they could talk sensibly before Harry arrived home from work. If anyone was going to tell Harry. it would be herself, not foul mouthed Sheila.

Sheila started again on her invective. "I'm ashamed to be part of this family. There's Dad walking around like he's blind and deaf, and you sitting around with your head in the bloody clouds, smirking and thinking you're so bloody clever in pulling the wool over everyone's eyes, dreaming about your latest romance. The priest used to tell me how many sins fornication added up to, and your soul is as black as pitch. You'll burn in hell forever, Mam."

Marian cleared her throat. "Sheila, can we talk about this? I've heard enough of your blather now. I know how you feel . . .,"

"You know how I feel?" she screeched. "How could *you* possibly know how I feel? How I've suffered all my life because you're a fallen woman? How often I've wanted to tell Dad, but I couldn't. It would have devastated him, and I thought more of him than that. I used some of my knowledge of your activities with you to get things I wanted, although I never told you I knew everything, now did I?"

Marian sighed. It was not going well, but why should it be? Sheila was a nasty young woman, no mistake about that. From this day forward she foresaw nothing but strain between them.

"No, Sheila, you didn't, but I'm sure you're going to spill the beans to your father now, aren't you? All I ask is you let me tell him first, before you put in the boot."

Someone rapped at the back door. Marian turned and looked out the window, praying it was not Matthew. She saw Ruth, her next door neighbour. "Come in, Ruth, the door's open," she called. At least with someone else in the house Sheila might stop her ranting. Ruth hurried in, her shawl wrapped tightly around her chest.

"Oh, Marian," she said, her face grief-stricken and streaked with tears. As she came into the kitchen, she wiped her eyes on her apron, and said, "Hello, Sheila lass," then blew her nose on a grubby duster.

Marian took her arm and seated her in a chair. "What on earth is it, Ruthy? You look upset. Here, sit there and I'll get you a nice cup of tea." Marian bustled around, glad to be doing something.

Ruth made sure they were both paying attention. "It was horrible, horrible. I saw gallons of blood all over the road. You never saw anything like it. They had to use buckets and buckets of water to flush it down the grid."

"All right, Ruth." Marian patted her hand. "What are you talking about? Tell the story from the start," She put an arm around Ruth's shoulders, comforting her. At the best of times Ruth succumbed to hysteria.

"I was coming back from the co-op and when I saw it," Ruth said, relishing having the floor. "They were standing looking at something on the ground outside Scrivens' house."

"Who were?"

"A bunch of workmen and that chap, the agent."

"What happened, Mrs. Beavis? Come on, spit it out," Sheila said. She waved her hands irritably as if it would hurry her.

"Leave off, Sheila, Ruth's upset enough without you chiming in," Marian said as she went to pour boiling water on the tea pot.

"W..e..l..l," Ruth related, her voice dropping because it was so horrific, "When I got closer I saw it was a man. He was covered in blood and it was running down into the gutter." She shuddered theatrically. "They said he was dead and someone had gone for the police and the doctor. 'It's too late for a doctor,' the agent chap said, 'he's a goner. That's his jugular vein. They can't sew that up.'"

Marian shuddered and saw Sheila agog. She loved disasters.

Ruth shook her head. "I was shocked the way they all stood looking at him like. 'Cover him over,' I said, 'show a little respect.' Then someone got a tarpaulin and they put it over him."

"What happened? Come on, tell us." Sheila asked, curious as always.

"Well, I noticed some workmen on the roof mending it and apparently four slates slid off on that side while he stood at the edge of the pavement watching other chaps on our side replacing slates. They said he was almost dee-capitated," she relished the word. "Dee-capitated means the slates almost cut off his head," she said by way of explanation.

"I know what it means, Mrs. Beavis," Sheila chirped. "I did go to school. I know you didn't, but . . .,"

Marian glared at her. "All right. Sheila, all right," she snapped. "No need to lash out at Ruth, she's done nothing to you."

Sheila shrugged and turned her attention back to Ruth.

"It was something to see, though." It was plain Ruth had enjoyed it, no matter how upset she was. "His arteries pumped out the blood and nobody could do anything. He was unconscious, they said, so that was a blessing."

"Huh! Some blessing. Almost got his head taken off and it was a blessing?" Sheila interrupted nastily. She sat with her head on her hands, elbows on her knees. "Tea ready yet?"

Marian glanced at her and saw the raised eyebrows, the smug smirk. She moved toward the teapot.

"A right nice gentleman he was, and all," Ruth wittered. "You liked him, didn't you, Marian? Aye, he fixed up these houses right proper, so he did. Might have known we couldn't be so lucky as to have him looking after us interests for long."

An icy hand wrapped itself around Marian's heart, squeezed hard and her heart skipped a beat. Now her pulse began to race, her heart to pound. No! Not Matthew, it couldn't be Matthew. She could not speak and her hands flew to her mouth. Her face a mask of horror, she plopped heavily down on a chair and put her head in her hands, numb with shock. "Not Matthew, please God," she muttered.

"You mean that chap who now owns these houses?" Sheila asked, her face suddenly smiling and happy. "You mean the new landlord, a tall chap with wide shoulders?"

"Aye, a right lovely chap, too," Ruth said, shaking her head. "His poor wife will be heartbroken. Mind you, he's got a pile of brass, from what I hear She'll be all right, I expect."

Marian heard her voice in the distance, muted and flat, twittering on and on and yet she felt numbed.

"Still and all, to lose your mate, it's hard. I know about that, all right. I know what it feels like to have your love taken from you in a split second." She snapped her fingers with a loud crack. "My Fred he was right as rain in the morning, yet he got felled by an 'eart attack as he was getting off the bus half an hour later."

Marian felt anaesthetized. Where her heart had been was an empty husk and her mind was blank. Matthew was dead and to think she pushed him out today because of Sheila. Her face was ashen and her eyes vacant.

Sheila, a nasty smile on her face, looked at her mother. "What about that, Mam?" She turned to Ruth. "Do have another cup of tea, Mrs. Beavis," she said chummily. "Then tell us about it again. I want to hear all the gory details."

Ruth did not need any encouragement. She liked an audience and Sheila hung on her every word, making her search her memory for every petty detail.

Marian let it wash over her like a tide of acid. She didn't want to hear it, oh God, she didn't want to hear. Yet what could she say? She could not tell Ruth to shut up, to stop relating her adventure. Her stomach clenched itself into a tight knot and she felt sick, deathly sick. Now her heart palpitated as if she had run a mile and she gasped for air. He was gone, her lovely love, he was dead. How could she go through life without him? Without his assurance one day they would be together?

Ruth eventually ran out of steam and started repeating herself. Marian stood, feeling like her limbs were heavy as lead. "It's been a great shock, this has," She looked at Sheila as she added, "to everybody."

Sheila smiled gleefully and Marian felt like hitting out at her, but knew it wouldn't solve anything. She saw Ruth to the door and patted her shoulder.

"You get some rest, love. It's been a shock to your system."

Not half as much as it's been to mine, she thought, her stomach cramping with the knowledge she would never see him again, never kiss him, never again make love with him. Her life was also ended.

As she sat at the table, Sheila looked at her, grinning malevolently. "So, he's kicked the bucket, your fancy man, eh? Gone to push up the daisies." She was almost laughing with glee.

"All right," Marian said, retaliatory energy flooding through her as she contemplated Sheila's evil expression. "That's put you all right now, hasn't it? You're chuffed because he's dead. Shows what a rotten person you are, you ill-tempered shrew. You were always cruel, cruel in words and cruel in deed."

Sheila tossed her head. "Aye, and I've reason to take it out on you now, haven't I?" Marian turned away to hide the tears. "Knowing what I know will make my life around this house a whole lot easier . . . or do you want me to tell my Dad what you get up to when he's out at work? Shows how thick he is, not knowing about you after all these years."

Marian whirled around to face her. "Don't talk about your father like that!"

"Oh, so now you'll come to his defence, will you? My Dad, who you've treated like a bloody door mat all these years. What about the years you've been carrying on and him not knowing what a two-faced bitch you are? If he is my real Dad, that is, and only you know that." She smiled as she heard Marian gasp. "The man has to be a few bricks short of a load not to see it. People hint it to him. I know, I've heard them, but he thinks the sun shines out of your arse."

Marian let the irritation wash over her, but made no move to rise. She simply sat with her chin in her hands and looked at her daughter.

"We must talk about this, Sheila." Unshed tears made her voice strained and it felt hard to talk. "Talk it out. Not today, I can't talk today. Leave me some time to grieve for him. We'll talk Saturday when your Dad goes on his dart match."

Sheila's tone scalded. "I'm supposed to feel sorry for you, I suppose? Well, that's not on for a start. Anyroad, it so happens I'm going out for supper tonight with a new fellow and I'll not be back until late. I got sent home from work because I felt sick, but this has perked me up no end." She pushed at her hair and stood to look at her reflection in the mirror over the fireplace. "He's a nice chap, is Arthur, and I wouldn't want to let him down. Don't wait up, will you? You know how it is when a chap wants some of the old slap and tickle." Roaring with laughter, she sauntered up the stairs.

Marian got tea ready, her body operating on automatic. She made a bacon, egg and onion pie and prepared the cabbage for the pot. How could she face Harry now, knowing Sheila was bound to tell him if she didn't?

Then she ran upstairs. Today when he arrived Matthew had given her a present of Columbine and Harlequin. Setting them down on the bedside table as she shed her clothes, she had regarded them with delight thinking them a lovely gift. Tiny and precious, made of china and hand painted, they each stood on a grassy hillock and around their feet were flowers and grass. Each had one hand outstretched, heads over the shoulder looking at someone, and when Matthew sat them down next to each other she could see they were striving to touch each other.

"Like us two, that is," he said, "I thought of us when I saw them in the antique shop. Reaching out, always reaching out, yet never able to be close on the same patch of grass."

"Oh Matthew, they're beautiful," she said as she picked them up and admired their colours. "I'll always think of today when I look at them. They'll go right into the china cabinet in a place of honour."

Then she put them down, stepped into his arms and they forgot the figurines.

Now she looked at them. So perfect, so tiny and so absolutely horrible. Tears filled her eyes. Yes, she would always remember today. Now she never wanted to see them again, and yet she did. They were all she had left of him, but they could not replace him in her heart.

Quickly she made the bed, straightened up the evidence of her infidelity and shed a few tears.

"So that was when he bought them. Your granddad said they were like us, always at arms length. He wasn't a demonstrative person, your granddad, lovey. He found it hard to say words of love or show affection. Still, like you said, he was a grand chap altogether."

Marian didn't know how she had come up with the story. The pain of holding the figurines was intense even now.

'Matthew,' her heart called, 'I'm thinking about you even as I tell this child a pack of lies.' Then she prayed mentally, 'Forgive me God, I lie to her all the time and yet she thinks I'm wonderful.'

"Lovely story, Gran," Rita said as she looked at the figures. "They must be worth a lot of money. They're so perfect."

"Aye, he said that, perfect, he called them." She meant Matthew, of course, not Harry.

"I know they were in a second hand shop, but they're so well made I think you should have them valued."

"No, put them back in the cabinet," Marian said. "When I die, they'll all belong to you and you can do what you want with them then."

She didn't want to think about what they meant to her. Didn't want this pain in her heart, didn't want to cry in front of Rita.

"I think I'd like an early night," she said, rising with some difficulty. "My rheumatics, or should I say as you told me, 'my arthritis' is bothering me today."

"Oh Gran, why didn't you say?" Rita said suddenly noticing her Gran's pallor. "Come on, we'll get you up to bed and I'll fetch you a hot toddy. That'll be nice, won't it? It'll help you sleep."

"Aye, only don't use so much whisky this time, love. The last time you made one I passed out, never mind slept, and my head was hammering when I woke. Talk about a hangover."

When Gran was in bed and nodding off, Rita went down to the front room where she put the figures back in the cabinet. She looked at the rest of the things. All this was to be hers? Of course she didn't want her Gran to die, but Marian was an old lady and death came to everyone. Full of joy at her inheritance and yet dreading losing her Gran, she picked things up and replaced them, thrilled now they belonged to her.

All her life she could recall being fascinated by the cabinet. Bow-fronted, each small window consisted of bubble glass like an oldfashioned shop front. The piece itself was worth a great deal of money and it showed in the fine lines and patina.

When it belonged to her, she knew she would never part with a thing. Each item would remind her of her grandparents, of her heritage. Everything had a happy memory attached to it, whether a cheap gimcrack or a piece of expensive china or silver.

CHAPTER ELEVEN

1938

Marian and Sheila eventually talked, though all it resulted in was an uneasy animosity. It was only after thinking it out, that Marian's argument won the day in her favour. What was the use of destroying Harry for nothing, she asked Sheila? The affair was over and done with Matthew's death.

Now they ignored each other, even while in the same room. Harry noticed nothing - he never did. As long as Marian served his meals on time and he had a clean shirt, nothing much bothered him.

Sheila became furious when her young man Arthur threw her over. As usual, she tried to find a way of blaming his renunciation on someone else, but in her heart realized it was her own fault. She had been too grasping, too greedy, too demanding. And, she told her Dad, his mother had a lot to do with it because it was on his mother's insistence Arthur said he wanted to stop seeing her. That had caused a terrible row.

"Not going out tonight, Sheila?" Harry asked. "You usually go to the pictures Wednesday with your young man, don't you?"

Sheila tossed her head."He's not my young man anymore, Dad," she said. "He's at home with his mother. A bloody Nancy boy. He's a Mary Anne."

Marian looked sharply at Sheila. So this was the reason she was in such a bitchy mood these last few days. Up to last Saturday, Arthur had been Sheila's knight in shining armour. Marian knew enough about

Arthur to know him as a caring person who probably stayed with his mother to look after her in her old age. That, in her books, made him nicer.

"Not like you to go out with one of them limp wristed chaps, is it, Sheila?" Harry said, lowering his paper.

"No, he was in disguise. Thinks more of his crabby old mother, than his girl friend."

Marian thought about it. Surely Arthur was an eligible young man? Hadn't Sheila been sounding off about his virtues for weeks after she started going out with him? Back then, according to her ravings, he was everything a man should be, tall, dark and handsome and with prospects. Arthur worked at Pemberton Mills and was well thought of by the management, being in lower management. He wore a collar and tie to work with a brown coat overall to signify his position. That made him better than the other chaps she knew who wore overalls to work.

Marian wanted to say something about the rift, knowing it almost had to be Sheila's fault if they fell out, but she didn't. Yet only two days later Sheila announced she had a date with a new chap - a fellow she met on the bus coming home.

Her face wore its nasty smirk as she said. "He knows you, Mam. His dad's Archie up at Hillside Farm."

Marian flushed darkly.

Harry dropped his paper to look at her. "Oh aye, I know old Archie," he said, "He belongs to the lodge. Aye, he's got four sons. Which one is this?"

"Berty, Albert," Sheila said, "He's older then me, but then I can't stand little boys."

Marian said not a word. She didn't dare, and now she heard Archie belonged to the lodge? How much had he let slip about her to Harry?

For almost a year the family lived in comparative peace. Sheila went out almost every night, and when she did stay home, she went to bed early. Probably catching up on her beauty sleep, Marian thought cynically, glad to have her out of the way.

One evening a young chap came to the door and passed Marian an envelope addressed to Sheila. When she gave it to her later, Sheila tore it open and stood so she concealed the note as she read the contents, screwed it up and tossed it on the fire. To make sure she burned every scrap, she held it down with the poker.

"What was that?" Marian asked, curious.

"Nothing to do with you, Mam." She lifted her chin and spoke sarcastically. "That's for me to know and you to worry about. Keep your nose out of things that are none of your concern."

Something niggled at Marian. "Who was that chap as brought it here? I never saw him before."

"You won't see him again, either. Forget it, Mam, it's nothing to do with you."

Sheila went upstairs and changed into a pair of slacks she'd bought the week earlier. Marian did not like to see women in trousers and the purchase sparked a week of argument. Now she said nothing, but tutted at the sight of Sheila dressed like a man.

"Off out again tonight?" Marian asked as she came down, tying a head scarf over her hair.

"Yes, so what? Who died and put you in charge of my love life?" She smirked as she looked at her mother. "At least *I've* got one."

Marian sighed. Things were becoming ever more difficult with Sheila now she had a weapon in her quiver. It would not take much for Sheila to run to Harry with a mouthful, so Marian needed to watch what she said.

"Still going out with Bert?" she asked.

Sheila snorted. "Bert? Give me a break. He's about as bright as a bag of soot. Wanting to marry me. Huh! As if I would even consider a knucklehead like him. No, I've got a new chap now. Ever so nice and he's got lots of money."

Marian cast her mind about the village and knew whomever Sheila was involved with either was from elsewhere, or married. She liked married men, did Sheila, as they supplied all sorts of treats and yet had no hold on her.

Years later Marian often thought about that unfortunate time in their lives, when Sheila and she were so antagonistic. Sheila was a real live wire back then, full of energy, full of the joys of life once away from the house. The neighbours often told her tales of Sheila being seen in Wigan or Bolton at dances or concerts. In the following years she changed a great deal, and had changed considerably by the time she was twenty-one and managed to snare back Arthur Goodwin.

A bus hit and killed his mother, which left Arthur with his own house. To land a chap who had property was a feather in her cap. He only rented it, housing being scarce in those days, but he had a house. So they married. Marian breathed a sigh of relief now that Sheila was out of her house.

1958

Rita was well into her twentieth year and looking forward to being twenty-one, an adult in her own right. Funny, she didn't feel any different and yet it was only two weeks to her birthday. She asked her Gran if being twenty-one, the magical age, suddenly gave you great powers or something.

Marian at seventy-three, was smaller and thinner. Her pure white hair stood out around her face in soft curls like angel hair floss. She was still good to look at and if you saw her from the back you could take her figure for that of a young woman.

Sunday they were having a birthday tea for Rita at Wisteria Cottage, and Marian baked a special cake in honour of the occasion. It had crossed silver keys on top and large candles shaped like twentyone. Rita, excited about the tea party, invited some friends from work. These days she worked at a new company that manufactured candelabra, both gas and electric. It was at the office she met Ian, the owner's son and they were courting.

Marian liked Ian. A good looking young man, he had a great deal of ambition. He obviously adored Rita as his eyes followed her every move. Oh yes, Rita could do far worse than Ian, Marian thought. It had taken the child long enough to find a boy friend and for ages there had been a steady procession of lads calling for her at the house that she never saw again.

Rita still lived with her Gran since Arthur had not asked her to move back to Wisteria Cottage. Not with Sheila on the loose.

Aye, Sheila. Marian was aware that Rita, often thought about her mother, wondering aloud where was she and what was she doing. Her Dad, overjoyed with his new life, shuddered when he heard her name. That was usually because Rita said something like 'my Mam used to,' or 'my Mam said,' but that was less often these days. To Rita it was like they had erased her mother from the family tree, as though she never existed. Yet she had existed and Rita, extremely well read these days, worried some mental instability inherent in her mother would rub off on her. She surely must have inherited some of her mother's genes and she prayed they were all good.

The possible transfer of defective genes bothered her now she loved Ian. She wanted children, lots of them, and to think a child of hers might turn out like her mother tormented her. Yet when she looked in a mirror she was the spitting image of her grandmother, which only went to show things could skip a generation. So while she was nothing like Sheila, surely her children might turn out to be like her mother.

One evening she decided to ask. "Gran?"

"Yes, lovey?"

"Don't take this the wrong way, Gran, but was my mother your real daughter?"

"What on earth do you mean, child?" Marian looked shocked. What a question to ask. What was going on in the girl's head now?

"What I mean is, was she adopted?" If they had adopted Sheila it would solve all Rita's problems, at least she thought it would. On the other hand it could be worse, for who knew what genes she might inherit?

"No. Indeed she was not, she was born upstairs in this house," Marian said, her tone insulted and sharpish.

Rita didn't want to upset Gran, but she needed to know. "Well, was *I* adopted? You can tell me, I'm almost twenty-one."

Marian found herself becoming angry and stared at Rita as if trying to see inside her head. "No, you were not and why would you ask such a terrible thing? Whatever is going on in that dizzy head of yours? What is all this?"

Rita sighed miserably. "I'm sorry, Gran, it's just that I love Ian and I think he's going to propose soon. I want to have children, Gran, lots of them, but if any of them are going to turn out like my mother, well, I wonder about it. I can't see me being a strict disciplinarian somehow."

The black cloud lifted. "Oh dear, you *are* getting yourself into a tizzy about nowt, aren't you?" Marian chuckled. Better to make light of it and set Rita's mind at ease, rather have a post mortem about what made her mother tick. "There is absolutely no way any of your children will ever be like your mother."

"Yet Gran, I'm like you," Rita pointed out, "I inherited a lot of your genes so that means things can skip a generation. How do I know my Mam's genes won't come out in *my* children?"

"It's like a soup, isn't it?" Marian searched her brain for a few words that would bring back memories of articles she had read on genetics. They were into that thing these days and obviously Rita had read too much for her own good. Unfortunately she realized that in her harlot ways Sheila had taken after her. "How many brothers and sisters does Ian have?" she asked, giving herself time to think.

"Two sisters and one brother," Rita was puzzled. What did that have to do with anything?

"His mother, is she nice?"

"Oh yes, she's lovely, a real lady."

"What about his father? What's he like?"

"He's tall, very much in charge and nice, too."

"A real businessman, you'd say?"

"Oh yes, Gran. He's a good boss and has a warm way with people," Rita said smiling, picturing him in her mind.

"Who does Ian take after. Think carefully now, his mother or father?"

"His father, of course. He's got the height and the looks and has the same way of talking to people. You know, able to converse easily with all sorts." Her face revealed her love.

"What about his brother and sisters? Who do they take after?"

Rita screwed up her eyes, then closed them, thinking of what little she knew of the rest of the family.

"Well, they're all very much alike. His brother Anthony is tall, but has similar facial features to his mother, while his sisters don't look like either of their parents much. Mind you, they wear lots of makeup, but there's some of both parents in there. If you know what I mean."

Marian smiled. "I don't see any reason for you to worry about Ian, then. Now about you. Who do you take after?"

"Me? I suppose I take after my Dad in temperament. I look like you, though."

"What does that mean to you? Think it out now." She set the tea cosy over the newly made tea.

"It means I take after my Dad in disposition, after him in the way I think, too. I take after you in looks, that much I got from my Mam. That's the only good thing I did get from her when you think about it."

"Yes, love, you're like me In a lot of ways. Yet are you like your mother in any other way?"

"Not that I know of," Rita said her brow still rucked.

"Then you have nothing at all to worry about. If you'd been born with any of her genes, don't you think they would have come out long before now?"

Rita smiled, it was only a small smile so Marian knew she had not convinced her.

"Right, let's figure it out, then. Do you chase after men? Do you smoke and drink? Do you stay out all night, or come home with some chap's by blow in your belly?"

"Gran!" Rita was shocked at her Gran talking that way.

Marian poured the tea and set a cup in front of Rita. "Look here, Rita, you're nowt but a child in many ways. However, I know one thing and so do you, you no more take after your mother than that old cat of mine." Both looked to where Napoleon lay in the hearth, basking in the heat, fast asleep. "No, I take that back. It would insult the cat. If you'd any of her genes that mattered, they'd have shown in you by now. That means that if they haven't, then you don't have any bad ones to pass on, doesn't it? Stands to reason." It sounded good, although Marian knew it was a lot of baloney. The thing was to set Rita's mind at ease.

"Will it be all right, do you think?"

"Aaw, come here, Rita, love," Marian hugged her and kissed her cheek. "It'll be more than all right, lass, it'll be wonderful. You're your father's child all right. Your Mam and Dad had been on holiday when they were first wed. She hadn't started eyeing other men then, so you needn't worry. You're your Dad's child all right and you've got more of him in you than of her."

She grinned now and held Rita at arms' length. "So you think you're going to be an engaged lady before long, do you? What makes you think that?"

For now the doubts were pushed aside, Marian could tell as she listened to Rita babbling about Ian, how he looked at her and what he said. Yes, the girl was smitten and Marian was glad. Time the lass had some real happiness.

"Tell you what," Marian said, "Fetch me the tin from the sideboard and we'll look at some family snaps. That'll show you what gene pool you came from."

Together they looked at the old photos. "This is your Great-Uncle Simon," Marian said, "He was my Dad's brother. A handsome man, he was, tall and straight. Lost his life in the first World War. We called it the Great War back then." She chuckled as she pointed out another shot, "This is your GreatAunt Matilda, on my Dad's side. Matilda was a suffragette and proud of it," And looked it too, Rita thought, all bust and chin, corseted within an inch of her life. "Died in the influenza epidemic, she did. She lived in London at the time and worked in the slums. A saint of sorts, I think. She was always a charitable woman. Her husband made his money in manufacturing biscuit and cake tins, you know, and she gave it away as fast as she got her hands on it." She pointed to another browned photo. "This is my older sister Emily. Now she was a real beauty."

Rita looked at the cracked snap. All she could see was a fat, expressionless woman with lots of untidy hair.

After they had looked through all the snaps. It suddenly occurred to Rita none of the people depicted were alive, apart from her Gran. Unanticipated tears came to her eyes. Suppose something happened to her Gran? Suppose she died when Rita married, died of loneliness, died because she had nobody to look after her?

"What on earth is the matter with you now, child?" Marian asked, regarding her with concern. She was all raw emotion, was Rita, her nerves were always on the surface these days.

"Oh Gran. I'll never leave you. Not for Ian, not for anyone." She sobbed into the tea towel.

"Oh dear, time for tea again." Marian got up, moving stiffly after sitting for so long, and put on the kettle.

CHAPTER TWELVE

1959

"Yes, that was a lovely party, wasn't it?"

Marian and Rita were talking about her twenty-first celebration and the gifts she received. Some of them now sat in the china cabinet that Rita was cleaning in time for Christmas.

How time flew, Marian thought as she watched. One day it was Easter, then it was August bank holiday, then it was Christmas.

When she was little, the days lasted months, the months dragged by on snail's feet. Even when she was a young woman, time was on her side and still dragged its feet, especially if she were looking forward to something. Yet what was there for her now? Nothing. Time accelerated, it shrank, days sped by quickly. Time decreased, never enough time for anything it seemed, though these days she was almost housebound.

The children were coming home for Christmas day. These days that meant Roger and his wife Mavis and their two bratty kids, Rita and Ian, Arthur and Molly. Yes, it would be a full house all right and she hoped she was up to it as she tired so easily these days.

Rita was a gem of a lass, always there, always cheerful, always willing. Ian came around to clean the upstairs windows and scrub down the back yard bricks. He even whitewashed the yard walls and the kitchen was much brighter for the reflection it gave. Molly also helped, she brought casseroles and cakes from her bounteous kitchen and did the heavy washing in her new washing machine.

Aye, she was blessed all right, blessed with good family. She shook her head at her thoughts. What was she thinking, complaining about the fuss of Christmas? How many more would she see? As tears misted her eyes, she blew her nose. Rita spun around to look at her with concern.

"Are you all right, Gran? Not coming down with a cold, are you?"

"Oh do leave off, Rita, and take your hand off me." She pushed Rita's testing palm off her forehead. "I know you mean well, but please stop treating me like a baby."

"All right, Gran," Rita said, deciding to watch her Gran closely. "Let's get these done. You wash and I'll wipe. We can dust and clean the cabinet after that."

Marian attempted to be cheery and merry as they worked. No use giving the girl anything to worry about.

As they were putting things back in the now clean and shiny cabinet, Rita said: "This is special, Gran," passing her the valentine card that usually sat at the back of the top shelf. It was old, lace trimmed and hand-painted. The rose looked so lifelike, raised and velvety to the touch. Rita looked inside, but saw nothing written there other than "Guess who loves you?" in spidery writing in faded violet ink.

"Oh it was, Rita, very special."

"Who sent it? Do you know?"

"It weren't sent to me, lass," she chuckled, "Someone sent it to your Granddad before we married. A young lady I suppose. He liked it, or so it seemed to me because he kept it in his shirt drawer under everything and at the back. I put it in the cabinet and, do you know, he never noticed it was gone from his drawer? To top it all, he never noticed it in the cabinet, either. That's why it was on the top shelf. I thought he was bound to see it, but he never did, and if he did, he never said."

Marian stroked the rose. Who had sent this to Harry and why had he kept it? It was expensive, she knew that, and who would Harry know who could have afforded to buy such a thing? It was another thing she didn't know about him and yet he was always transparent, was Harry. It intrigued her, this valentine. It gave him an air of having a secret and he still did, because he died before she asked him about it.

1909

Harry Haydon was in love with Mary Gillespie. It wasn't a crush, either. He'd had lots of those. This was plain and simple love in its highest, purest form. She danced in front of his eyes each time he blinked. He saw her in every other young female with whom he came into contact. He dreamed of her, constantly daydreamed, and over the past week lost his appetite.

Harry, now twenty, worked for his uncle who ran a small construction company. It was while they were doing some alterations to Gillespie House when he first saw her.

Mary Gillespie celebrated her sixteenth birthday six months earlier. Shapely, pale complexioned with pink cheeks, she possessed a cheeky smile that warmed your heart. He noticed her reading a book as she sat on the lowest branch of an old pear tree outside the conservatory Mr. Gillespie had contracted his uncle to add a raised bed inside the conservatory with a gold fish pond and fountain.

"A pond for fish, how posh can you get," he said when his Uncle Sam told him what the job involved.

Gillespie House, a fine place, stood in acres of carefully cultivated and groomed land. Old man Gillespie, a banker, built the place only ten years earlier and each year he added yet another attraction to the already splendid house. Still, a pond for fish? And to also have a fountain! Well, Harry supposed if you had the money, you could buy anything, no matter how silly.

She giggled and he glanced up from his crouch as he mixed cement on a large board.

"Hello, down there," she said, smiling her cheeky smile.

He had to respond in kind. She looked so doll like in her full skirted organdie dress with the bows and frills.

"Hello. You live up there, do you? Are you a fairy?" he asked, cheeky too.

"Oh no," she laughed and it sounded like the tinkling of silver bells to his ears. "I sit here when I want to avoid my governess. She will make me go indoors and read at the table, or sit up straight in a hard backed chair."

"That doesn't sound too awful to me," he said, turning to the mixture and adding sand. Imagine having time to sit around reading?

"Oh, but it is, you see. She is very strict and even my Mamma can't move her once she has made up her mind. Never mind, I shall not need a governess soon and they will dismiss her."

Harry glanced up again. She seemed unconcerned about the woman, and why shouldn't she be? From the look of her, they had raised her to treat servants as expendable. If you tired of them or didn't like them, you simply sacked them and thought no more about it. Oh yes, he knew well of such people for twice already in his young working life men had sacked him.

"Why do you shake your head?" she asked.

"You wouldn't understand, Miss," he said sadly.

"Try me, go on, tell me and we shall see." Jumping down from the branch in a welter of flounces and frills, she stood at his side smoothing down her gown.

"Well," Harry glanced around to see if they were alone. He could get in big trouble for what he was going to say. His face flushed when he saw how close she stood. "You don't care that the woman, your governess, will lose her position. What will she do then, do you think?" He wiped his wet hands on his pants.

"Oh, I expect she'll find another girl to tutor," Mary said flippantly.

"How old is she, this governess, would you say?"

She wrinkled up her nose delightfully as she thought about it. "At least twenty-five or maybe older. I'm not good with the ages of old people."

Harry looked down, thinking her absolutely beautiful. Her complexion was so flawless it resembled fine porcelain. Her hair shone with health and he'd never seen such shining hair. As she lifted her arm he saw how fine the skin was on the inside and his heart leaped in his chest as she put a soft, warm hand on his arm.

"Why does it concern you?"

"Well, Miss," he stammered, "When you sack people they don't walk into another position. It takes time to find a place and then that doesn't mean they'll be kept on. People like her can't survive without jobs." He gestured around at the magnificence. "They don't all live in big houses like this, and have things like goldfish ponds and fountains."

She regarded him seriously. "Hm. You sound bitter for such a young man. Do you have a hard life?"

Harry felt like telling her what a hard life he had, but thought better of it. "Aye, I do, Miss. Now I'd better get back to work afore I get sacked meself."

He started to shovel the cement into a wheel barrow prior to taking it into the conservatory.

Mary observed him with great interest. She liked this lad, handsome and tall, he had wonderful muscles in his arms. He was much nicer, she decided, than the boys she met socially with her parents, boys who were decidedly soppy, boys who loved their mummies and daddies and cried if they as much as cut a finger. This young man was strong and he was manly. Oh yes, she liked him a lot.

"Miss Mary? Miss Mary? Where are you? Come inside at once," Miss Ince, the governess, came walking quickly around the side of the house. Harry looked up and saw a grey clad young woman who wore her hair in braids around her head. "What are you doing, child? It is time for your piano lesson, come along at once. Mr. Sutton is waiting." She glared at Harry and did not like what she saw.

"Miss Mary, please come away from that dirty thing," she gestured to the cement on the board, "I do hope you were not talking to that workman. Well bred young ladies do not converse with the lower classes. Come along."

Mary smiled at Harry over her shoulder and waved a dainty hand as she followed the muttering and grumbling Miss Ince. He waved back smiling broadly, liking her trim shape and her dancing curls. By, but she was a right gradely lass, a lass he could never hope to know better. Still, he could dream, couldn't he?

"Oy! Stop tha lollygagging and get on wi'it," his uncle said sharply as he came back into the conservatory. "Take tha eyes off the young miss. She's not for the likes of us, tha knows."

Harry smiled bitterly. No, she wasn't for him.

As he worked, his gaze cast around for a glimpse of her. He began to dream of her and wondered if he would ever again meet anyone as lovely.

Some days later she came into the conservatory from the house and touched him on the shoulder as he knelt smoothing the cement floor of the pond. It was when he was thinking of her, too, and it made him start mightily.

"Sorry for startling you," she said, laughing at his expression.

"Aye, well, you almost gave me a heart attack," He had to laugh with her. "I was thinking about you in fact, and then, there you were."

Today she wore a green muslin gown with a yellow satin sash at her tiny waist. The balloon sleeves made her waist seem even smaller and the sweetheart neckline suited her. This was her best dress and she had worn it for him, wanting to impress him.

"What were you thinking?" she asked, flirting with her eyelashes and dimples.

He blushed. "Oh, that I hadn't seen you around. I thought maybe your governess locked you up for being near me."

She giggled. "Miss Ince? She is not that bad, even if she is old-fashioned. My father told her she must treat me as an adult now, not as a child."

"But, you . . .,"

"Don't say it!" she warned, raising her hands and flapping them. "You are going to say 'but you are a child' and yet you do not even know my age. I'll tell you I look far younger than my true age. So how old do *you* think I am?" She stood as tall as she could, trying to look older.

Harry gazed at her, finding it difficult not to smile. Then his mind reeled at the nearness of her and he felt his heart pounding like a jackhammer.

"I'm not good at ages, either," he said eventually, wondering whether to say what he thought or add a couple of years. Would he insult her? He must be diplomatic. "I would say you're eighteen." He added a couple of years. She looked more like fifteen to him, but he knew youngsters were always in a rush to grow up, as he had been.

Mary clapped her hands joyfully. "I always suspected I looked older. I am sure I developed faster intellectually than my peers who bore me terribly."

Harry smiled. She was all of sixteen and a half, he thought, but she did look older, especially wearing that particular gown, and with her hair pinned up that way.

"You guessed exactly right," she crowed, her dimples coming and going. "Being eighteen, no person should treat me as a child because I am fortunate to look younger."

"Miss Mary!" Miss Ince gasped. "Come away at once, you will soil your dress, and you, young man, get on with your work. They do not pay you to talk to those who are your superiors. I shall inform Mr. Gillespie of your temerity." Taking Mary's arm, she led her away.

The next day Mary came again, only this time when she entered the conservatory, she shut the house door and locked it in case Miss Ince spotted her.

"Yoohoo," she trilled as she came down the short tiled walk dressed in a white organza gown with an orange sash that made her look like a luscious tropical flower. "Here I am again."

Harry straightened up and looked at her. "I do wish you wouldn't, Miss. I can get into a lot of trouble." He worried about his job.

"Oh, don't be silly. I can handle Daddy if Miss Ince says anything. Your boss has gone down the drive in the trap so nobody will disturb us."

Harry stood up and looked around, both to the house door and outside in the garden.

Mary laughed her tinkling laugh. "Now don't worry. Miss Ince is talking to my art tutor, and I think she's sweet on him." She smiled up at him from under her brows and put out a hand. "By the way, I don't know your name and I can't keep calling you 'young man', can I?"

"It's Harry, Miss Mary, Harry Haydon."

They shook hands as formally as if at a ball.

"Is it short for Harold?" she asked.

"Could be." He shrugged. "I don't rightly know as I was allus called Hal was I was a young 'un."

"How strange. I know they named me after my grandmother. For whom were you named?"

"I don't rightly know," he said. She was making him feel stupid and he wasn't, he knew.

She smiled and his heart soared. "I like you, Harry, I like you very much. You have such lovely muscles, and you are so tall."

Harry turned bright red. For a well bred young lady she seemed so forward. None of the village girls talked in that manner, and if they thought he had muscles they never said so.

"Oh dear, now I have embarrassed you," she said as she sat on the low retaining wall and spread her skirts. "Mummy says my tongue is going to get me in trouble one day, but I do not see why I cannot say what I think. It is a much nicer way to be than talking a load of rubbish because society dictates."

"Aye, that's as maybe, but you can hurt people being that way as well. You might say the truth, Miss, and that's not what people want to hear."

"I could never be a hypocrite," she said firmly, "Have I said something to hurt *your* feelings, Harry?"

"No, but I don't think it's right that a young lady such as yourself tells a strange man he has nice muscles. It's not done."

Mary laughed. "I always say what I think, Harry, and, yes, it has landed me in a great deal of trouble, but at least people know where they stand with me. I never lie or exaggerate."

"Oh aye?" he smiled.

"When I am twenty-one, I will take my inheritance and use it to further my education and become a teacher. The time is coming when the world will treat women as equals, the time when we need to show we are as good as, if not better, than some of the men who run things."

Harry gaped at her. What she talking about?

"Christabel Pankhurst and Annie Kenny, the suffragettes, and their Women's Social and Political Union are my idols and I support their ideals wholeheartedly. My father stands against everything for which they aim, while my mother can see nothing wrong with the status quo. No, I have ambition and intelligence and plan to change things for the better when I am able."

Harry stood looking at her, his hands hanging loose, work the furthest thing from his mind. His uncle would be gone an hour and, as a fast bricklayer, he could soon catch up. If he only knew what she was talking about, what she meant.

"What a young lady should, or should not do or say, was surely not part of the educational curriculum at your school, or was it?" she asked then, wounding him to the quick, although she could not know.

Harry's education was minimal. Illiterate, he could not even write his own name. She was right, who was he to tell her what she would and should not do or say? "No, they didn't teach us about that, but I do know young ladies shouldn't be so forward. It isn't ladylike," he said obstinately, his face flaming.

She was playing with him, this young lady was, playing with him for her own amusement. He knew why, though, it was because of her upper crust background and him an ignorant labourer. To her he was an animal, and he could bet she had a good laugh after she went back to her part of the house. She probably told her snooty friends so they could all laugh at him, too.

Whether or not he was being rude, work came first. "Time I got back to work. That's what I get paid for, not talking to you," he said, turning his back on her.

"Oh dear, I must have said something to upset you," she said, her voice quivering. "I am sorry, Harry, I do like you so very much, and you are right, I should not say the things I do."

"Aye well," he said as he picked up the trowel and applied cement to a layer of bricks.

Mary sat watching, her chin on her hands. She had never looked at a man before in a sexual way. Her father, a fat man, had no muscles at all as far as she could see. Her uncles were also stout and the boys she met, well, they were little boys. She sighed with the pleasure of her thoughts and he turned to look at her.

"Don't you have something else to do?" he asked, now annoyed at her constant scrutiny. "Practising the piano, or having a dance lesson?" He saw no future in talking to her, lovely though she may be, no future and much heartache.

"No. Nothing at all." She smiled gaily and flung out her arms. "I can sit here all day if I wish. You do have such lovely muscles, Harry, like David."

He snorted. "David who?"

"David, that's all, Michelangelo's David."

"Oh aye?" Who the heck was she talking about now?

"Have you ever seen the statue, Harry? I know you cannot see the real thing as it is in Florence, but we do have a small copy in the library. I will show it to you tomorrow."

Harry had thought a lot about Mary Gillespie. After less than a week he had fallen desperately in love with her. What would he do when the job finished? When they finished here, he would never see her again. His Uncle Sam constantly carped about his daydreaming, about his gazing off into the distance as if gobstruck. Harry knew he must to try to forget the beautiful young woman as fast as he could, so the sooner the job finished, the sooner it would be possible.

Even as he worked, his mind told him to slow down, to make the job last longer. To see her again every day, to have her touch his arm again, or let him touch her.

Mary took her book out into the garden and sat on the pear tree branch. From her perch she could see inside the conservatory where Harry applied tiles to the outside walls of the planter and pool. It was a hot day with not a cloud in the sky and inside the conservatory it had become extremely warm. Harry, thinking himself alone, removed his shirt and wiped his brow with it.

Mary's breath came fast and her heart beat rapidly as she gazed at him. "Why," she murmured, "he looks better than David. In fact, Harry is gorgeous." Yes, she decided, jumping to the ground, she would fetch the statuette and show it to him now.

"Hello, Harry," she said, smiling up at him as he stretched his weary back.

"Hello," he said, hurriedly picking up his shirt and donning it.

He knew one didn't stand around bare chested in front of females and especially not well brought up young ladies. It surprised Harry when her face fell.

"I am sure it must be extremely warm in that shirt," she said, "You may take it off again, if you like," She smiled sweetly and his heart swelled with the feeling of love that swept through his being. Her beauty took his breath away.

She raised a hand from her billowing skirt and showed him a statuette. "Look, Harry. This is David. The one I was talking about. Michelangelo carved it."

Harry looked at the small statue. It was of a naked man and although it wore a fig leaf, he felt so embarrassed he had to turn away. Did she think *he* looked like that? On one hand his heart sang with the knowledge. He felt proud, yet on the other hand he felt shocked a young lady would walk around with such a thing and think nothing of it. So it was true what they said about the upper classes, they had no morals.

He shook his head angrily. "Take that back, Miss, back to where you got it. I don't think it's right. You shouldn't be looking at such a thing."

Mary laughed merrily. "Harry, don't be such a blue stocking. We have paintings on the walls of both naked men and women. This statue is one of the world's greatest sculptures and everyone knows about it. I think most homes have a copy of their own. I do think your school didn't do you any favours by not teaching you about great art."

Harry walked to the outside door and stepped into the garden. The sweat poured from him and made his sodden shirt transparent. Why was this young woman torturing him? Yet he wanted her to torture him, wanted to know she liked him.

Mary followed and stood at his side. He heard her sniff, but would not look at her, knowing his ignoring her annoyed her.

"Harry? Look at me, Harry!" she ordered.

As Harry turned another few degrees, she skipped around until she faced him and grabbed at his arms.

"Please," he said in a strangled voice. He put his head back and looked over her head. He dared not lower his gaze.

"All right, I will," she said, as she stood on tiptoe and kissed his chin.

Her action flabbergasted Harry, but he did not move away. Then his arms went up on their own volition wrapping themselves around her tiny waist and he returned the kiss on her soft lips. If his uncle sacked him now, he didn't care. He was kissing the most beautiful young woman in the entire world.

"Oh Harry, I think I love you very much," she breathed as she held up her face for more. Harry obliged. His body was on fire for her and he didn't care about anything else.

"Miss Mary!" Miss Ince grabbed her arms and pulled her away. "What on earth do you think you are doing, young man?" she shouted at Harry.

Mary struggled to get free. "No, don't. Take your hands off me," she cried, but Miss Ince held her even more firmly.

Sam came into the garden from the drive and saw an angry Miss Ince with Mary's arms firmly grasped and Harry standing red faced and embarrassed.

"Now, now, what's all this to do?" he asked looking from one to the other. "What's going on?"

Miss Ince glared in his direction. "This . . . this . . . this employee of yours has tried to take advantage of Miss Mary. He had his arms around her and was kissing her. It's a good job I decided to come looking for her, or I shudder to think what this lout would have done."

"I didn't . .," Harry started to say.

"No, he didn't," Mary said simultaneously.

"You're sacked, Harry," Sam said, his face grim. "Sacked as of this instant. Get your things and leave the premises immediately."

"He didn't do anything," Mary protested. "I was the one who kissed *him*."

"Miss Mary, please do not lie to save this man's job," Miss Ince said shaking Mary so hard her head wobbled. "He is a disgrace and must leave the premises. His employer is perfectly right to dismiss him."

Harry walked down the drive without looking back. His lovely daydreams were gone. Now he had lost his job and if his uncle stewed on it, would tell his mother about his disgrace. Nevertheless, he had kissed Mary. In fact, she had kissed him first and how wonderful to think of that. His being sacked seemed fair punishment for kissing a lady. Miss Ince was right, he hadn't known what would have happened next for he was mad with love for the young woman who had said she loved him.

He went to walk in the park and spent several hours staring moodily at the trees. Hunger drove him home and when he arrived, he found his Uncle Sam sitting in the kitchen talking to his mother. His heart sank - now he was for it.

"Where have you been, lad?" Sam asked grimly.

"Walking," Harry said as he took a mug of tea from his mother. She eyed him strangely but said nothing.

"Walking? We have work to be done, my boy, lots of it, too. I can't have you taking walks when I've got things to be done. Tomorrow you can start on that retaining wall for old man Whittier."

Harry gulped at his tea and looked at his uncle. He had not sacked him?

Sam punched Harry's arm with a gentle fist. "About the to-do this afta, Harry. Don't take no notice of the old harridan, Ince. She's nobbut a dried up old maid."

Harry smiled. "Thanks, Uncle Sam,"

The next day they talked about what had happened and Sam felt chuffed the daughter of the house had taken up with Harry.

"By the heck, I wish she'd'a kissed me. I'd have done more than kiss her back, I can tell thi. What a brazen bit of stuff she is! Just think, going around kissing the likes of us. I wouldn't like to be wed to such a woman, though, she's trouble with a capital T."

"Aye, I reckon she is," Harry said smiling, his mind going back to the feelings she had awakened in him. The touch of her soft lips, the perfume from her hair and the look in her clear eyes when she opened them wide. Oh God, but she was lovely and desirable. Still, no way he would he ever see her again and now he must forget her.

He received a valentine that year when it wasn't even Valentine's Day. It had to be from Mary. Carefully he tucked it back in the envelope and hid it in the bedroom. She had not forgotten him and his heart sang with joy.

Resolutely shutting her image out of his mind, he practically forgot her, until he met Marian Steadman.

When he first spotted Marian at the barn dance, his heart lurched in his chest as she seemed the spitting image of Mary: the Mary always at the back of his mind. He compared every young woman he talked to, to the image of his ideal woman, though, of course, none of them ever measured up and now to his immense delight was her double standing across the floor.

Harry asked her to dance when he got over his elation. This was his future wife.

"Shall I put it back?" Rita asked softly, breaking into her thoughts.

"What? Aye, put it back in the same spot. I shall think of your Granddad when I see it there. He must have been a right playboy before we wed, you know?"

Rita chuckled. "Oh Gran, Granddad? A playboy? You might as well think of yourself as a courtesan." To her, her Granddad seemed such a quiet man, taciturn. He never said much or showed much emotion and rarely smiled. While she knew in his youth, he was handsome, she always thought of him as old. His face was so weather beaten and lined, she could not imagine it any other way.

A playboy indeed! Marian smiled as she watched Rita put her treasure away. To think she often thought of herself as a courtesan, and now Rita had come out and said the same thing. One day soon she would tell Rita more about her life, about the other things in the cabinet.

Aye, to think Harry kept the valentine card. They were married all those years and yet she never asked. He had never told. Well, the best thing to do was tell Rita as much as she could. Yes, that's what she must do.

Maybe it was her age or her health, but this year Marian found Christmas a definite strain.

Roger's wife seemed snootier than ever since they promoted Roger to General Manager of his company and nothing seemed good enough for her. She regarded the clean house as little more than a hovel, making remarks that wounded, remarks that made Rita want to slap her face.

"Don't touch that, Neville," she said to the eldest boy when he stooped to touch the shiny brass coal scuttle. Neville had never seen a coal scuttle before as his home had gas and electric fires. "That thing is filthy and will soil your hands."

"The scuttle is shining clean," Rita said heatedly, not caring if she were discourteous, glaring at Mavis like a combatant. "This whole house is spotless."

"Now, Mavis," Roger said, ever the peacemaker.

Mavis tossed her head. "Roger, this house is simply awful. To think your mother lives here, it's deplorable."

"Do I take that as an invitation to come and live at your house, me and Rita?" Marian asked, eyes full of mischief.

"Now, that's a grand idea," Roger said, slapping his knees and grinning.

"Roger!" Mavis looked horrified. Marian knew she would not want her, an old lady and Rita, a young woman, living in her lovely home.

"No, thanks all the same, Roger," Marian said, mentally laughing as Mavis blew out a relieved sigh. She decided to get a dig in, something she would not do normally. "Your wife won't want that. Why, we'd mess up her place, what with our coal fires and the likes. Rita likes to come and go to her own schedule. As for me, I like meals served at proper times and proper food, too. Not that diet stuff, but food that sticks to your ribs. Anyroad, I couldn't live nowhere without my fireplace. No thanks, we like it here. It's a nice house."

"It's a lovely house, Gran," Rita said hugging her. She turned to Mavis. "Why don't *you* sit in the front room?" Her lip curled as she added, "We sanitized it for you."

Mavis glared back, her chin rising imperiously. "No, thank you.

As you have no fire worth mentioning, the room feels damp. Damp affects Neville's asthma, you know."

Roger snorted. "Asthma? Give over, Mavis, the lad had a sniffle." He appealed to his mother, "A common cold it was until a minute ago," Turning, he faced Mavis, "Or are we too high class these days to have common colds? Maybe only people who live in these houses have colds. People like us have asthma and allergies or anything else with a fancy name."

Mavis sat in aggrieved silence. Marian smiled; she could almost see what Mavis was thinking, that it was not going well, not at all well. Stupid woman, she was, thick as two short planks when it came to getting along with her fellow man. Oh yes, yoo full of herself, she thought herself better than anyone else.

"Come on, let's go into the parlour and play charades," Molly said cheerily. "Let Rita and Marian get on with the meal. We're only underfoot here. Anyway, Arthur banked up the fire earlier with anthracite and it'll be warm."

Rita giggled as she watched Mavis because her face looked a picture of misery as she dragged herself to the front room.

"What my boy sees in that woman beats me," Marian said as she grated cheese for the cauliflower.

"She must have something we can't see," Rita said, poking at the potatoes to check if they were ready for mashing. "Uncle Roger is so nice, although I can't say the same for those two boys. They're proper little snobs. Their mother has seen to that."

Arthur came in, tugging down the waistcoat he had worn for the occasion. His suit was his wedding suit and he rarely wore a waistcoat. Marian admired him now as he spoke. "I'm off to the pub to pick up some sweet sherry for her ladyship and something stronger for us men."

"Aye, and don't waste too much money on that sweet stuff," Marian said. "She'll only sip it and say some'ats wrong with it. There's no pleasing her ladyship."

"You're right there, Gran," Rita said, pouring the potato water into a bowl to use for making gravy. "We will waste this lovely meal on her. She should have brought her own crustless watercress sandwiches and a thermos."

Marian laughed and pushed at her. "Aye, I reckon you're right. Now lovey, how's that bird doing?"

All afternoon Molly played peacemaker and Rita felt glad her stepmother was such a lively person. She kept them in stitches with witty impressions of people she knew. This jovial audience did not, of course, include Mavis, whose face could have stopped a clock.

They enjoyed a grand meal. Everyone ate too much and lay around puffing like grampuses, while Mavis sat bolt upright, sipping tea with no milk or sugar. She pushed the food around the plate and ate two tiny mouthfuls with a great deal of disgust. Nevertheless, the boys ate a huge meal and each scoffed two helpings of Christmas pudding with brandy butter. Afterwards they ate tangerines and chocolates, cakes and biscuits. Then they drank cocoa and pop and milky tea.

"Mummy, I have a tummy ache," the youngest boy Granville whined, rubbing his stomach.

"We'll have to leave right away," Mavis announced getting to her feet with more energy than she had displayed all day. "The boy is ill. Probably botulism from the under cooked bird. We must take him to the emergency ward. Where did you put my purse?"

Roger turned his head sharply and glared at her with narrowed eyes. "Sit down, Mavis, we'll go when I say we'll go. This is Christmas Day and I spend it with my mother. Neville, take your brother outside and run around. All you've got, lad, is indigestion from all the food you stuffed into your greedy little gob."

The colour rose to Mavis's face and she looked pained. Now she regarded Roger, who she considered had drunk far too much wine at the table, spirits and beer later, with disgust. A look not missed by those watching the interplay.

He looked at her, shrugged, then looked over to his mother and laughed. "They don't get food like that at home, you know, Mam, only weighed out portions of everything that's good for them. I keep telling her that growing boys want food, good solid food, stick to the ribs food like you said. Food that will make them big and strong."

Mavis glared at him stonily, her expression saying the man was a peasant.

"You should see what she puts in front of me when I get home from a hard day's work, Mam. It's enough to make a grown man weep." He laughed then and said in a quieter voice, pretending to whisper, "I have to stuff myself at the work's canteen at lunch time or I'd be as thin and angular as her."

He turned to look again at his simmering wife and while Mavis said nothing, he knew he'd hear about it all the way home. Tomorrow, and the day after . . . hear about it forever. Mavis always had to be top dog, always had to call the shots. Well, he wasn't having any of that in the house where he was born, nor in front of his mother.

"Uncle Roger is unhappy with her, isn't he?" Rita asked later after everybody left and they were putting away the best dishes.

Marian paused and stood with her hands on the dresser as she thought."Aye, he is at that." She opened the drawer and started to put away the cutlery. "My Roger is an honourable man, though, he wouldn't leave her, not with two growing boys at home. Some people honour their commitments, Rita, love. They stick with it even when things get tough."

"Like you and Granddad, you mean?"

"Aye, I suppose I do." Marian paused with her hands in the cupboard where she was now stacking the plates. "We went through a lot, although it only served to bring us closer together."

"Will Uncle Roger always stay with Mavis?"

Marian chuckled. "If he has any sense, he'll find another woman and simply stay with Mavis for the roof over his head. Look, Rita, I'm sure you've realized by this time that not all marriages are happy. Some people change, others don't. Look at your Dad, he changed a great deal once they gave him more responsibility, but your mother, she never changed, she stayed narrow minded and self-centred. The best thing that ever happened to your Dad, Rita, was Molly."

Rita nodded. "Yes. I couldn't see that at first, Gran, but I do now. He's happy, is Dad," Rita looked into the future when Ian and she would have their own cottage in the country, when they would be as content.

"Aye, there's not many as get a second chance at happiness, Rita. You'll learn that as you get older." Her voice changed, she sounded forceful now. "When the opportunity presents itself, you have to grab it with both hands and to heck with what people think or say. You know what they say, 'you're a long time dead'."

"Yes, that's true enough, Gran. Funny how I don't seem to have understood that a year ago and now I do."

"It's the key of the door as they say, lass, but I figure it's the key of the door to understanding that you get when you're twenty-one. They say 'you can't put an old head on young shoulders' and 'you have to learn the hard way'. Oh, that's all platitudes, of course, but it's true. By the time you're thirty you'll know a lot more, and when you get to my age, why, you'll know everything."

"Oh Gran," Rita put down her towel and kissed her, laughing, "What will I ever do without you?"

Marian put her hands on Rita's shoulders and shook her gently. "A heck of a lot better, Rita, a lot better. I've lived my life, so it's your turn now. Don't you dare turn Ian down because you think you have to stick here with me. Promise me."

"I promise, Gran." Somehow she felt like crying as she'd already told Ian they would have to wait because of her Gran. Ian, desperately in love, pleaded, saying they would live with Marian, but Rita didn't want that. She wanted her own little cottage, a cottage with a garden and a lily pond. In her mind she had already furnished it down to the soap dish. No, she wouldn't want to start her married life in a terraced house with neighbours like those around here. As much as she loved her Gran, she didn't want to start married life with her sleeping in the next room.

Marian glanced around the now tidied kitchen as she sat by the fire and held her hands to the flames. "It's about time for your Christmas story, lovey. What'll it be this time, do you think?"

As Rita went to make her choice, Marian relaxed in the armchair as the fire warmed her legs. She felt bone tired, flat as an empty sack. It was like the life was slowly oozing out of her, like a tire with a slow puncture. Time to tell my granddaughter things I would never have dreamed of telling before, she decided, time to ease my mind, time to wipe the slate.

"This Gran, I chose this." Rita handed her a small brass framed desk clock, long stopped. "Why don't you get it fixed?"

The hands pointed to two-thirty. Marian had moved the hands to that position later when it ran down. That marked the time when Harry left her.

1922

They had a terrible row that Saturday afternoon and it ended with Harry leaving her.

"I'm leaving and I'm leaving now," Harry shouted angrily as he went down the flagged passage. At that time they hadn't lino or a runner laid as they couldn't afford it.

She rushed after him, grabbing at his sleeve. "Don't go, Harry, don't leave me. Please don't go," Tears streamed down her face. How could he leave her, leave her with two small children? What was she going to do? Surely he should stick by his vows as she was sticking to hers?

Harry shook her off. "Look Marian, I've got to go. How often do I have to tell you? She loves me and I love her."

"Who is she?" she screamed, "Tell me her name."

He blew out a sigh, tired of her questions. "You wouldn't know her even if I did. You've never seen her. She lives in Ekersley."

"Harry, don't go," she cried, "please don't go. I don't care about her, honest I don't. You can still see her, but please stay with me. Please don't leave me. I couldn't stand it." An icy hand gripped her heart. While she felt no guilt about her own affairs, she would never consider leaving him for the other man.

"There's nowt for me here, is there? You live on another planet as far as I'm concerned. You don't even notice me when I am here. I could be lying dead in that kitchen and you wouldn't notice. It's only the kids you care about."

He spoke the truth of it and she knew it. "Harry," she begged, "I'll change, I promise you."

Harry put back his shoulders, seeming to grow inches before her eyes."That won't make any difference. I love Maggie now. I don't know how often I have to tell you. I'm off." He picked up a packed suitcase she hadn't seen behind the door.

"No," she shrieked, realizing he really meant to leave. "No, please don't leave me."

"I'll send you some money every week," he said his voice thick with emotion, "but I can't stop here, not now."

After he closed the door with a spine chilling thud, she stood in the hall, stunned. The awful enormity of it flooded over her like a waterfall as tears streamed down her face and a great fear filled her heart. A man she always considered so reliable had deserted her, and him such a good provider. How could he do this to her? Not once had it entered her mind to that point that she had caused the rift by her ignoring him and his needs.

She heard the children in the back yard playing and moved to the kitchen window, tears rolling down her cheeks as she watched. Poor innocent children, now fatherless. Playing with coal, they were, both blacked and soiled, happy with it, though. The wireless played softly, a BBC offering of Gregorian Chants sung by the Benedictines of Solesmes. The music seemed appropriate, gloomy and dolorous.

What had she done to deserve this treatment from Harry? She'd always been there for him, hadn't she? Then she shook her head, no, she admitted bitterly, she was well aware she hadn't been a good wife because for months she'd treated him more like a lodger than a husband. He must have been suffering in silence. Well, now Harry had found someone who noticed him all right, someone who made love with him. Suddenly jealousy filled her with bile such as she'd never known. Another woman lying with *her* husband?

Yet what about her? Hadn't she lain with other men? What would Harry think if he knew that? A chill ran over her and she shivered.

Suppose he'd found out about her adulterous affairs? Suppose her licentious behaviour was the real reason he left?

Yet castigating herself would not solve the problem. Knowing Harry as she did, she also knew chasing after him wouldn't fetch him back. No, she decided, making a plan. She would avoid his haunts, avoid his work area, give him time to think about what he had done. She had no doubt the other woman would fill his mind. Harry was a loyal sort and may come back to her, but never if she asked him.

For four days she stayed inside the house. The children were out on the street playing on fine days while she stayed in the kitchen and thought about her life. It was like it was over already. While Harry was here, she had ignored him, but now he was gone, she missed him sorely. A deserted wife.

It all came down to the type of person she was, and she tried to analyse what it was that made her tick. What was wrong with her that she looked and lusted after other men? Were all women like her? She doubted it, but who knew? After all, she couldn't go around asking people about such personal matters. Other women seemed content, didn't even look at other men, but she did, she looked at all of them and lusted after most. It had to be wrong. She had to be mentally deficient somehow. Strange how now she was alone, she didn't want any other man, she wanted Harry.

At odd moments she sought relief in reading the Bible, but all she seemed to find were passages about wanton women and punishment for sins. In two days she felt like she had passed her entire life shut away in the house. Only her anger made her feel alive, only the needs of the children gave her days any structure.

What would she do about expenses? Obviously she would have to find a job soon because she had no idea if Harry would honour his commitment to send her money. Once he was with his lady love, he might forget all about her, about the children. Aye, she knew from experience that when one was in love, other obligations were the last thing you considered. Hadn't she always spent every waking second thinking about her lovers?

Fortunately she got a job with the newsagent at the end of the street.

It was convenient, the hours were good and Ruth next door took in the kids while she was at work. Ruth Beavis, a good sort, listened to her tale of woe, offering a shoulder and sympathy.

Marian felt terribly lonely. It didn't help that the kids kept whining for their father, that she kept thinking he would suddenly open the door and sit in his chair to take off his work boots. Every time footsteps slowed on the street she would stop and wait, and every time somebody knocked on the door her heart leaped with hope. For two weeks she saw no money from Harry and thanked God she had a job. Then, one evening on the third week he knocked at the door.

"Harry," she said with surprise as she opened the door to find him standing there, shamefaced, nervously shifting from foot to foot. "Well come in, Harry, don't stand there." Better, she thought, to be matter of fact, as if nothing had changed, treat it lightly. As she led the way to the kitchen, her face broke into a grin that she quickly erased as she turned to look at him.

Harry stood in the kitchen and wound his cap around in his hands. He appeared agitated, ashamed maybe, and Marian had never seen him that way before. She turned away to put on the kettle, not wanting to see his embarrassment, and shut her eyes for a moment as she uttered a silent prayer.

"Nice to see you, Harry," she said. It would never do to show how much she wanted to throw herself into his arms and beg him to stay. Joy raced through her veins, she felt like shouting, but she turned and simply smiled up at him.

"Would you like some parkin?" she asked as if he were a visitor or casual acquaintance, showing him the cake she had baked that afternoon.

"Aye," he said gruffly, putting down his cap and sitting at the table.

"Dad!" "Dad!" Two small forms flung themselves at him and he gathered them to him and kissed them on their cheeks. The tears in his eyes surprised Marian.

She smiled. Harry wanted to come back. "Come on you two, get out of it," she said now laughing, "Wash your hands. Tea will soon be ready."

Harry blew his nose and Marian averted her head to hide her happy smile. He missed the children, did Harry. She still had a hold over him, if only through them.

They ate buttered parkin and drank tea. The children chattered and giggled, telling him everything had happened since his departure. She could tell he was wanting to say something, but the children were so excited they gave him no chance. Then a sudden thought struck chill into her heart. She watched him as he chaffed with the pair of them, laughing now, happy. If he wanted to take the children away, it would devastate her. Prickles of anxiety ran through her.

The kids raced outside after their tea, confident when they came back their dad would still be there.

"They've grown," Harry said. "It's been only three weeks, but they've definitely grown."

Marian kept her voice steady, nervous as she felt. "They do that, children. You never did say, has she children, your lady?"

As his head was down, Harry's voice sounded muffled. "She's thrown me out, Marian," he muttered, embarrassed. "She didn't want me. She just wanted a meal ticket. Oh, I saw through it quickly enough and was wondering what to do, but then I heard the talk at the pub. I was mortified, Marian. I was the subject of a lot of gossip and they all knew about her, every man jack of them. Too bad I never listened to idle chatter before I got involved. I never listen to gossip because it always hurts somebody." He raised his head and looked straight at her. "Look, I'm sorry, Marian. I'm so sorry I put you through this."

He looked so ashamed of himself her heart went out to him. Harry had made a big mistake and much to her amazement he was man enough to confess. How she had misjudged him. Would she be as forthright if the shoe was on the other foot? What would he have done if it ever happened she left him and returned? Yet she knew he would take her back whatever, no matter what her sin because he was that type of chap. Now the guilt of years flooded her being.

Smiling joyfully, trying to make it all right again, she said tremulously, "Oh, Harry, there's nothing to be sorry about. I'm sorry I ignored you and I'm sorry I took you for granted. I realised it was all my fault. I did so want to see you and beg for your forgiveness, but something stopped me. We both made a big mistake. Surely you can forgive me? I forgive you."

Harry looked at her with tear filled eyes. "Aaw, Marian, what did I ever do to deserve you? You understand and you can forgive me," He stood and took her into his arms, tears running down his cheeks. They kissed and heard childish giggling from the door.

Sheila and Roger were watching.

"So I took him back," Marian said, misty eyed, "Harry was so ashamed of himself, Rita. Mind you, I had a lot to be sorry about, I freely admit that. I was so wrapped up in the children as every mother is, I had pushed him aside. Remember when you have children, now, take a lesson from this, Rita. Anyroad, we were happy afterwards and he never again looked at another woman. It's a hard lesson I learned and it caused a load of heartache, so I'll say this, Rita. You listen well now . . . all men look at women. It's only when they stop to touch you need to worry."

"This clock?" Rita extended it on her palm. Gran had not mentioned it. "What has this to do with the story?"

"Oh, that's the time he left me, Rita. I set the hands much later when it ran down. Harry and I took the clock out any time we had anything serious to talk about and we looked at it before opening our mouths. It stopped a lot of anguish and heartache, that little clock did. You see it's like this, love, and as I've always told you, you must always think before you speak. You can never ever take back a bad word, or a word spoken in anger you didn't mean. In everything you say in anger, there is a spark of truth and the other person knows that."

"A nice story, Gran. Imagine, my Granddad with another woman. Well, I never!" Rita shook her head. What other secrets had Gran not told her?

The mystery surrounding her mother still niggled away at the back of her mind though she had convinced herself one day she would get her Gran to tell her the truth. It well might be something in the cabinet told the story.

"Bed for me," Marian said standing shakily. "It's been a long hard day."

CHAPTER THIRTEEN

As the new year eased into February, Marian became bed ridden. Arthritis severely inflamed her joints and it soon became agony for her to stand for any length of time.

She looked now at her hands where they lay on the counterpane, seeing them as claw-like. Where were her slim hands, the tapered fingers, the rosy fingernails, the grace? Now grave marks splattered the backs, her nails were like ridged old ivory, the skin, paper thin, showed every tiny vein and the large ones stood out like ropes. She sighed fitfully. Growing old was horrible, aye, horrible.

As she lay in bed she had all the time in the world to think back on her life, and think she did. What would they think of her now, those young men who once lusted after her? After whom *she* lusted? What did they look like now - supposing they were still living? So many young men died in the great wars, many died later of old age, hard work and disease. Aye, many of her peers were long gone.

As for herself, she often wished she had died with Harry. It had been miserable without his company, because though a dull man, it hadn't been so bad when she had his company. She admitted that fact when she lived alone.

Rita, bless her, did her best, but a man around the house was something special. Young Rita could never make up for her losing Harry. She'd stuck with him for all those years, even when she could hardly stand to look at him, even when he hated her. Aye, he hated her sometimes, she realized well enough and knew she had earned and deserved his hatred. If Harry had not been such an easy going chap who lived up to his vows, she didn't doubt for a second he would have left her for good. Even after his one affair, she knew she was not home clear, not if she ignored him. Overall, she had not exactly been a caring wife.

Why had she not remarried after his death? She often wondered about that as she had been free as a bird and not so old, not too old that men didn't follow her with their eyes. Strange, though, all the time she was with Harry, her gaze was slithering around the men, then when he died, she went right off them. Of course, Matthew died long before Harry passed on, and Matthew had been her one and only, if she told the truth.

Rita came into the bedroom carrying a double handled cup of soup. Marian found it difficult to holding a spoon because of her arthritis and the double handled cup allowed her some little freedom. How hateful, and how she resented it when Rita cut her food and fed her like a baby. When was this going to end? When would she be free of the body that had betrayed her? Yet when she looked at Rita with her young happy face and her look of concern, she didn't want to go. Aye, she wanted to see Rita wed, maybe see some great-grand-children. What else was there to look forward to at her age?

Rita grinned widely. "Lunch time! Here we go, Gran, mushroom soup, your favourite and before you ask, it *is* home made. Molly made it for you yesterday."

"Good, and since when is dinner called lunch? It's been dinner ever since I were a lass and there's no reason to go changing it now." She felt decidedly cranky as Rita helped her sit up, plumping the pillows behind her. "Anyroad, does it make it taste any different?"

"Not at all," Rita laughed, "I guess I'm getting to be a bit of a snob, Gran. Lunch is what Ian's mother calls it."

"Huh! Some difference. I suppose now they have a new name for tea and supper as well."

"Well, seems like tea is still tea and high tea is essentially what you call supper, but supper, as you call it, is now dinner. Supper, they tell me, is a late night snack, in polite circles. I got a book on it from the library. I'll have to watch myself, Gran, when we're entertaining Ian's parents, you know."

"Utter hogwash, piffle, that's what it is," Marian said. "You call it what you've always called it, and if they don't like it, they can lump it." Marian sipped the soup and found it delicious..

Rita laughed. "My word, somebody is grouchy today. Are you feeling all right?" She regarded her Gran with concern. Any slight deviation from the norm worried her.

Marian made her voice stronger. "Of course I'm all right, as right as I can be stuck here in this bed with nobody to talk to all day long." As much as she tried to sound cheerful, her tone sounded peevish.

"Now, Gran, all you have to do is bang on the ceiling and I'll come running. Don't try to play the martyr with me. You know we've told you we'd put the bed downstairs, so you've only got yourself to blame if you insist on being up here."

Rita regarded her grandmother with love. Marian would like to be downstairs, Rita knew that, but also knew she didn't hold with having beds on the ground floor. Beds were for upstairs.

"You know you can go to stay at Dad's. You've not been short of invitations from him and Molly. No stairs at all there."

"Aye, well," Marian drank more soup. "This is grand, full of mushroom chunks, almost, but not quite, as good as I make meself" She chewed on a mushroom slice.

"So do you want to move downstairs?" Rita asked, standing with hands on hips, in what Marian called her 'bossy-boots' pose. "Or would you prefer to go to Wisteria Cottage?"

Marian thought for an entire second. "I want to stay here where I've lived since I was eighteen. This is my home and no, I don't want to move the bed downstairs."

"Well, it's up to you, Gran," Rita said, shaking her head. "If you change your mind, just say the word."

"I won't change my mind," she said as firmly as she could. Her voice had lost its force and it quavered a lot. Another sign of old age, one she detested.

"Yes, we all know that well enough. You're as stubborn as a mule,

Gran, and silly with it. You know you'll like it better down there where you can keep an eye on what's happening in the house."

"No, I won't," she said testily. "I'll want to do everything myself. Better I don't see what messes you're making before I get my food. I bet half of it's been on the floor before you fetch it up here."

Rita chuckled. Sometimes pleasing her Gran seemed impossible, though she knew most of her nattering was only time wasting. Gran liked to talk these days, she had little else to do, although she tended to fall asleep in the middle of a story. It frightened Rita to see how old her grandmother had become, and how rapidly she was failing.

Leaning over, she gave her a cuddle. "Right, bossy britches, lie down now, have a nap and I'll come up with the paper and read to you in half an hour."

"Thanks, love. You know I love you, don't you?" Her eyes misted over, she felt so soppy these days. A stray sunbeam could make her cry.

"Oh yes, I know, Gran and I love you, too."

When Rita got back, Marian was fast asleep, so she sat in the bedside chair and skimmed through the paper looking for items of interest, knowing she would soon wake. Marian slept little these days and then only in cat naps.

"Rita, love?" Her voice creaked. She swallowed trying to moisten her throat.

Rita smiled. "Oh, so you've finally woken, have you? Me sitting here waiting and all, and you snoring like a pig in clover."

"Aaw you!" Marian grinned and chuckled. "I don't snore. I've never snored."

Rita grinned. "Oh? Next time I'll record it, then you'll hear for yourself what I have to put up with. It almost shook the tiles off the roof."

Marian started to chuckle, then burst into tears. Tiles off the roof, now why had Rita said that?

"Gran," Rita regarded her with alarm. This was not like her grandmother. "What did I say?"

Marian wiped her eyes on the sheet and sat up straighter. "Sit down, Rita. I'm going to tell you a story, an honest to God true story this time."

Marian talked for nearly an hour and told Rita about Matthew, about the roof tiles that killed him and of her great love for him. She didn't say anything about their intimacy because that wouldn't be right. Even now she was reluctant to tell the entire truth about her affair.

"Oh Gran, how awful for you." Rita felt dismayed. Poor Gran, poor Matthew, poor Granddad.

"Yes, it was," Marian nodded, "I've decided I'm going to tell you something else every day, Rita. You should know about your mother and me. I can see that now. The closer I get to death's door, the more I realize I should tell you."

Rita's jaw dropped, closer to death's door?

"Gran! Don't talk like that, you've got years yet," she said heatedly, as if denying it would make it go away.

"Now who's telling tall tales? You know and I know I've only a short time left and don't deny it," She closed her eyes wearily. "I want to sleep now. It's right tiring, all this confession stuff." Her face wore a small smile.

A good girl, Rita was a good girl, she ruminated as she dozed. A girl with brains and spunk, aye, she would survive anything I could tell her. Morals are different these days. Youngsters hop into bed with complete strangers from what I've heard on radio and read in the papers. A good job Rita isn't that way inclined, though maybe she's inherited my hot pants, she thought, smiling and chuckling as she napped. Rita smiled, thinking Gran was having a lovely dream, a happy dream.

Molly came over later fetching an apple pie. Her flaky pastry was light as a feather. Even Gran raved about it, and Gran was hard to please.

"How is she?" Molly asked as she put the pie in the pantry.

"Getting ready to die," Rita said, her eyes filling with tears. "She knows she's not got long." She blew her nose. "Says she's going to tell me things. Oh Molly, what will I do without her?"

"Now, Rita, you've got me and your Dad and Ian. What more could you want? She's old and sick. Would you want her stuck in bed for another five years or more?"

Rita sat by the fire and poked it to a blaze. "No, but it's hard to see her slipping away like this, slowly. If she's going, I hope she dies in her sleep," she said fiercely, "I don't want to see her wasting away, and

I don't think she'd want that either." Her eyes filled again. "She said she wished she'd died with Granddad."

Molly took her hand and stroked it gently. For a young woman Rita took things seriously, and she didn't know of many youngsters these days who would worry about an old lady.

"Now, Rita, you've got to be strong," she said, "She doesn't want you looking at her like that, all spaniel's eyes and tears. Make sure you stay cheery and make her last days happy. I'll come every day, you know, and between us we'll keep her smiling."

Rita wiped her eyes. Molly was a good sort. That she'd always known though not acknowledged it to herself at first. How different things would have been if Molly had been my mother, she thought.

"Thanks, Molly, if anyone can make her laugh, you can. It's just . . . it's just, so difficult for me because she's been more than a mother to me all these years."

"It's hard for anybody, lovey. Keep your chin up, Rita. She won't thank you for your tears."

Rita put back her shoulders and dried her eyes. Molly was right, in her own mind, she was almost an adult and had to show what she was made of, show she could handle things.

"No, you're right, Molly. No, she won't thank me for being gloomy. Right! From now on I'll be a ray of sunshine."

Molly nodded. Rita would carry it off./ S, she was made of the right stuff.

"Good, make sure you are. If you want to cry, come to me and I'll join you. Now I'll go up to see her, but then I'll have to rush off. Enjoy the pie."

Molly sat with Marian for half an hour and left as Rita after made the tea.

"Here we go. Tea for two and two for two," she sang merrily as she entered with the tray.

Marian chuckled creakily. "Keep your day job, Rita, keep your day job. That voice would sour milk," Marian felt better after having a chat with Molly.

"Now, would you like a biscuit or a piece of cake, Gran?"

"Nowt. I'll have my tea, thank you. Then I'm going to tell you some'at."

Marian told her about how she met Harry, about the china cup and saucer his mother gave her for her birthday: how they managed through both wars, about Harry's stint in France, of the dreary depression, about the Spanish Flu and the thousands who died. She told of World War Two when the government rationed food, although they had access to many things city dwellers could not get. She told of the bomb damage sustained in the village. Then she fell asleep in mid sentence. Her words had been getting slower and slower and simply stopped.

Rita took the cup and saucer out of her hand and covered her with the eiderdown. Switching on the night light, she took the tray downstairs.

How much Gran had lived through, how much she had experienced and not all of it pleasant, either. Tomorrow, God willing, she would hear more.

After an hour Marian woke. She squinted to see the bedside clock in the glimmer from the night light. Now was it seven in the morning or evening? Telling time with the curtains drawn was hard.

She lay still for some time and heard Rita moving about downstairs; then came the clatter of china. When she heard the poker being rattled in the grate to clear the ashes she realized it must be evening. Picking up the cane, she rapped on the floor.

Rita came running at her summons. "Gran?" she gasped, out of breath from her headlong rush up the steep stairs.

"I wish you wouldn't do that, Rita," she said irascibly. "You come around the door as if you expected to see me dead as a door nail. There's horror on your face when you come in here. If I rapped, I must be all right. Try not to do it, Rita, please, for my sake." She chuckled. "I feel like I've disappointed you, being alive and all."

"Oh Gran, I *am* sorry," Rita laughed. She mustn't upset her Gran, she told herself, she must put on a cheery face. She stood to attention. "Well then, and what did her Royal Highness want of her loyal servant?"

"Don't be so cheeky. Sit down and I'll tell you some'at."

Marian talked about her young days, of working at the manor, of how she fell in love with Lord Gerrard when she first worked there.

"He's dead now, is Lord Geoffrey. Aye, good food and a love for port wine took him. Old Lady Cynthia is still ruling the roost although the Manor isn't what it used to be. Most of it's in disrepair and closed off."

Her mind flitted over the manor and its inhabitants. Old Lady Cynthia, the only one left because Geoffrey and Cynthia never had children, lived in two rooms. Gossips said the new kitchen was built on the ground floor and the size of a closet, and one servant did everything. Death duties and taxes had taken the vast fortune Geoffrey thought would last forever and whittled it down to a mere subsistence.

Marian talked about Manchester: a city she hated with a passion.

"Aye, after my parents moved there, I stayed with them. (She stayed only a day, but she had said otherwise in another story and thankfully remembered). The air was full of smoke and soot, smuts covered my clothes and I caught a cold that hung on for a month. Aye, I hated Manchester. It seemed so dark, dirty and depressing." It was high time she told Rita the truth about the industrial city and not made it sound inviting.

By this time she was tired again and Rita left her to doze. By, but her Gran had led some life, a life of variety for sure. She seemed to have tried everything at least once.

Marian lay in the state that is not sleep and not yet wakefulness; feeling as though suspended in another world where her body felt warm and cosy. No pains bothered her and she felt like if she had the inclination, she could run a mile. Her mind flipped back to the days when she could run, run like the wind and often did, ran wild on the moors simply to let off pent up energy. Now she couldn't walk, and a run was beyond her capabilities.

Aye, the moor, the wide open clean aired space where the villagers walked for pleasure and exercise. The hidden copses where she had lain with some handsome chap as if it were another planet. The wildlife she had often watched, deer, badgers, rabbits, stoats, foxes: they were still there, breeding and proliferating. God knows the county needed the moor as a retreat for the thousands who lived and worked in the cities, and who never otherwise got a breath of fresh air.

As her mind wandered through the labyrinth of her memories, she thought back to when she met Harry. By, but he was a handsome lad, his brown eyes warm and full of admiration for her. Aye, she had been trim and good looking back then.

Oh, she knew the lads went for her, knew all the tricks. How to flirt with her eyes, how to cause the adorable dimple in her cheek when she smiled, how to cast those admiring glances and small sighs of pleasure. How to make a lad think he was special. I still know how, too. Aye, give me a man and I could stand him on his ear right enough. Oh, not with looks any more, but I know I have the knack of making a man feel special, even now. In her reverie she was again young.

From the first second she laid eyes on Harry, she had liked him. Him, he was smitten right enough, and her, she fell in love with him even as she saw him. Not that he had been the first by any means, but he was the first man she'd taken a shine to after Geoffrey. Poor Harry, he should have known better as she had not been a good wife. Oh, she gave him two children and stood by him. Nevertheless, her heart had not been in it, or why would she have chased after other men? For many years before his death they lived more like brother and sister than husband and wife.

While she knew after years of marriage, the first mad all-encompassing passion faded never to return, she always felt a need for the nearness of another person, of the special feeling engendered by the irrefutable look in a man's eye. Obviously Harry forgot such feelings after they were married a while, and Marian did not count Agnes Reilly as a grand passion, or the woman for whom he left her. Still, Harry had not played away much she knew of and basically stayed true to her.

As for me? I was forever casting my eyes around and looking at other men in a way I now considered calculating. That makes me feel ashamed, it does, the way I threw myself at men. A trollop, I am, right enough. Sheila was right, I was a harlot even while I walked around looking like butter wouldn't melt, yet the village knew about my shenanigans. How stupid I was to think I could get away with anything.

She sighed deeply. Aye, well those days were over. No more would she be a predatory female, no more would she spend her days full of longing that needed assuaging. She was old, old as the hills, so old she would never lie with another man. Strangely, though, all her dreams were of youth. Sometimes God could be so cruel.

Marian dozed and in her half dream ran down the bluebell-covered hills of the beech wood, laughing as some young chap chased after her, they kissed and laughed with the joy of being young and alive. The world was new then, held so many wonders she had not experienced, held so many things far in the future.

"Good morning. Had a nice sleep, Gran?"

She opened her eyes blearily. Rita stood with a tray in her hands and Marian glanced at the window, saw the sunshine.

"Good morning, Rita, love."

"Top of the morning to you, Gran. Tea and toast coming up, your majesty."

She smiled at Rita as the girl plumped up her pillows and straightened the coverlet. "I was having a lovely dream then, Rita."

"Yes, you were smiling."

Her crooked hands took the mug of tea and clasped it, relishing its warmth in her cold, old hands.

"It was all about when I was a lass, younger than you. We were in the bluebell woods in May and it was right grand."

"It's a shame but the bluebell woods have gone now. They built houses where they used to be," Rita said sadly shaking her head. "I used to play in those woods when I was little. I remember the little brook where I used to fish for tiddlers with a piece of string and a bent pin."

Marian chuckled. "Remember when you ran all the way here with a stickleback in your hand? The sweat from your hand almost cooked it by the time you got here. We put it in a jam jar and you sat at the table and stared at it for ages, willing it to wake up. Ooh, you cried and cried when it didn't. I had to flush it down the lavvy and you said a prayer over it."

"Oh yes," Rita laughed as she said, "I was sure it was asleep. I was silly back then."

"Aye, all things change," Marian said sadly. "Not always for the better, but they change. My old school has gone, too. It's a mini mart now. The place where we used to play after school, a big field full of buttercups and daisies, now it's a shopping precinct."

"Yes, sad, isn't it?" Rita said, "I still remember the Baptist church hall where the dance school put on their recitals. It's now a parking lot." She chuckled, thinking back. "Remember, Gran, when I used to take tap lessons?"

Marian laughed, thinking even her laugh was little more than a croak these days.

"Aye, you were about as graceful as a fairy elephant, you were, Rita." She lay back on the pillows and chortled. "All that clatter, what a din! How you mythered for them tap shoes, then wore the plates away outside on the concrete pavement showing off, and you soon managed to ruin them. So much for your ambitions of being the next Shirley Temple."

"Yes, wasn't I something? 'Course it was my Mam who put it into my head." Rita laughed and shook her head at the thought of it, "By, Shirley Temple! I bet my Mam saw pound notes by the barrow load if she could get me to dance like her. I used to hate it when she tied my hair in rags at night so I'd have ringlets the next day. It was too curly to start with but she wanted it in smooth ringlets, not a curly top like Shirley used to have when she was younger, but like when she got older."

"Aye, your Mam had lots of ambition if she didn't have to do anything other than make you look pretty. It was me who bought you the shoes, though love, she didn't want to spend money on making you into a movie star, even if that were her ambition."

"I never knew that!" Rita gasped. "I thought she bought them. She took me into town to get them." Rita thought back, her mother had said nothing about Gran paying for the shoes. Now she felt guilty because she ruined them by sliding on the pavement and then on the paved hill, clattering inept tap dances on the paving stones, showing off to her friends. Yes, she had wanted to ruin them, thinking it would irritate her mother. Strange how she would do anything back then to annoy her Mam. It was, she supposed, her way of getting her own back.

"Aye, but you still used to clack away in your clogs, lovey. You showed me in the kitchen often enough, didn't you? By, it took me years to get rid of my headache. Your Granddad was fit to be tied when you started the racket because we couldn't put music on the wireless, or you'd be at it again. Thank God you grew out of it fast or we'd have no ear drums left." She chuckled, thinking back.

Rita laughed, glad her Gran felt better. "I must have been a rotten kid, Gran. What I got up to sounds like a made up story."

Marian stretched out her hand. "No, Rita, you were a normal child. You got a lot out of life and made us feel young. Don't ever regret anything you did at that age because you were learning about life and you made us laugh. By, did we laugh about you when you'd gone home." Marian grinned. "Remember when you tried to make chewing gum out of toothpaste and sugar and put a whole baking tin full of it under my gas stove? Millions of black beetles were running around the kitchen after that, I can tell you." Rita had done some hilarious things, and look at her now, a lovely young woman, engaged to a nice young man.

"How about the time I tried to make fur mittens out of the rabbit skins the butcher gave me? The back yard was full of tomcats for weeks. I never did figure out how they could smell the skins."

Marian nodded. "Aye, you were supposed to nail them to a board, scrape them clean and then cure them with saltpetre and since we didn't know where to get any, you used plain old table salt. Them moggies lined up for miles in all directions. Remember how they all sat on the coal shed roof, howling? Your Granddad threw buckets of water at them, but they wouldn't budge."

They laughed, thinking back. "I never did get the mittens, either."

"How about the time you made a bikini top out of two of my scarves and went sashaying up the street with all the lads gawping. Remember young Eric calling you Dorothy Lamour?" Rita recalled and laughed like crazy. "By, but you was mad at him. You came back here and gave me a mouthful as if I had owt do with it. I would never have let you out of the house half dressed like that. It was just as well you had nothing to hide back then other than a lot of skin."

Rita wiped the tears from her eyes. Imagine her doing such a thing. "I'm glad I made you laugh, Gran," she said, "because those days were not days of laughter, what with the war and rationing and shortages and all that carry on. Of course I didn't realize what was going on, but then none of the kids did."

"That's the way it should be, children are innocent victims of man's stupidity," Marian said. She felt well today, better than she had felt in a long time. "Now, can I get up today? The sun is shining and I think I want to go downstairs and sit by the front window."

"Of course you can," Rita said, her face shining with pleasure. She liked to see her Gran up and around. "I'll get out your best woollen dressing gown and your new bedroom slippers and you can sit there like the queen looking from her balcony. At least it's warm today, and we maybe can open the window so you can have a crack with people as they pass."

So dressed in her best, she sat at the window. The window, it brought back a painful memory, she thought, as she assessed the still solid, white painted wood. The window Matthew installed. Even now it looked new as he had not stinted on materials, used only the best. She ran a gnarled hand over the frame. Matthew, Matthew . . .

Suddenly she recalled her pal Ruth Beavis from next door had passed. Only a week ago Rita mentioned it, and only by accident. How sad to think she'd been unable to see her best friend off with a fitting farewell as she hadn't enough strength then to attend the funeral or even go to the laying out. Ruth and she had grown up together, had been neighbours since they were both lassies. Aye, Ruth, she had been a true friend. She quickly wiped the tears from her eyes as she heard Rita's footsteps.

"All right, Gran?" Rita said fetching her a mug of tea and setting it on the sill.

"All right, love, but you know, there's not a soul I know has passed at all."

Rita nodded, saying nothing. Most women worked during the day now. Few stayed home to raise kiddies and those who worked farmed them out to nurseries. Sadly, most of Gran's contemporaries were dead or ailing like herself.

They had been a strong generation, her Gran's, had survived through a terrible time. They possessed stamina, too - intestinal fortitude as her Gran called it - and work ethic; none were afraid of hard work. Wars saw a lot of them off and years of bad diet caused many to develop horrible diseases in their old age. Yet they were fighters, like Gran, their life urge was strong.

As her grandmother sat in the light, Rita saw it would not be long now. Marian looked almost transparent in the strong sunlight, the flesh had melted from her bones and she looked gaunt. The strong lines of her cheek bones showed: cheek bones that were not there in the past. Gone was her rounded, plump granny and all that remained was this tiny shrivelled likeness. Rita sighed, dreading what was to come.

"What's up?" Marian asked, holding her double handled mug in both hands as she sipped. "What's the long sighs about?"

"Nothing, Gran," she said, swallowing the lump in her throat. "I was thinking about something. Did I tell you that . . ., " She went into a rambling story about what Ian's Dad said, anything so she didn't have to think about Gran's death, anything not to cry out loud, to shed tears.

Molly arrived shortly after and she left them to have a natter while she went for the day's groceries. When she got back Molly left to do her own shopping, leaving Marian in the kitchen sitting by the fire. It was well banked up, Rita saw, recognizing Molly's fine hand with a fire.

"Nice fire," she said as she held her hands out to the warmth. The kitchen never saw sunlight, being on the north side and overshadowed by the houses at their back. The whitewash had long gone from the walls, washed off by constant rain. Only patches remained.

"Aye, I like a good blaze, it warms the cockles of my heart, it does," Marian said feeling peaceful, mercifully free for once from the pain of her joints.

Rita made tea, the inevitable tea. It was strange that tea must accompany everything they did. Not that her Gran could drink much of it these days. Hers was always more milk than tea, fortified with the sugar she had detested as a young woman. Still, it was sustenance of a sort and she was rarely without a mug at her hand.

"Shall I tell you about your Mam and me today?" Marian asked.

Rita looked up sharply, her face full of expectation, eyebrows raised.

"Oh, don't look like that lass, it's not a nice story. Nothing involving your mother is nice, may God forgive me for saying such a thing."

"Go on, Gran." Rita sat on the edge of the chair, eager to hear the tale.

Marian sighed knowing it would not be easy. Her mind ran around the edges of it, thinking of how to start and how to make it easier on the girl. Please God, let me get through this without falling asleep or making a mess of it, she prayed. It was bad enough as it was, without making it worse.

"Well, it all started when your Mam met your Dad,"

Rita sat like a statue, this was what she wanted to hear and she hoped Gran would get on with it. Marian rambled on so about minutiae, things that made no difference, kept going off on tangents so Rita continually had to draw her back to the gist of the story.

". . . and so she started going out with a young man from Hillside Farm, well, not from the farm, but his father worked there. Archie his name was, his Dad. I remember how Archie asked a chap to ask me to sleep with him. By, I was that taken aback, I can tell you. What an insult and me a married woman! This other chap . . .,"

"Gran, about my Mam and this chap Archie," Rita prodded gently.

"No, no, his name weren't Archie, that were his Dad." Why didn't Rita listen? "His name was Bert. Aye, he was not much to look at, Bert, and not much inside his head but dust and cobwebs from what I knew of him, but he had muscles like you wouldn't believe. All the farm work was the making of him and all the girls were after him. Mind you, once they'd talked to him for a minute or so they realized he had a head full of space. He was the sort your Mam liked, someone she could drag around by the nose, like."

Marian passed Rita the mug and Rita poured her more tea. Talking was thirsty work and the fire was so warm and toasty. She dozed even as Rita turned to pass the mug back.

"Oh Gran," Rita said with some exasperation, and when they were getting into the story, too. She decided to hand wash some things while she waited for Gran to wake.

It was a quarter of an hour or so before Marian woke, knowing she was not in bed. Her neck ached from being on one side and she groaned as she moved.

"Well, at last. Back with us, are you? Here we go." Rita helped her sit up, put a cushion at her back. "You had a lovely nap, Gran, feel better now? Cup of tea?"

"Tea? No, no tea. One day I'll float away on a sea of pee, the way you keep pouring it into me."

Rita sighed. Gran seemed crotchety, so no more story today for her. Glumly she sat in the other chair and gazed into the fire.

"Why the long face, young lady? What's up?" Marian asked.

"Nothing, Gran, you rest a while and then I'll read the paper to you."

She did and as Rita read, Marian's mind wandered, not hearing. Then it came back to her she'd been telling Rita the story about her mother. Rita had always wanted to know about the fight and about the soapstone seal. She must tell her.

"Rita. Put the paper down, love. Why didn't you remind me I was telling a story? You know my memory's bad these days. I'll forget my own name next."

Rita smiled and folded the paper, putting it at the side of the chair. "Thanks, Gran. I didn't want to bother you. I thought perhaps you didn't want to go on with it. You said it wasn't nice."

"Nor is it, but where was I up to?"

"Bert, Archie's, son, the one with the muscles and empty brain box."

"Right. Well now, this Bert was going out with your Mam and she was seeing him almost every night. Up to no good, she was, and her still single, too. You can bet she had only one reason for seeing him, mind."

"You mean she wasn't a virgin when she married?" Rita chuckled, "Oh Gran, not many girls are these days and nobody thinks anything of it. Nevertheless, I suppose back then it was terrible."

Marian looked shocked. "It still is terrible. What this world is coming to, I do not know, and a girl should stay innocent until she weds. There's nowt wrong with that." She eyed Rita speculatively and wondered whether she was sleeping with Ian.

Rita saw the look and knew what she was thinking. "It's all right, Gran, I'm not sleeping with Ian." She chuckled. "You've got a dirty mind, you have."

Aye, I have an'all, Marian thought. Aren't I the one who knows what goes on in a young girl's heart, the longing for the nearness, the want for the touch of a man's hand?

"Good, now where was I?"

"My Mam sleeping with Bert."

The front door knocker rapped into the quiet.

"Oh, for heaven's sake! Right, keep your place now, Gran, I want to hear the rest of it today, no excuses." Exasperated, Rita stood and went to answer the summons.

When she opened the door, an officious looking man stood on the step holding a clipboard.

"Mrs. Haydon?" he asked.

"No, that's my grandmother, but she's sick. Could I help you?"

"I'm from the council offices. My card," He proffered a card reading, "Frederick Hardcastle - Chief Planning Officer."

"What's this about?" she asked mystified.

"The council recently purchased these houses from the estate of Matthew Harding. We've slated them for demolition."

Rita gasped. Pull the houses down?

He saw her face and hastened to reassure her. "Oh, no need for alarm, we'll rehouse you all in the new council houses we'll build on this site. Semidetached, modern, indoor plumbing, small gardens, all mod cons, you might say."

The news horrified Rita. What would her Gran say? "Yet suppose people don't want all that, suppose they want to stay right where they are? A lot of the old people on this street were born in the house in which they still live. It's like taking away their heritage."

"Now, now, Miss," He showed all his teeth and smirked. "I didn't catch your name."

"I didn't throw it," Rita said nastily. Smarmy man, she thought, all slime and teeth, coming here, telling her they would be pulling down the house.

Oh, it needed pulling down, she thought, it did, and the new council houses were nice, though the rent was higher, but she knew old age pensioners got a discount. She glanced up the street. These terraces were old-fashioned and cold, not well insulated, the whole shebang outdated. No wonder it was only the older people liked them, but then they had never known anything else.

The arrival of a TV in almost every home showed the youngsters what life was like outside Trawton. They now rented council houses in other areas, or moved to flats in the towns and cities. Who could blame them?

She looked at the man. "When's this going to start and where will the people live while they're homeless?"

He smiled. The young people understood. Fred hated it when an old age pensioner opened the door. It was no use sending letters as half the oldsters could hardly read. It was his idea, this door to door business and it was hard work and all, hard work trying to make some of them see it was for their own good.

"We'll pull down the end row, Roland Street, in six months. By that time they'll have built the first row of council houses on the spare land that abuts the street. Nobody will find it a great strain as they'll only have to move about thirty feet or so. Then we'll pull down Roland Street houses and build another row of council houses, and so it'll go. No fuss, no upheaval other than moving a few feet."

Rita looked sceptical. "It sounds fine in theory, but I bet it'll be a right mix up, even if you can find workmen willing to work to order instead of their own speed, which is practically snail-like from what I've seen of the current generation of tradesmen."

"We'll be using our own builders, Miss Goodwin. That makes a difference. You'll see, it'll be painless."

"So you say, but what is my grandmother going to say when I tell her you're pulling down her house?"

"I can tell her if you like," he offered.

"No, thanks," Rita sighed. "She's got a weak heart and this will be more than she can take from a stranger."

Rita shut the door and stood with her back against it for a moment. She would not tell her grandmother, not the complete truth, it would upset her.

"Who was that at the door? You were gone a long time," Marian asked as Rita entered the kitchen.

"A man from the council, Gran." She busied herself with the fire. No, she wouldn't tell her Gran as it could take years for them to get around to doing anything. The people of Trawton knew the local council didn't make hasty decisions, although it did seem like they were going to do it at some point in time.

"Well?" Marian said. "Like pulling hens' teeth, it is with you sometimes."

She decided not to worry her. "Not much, only that they have sold the houses to the council. It won't make any difference to us."

"No," Marian said sadly. Matthew had owned these houses, she'd always known that, even when she didn't think about it. The fact he owned it and fixed it up meant a great deal to her and they had lain upstairs on her bed and made love. To think only this morning she'd remembered him when looking at her nice front window.

"Gran, you all right?" Rita broke into her thoughts.

"Aye, I'm fine. Now how about a spot of tea?"

Rita watched her Gran's expression. It bothered her, she could tell, that the council owned the house. Of course her Gran knew the past owner, the man who fixed up the street, and, in fact, loved him. Oh, she'd heard about him more than once since her Gran confessed love for him, about his terrible death right on the street, about his height and his crystal blue eyes. Over the years she supposed Gran's memory made him more handsome, more charming. Her Gran's face when she talked about him was something else, full of lost love and sadness.

After Marian used the commode that now sat in the corner of the scullery - supplied by the local health department through the doctor's office - Marian wanted to go back to bed. It had been a long day for her, sitting here for hours.

"I'm sorry, lovey, I promise I'll get back to the story when I've had forty winks. I can't keep my eyes open right now. I'm jiggered."

She hated to see the disappointment in Rita's eyes, knowing the child had always wanted to know about the family argument.

With a sigh Rita went back down to make their evening meal and pondered on the halffinished tale. Gran would not tell her more tonight and she knew that. What was going to happen? What did the muscle-bound Bert have to do with things? Her father, where did he come in? The soapstone seal, what had that to do with anything?

Marian dozed off and on and wondered how she was going to finish her story, wishing she hadn't started it. She must find a way to frame it so Rita wouldn't hate her. Sheila was the real villain of the piece, although it didn't bother her much to have to state her daughter was a nasty piece of goods.

It was two days before she felt up to picking up the thread of her tale, two days while she tried to concentrate on it while the thoughts kept sliding away. Time though, time to spill the beans as they say, time to get it off her chest. After her morning wash, she felt up to telling the tale.

"So where was I up to, love?" she asked, "What part did I get to?"

Rita perked up. At last. "Bert the muscle man and my mother, Gran, before we got interrupted by the man from the council."

"Right, let me cast my mind back while you make a pot of tea and I'll have a spot of whisky in it this time. That should keep me awake."

Rita brought up the tray and they had tea and biscuits. Arrowroot, her Gran's favourite that she dunked in the cup. Rita added a tiny spot of whisky to Gran's tea. Not too much or it would put her to sleep.

"Now, before I start, you must realize your Mam and me had a terrible altercation. After she saw me with Matthew, she was judgmental, as usual, and for days after she threatened to tell your Granddad, so I was frightened. Now before you say anything, I know Matthew was dead and maybe nobody would have believed her. Nevertheless, morals were different back then and it was more about my state of mind at the time. I'm not making excuses, mind. I was simply thinking about your Granddad. My Harry wouldn't have liked to know his wife was an adulteress. What could I do? Adultery can be committed in the mind as well as the body, you know, and it was all true, after all." Sadly she shook her head thinking back to those dark days. Even now she could not tell Rita about their physical affair, did not want to reveal what a terrible person she was.

"So what happened?"

"She would have me at her mercy for the rest of my life, she said, said I would dance to her tune from then onwards. I was upset, as you can well imagine. The loss of Matthew just about finished me off, I was that depressed, so I made up my mind and told her I was going to tell Harry myself. I figured that would give her less ammunition, although I knew she would blacken my name in the village right enough, but if Harry knew and forgave me, then it would be all right."

"Did you tell him, Gran?"

"No, Rita, I never did," She sank back against her pillows, her face sad. "I allus wanted to, you know. Aye, I started to a couple of times, but you know your Granddad loved me a lot and I didn't want to see the hurt in his eyes. Can you understand that?"

"Yes, I can," Rita said patting her arm. "I can understand that, all right."

No, she never told Harry, no more than she could now tell Rita, because she was afraid of what might happen: of what they would think of her. She was scared to confess her sins to her husband, a man who trusted her, whose trust she had betrayed. She would never want to destroy him and it would have devastated him, because Harry was not strong, Not like she was when she forgave him for straying. He was ostrich-like, putting his head down and hoping his problems would go away if he pretended they did not exist.

Aye, often she had taken up the reins in their marriage. She had always found that strange. He'd been forceful enough when they were first married and after all, he had enlisted in the army and fought alongside his mates. What, she wondered, changed him? Why had he become a shadow of himself? She shuddered to think it was because of her gallivanting, but then he never mentioned it.

"So what happened, Gran?" Rita broke into her musing. "What

did she do? What did my Mam do when she found out you hadn't told him? Or did she ever find out?"

Marian sipped her tea and smacked her lips. "Lovely, this is," she said, with a trace of her merry old smile. "Well now, she didn't find out I know of, but I was allus there then, allus at his side. I never gave her a chance to talk to him alone. Then Bert as well, that kept her occupied."

"So what happened next?" Rita could see Marian was having difficulty concentrating.

"Well, I knew she was up to some'at. What it was I didn't know, but she was always a cagey one, was our Sheila. She was being secretive and going out at peculiar times so I asked her what she was up to, but she wouldn't tell me owt. I was suspicious, what with young chaps coming to the door fetching secret messages that she read and threw in the fire. After it happened two or three times, I became distrustful of her and besides I was dying of curiosity. Well, one night Harry was at the lodge, or the pub, anyroad he was out, thank God, when I decided to follow her."

"And?"

Marian sipped her tea, her eyes half closed as she remembered. "I put on my coat after she went down the street and I dodged in and out of doorways." Marian laughed thinking back on it. "It were like a detective film. By, but I must have looked funny. Mind you, nobody was about, or I'd have been the talk of the place. They'd started the blackout so people began to stay home at night."

Rita smiled, yes, it must have been a sight, her Gran tailing her Mam.

"And? What happened then? Where did you go?" Rita urged.

"Oh, she went to the blue bell woods and along the footpath. I wasn't young then, mind, I was over fifty and didn't get much exercise apart from housework. My legs were tired by the time I got half way through the woods and I stopped. I couldn't move for a minute or two, what with gasping for breath and all. Then when I started walking, I twisted my ankle on a stone, fell over it and landed on the gravel. By, but I was livid, not able to hightail it after her, and me being nosy like."

Marian sank back on her pillows and closed her eyes for a minute and Rita realized the tale telling was taking a lot out of her. "You rest for a while, Gran, we'll continue this at dinner time." Her Gran was already dozing so she covered her with the eiderdown and made to go downstairs.

"Cooee!" A voice called from the foot of the stairs as she left the room. Molly. Rita smiled, time for tea and talk.

It was nearly two by the time she sat again at the bedside waiting for her Gran to pick up the story, but by this time Marian was choleric and decidedly cantankerous. No matter, she wanted to hear the rest of the story.

"Now Gran, we were up to when you went through the blue bell woods and you twisted your ankle. Then what happened?"

Marian grunted irritably. Why was the child always on at her with questions, always questions? Oh yes, she'd promised to tell her and she wanted to, yes she did.

"You were in the woods, Gran, and twisted your ankle," Rita prompted.

This walk down memory lane had been her idea, so why was she taking her spleen out on Rita? She made a concerted effort. "Oh, aye, I recall it now. I was sitting on the damp path rubbing my foot, wondering whether to go on or return home, but then I decided to go after her, knowing whatever it was she was up to, was something nasty. I hobbled along as fast as I could and managed to get her in sight as she'd slowed down. We'd come to the outskirts of the farm by this time and I hid in the bushes and watched where she was going. Well, she ran to the barn door and went inside. Strange, I thought, why would she go into the barn? Just like her, I thought, to mess around in a dirty barn. She never did have any class."

It was easier now, the telling and she wanted to air it all, say it aloud after all these years.

"Then someone rode up on a horse, tied it to the hay wain by the barn and went inside. Even stranger, I thought. Then another two men came from the woods on the other side and went into the barn. I felt very puzzled by that time."

Rita wondered where the story would lead. How exciting it seemed. What on earth had her mother been doing?

Marian saw Rita's rapt face and continued. She must tell the story before she felt sleepy. Now she sipped at her laced tea and nodded. "I sneaked close to the barn and peeped through a space in the barn boards and saw them, about fifteen or so men, and there sat our Sheila and another woman. They had lit lanterns and while it weren't very light inside, I could make out their faces. When I heard someone else coming, I ducked behind a wagon and hid. Anyway, I crept back to the hole and listened and heard what they were on about. They were fifth columnists." Even now she felt the prickle in her nerve endings as she had on that terrible night. Her heart beat faster and her face felt flushed.

Rita had never heard that expression. "What's that?"

"They were spies for Germany working for Hitler against England, Rita. The war started in September 1939 and Hitler, the nasty piece of goods that he was, wanted to be prepared. Hitler was here in England, you know, in 1912 and 1913. He stayed with his brother, his half-brother who owned a small restaurant in Liverpool. So Adolph saw the ships coming and going when he was here and wanted to put a stop to it when he came to power and we were at war.

"Anyway, here in England were German men who'd been educated here, or maybe their parents were German, or they were English but believed in Hitler's vision of a master race. Whatever, they were here all right."

She wandered off on a tangent as a thought struck her, her mind taking her back to those terrible times. "Aye, it wasn't only the nobodies who liked Hitler. Look at Edward the Eighth, the Duke of Windsor as he was then, they say he was a good friend to Hitler, him and his American wife."

Rita nodded. Her mind was trying to get around it, the knowledge and dread of knowing her mother was involved with spies. A million questions were boiling in her mind, but she said nothing, knowing she would learn more by letting her Gran talk.

Marian thought back."Aye, I read a lot about those days 'cos I was curious to know what had been happening. It came out after the war, love, that Hitler offered Edward millions of Swiss francs and proposed to put him back on the throne of England. I suspect Edward was probably mad at the English who had turned their backs on him, as had his family, and I bet Wallis Simpson wanted to be Queen," Marian grinned, thinking of it. "Aye, they didn't give her a title after she married him and that must have stuck in her craw. Old Queen Mary shunned her too. You can bet Wallis would have pushed Edward into going along with the Führer, all right. You know what they said about her?"

She didn't wait for an answer and Rita didn't interrupt.

"They say she liked the fascists, did Wallis. Although Edward was madly in love with her, she liked men, lots of other men. She spent a lot of time with Albert Trekk and he spent a lot of his time in England spying on everything going on at the airports, ship yards and big factories. When Hitler sent Ribbentrop to England, Ribbentrop befriended her because she was close to Edward, although she and Edward wasn't married yet. Anyroad, it turns out old Ribbentrop was getting information that could only have come from Trekk via Wallis. That's when they started being careful what they told him, so I heard."

Gran's knowledge about this period amazed Rita. How did her Gran know all these things?

"I always thought of Edward as such a romantic figure, Gran. He was a lovely man."

Marian snorted. "I think he was a fool and a pawn in Wallis Simpson's quest for glory, that's all he was. An ambitious woman, she'd do anything to get what she wanted. Well, as much as I love the Royals, I'm glad the British government saw to it she got nowt. They jammed a spoke in her wheels, all right. Now, where was I up to in the story?"

She lay back and closed her eyes. Thoughts were there in her mouth a second ago, seemed to leave her mind and she had to concentrate hard to fetch them back. She sat up straighter and sipped her tea.

"Do you know when Edward married Wallis they went to France to live and decided to make a tour of Germany?" Rita nodded, she'd seen that in a documentary. "What a surprise, eh? The British Government was watching all this, mind, and they'd got spies watching the Windsors.

"I read that famous people like Errol Flynn, the film star, was a Nazi sympathizer because he went to France and met with the Windsors," Rita said.

"Who'd have believed it, eh? Mind you, they were all friendly with Hess. Hess thought the Windsors would help Hitler take England without any bloodshed if he could put Edward in charge of the operation."

"Yet the man was born to be King. What happened to his loyalty?" Rita asked, bewildered. They'd never taught her any of this at school and she hadn't read any articles showing Edward in this light, not that she had ever been particularly interested in recent history.

"Don't you forget now, Rita, his family turned their backs on him and his wife, and he did love the woman, loved her enough to give up the throne. He had nothing, a measly allowance from the government, but no property of any kind, so he was homeless, stateless and jobless. Look at it from his point of view. So when Hitler dangled all those millions in front of him and promised to put him back on the throne of England, what do you think he would do?"

"Still and all, Gran,"

"Aye well, we shouldn't judge. They'd brought him up in luxury with people bowing and scraping and now he was just about a common man. That must have been an awful shock to his system. I think he thought the English people would have forced the government to let him stay on as King, but they didn't. The government decided and public opinion stood for nowt back then. Anyroad, a woman like Wallis Simpson could never give him what he wanted, and that was to live in England, the land of his birth which was now off limits. We were lucky he abdicated, I can tell you. I remember when . . .,"

"Gran! Stop that, you're wandering off again. What about the spies in the barn?"

Marian pulled herself up. She must tell the story. "Sorry, love. Well now, I listened and peeped and got scared. It was a dark night, cloudy with rain in the air. I can remember because the cold struck right at my innards. All that creeping through the farm yard to the barn and around the front, jumping from shadow to shadow. It was awful, trying not to make any noise, and my ankle hurting like billyo." She put her arms around herself and hunched as if feeling the cold. "Aye, I can see it now. They was all sitting around a big lantern. Bert was there and his dad, Archie, that blackguard." She snorted remembering. It was like yesterday to her now, seeing them there. "I saw one of the councillors, even the vicar from St. Edmund's. By, I was shocked to see him sitting there, grinning and rubbing his hands. I also saw a man I knew well, a merchant seaman, Howard, his name was. He's the one who gave me the soapstone seal and it was a real shocker to find out he was a spy. Imagine, all the time everyone thought he was coming to visit his brother, he was messing about with those blackguards."

Rita's eyes widened. So that's why Gran never told her about the seal.

"The man who did most of the talking was one of the local gentry. He owned mines and mills and an iron foundry, and a right bigwig, all right. Right toffee nosed twit, spoke like the king, all posh. King his name was locally, although this lot called him Koenig. I later found out his parents were Germans."

Rita gasped, taking it in all at once was difficult. "How terrible. Imagine that, spies in Trawton!"

The whisky was making her garrulous, but that was good. She had to finish the story. "Aye, that's what I thought at the time. What could they do in a sleepy English village, I thought? Yet it wasn't what they were going to do here, was it? Oh no! This was what they called a cell, where they were teaching them spying and sabotage . . . and who'd ever suspect a small village to be hiding such people? Come to that, who would ever suspect they would get my own daughter involved in such a terrible thing? Not me, for one. Still, it happened because we were right in the thick of things, what with the Manchester Ship Canal and then the docks at Liverpool where over half the country's food supplies came in, along with other stuff. The man I knew, Howard, would know all about ship movements and cargoes, seeing as he was sailing in and out of there all the time, and I suppose he had his sources of information. Then we had many airfields and factories between here and Manchester."

"Were there any real Germans in the barn? How would they get into England?" Rita asked, puzzled.

"No love, not that I heard. They all spoke local English or had university accents and a lot were of German descent, I expect. The others were probably fanatics of one kind or another, always willing to hop onto a band wagon if offered the chance. These cell leaders paid them, and don't forget money was tight in these parts. Mind you, as I said, some of them were from other places. They weren't local bods."

"It seems strange an Englishman would want to help Hitler conquer his home."

"No, love, they thought if he won they'd be one of the lucky ones, the ones who got the cushy jobs and the perks. They never thought we'd beat the bastards, you can count on that. Anyroad, when I listened they were talking about getting information on the new liner Queen Elizabeth. Recently launched, she was, due to go to Southampton to be completed, away from the Walker Dock at the Clyde. It seemed this lot didn't believe that plan as it would put the ship in range of German bombers, so they were trying to find out if it was coming to Liverpool. Then they talked about the Queen Mary. Aye, that was a ship they'd have loved to put out of service. A ship of that size was faster than anything the Germans had and could carry thousands of troops. Now, where was I up to? Could I have some more tea and whisky?"

Rita poured the tea and added a spot more liquor as she prompted. "You were hiding outside the barn, Gran."

"Oh aye, and our Sheila was inside with them spies. Well, I hid there dithering, wondering what I should do and pulled back under cover of a cart trying to decide, when I heard raised voices and peeped back inside.

"They were arguing and one man was trying to leave. 'I won't do it,' he said, 'This is diabolical.' He turned again to leave and a man from outside our area pulled him back.

"You stupid fool. You took an oath, remember?" he said.

The man stood his ground then. "Aye, Mr. Snow, and I'll soon forget that, you bastard. Innocent women and children are going to be hurt and I can't go along with it. I'm getting out of here." He turned to go, and one of the others, he was one of our local shop keepers, took a revolver out of his pocket and shot him dead."

"What?" Rita's hand flew to her cheeks; she was thunderstruck. Her Gran had seen a murder? "What on earth did you do, Gran?"

"I started to move away and was all for fetching the police, but then it dawned on me our police sergeant and Trawton's chief constable were sitting right there with the Chief of Constabulary from Pembleton, and not one of them moved a muscle when the man was shot. I spotted a judge, too. I'd seen his picture in the paper. The Chief Constable was an influential man, knew everything going on and helping make most of it happen, seems like. Two of the other men tossed the poor sod into the hay and they went back to their meeting."

"Good grief."

"Callous it was, dead callous and I'd seen it. Then they talked about getting rid of the body. They decided to bury it under the manure pile in the field. It's still there, I expect 'cos who would start digging in manure and why? If someone does find it after all this time, who's to say who did it?"

Rita was agog, sitting on the edge of her chair. "So what did you do? Who did you tell about it?"

Marian shook her head sadly. "That's it, love, I couldn't tell anybody. I mean, who could I trust? It might have been me next that got shot. I was no hero, only a housewife, and my daughter was mixed up with them. So if I told on her, I would tar myself and Harry with the same notoriety. They'd think we were also spies. Two or three locals had nasty accidents around that time and I figured it was because they had talked about the group. I thought about writing an anonymous letter to the newspapers, but had second thoughts. Well, I wasn't as educated as you are, love, and thought they would trace me by the paper and the writing and the post mark and all that. I was wrong, I know that now."

"Still, did anything terrible happen?" Rita asked.

Marian nodded grimly. "World War Two, that's what happened, love. The war to end all wars and I was responsible for many lives being lost."

"No, you weren't," Rita cried, "Don't say that. You didn't do anything."

"Aye, nor did I, but I *should* have done something. It was only right. Instead, me and Sheila made a pledge to each other we'd never tell another living soul. Neither of us trusted the other and it was my idea about the paper we signed. We signed saying we would never tell and swore it on the Bible. I was never easy about it, though, I must admit. Sheila was forever fetching it up as though she were going to tell people. I didn't think she would, though she allus threatened. Her point of view was I was more responsible than her because she wasn't twenty-one and still a minor." She sighed bitterly, "I suppose she was right, although I had more on her than she ever knew. Not very smart our Sheila, not smart at all. Yet then neither was I, now I come to think about it."

"So that was what was between you and my Mam?" Rita was shocked to think her mother was working against her own country. It was not at all what she had expected. "That's the reason why you didn't speak to each other?"

Marian nodded. Some things she couldn't tell Rita, the bitter hatred she felt for her daughter, the burning hatred that made it difficult to speak to her traitorous child. A child who would have turned in her own mother if it earned her a few brownie points and a couple of pounds.

"Aye, gl t'were, and wasn't that enough? I hated her for it, I can tell you. I could hardly stand to look at her, traitor that she was, and yet I couldn't hand her over, love. She would have been incarcerated, you know, and maybe hung. What a deplorable thing to leave to your relatives, to leave to you, Rita, having a mother that was a traitor. You'd have lived with the shame of it all your life, and it could have ruined your chances for happiness, so I couldn't do it. Of course that was the largest part of it. It made me feel rotten, all that guilt. I was as bad as them fifth columnists, keeping my mouth shut and letting that lot wander around free."

"Well, if you had told, what would have happened?"

"They would have jailed most of them for the duration and hung them after the war. A lot would escape the net, and the Germans would have looked after them, unless they were small-fry. A lot of the people you know today would have lost their fathers, Rita, a whole lot of people who you'd never think would have such leanings. Yet we let them live their lives as if they were like us. It was wrong, lass, dead wrong. It got so that I could hardly speak to any of the locals. Who knew what they were involved with?"

"Yet this is now and you shouldn't worry about what happened way back then," Rita said sitting on the side of the bed and putting her arm around Marian. "You should let it go, Gran, don't worry about it. You did nothing wrong that I can see. I would probably have done the same thing because I'd have been scared to death of them."

"Aye, I was scared something rotten. So was your Mam, but in her case, she was petrified in case I told. You know, I never told your Granddad either, and that niggled at me something rotten for years afterward. Anyroad, I've got it off my chest now and you can do what you like with it." She smiled up at her lovely Rita. Rita had not blamed her and she felt relieved.

Rita smiled. "Don't worry about it, Gran. I've read books about spies, although it surprises me you had any around this neck of the woods. That man you mentioned, Mr. Snow, that was his code name." She sounded proud she knew. "He was a double agent. Right, missus. Time for your nap." Rita said firmly, hugging her.

"Look, lass, fetch me something first. In the pantry, behind the potato bin and under a loose flagstone, you'll find a tin box. Fetch it here."

Rita ran down the stairs. To think her Gran had seen German spies, had seen a man shot dead . . . and her own mother was involved with the Germans. How shocking but no matter what, she thought her Gran wonderful. What a life. Maybe now she had told the shameful story Gran would tell her more of her life. What else could possibly be that bad?

After she moved the wooden potato bin her Granddad built donkey's years ago, she pushed at the flagstones with the toe of her shoe. One moved. Taking a kitchen knife, she prised it up and laid it aside. Underneath was a metal box, a box that once held candles by the length of it.

"Here it is, Gran," she said holding out the dirty item. She had wiped as much muck off it as she could with an old newspaper.

Marian tried to open it, but her hands had no strength. "Here, you'd better do it," she said, passing it back thinking, 'useless this body is, useless.'

Rita finally fetched a knife and worked it under the lid all the way round before she could remove the top. What was so important that it had been hidden all these years, she wondered? She passed it to her Gran who looked at the oil cloth wrapped roll inside. Marian pulled off the cloth and inside was a paper and an old newspaper. Passing the newspaper to Rita, she said: "See that?"

The date was January 15 and the headline read 'Councillor Cunliffe Charged With Treason.' The story reported he had been found guilty and sentenced to jail for the duration.

"Was this one of the men at the barn, Gran?"

"Aye, right bastard he was and we all trusted him." She smiled grimly, looking at the photo. "He got caught out by his own wife who blew the whistle on him. They held the war crime's trials after the war, you know, and he was hung later. In 1947, I think. Hanging was too good for him, if you ask me. Mind you, him and his missus didn't get along, and he was having an affair with our Sheila at the time they caught him."

Rita gasped. This story was something she would never have thought of in her wildest dreams.

Her voice was high and squeaky as she asked: "My Mam was going out with him?"

"Oh aye, she didn't care about his political leanings, and he's probably the reason she took up with that horrible lot. She only cared he was wealthy. He could have had one leg and half an arm and be black as the ace of spades and it wouldn't have mattered to her, if he had brass in his pocket. She'd gone off muscles by then," Marian laughed mirthlessly.

A sudden thought struck Rita. She had to know. "Gran, when did she marry my Dad? Was it before or after this time?"

Marian said it like it was. No point in prevaricating now. "It before, lovey, before you was born. Look at the date on it."

Rita shook her head sadly. "Not a very nice person, my mother.

She was going to marry my Dad and was still playing around," she said bitterly. "Did Dad know about it?"

"No, not then, he was away in the army, although I knew. She liked to flaunt her affairs in front of me because she knew I would say nowt, not unless I wanted to be shot, too."

Rita mulled it over for a second. "Oh Gran, and to think of the grief I gave my Dad when he wanted to marry Molly. If only you'd told me about my Mam then."

Marian smiled at her fondly. "I couldn't do that, love, now could I?"

"No, I suppose not. Anyway, what's that paper you've got there? Is there more to this story?"

Her grandmother looked tired, Rita noticed, her eyelids were beginning to droop. Rita knew she should let her rest, yet somehow knew she had almost ended the story.

Marian blew out a long breath and pulled herself upright, knowing she must find the strength to finish the tale. "Aye. This is the paper we signed. The paper I signed and gave to her, she's burned, she told me that much. That was another reason she wanted to come back here, to find my copy."

Marian passed it to Rita. "Read it, love, read it and weep."

It was brown with age and badly creased although the ink had not faded too badly.

"We, the undersigned, do solemnly swear we will never divulge the events we witnessed at Hillside Farm barn. We will never mention it either accidentally, or purposely, nor use it as blackmail in any way against the other.

"Marian Haydon does solemnly swear she will never divulge the actions of Sheila Goodwin under pain of legal prosecution, in return for which Sheila Goodwin does solemnly swear she will never tell anyone of the affair between Marian Haydon and Matthew Harding."

It had both signatures.

"What is this bit about, Gran, second edition? Was there another one?"

Marian nodded. "Aye, and that was before other stuff happened where we had to swear about the other."

"You mean this bit here where it says you wouldn't tell anybody about Sheila Goodwin's actions?"

"That's it. Tomorrow, love, I'll tell you tomorrow, Rita. I want to sleep now. Wake me for my tea." Already her eyes were closing. She found confession enervating.

Rita took the papers downstairs and put them into the china cabinet. They were suddenly precious to her. Yet to think her grandmother and mother were eye witnesses to such terrible things, and realize her mother was a whore. No other word for it, she told herself. Playing away she was, and herself only a baby. Her mother was a rotten person and a traitor. Idly she wondered where her mother was now and whether she had remarried. Since Dad threw her out nobody had seen hide nor hair of her.

Why had Dad married her? Tomorrow she would ask Gran about that. Her father, if she told him what she knew, what would his reaction be? Hmm, she would have to sleep on that particular problem.

Putting on her coat and locking the door, she went to the grocery store newly opened on the corner, only a hundred feet away and so convenient. It had been a house only two months ago and, knowing what she did about the council's plans, she wondered how much they would compensate the owner, an immigrant from Pakistan, or if they would even bother. Still, they had granted him a business licence, despite the fact they knew what was going to happen to his business in a short time.

"Missy Rita." The owner, Ali they all called him, beamed at her from behind the counter.

"Hello, Ali, anything tasty in the deep freeze for Gran's tea?"

The shop being cramped and cluttered, Ali kept a large freezer in his living room.

"Oh yes indeed. I've got some lobster Newburgh, some cracked crab, expensive but very good, and then some various dishes already made up."

"Lobster Newburgh, eh? How much is it? Gran needs a treat."

Ali brought out a small package. Enough for two servings, the package stated. Well, on toast it would be more than enough for their teas. It was expensive all right, but today Gran had set her mind at rest to some extent, although Rita dearly wanted to hear the rest of the story.

The lobster was rich, Rita admitted as she finished it later. Marian ate quite a lot, saying repeatedly what a treat it was, lobster. Aye, what a treat she kept saying although she'd never liked lobster, but she couldn't tell Rita, not with her sitting there with shiny eyes, pleased she had bought her Gran something so fine.

Arthur it was, she must thank soon, Arthur who paid Rita to stay home and look after her. She could have been at work, working alongside her fiancee, Ian.

The poor souls did their courting in the kitchen. Not that the youngsters were in the house all the time, Marian wasn't having that. Molly and Arthur would come to visit and let Rita go with Ian to a movie or a show in Wigan. Yes, Marian mused, she was blessed, she was. Good company all day and night and people who cared about her. What more could she ask?

Rita and Ian sat in the kitchen that night, close together on the old settee and talked of their wedding and the future. Often Rita asked herself how long Ian was willing to wait as it had been a long courtship for the day and Ian patience personified. It must be difficult for him, she knew, for she longed to sleep with him. She told this to Marian who agreed Ian was a prince among men, waiting like that.

Now she sighed sadly. "She's fading fast, Ian," she said. "Do you mind if we don't go out tomorrow? I don't want to leave her."

Ian sighed with annoyance, his impatience showing. "Oh Rita. She's been down before and she's always bounced back. She's a strong old lady and we'll probably have to beat her with a stick to make her go."

She pushed him away. "Don't joke about this, Ian. She's not going to bounce back this time."

"How did you reach this conclusion, Doctor Goodwin?" he said, noting she didn't look at all pleased he was trying to lighten the situation. She looked stricken with it.

"Because she's making her confession," she said as she burst into tears.

Ian comforted her. Maybe Marian was not going to last long now. Soon they would be married. Soon they would move away from Trawton and into the small house in Pemberton on which he had put an offer.

Later they went up to check on her Gran and found her sleeping peacefully.

"See, she's fine," Ian whispered.

The following morning Marian seemed grumpy. Waking herself was difficult today as most of the night she lay awake, plagued by leg cramps she could not reach to ease.

"Come on, Gran, time for breakfast," Rita said as she pulled her up and settled her against the pillows.

"I'm not hungry, lass. Take that away." Her nerves were close to the surface and even words irritated her. "A cup of tea, that's all I want, a cup of tea and some of my medicine."

Rita looked at her. Marian's eyes seemed cloudy. She looked frazzled, as she would say herself and Rita wondered whether to call the doctor.

"I'm going to get up today, Rita," she said in her old lady's voice, the voice that whined so much and she hated to hear. With an effort she made it stronger, drawing on her remaining strength. "Don't start your argufying. I want to sit by the fire."

"Yes, Gran," Rita said obediently, glad she felt better than she looked.

As they sat by the fire, and after Molly been and gone, they talked. How they had talked over the years, Rita thought. She talked and listened, and listened and talked, for all these many years and still had things she wanted to know about her Gran. Her Mam of course, oh yes, her Mam. It was almost too late and all the things she been going to ask fled from her mind, replaced by the worry about her Gran's health. Her Gran had taught her so much, practically made her into the person she was today and for that she thanked her.

She decided she must hear the end of the story. "Now, about the paper swore you wouldn't tell about my Mam's actions."

"Aye, I'd better finish that tale off before I start another, eh?" Marian said, her mind going back to those dark days of the war. "Well now, your Mam, a trollop of the highest order, was having an affair with another married man. That was after the councillor got caught and jailed. This other man was a nasty bit of work. He was a crook, a wide boy, a spiv as they called them back then, and he sold stuff on the black market. Well, she did him in, then told me about it, as if I could do anything for her."

Rita's mouth dropped open. "She did him in? You mean she killed him?" Horror held Rita stupefied. Never had she expected anything like this. Her mother a murderess? God grief, what *hadn't* her mother done?

"Aye, she shot him with his own gun," Marian nodded as she gazed into the fire, seeing it again. "It was an accident mind, love. She didn't do it on purpose."

Rita felt horrified. Her forehead felt cold and the hairs on her arms stood on end. Her mother was an absolute monster. "But what did you do? What did *she* do?"

"Well now, she was in his flat. One of them that were part of a big old house, you know the sort they had before they started building them concrete things all over. Apparently nobody else had moved into the place at that time because he owned it and he'd only begun knocking out walls and putting them up again in another place. Our Sheila was playing with his gun. Stupid sod him, leaving it where she could see it, and it loaded too. Laughing and pointing it at him, she were, saying 'your money or your life' like a highwayman, and it went off. Shot him in the chest near enough to his heart to kill him. She got out of there fast and came and told me. Fetched me the gun, as if I wanted the murder weapon. I got panic struck and tossed it in the duck pond that night."

"What happened? Did the police know she'd done it?"

"No, of course not; they would have arrested her if they had. The chap belonged to the underworld, so they obviously thought it was a gang thing. I don't suppose they bothered doing much investigating, although your Mam was scared stiff for weeks in case they came after her. It was a long time afore she started playing away again, I can tell you." She sighed, thinking back. "I was an accessory to that murder as well, Rita. So you can see where I was with her."

"Yes, in trouble no matter what you did. You couldn't tell the police because she was involved in a murder with the fifth columnists, and they would have arrested you for treason as well as her, and she wouldn't confess, if I know her. Then she also blackmailed you into getting rid of the gun, so you were an accessory after the fact in another murder."

Marian nodded. "That was the long and short of it. We were our own worst enemies, me and your Mam. Terrible for me not to tell on her, other than I liked my own comfort too much and if I went to jail your Granddad would be all alone."

"What about my Dad? Didn't you tell him? Didn't he suspect anything?"

"He was away in the army, as well you know. What fighting man would want his mother-in-law writing such news about his wife? I couldn't do it, love, nor would you have done it either, so don't look at me like that."

Oh Lord, the look on Rita's face, Marian thought. I've tarnished my image with my granddaughter and I hate what I've done to her. Quickly she tried to smooth it over. "I was thinking of Harry more than anything, lovey, you have to believe that. I had you to consider as well in later years, you and your Dad."

Marian knew she was making excuses for her own stupidity. Clearly she should have reported both incidents, she had no real excuse, but it was too late now. She shook her head sadly. "My Harry never harmed anyone in his life and look at what I did to him."

"Aaw Gran, Granddad loved you so much. I know he did, and anything you'd do would never be done to hurt him. He would have understood."

Marian knew he would not. He would have taken her to the police right away. "That's speculation, Rita, pure speculation. You never knew your Granddad like I did. My Harry was a funny man in many ways and, while he didn't say much, he was a thinker, all right. He had his own opinions on everything, although I was the only one he confided in, as far as I know."

Rita smiled, seeing in her mind's eye the Sunday afternoons when they took her for a walk, seeing them strolling through the park arm in arm, Darby and Joan, while she ran around chasing a ball or a butterfly, secure in the knowledge of their love.

Rita sighed and took Marian's hand. "My Mam was not, or should I say, is not, a nice person."

Marian decided not to tell Rita that her mother had died because the child had heard enough bad news for one day. A nasty woman who lived on one of the other streets told Marian that Sheila died in a TB clinic only six months earlier and had another baby born dead. Marian kept the knowledge to herself, nursing the ache of a mother for a wayward child. No matter how badly she felt of Sheila, she was still her child and every mother loves her child.

Rita caressed the old worn fingers. "She's made you unhappy and I'm glad you didn't tell me before now. I wouldn't have been able to keep my trap shut."

"That's the truth, Rita, you always did need a glass of water to hand to wash down your foot. I know there's no harm in you, though. Never was, always was a good girl, you were."

Marian closed her eyes, her hand in Rita's and slipped away in sleep, her mind finally at rest.

EPILOGUE

"It's a handsome piece, all right," Ian said, as they admired the china cabinet that now stood in the front room of their new house. "We'll have to buy the rest of the things to match."

The room was empty except for the cabinet. As yet, they had only furnished the kitchen with things from Gran's house plus their bedroom, but what did it matter? They had the rest of their life to fill the house with furniture.

Rita stooped and moved a few things around. On the top shelf was the topper from their wedding cake, a bride and groom holding hands. Next to it stood two figurines, Columbine and Harlequin. She moved them so their outstretched fingers touched. Together at last, she thought, they are together again at last, my Gran and Granddad.

Everything was there, every memory of her Gran's. Now they were *her* memories and her future children's memories. Gently she touched the clock still set at the time her Granddad left; she and Ian would have something they would use to break the ice after a quarrel. She smiled. It was too soon after the wedding for that.

Turning, she moved into the warm circle of his arms and felt at peace.

"I'll tell you all about everything in the cabinet," she said, swallowing her tears "Only one thing at a time, though, and only on Sunday after tea."

-end-

CPSIA information can be obtained
at www.ICGtesting.com
Printed in the USA
BVHW030513121221
623798BV00001B/8